"G...

Concentrate your ... ...rcraft and the Galleons," Fuller call... ... communications channel.

The brilliant blue energy blast of Jaffray's PPC sheered the hovercraft *Pegasus*, sending a spray of steam and boiled-off armor into the air. The impact was so hard on the *Pegasus* that the hover tank drifted to the shoreline where it collided with a tree stump and slammed to a halt.

Loren fired his PPC again, feeling the wave of heat in the cockpit as the weapon discharged. There was another flash of light as the armor exploded off the *Pegasus* and showered into the river. The wounded hovercraft teetered slightly in the middle of its turn as its driver fought to control it.

Still his target did not flee but instead accelerated and cut across the river, taking a direct interception course with Loren's *Gallowglas*.

What in the name of Liao is this guy up to? Although it's obviously suicidal, not just one, but all of the enemy craft are pressing into us. Why? Unless they know something that we don't....

"Trap!" Loren transmitted to every friendly 'Mech within range. "It's a trap!"

FASA (0451)

EXPERIENCE THE ADVENTURE OF
BATTLETECH

- [ ] **BATTLETECH #1:** *Way of the Clans* by **Robert Thurston**. It is the 31st century, where the BattleMech is the ultimate war machine ... where the Clans are the ultimate warriors ... and where a man called Aidan must succeed in trials that will forge him into one of the best warriors in the galaxy. (451015—$4.99)

- [ ] **BATTLETECH #2:** *Bloodname* by **Robert Thurston**. The star captain locks in deadly combat on the eve of the invasion of the inner sphere. (451171—$4.99)

- [ ] **BATTLETECH #3:** *Falcon Guard* by **Robert Thurston**. A clash of empires ... a clash of armies ... a clash of cultures ... the fate of the Clan Jade Falcon rests in Star Colonel Aidan's hands. (451295—$4.99)

- [ ] **BATTLETECH #4:** *Wolfpack* by **Robert N. Charrette**. The Dragoons are five regiments of battle-toughened Mech Warriors and their services are on offer to the highest bidder. Whoever that might be ... (451503—$4.99)

- [ ] **BATTLETECH #5:** *Natural Selection* by **Michael A. Stackpole**. A terrible secret threatens to begin the violence anew—in the bloodiest civil war man has ever known. (451724—$4.50)

Buy them at your local bookstore or use this convenient coupon for ordering.

PENGUIN USA
P.O. Box 999 — Dept. #17109
Bergenfield, New Jersey 07621

Please send me the books I have checked above.
I am enclosing $_____ (please add $2.00 to cover postage and handling). Send check or money order (no cash or C.O.D.'s) or charge by Mastercard or VISA (with a $15.00 minimum). Prices and numbers are subject to change without notice.

Card #_____ Exp. Date _____
Signature_____
Name_____
Address_____
City _____ State _____ Zip Code _____

For faster service when ordering by credit card call **1-800-253-6476**

Allow a minimum of 4-6 weeks for delivery. This offer is subject to change without notice.

BATTLETECH.

HIGHLANDER GAMBIT

Blaine Lee Pardoe

A ROC BOOK

ROC
Published by the Penguin Group
Penguin Books USA Inc., 375 Hudson Street,
New York, New York 10014, U.S.A.
Penguin Books Ltd, 27 Wrights Lane,
London W8 5TZ, England
Penguin Books Australia Ltd, Ringwood,
Victoria, Australia
Penguin Books Canada Ltd, 10 Alcorn Avenue,
Toronto, Ontario, Canada M4V 3B2
Penguin Books (N.Z.) Ltd, 182–190 Wairau Road,
Auckland 10, New Zealand

Penguin Books Ltd, Registered Offices:
Harmondsworth, Middlesex, England

First published by Roc, an imprint of Dutton Signet,
a division of Penguin Books USA Inc.

First Printing, June, 1995
10 9 8 7 6 5 4 3 2 1

Copyright © FASA Corporation, 1995
All rights reserved

Series Editor: Donna Ippolito
Cover: Romas Kukalis
Mechanical Drawings: Duane Loose

REGISTERED TRADEMARK—MARCA REGISTRADA
BATTLETECH, FASA, and the distinctive BATTLETECH and FASA logos are trademarks of the FASA Corporation, 1100 W. Cermak, Suite B305, Chicago, IL 60608.

Printed in the United States of America

Without limiting the rights under copyright reserved above, no part of this publication may be reproduced, stored in or introduced into a retrieval system, or transmitted, in any form, or by any means (electronic, mechanical, photocopying, recording, or otherwise), without the prior written permission of both the copyright owner and the above publisher of this book.

BOOKS ARE AVAILABLE AT QUANTITY DISCOUNTS WHEN USED TO PROMOTE PRODUCTS OR SERVICES. FOR INFORMATION PLEASE WRITE TO PREMIUM MARKETING DIVISION, PENGUIN BOOKS USA INC., 375 HUDSON STREET, NEW YORK, NEW YORK 10014.

If you purchased this book without a cover you should be aware that this book is stolen property. It was reported as "unsold and destroyed" to the publisher and neither the author nor the publisher has received any payment for this "stripped book."

To my wife, Cynthia, and my children, Victoria and Alexander ... without whom this book would mean nothing. To my mother and father, Rose and David, for allowing me to play all of these games when I was a kid. Bill Murphy deserves credit for teaching me to appreciate the classics and for encouraging me to be a writer. The Hartford brothers deserve their due as well.

I want to thank Sam for this chance; Donna and Sharon for taking the time to teach me how to be a better writer. And Mike Stackpole for his encouragement.

And finally to Central Michigan University ... home of the mighty Chippewas and *The Central Michigan Life*—for some of the best experiences of my life.

As I have said, when those states that are acquired are used to living by their own laws and in freedom, there are three methods of holding on to them: the first is to destroy them; the second is to go there in person and live; the third is to allow them to live with their own laws, forcing them to pay a tribute and creating therein a government made up of a few people who will keep the state friendly toward you.

—*The Prince*, Niccolò Machiavelli, 1514

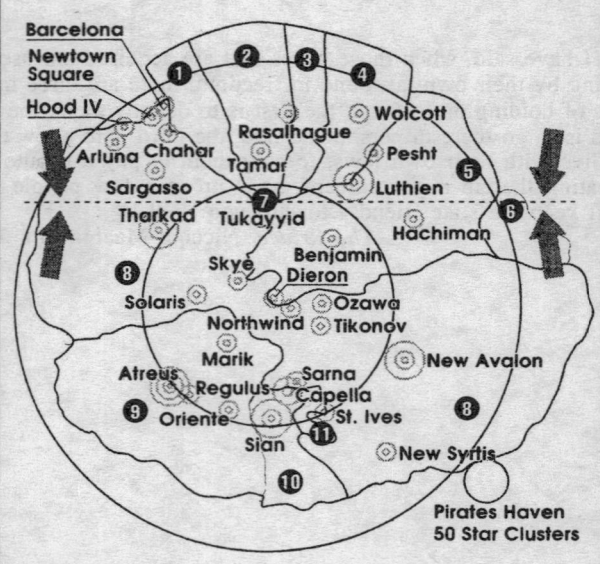

MAP OF THE SUCCESSOR STATES
CLAN TRUCE LINE

1 • Jade Falcon/Steel Viper, 2 • Wolf Clan, 3 • Ghost Bear,
4 • Smoke Jaguars - Nova Cats, 5 • Draconis Combine,
6 • Outworlds Alliance, 7 • Free Rasalhague Republic,
8 • Federated Commonwealth, 9 • Free Worlds League,
10 • Capellan Confederation, 11 • St. Ives Compact

Map Compiled by COMSTAR.
From information provided by the COMSTAR EXPLORER SERVICE
and the STAR LEAGUE ARCHIVES on Terra.

© 3056 COMSTAR CARTOGRAPHIC CORPS.

Prologue

DropShip *Stonewall Jackson*
Orbiting Elgin
Tikonov Commonalty, Capellan Confederation
21 December 3028

"Lads and lasses, after centuries of waiting, our time has finally come. We are soldiers, mercenaries proud of our independence and prowess. We have fought long and hard, won and lost many battles in service to others. Now, under your eyes, the eyes of the warriors of the Northwind Highlanders, we must choose our destiny." Colonel Alastair Marion of Marion's Highlanders spread his arms wide to include every member of the Warrior Cabel gathered around him in the bay of the DropShip *Stonewall Jackson*. As he spoke the music of several bagpipes booming in the background gradually drifted into silence.

There was something poignant about the choice of Marion as a spokesman, for his regiment, Marion's Highlanders, had been nearly destroyed by the Third Royals RCT on Ningpo.

But he would rebuild his regiment and like the commanders of all three other Highlander regiments Colonel Marion had responded immediately to the call by the Clan Elders for a Cabel. With them had come delegates to represent the will and interests of every Highlander, no matter his or her rank. They'd chosen the Elgin system, where MacCormack's Fusiliers were in the fight to save the Tikonov worlds, as their meeting place. The Fusiliers' DropShip had met them at the jump point, and that was how they came to be assembled aboard the *Stonewall Jackson* this day.

Marion let his gaze wander over the faces gathered around him. "Hanse Davion of the Federated Suns has made us an offer that we, as a military unit and as a people, must vote on. He has offered us something denied our blood for decades—the return of Northwind!" Wild cheers and applause greeted these words. As the cheers echoed off the metal walls of the vast bay, it sounded like hundreds more MechWarriors and support staff were present. And, in a way, they were. The Highlanders were loyal to each other above all other things and they always acted as one.

"Never in all my years did I dream we might one day be considering such an offer, yet we have received word from Prince Hanse Davion that he is willing to turn control of the planet Northwind over to the Highlanders. It is a dream come true, yet even dreams have their price. The only way to accept this offer is to abandon our long-standing contract with House Liao and the Capellan Confederation. Turn our backs on a people we have defended since the days of the Star League. Desert a government that has sustained us and our families in both good and bad times."

The hint of regret in his voice changed quickly with his last words: "That is the price for once again regaining control of our homeworld!" A hush seemed to fall over the bay as the Colonel triumphantly raised both arms in the air.

Then another voice rose from the floor, booming loud and deep. "This is an opportunity we Highlanders have only dreamed of over the centuries. But I contend that the cost is too high. The price is not a change in contract, fellow Highlanders—the price is our honor. My honor is not for sale, even if the prize is the return of our homeworld."

"Major Jaffray is right," came the voice of another Highlander, a female wearing a warrior's sash of bright blue and orange tartan. "But if we don't accept, what chance have any of us to ever see Northwind in our lifetimes? Even now, as we meet here, the Capellan Confederation is in flames, under attack by the armies of Hanse Davion. There is little hope of the Capellans ever winning Northwind back and turning it over to us again. No one in my family has yet set foot on the soil of Northwind. Nor can any of our children look forward to ever knowing Northwind unless we accept this offer. Before I die, I must see with my own eyes the rolling green hills of our heartland."

Colonel Henry MacCormack of the infamous Fusiliers climbed up on a transit crate next to Colonel Marion. "Let there be no illusions, Highlanders. Hanse Davion's surprise attacks have the Capellans on the run, but we might still be able to save the Tikonov worlds. Perhaps even turn the recent series of routs into a Capellan victory. That is ... if we decline the Davion offer." A chorus of "no's" rang through the DropShip bay, drowning out the few assenting "ayes."

Corwin Jaffray spoke up again from the floor of the bay. "Do not delude yourselves, fellow Highlanders. Hanse Davion dangles the offer of Northwind before us only because he knows the threat we represent. If we jump ship now, the Capellans will lose dozens of planets that we now defend, and all it will cost the Federated Suns is one world—Northwind."

Colonel MacHenry of the Second Kearny Highlanders, unable to wade through the crowd to the makeshift podium, had climbed up on another crate at the back of the gathering. "We've been warring with the Davions for years, lads. We know them for the dogs they are. What good is the word of someone like Hanse Davion? How long do you really think he will let us rule Northwind? Only 'til this little donnybrook is over. Then we become his lap dogs.

"I say we dunna trust this devil. Think about what they're actually offerin' us. Northwind will not be ours free and clear, but will remain a Federated Suns world, with us at its head. That is not what the Liao has promised us—that Northwind would be an independent world under our total control. Mark my words, once this war is over, the Fox will forget all about this agreement, like as not exchanging the carrot for the whip to make us dance to his tune."

"Aye," came the voice of another female in the crowd, one whose sash marked her as a Sergeant Technician. "Hundreds of our kin have died at the hands of Davion's dogs. Now he expects us to bow to them as our lords, or worse, as consorts. My honor is no' fer sale!"

Another officer, a rough-faced major of the First Kearny

Highlanders, garbed in the tartan of the MacLeod clan, spoke up from the floor. "I hear your words, brothers and sisters. But the one bond that has held us together as a unit over the centuries was the thought of once again returning to Northwind as a free people. Now, finally, after centuries of war, we have a chance to fulfill that dream. I, for one, do not want to lose that chance. I will stand on the soil of our beloved Northwind!" Cheers filled the dim confines of the bay as the assembled warriors began to stomp so hard against the plating of the deck that the whole ship seemed to vibrate under their boots.

Colonel Marion again took the floor of the Cabel. "This debate could continue until the end of time, but in case we've all forgotten, there's a war going on out there. Every man and woman here understands the issues we face. There is not a lad or lass among us whose heart is not torn by this offer. Some of us will break ranks with the Highlanders, regardless of the decision we take today. But no matter what the outcome of the vote, I ask that each one of us remember our code of honor."

Colonel Marion's voice rang out like a bell. "Remember that once a Northwind Highlander, it is with you for life . . . and beyond. Those of you who decide that our decision today calls for a parting of the ways, remember that a place for you or your kin will always exist among our ranks. Blood is the only bond that cannot be broken, not even by the mighty lords of the Inner Sphere. When all is said and done, nothing can destroy the Northwind Highlanders!"

The voting was done by hand and took less than twenty minutes. When it was over the Cabel voted to ratify the Northwind agreement. All four colonels immediately issued orders for their regiments to pull out of the Capellan Confederation and to make posthaste for Northwind, acknowledging Prince Hanse Davion of the Federated Suns as their liege lord. In the weeks that followed more than two hundred dissenting MechWarriors, technicians, and their families left the Highlander ranks. There was no mutiny, no bitterness. Those who chose not to return to Northwind would continue to long for the day when they could, and those who went grieved at this parting with dear friends and comrades.

The desertion of the Capellan Confederation by the key regiments of the Northwind Highlanders sealed the fate of the Capellans in the Fourth Succession War. Millions died and millions more came under the dominion of the seemingly unstoppable Davion war machine.

1

Marik Palace
Atreus
Marik Commonwealth, Free Worlds League
8 August 3057

Sun-Tzu Liao studied his host very carefully as he and Thomas Marik sat talking in the study where Marik carried out most of his official business as Captain-General of the Free Worlds League. Though his eyes never left Marik's scarred and somber face, the younger man was also taking in everything around him—the candles, the tapestries, the hardcopy books, the antiques, the models of ancient aircraft. It was not the first time he had been in his chamber, but like any predator, the Chancellor of the Capellan Confederation knew he must be ever alert to his surroundings, ready to respond to any clue, any hint of possible danger, possible opportunity.

"You maintain and support a variety of subversive groups and revolutionary forces in the Sarna March, do you not?" Thomas was saying, slumped deep in his massive chair as if it were the only thing in the universe that could support him and the burdens he must carry. Sun-Tzu noticed that Marik's gaze seemed to wander as he spoke, as if his thoughts were light years away from this conversation. But there was no mistaking the gravity of his tone.

"I do," Sun-Tzu responded. "My Zhanzheng de guang are

HIGHLANDER GAMBIT

active on a number of Davion worlds. I also have ties to certain tongs and Liao loyalist groups." *What is Thomas up to?* he wondered. *He knows perfectly well that I've been busy stirring up trouble for Victor Davion in the Sarna March for some time now.* The only possible answer was that Thomas had taken the bait his agents had planted—a fake blood sample that "proved" Davion had replaced Marik's dying son Joshua with a double. The boy had been ailing for some years and been sent to the doctors on New Avalon in a last desperate hope of saving him.

"Good," Thomas said thoughtfully, his attention now turned full force on his visitor. "A situation has arisen that will require me to enter 'negotiations' with Victor Davion." Marik's emphasis on the word "negotiations" made it obvious he meant much more than the word usually implied.

Thomas paused and seemed to study Sun-Tzu curiously for a moment before going on. "I would like to use your agents in his Sarna March to pressure him in a way that will incline him to speak in good faith with me. To do this, I wish to create the impression that we have had a difference of opinion on certain matters. You will leave immediately and return to your capital on Sian."

Sun-Tzu chose his words carefully, speaking slowly and evenly. "I know you do not intend this, Captain-General, but some might interpret what you have suggested so far—a feigned split and my forces stirring up trouble in the Sarna March—as an attempt to force me away so you can conspire with Victor Davion to split my realm. I do not think this of you, but there are those who might."

Thomas straightened up and looked directly into the Liao's eyes. "It could seem that way, I agree. What sign would you have of me to prove that I do not intend to throw you to that rapacious wolf?" If Sun-Tzu had doubted Thomas, he did so no longer.

The young Chancellor held up one of his hands and casually studied the fashionably long fingernails of the last three fingers. The intricate designs painted on them in black lacquer and gold leaf caught the flickering of the candles like tiny stars. "There is the matter of setting a date for my wedding to your daughter." Thomas had been stalling on Sun-

Tzu's marriage to Isis Marik for five years now, a fact that had given Marik the upper hand in all their dealings.

The Captain-General gave the slightest of smiles, like a chessman acknowledging the rightness of his opponent's play. "Yes, Isis," he said softly. "Six months from now we shall announce that the wedding will take place roughly another six months hence."

Sun-Tzu hid his surprise. It was as if a crossroads had been reached, a milestone passed. "That is acceptable, but covenants are easily broken. Not that I would accuse you of such a thing, but if there were a coup . . ." This was his moment, and Sun-Tzu did not let it pass. Another chance like this might never come.

Again Thomas studied him, the light of the candles making his fire-scarred face look like a ritual mask. "Take Isis with you to Sian," he said, and it was obvious to Sun-Tzu that this was no snap decision. "You may hold her hostage as Victor has my . . ." The hesitation at the mention of Joshua's name struck Sun-Tzu hard. Proof positive, he thought, that his agents had succeeded.

"She will not be a hostage, but cherished as my bride-to-be."

"Yes, I know that you would keep her safe. I will cover your expenses for creating this added pressure, and my troops will stand by to repel Davion invaders if they decide to strike at you. I will also coordinate with the Capellan military to move troops to make life more difficult for Davion intelligence."

Sun-Tzu listened and understood. These were not rash decisions on the part of the Captain-General, but carefully calculated and coordinated moves. Had he underestimated Thomas, the man he'd considered an idealistic old fool? "Very good. When do I leave?"

"Within the week. Precentor Malcolm can help you send our orders to your subversives so their activities can begin before you arrive in Sian. You should be there by mid-September, I would think, but I need matters underway before then."

"It shall be done, Thomas." Sun-Tzu wanted to shout in elation, but all he did was imitate Thomas's slight smile.

HIGHLANDER GAMBIT 17

"Together we will teach Victor lessons his father never learned."

"Yes," the Captain-General replied. "The time has come and the lesson to be learned is that of justice." The anger is his voice was sharp and cold as a knife.

"If you do not mind, I will take my leave of you now," Sun-Tzu said, bowing his head. Thomas nodded slowly, rising as he took the Liao's hand in a firm handshake.

Sun-Tzu Liao paused in the corridor outside the Captain-General's office, trying to compose himself after this astounding interview. Looking around, it was not the first time he was struck by the way Marik had turned these walls into a gallery. He'd never understood Thomas' love of antiques and had assumed it was a throwback to his days in service to the mystical ComStar. Walking slowly as he examined the ancient paintings and maps, Sun-Tzu came to a sudden stop in front of a large old map of the Inner Sphere.

Apparently dating back to the time of the Star League, the map showed the Inner Sphere as it had been in the days of the Star League, the golden age of humanity. In the area around Terra were many of the worlds the Davions had stolen from the Capellan Confederation some thirty years ago, places where Sun-Tzu had been setting up guerrilla movements and tongs for the past two years. There would be no problem activating them to make trouble for the Federated Commonwealth.

His eyes wandered across the worlds of the old Terran Hegemony, once the heart and soul of the Star League. The planet Northwind seemed to leap from the map, and the sight of it set the young Chancellor's thoughts to racing. *Northwind.* Sun-Tzu had been planning an operation there for sometime in the future. But now that Marik had asked him to step up his subversive efforts, Northwind just might offer a rare opportunity for a very special operation. The planet sat in the middle of the so-called Terran Corridor, the narrow swath of worlds that provided a connecting link between the two great halves of the mighty Federated Commonwealth. A strike there would catch Victor off guard and deprive him of a world that was both strategically and military important.

It would also be a stroke of revenge against the mercenaries who claimed Northwind as their homeworld. The Northwind Highlanders, who had deserted the Capellans in their greatest hour of need, letting the Davion invaders seize half their worlds. Fate had handed him a chance to make them pay for their treachery.

Sun-Tzu knew that two of the elite Highlander regiments were currently assigned along the Clan border, while MacLeod's Regiment garrisoned Northwind and Stirling's Fusiliers was posted to the nearby Ozawa. He considered the possibilities carefully as he stared at the map. *If my operative can infiltrate the Highlanders I can use him to destroy them. One man, from the inside, can cause more damage than a battalion of BattleMechs—if he performs properly. With only one regiment on the planet, even a small number of my forces, once dug in, could prove nearly impossible to uproot. I will destroy the Highlanders and avenge House Liao on the unit that betrayed us and the boy-prince who threatens me.*

Sun-Tzu lifted his wristcomp up and carefully punched in his access code. His intended operative's name came up on the tiny screen. "Jaffray, Loren". He smiled, remembering where the Second Death Commandos were stationed. Loren Jaffray's history made him the perfect tool for this operation. Not only that, he was a member of the Death Commandos. Sworn to die at the Chancellor's word, the Commandos were beyond elite in their devotion to the Capellan Confederation.

I will tell Isis that this is a good opportunity for us to make a tour of my realm so she can come to know my people and my worlds. And it will give me a pretext to make a stop on Krin. Loren Jaffray doesn't know it, but he and I have an appointment to keep. A very important appointment. An appointment with destiny.

2

Lake Fairfax
Krin, Capellan Confederation
1 September 3057

"What is the exercise I'm watching here, Colonel?" the lanky robed figure asked from the bunker viewing port, not lifting the macro binoculars from his eyes. All that was visible to the naked eye were the frozen surface of Lake Fairfax and a small cottage flanked by a dozen BattleMechs painted the dull gray and white of winter camouflage. Using the enhanced binoculars the robed man was able to make out a *Hussar* hidden near a steep stone cliff that hid the 'Mech from view of the cottage. The *Hussar* was running in low-powder mode, but it stood out against the snow despite its own white and gray-striped paint scheme. The pilot was not in his 'Mech, but on the ground digging in the snow and dirt, seemingly oblivious of the men watching him from the distant bunker. If not for the filter provided by the binoculars, the reflection off the snow of Krin's bright sun would have made viewing the scene intolerable.

Colonel Hertzog of the Death Commandos was also following the progress of the operation across the lake. "The cadet team is led by one of our best officers, Your Excellency. One Major Loren Jaffray, the one about whom you inquired. The scenario we're running simulates a rescue operation. In this drill, the enemy has taken one of our people hostage and is holding him in the cottage. They have a full company of medium and heavy BattleMechs and a platoon of infantry at their disposal. Major Jaffray and his team have only a lance of medium and light 'Mechs and two platoons of ground troops to execute the rescue. These warriors have all failed this exercise previously."

"Failed?" Sun-Tzu Liao lowered the binox and stared incredulously at the Colonel.

Hertzog smiled slightly and nodded. "As you are aware, our training is rigorous and not everyone can measure up, not right away. I'm confident that the Major will demonstrate why we test new Death Commandos in this manner."

The Chancellor returned to surveying the scene through the binoculars. "Where are the Major's other 'Mechs? I see only a lone *Hussar*, hardly a match for his opposition."

"He deployed several under the surface of the lake three days ago."

The tall, dark-haired young man smiled as he watched the 'Mech pilot leave off digging in the snow and begin the long climb up the side of the 'Mech to its cockpit. "I see, so the good Major will have his troops attack from the lake to create a diversion while his infantry crosses the minefield he has carefully disabled by hand. The enemy 'Mechs go after his comrades in the lake, and his infantry squads make off with the hostage."

"Possible, Excellency," said Colonel Hertzog, "although that approach might seem too obvious for Jaffray. And the risks he took in keeping three 'Mechs underwater for three days indicate he might have other plans. As I told you before, he is known for being, shall I say, unconventional."

Sun-Tzu set the electronic binoculars on the window ledge, and crossed the bunker to the massive green table set in its center. It was obviously much more than a simple table, judging by the computerized control surface and the delicate lighting system built in. "How does this work, Colonel?"

Hertzog flicked a switch and the surface of the holotable flickered with light and life, producing a holographic image of the terrain surrounding the cabin and lake in miniature scale. The scene was precise in its detail, every tree and even the crisp white of the Krin snow appearing as if the observer were looking down onto the real-life hilltop. The relocated mines showed as small blue dots on the holographic field. The BattleMechs, standing only five centimeters tall, looked more like children's toys than the deadly, ten-meter-tall weapons of war they were. Even Major Jaffray and his concealed infantry showed up as tiny figures huddled in the seemingly solid holograph snow.

"Obviously we don't use live ammo in this kind of exercise. All missiles and shells carry flash warheads, and the lasers and PPCs are rigged at three percent, just enough to make it *look* real. Our engineers have electronically mapped the hillside, which has been equipped with monitors that feed through fiber-optic lines between here and there. Each BattleMech has a core computer known as the DI, or diagnostic interpreter. It literally gives the 'Mech life. It controls, either directly or indirectly, all weapons, sensors, and movement of the 'Mech. The simulator system is tied into a program we have loaded into the DI systems of the 'Mechs. When the 'Mech is hit by simulated fire, the damage is also simulated, right down to the BattleMech quaking under the impact of the hits. Similar systems are rigged into the infantry's helmets and weapons as well. It will look and feel real to them, with our master computer calling the shots as to who is alive and who isn't."

Sun-Tzu clasped his hands behind his back and nodded thoughtfully. "An excellent training tool. To show a warrior his or her mistakes."

"Or to teach him what he's doing right. Centuries ago they called this virtual reality, but our techs prefer to think of it as synthetic reality. To those taking part, this is as close as you can get to battle without getting shot to pieces."

The tiny image of Major Jaffray returned to his 'Mech while the Colonel and his lord watched as the infantry squads moved through the opening in the minefield. "Jaffray has done quite a job with their mines. He's rearranged them in narrow lanes to pull in their infantry and 'Mechs." As Hertzog spoke, the infantry suddenly leaped into battle against the hostage guards. As troopers of both sides fought and died, their images fell and turned black against the stark white ice and snow.

"It looks as if they're going to get the hostage any second," the Chancellor said, leaning over the large table to improve his view.

Suddenly the BattleMechs of the hostage-holding team seemed to come to life. A *Griffin* and *Warhammer* went into action from their vantage point beyond the cabin. The *Warhammer* took only a few steps, but the *Griffin* moved in to engage the infantry.

The *Griffin* was a classically configured BattleMech. Towering over the snowfield, it carried a particle projection cannon in one massive armored fist and a missile pod on one armored shoulder like an infantryman's bazooka. The 'Mech took several steps down the trail and then veered off, moving straight into the mines. The holographic map displayed a series of explosions and simulated smoke as the *Griffin* staggered slightly, caught off guard by the blasts. Then it peppered the attacking infantry with a barrage of LRM fire that raced across the stark white background in a flaming spray. The infantry broke and retreated down the hillside, leaving several dead troopers along the way. The image on the holotable was eerily silent.

"Is there any way to reproduce the sounds of the fighting?" the Liao asked.

"Of course, Excellency. The monitors in the 'Mechs reproduce the sounds of impact for added realism. External monitors on the hillside can give us the audio feed." Colonel Hertzog pressed some control studs at the head of the table, and soon the crackling of lasers and explosions filled the bunker.

Sensing that they had their foes on the run, the defending infantry went hot in pursuit and ran directly into their own mines. The explosions on the surface of the holographic display brought them to a grinding halt. Still, Jaffray's light *Hussar* remained motionless and hidden behind an outcropping of rock near the shore. Several other defending BattleMechs had by now also powered up and begun moving down the trail to the shoreline.

"He's leaving his infantry squads to die," Sun-Tzu noted. "Even with those mines they're in a rout away from the cottage and the hostage."

"Diversion, Excellency. Observe."

The leading *Hercules* spun off the trail and started down

HIGHLANDER GAMBIT 23

the hillside to intercept the attacking infantry's escape. The *Griffin*, slowed by the mines, was attempting to backtrack out of the minefield to join in. As the *Hercules* opened up on the infantry with its short-range missiles and a barrage of autocannon fire, the holotable showed three attackers dead in the assault and the others returning fire as they drew closer to the frozen surface of Lake Fairfax. Their shoulder-launched missiles scored against the *Hercules*, but did not stop it from continuing its attack on the hillside.

The *Warhammer* and the *Griffin* followed the lead 'Mech down the far left side of the hill, away from the cottage. That left a lone squad to guard the hostage. Closing in for the kill, three other defender 'Mechs also started down the left side of the hill. But the raiding infantry put up a strong defense, constantly moving farther and farther from the cottage and their objective.

Suddenly the lone *Hussar* powered up, moving across the now-opened minefield without incident. Once it was out in the open, the sensors of the defending BattleMechs quickly picked it up, and three of them began to move toward the smaller, faster *Hussar*. Major Jaffray did not fire at them but instead concentrated on the cottage. The defending infantry squad began to fire once he came into line of sight, their shots showing as thin streaks of red on the holotable. The *Hussar* ignored them, running straight into the midst of their formation until the tiny figures broke and fled, apparently hoping to regroup in a cluster of pines nearby. Their man-to-man weapons were no match for a BattleMech.

Using its two stubby arms, the pod-shaped *Hussar* punched its way through the roof of the cottage. Detailed and realistic, the holotable image immediately showed wood shingles and timbers sliding off what was left of the roof and into the snow. The stubby body of the *Hussar* leaned forward as it reached into the structure and carefully pulled out what appeared to be a golden figure, obviously the hostage, through the hastily ripped hole. The war machine's actions were smooth, evidence of good 'Mech piloting and programming.

"I'm surprised," the Chancellor muttered, more to himself than for the benefit of the Colonel.

"Sir?"

"He will not escape at this point, even if the rest of his lance joins in." In the distance the table showed the first of the defenders, the *Griffin,* bring its weapons to bear on Jaffray's *Hussar.* It opened up with its PPC and long-range missiles, hoping to wreak some revenge for its earlier trip into the minefield. The PPC shot went wide and into a cluster of trees to the right of the hillside. The missiles came closer, hitting in and around the tiny holographic image of the *Hussar.* Those that missed buried themselves in the snow and erupted like fiery mushrooms on the three-dimensional display. The sounds reproduced by the holotable were realistic and perfectly timed to the blasts. Those warheads that hit the 'Mech showed as tiny red dots, like wounds on a man's flesh.

The line of defending 'Mechs was spread down the left side of the hill, pursuing Jaffray's diversionary infantry force. Now they suddenly turned their attention to the real threat, the *Hussar* and the hostage they were supposed to be guarding. They had all but ignored Jaffray's remaining infantry, who now stepped up their missile attacks against the 'Mechs now leaving them behind.

The light BattleMech turned away from its attackers, exposing its thinly armored rear to the approaching horde of 'Mechs. Instead of making his way along the shoreline and possible safety, Jaffray charged the fast-moving *Hussar* down the hillside. Several of the defenders' laser shots also went wide, burying themselves in holographic snowdrifts. The path leading down to the shore was tight and winding, opening up only at the shoreline itself. The Krin winter had totally embalmed it in ice and snow, and the fast-moving *Hussar* slid several times as it raced down the trail to the frozen surface of the lake. The 'Mechs shooting at the *Hussar* seemed to get closer with each shot. Time was running out.

The closeness of the shots seemed to shake Hertzog, who quickly concealed his flush of fear. The Colonel stood straighter and pulled his green dress uniform taut against his muscled frame in an attempt to regain his composure. "With all due respect, sire, I wouldn't rule Jaffray out just yet. I usually give him charge of a failing group of trainees so they'll learn to fight with their heads as well as their

'Mechs. Tactics have to be instinctive for a Death Commando. Only he would have had the brains to check to see that the shore ice was in shallow water and is solid for a pretty good distance ..." Suddenly Colonel Hertzog caught himself in his admiration of his officer. "But as I said before, sire, Jaffray is not the kind of man you would need for this mission."

The figure in the red and gold silk robe did not lift his gaze from the scene unfolding on the holotable. "Indeed." His tone was dry and disbelieving.

Major Jaffray's *Hussar* ran out onto the solidly frozen surface of the lake, a rain of laser and PPC fire pouring down the hillside around him. Two Streak missiles fired from the pursuing *Hercules* dug deeply into the back of the *Hussar*, which reeled from the impact of the warheads. The holographic image of the 'Mech showed it glowing more red from the fire it was taking than gray from its original paint scheme. A thin but brilliant lightning-blue blast of PPC fire from a *Warhammer* just narrowly grazed Jaffray's 'Mech and struck the ice on the lake surface. The holographic image displayed the impact as an explosion of steam and frozen shrapnel. If not for the speed of its run, the *Hussar* would have fallen into the hole blasted by the PPC. As it was, the 'Mech was running toward the deeper water and the much thinner ice.

The *Hussar* proceeded nearly thirty centimeters on the holographic display of the lake surface before the ice collapsed under the 'Mech's heavy tonnage. As the *Hussar* pitched forward into the hole Jaffray was already drawing the 'Mech's arm back and then flinging what the hand held just ahead of the gaping hole. The "hostage" landed out on the slick surface ice of the lake in a rolling and churning slide. The force of Jaffray's toss was incredible, sending the hostage only a few scant centimeters from the opposite shore of the holographic lake.

"Most interesting," the Chancellor said, his eyes fixed on the display. "I would have expected him to use his infantry to retrieve the hostage. To employ his 'Mech in this fashion is most unusual, I would think."

"I concur, sire. That little maneuver by Jaffray will cost our hostage more than a few broken bones, but she's safe and it looks like one of Jaffray's troops is already picking her up." Colonel Hertzog pointed to the spot on the holotable where the golden image of the hostage was encountering one of Jaffray's infantry. In the icy waters of the lake, Jaffray turned to face his pursuers as three bursts of laser fire dug into his 'Mech's torso and arms, burning red on the display. In real life, the water was only five meters deep, but left more than enough of Jaffray's *Hussar* exposed to fire from his foes. The smaller, faster 'Mech was no match for any one of its pursuers in a prolonged stand-up fight, but that looked like exactly what Jaffray was preparing to do. A move that seemed nothing short of suicidal.

The pursuit force moved down the hillside toward the shore, only to stumble into more of Jaffray's mines. As the speakers in the holotable played the roar of mock explosions, Jaffray's infantry ambushed the *Warhammer* on the left flank of the field, wracking it with short-range missiles and the blasts from satchel charges. The *Warhammer*'s weapons were ill-suited for anti-infantry combat, and as the 'Mech turned to face its attackers, one of the blasts tore its leg off at the knee. The mighty war machine fell like a drunken sailor, sliding down the snow-covered hill to the shore.

Its fellow defenders waded across the line of mines, training their weapons on the seemingly stranded *Hussar*. The defenders were carefully lined up like a firing squad, several of them taking positions behind rock outcroppings flanking the shore. The Major's infantry kept a pressing attack on the left flank, striking at the *Griffin* and a *Phoenix Hawk* in the ranks. The row of 'Mechs did not return fire immediately, but looked almost as if they were savoring Jaffray's defeat as his *Hussar* poked up through the hole in the ice.

Without warning the frozen surface of the lake bed exploded to life as Jaffray's three other lancemates broke upward through the surface and opened fire at the *Hercules* standing in the center of the pursuers' firing line. To Colonel Hertzog and his distinguished guest the attack was just as surprising, for the holographic images of the miniature 'Mechs did not appear on the display until they broke through the surface of the lake.

Jaffray joined in the assault, firing his large laser into the legs of the *Hercules* while his lancemates pummeled the same target with lasers and short-range missiles. The air on the surface of the holotable was ablaze with simulated laser and PPC light. Missiles and autocannon explosions splattered the winter snow on the hill. Overwhelmed by the barrage against its legs and chest, the *Hercules* staggered backward for a moment, looking like a wounded knight in heavy armor, then spun slightly as its pilot lost balance and thus control of the massive machine. The 'Mech tumbled backward against the hillside, burying itself in a deep snow bank.

Lined up so neatly against the snow-covered embankment, the pursuit force realized they were perfect targets for Jaffray's rescue team. With the rock outcroppings blocking their shots, the flanking 'Mechs could not bring their weapons to bear on some of the 'Mechs. Instead of pressing their positions, the pursuit force began to pull back to a small ridge halfway up the steep hill, back toward the main trail between the cottage and the shore.

As if on cue a series of explosions erupted on the ridge line as the 'Mechs reached their high-ground positions. The blasts sent two of the 'Mechs falling and sprawling down to the shore of Lake Fairfax at the feet of Jaffray's attack force.

Colonel Hertzog and his guest were not surprised by the blasts, for they could see the mines on the surface of the holographic hillside. The explosions pushed the pursuers back across the hillside again. They fired wildly at the 'Mechs in the freezing water but most of their shots seemed to miss or do only light damage. The pilots of the fallen 'Mechs were trying desperately to get their 'Mechs standing or out of reach of Jaffray's 'Mechs. One of them, the *Griffin,* floundered on the slippery surface of the lake like a fish suddenly cast onto dry land. With almost perfect timing, Jaffray's lance turned about face and plunged into the icy waters, disappearing beneath the surface once more. The battle was over as quickly as it had begun, and suddenly the rolling thunder of battle from across the lake stopped altogether.

Colonel Hertzog chuckled slightly. "Major Jaffray knew how his enemy would respond and set up a perfect trap. Keeping his 'Mechs underwater for three days was risky, but it let them creep into a perfect position along the shoreline.

Our planetary survey showed an underwater ledge with a steep drop-off there, but I've never seen anyone make use of it quite that way in the rescue scenario."

Slowly the robed man raised his eyes from the holotable image and gazed at the commanding officer of the First Death Commandos. The Chancellor's eyes narrowed as he leaned over the table and fixed Hertzog with his gaze. "You will have this Major Jaffray of yours report to me within the hour, Colonel. He and I have much to discuss."

3

Lake Fairfax
Krin, Capellan Confederation
1 September 3057

Major Loren Jaffray was still bathed in cold sweat as he stepped into the antechamber of the observation bunker. Clad in field shorts, and light boots, he looked wan and tired. Bags puffed under his eyes and several days of black stubble covered his face. He was still wearing his cooling vest, which crackled slightly as he came into the room.

In the 600 years that the BattleMech had dominated the battlefields of the Inner Sphere, the problem of heat buildup was still its biggest dilemma. Though the ten-meter-tall goliaths wielded enough firepower to destroy a platoon of more conventional armored combat vehicles, they also generated tremendous amounts of heat just moving about. The cooling vest, dripping wet with condensation, was not just a common sight among MechWarriors, it was often the difference between life and death in battle.

Loren pulled off his plaid headband and tucked it into his belt, then pressed his hands into the small of his back to stretch out some of the tension from the recent simulation. His eyes stung from his own perspiration, and the cool air of the bunker made him shiver. When the door to the area opened and Colonel Hertzog stepped the room, Loren snapped to instant attention. Hertzog nodded back informally.

"You wanted to see me, sir?"

"Yes, Major. Outstanding performance. I received word that our simulated hostage would have suffered three broken ribs and a fractured arm from your rescue."

"Fortunately we use dummies for these drills. In a hostage situation, the alternative to such injuries is death. I would say the hostage got off rather well."

Hertzog smiled slightly. "True enough. No doubt Major Quaid's defending team is more than slightly humbled by your success in this test." Jaffray knew that his commanding officer encouraged competition among his troops and that Quaid would have trouble trying to live down his defeat. "But that's not why I wanted to see you, Major."

"What can I do for you, sir?" Loren asked, taking a towel from the wall peg and using it to rub down his dripping black hair. There was usually only one reason for a CO to make such a visit—a new assignment. Then he saw that the Colonel was not alone. Now coming through the door was the tall, slim figure of a man dressed in the formal red and gold silk robes of his office. Chancellor Sun-Tzu Liao, ruler of the Capellan Confederation, was Loren's liege lord, and he would have recognized him anywhere. To a Death Commando like Loren, the Chancellor was much more than a mere head of state. The Death Commandos reported directly to him, were sworn by a blood oath to serve and even die at his command. The Chancellor represented more than leadership, he was their very reason for existence.

Within a beat of his heart Loren Jaffray dropped to his bare knees on the cold bunker floor and bowed his head. "Your Excellency." He had always hoped to one day meet the Chancellor, but had not expected to be covered in sweat and dressed only in the skimpy shorts favored by MechWarriors in the cockpit. For a fleeting moment he wondered just where he had stashed his dress uniform.

"Rise, Major Jaffray," the young Chancellor said. Loren quickly rose to his feet and to attention, but lowered his eyes slightly in respect. "I witnessed the training exercise and was deeply impressed. You took extreme risks in that little scenario."

"I knew my foe well and took advantage of that." Loren spoke with confidence despite his nervousness at this unexpected audience.

"So it was not luck but cunning that led to victory." The Chancellor's expression was impossible to read.

Loren smiled, hoping to break some of the tension he felt. "Luck played some role, sire. In battle it is always a factor. But I believe it's how one *manages* luck, turning and twisting it to meet one's needs, that is the key to any victory."

Hertzog stepped forward quickly. "Mind your words, Major Jaffray. This is the Chancellor you are addressing and he has not come here for a lecture on how to fight wars."

Sun-Tzu turned toward the Colonel, but did not take his eyes off Loren until the last possible moment. "You may leave us now, Colonel. I have important matters to discuss with Major Jaffray." He returned his gaze to Loren and for a moment, however brief, gave him a smile.

Hertzog was obviously shocked at being excluded from a discussion between his superior and a junior officer. "Sire?"

"That will be all," Sun-Tzu said curtly, waving his hand impatiently toward the door. Hertzog bowed his head slightly and backed out of the chamber, only turning around at the door, which he reluctantly shut behind him. The thud it made upon closing echoed in the room for a long moment.

The Chancellor moved to the now inactive holotable in the center of the room and carefully lifted the hem of his silk robe off the floor as he lowered himself into the chair. He gestured to the seat at the opposite end of the table. Jaffray draped the towel around his neck and also sat down. Another chill ran through his body, and he wondered if it was from contact with the cooler air of the bunker or the cool stare the young leader of the Capellan Confederation was giving him.

"This is a very great honor, Chancellor," Loren said nervously as he took a seat. There was good reason to fear. In recent times members of the ruling family of House Liao had been known for their homicidal tendencies. Sun-Tzu's own mother Romano had purged thousands of her subjects— all in the name of national security. Not to mention that it was her own father's complicated schemes that had goaded Hanse Davion into attacking the Capellan Confederation in the Fourth Succession War. A war that had cost the Capellans half their realm and millions of lives.

Then there was the other possibility. The Death Commandos were the Capellan Confederation's elite strike force. Loren's last assignment, a raid on a ComStar data depository, had been highly successful. He and his team had managed to frame the quasi-religious Word of Blake for the crime while netting much useful intelligence for their nation. Perhaps Sun-Tzu had come to commend Loren for the effort or perhaps to offer him another mission.

"I have come," the Chancellor said, steepling his fingers, "to ask you to undertake a mission in the name of the Capellan Confederation." Loren noticed the intricate gold inlay on Sun-Tzu's talon-like fingernails, which glittered in the yellowish light.

"Ask, sire? I am a Death Commando, sworn to obey you without question and to the death. Command and I obey."

Sun-Tzu studied Loren, but his expression was as unreadable as ever. "The nature of this mission is in many ways personal, Major Jaffray. And, for all intents and purposes, it is a mission that our government is not 'officially' undertaking. I cannot afford the political implications and protocol breaches of sending you out under a diplomatic flag. You will undertake this mission as a private citizen, with all the risks such an action entails."

Loren felt his back and shoulders tense slightly at the Chancellor's tone. For a Death Commando, special missions were not uncommon. What made this different was that the Chancellor himself was doing the asking, *in person.* "I live to serve, my lord. What would you have me do?"

"I want you to right a wrong against the Capellan people. I want you to win us not only justice, but revenge.

"In 3028 Hanse Davion lured the regiments of the Northwind Highlanders away from us, promising them rulership of their native Northwind if they would serve him. And then the Highlanders deserted us when we needed them most.

"The withdrawal of the Highlanders from their garrisons left the Terran Corridor worlds of the Confederation virtually defenseless. The Federated Suns military devoured our worlds in a matter of months. The defeat of the Fourth Succession War still eats like a canker at my people, Major. But now, the time is ripe for revenge."

Loren said nothing for a moment, taking in the words and turning them over carefully in his mind before responding. "The loss of the Highlanders did cost our people a great deal, my lord. How may I help right such a wrong?"

The young Chancellor smiled slightly. "History has granted me a unique opportunity. Although Victor Davion managed to quell the rebellion in the Skye March last year, I don't think he will deal so easily with the discontent of the people in the Sarna March. Armed resistance to Davion rule has broken out on a number of planets. And with the greater part of the Northwind Highlanders away defending the Lyran border with the Clans, the time is right to strike at my enemies, a blow that will bring us the retribution we have waited for so long."

Loren's mind raced with excitement. A direct attack, perhaps against Northwind itself? Somehow embarrass or humiliate the Highlanders? An assassination of the mercenary unit's leadership, perhaps? Then he realized that he was viewing the Highlanders as enemies when in reality Sun-Tzu was speaking of other, greater foes. Perhaps even Prince Victor Steiner-Davion himself. Jaffray's face flushed for a moment as he pondered the potential scope of what his lord might ask him to do.

Sun-Tzu's crafty smile broadened. "I want you to travel to Northwind to offer the Highlanders full independence of their planet from Davion rule, Major Jaffray. The goal of your mission is a simple one, remove Northwind from the Federated Commonwealth and neutralize the Highlander regiments."

For several heartbeats Loren sat in silence, his eyes fixed on the Chancellor as he took in the words. "Independence. Sire . . . such a mission is—"

"Outlandish, outrageous perhaps? Based on what I saw today, you of all people understand the power of audacity in both diplomacy and on the battlefield. I want you to go and convince the leaders of the Highlanders that the Davions have not fulfilled their contract with them. Rather than ruling Northwind free and clear, as my forefathers promised them, the Highlanders are no more than vassals of the Federated Commonwealth. Centuries ago we Liaos promised that the Highlanders would one day again rule Northwind as their own. The Davions have also made them the same promise, but it is they who are the lord and master of Northwind, not the Highlanders. You, Loren Jaffray, will open their eyes to this reality.

"Tell them that both the Capellan Confederation and the Free Worlds League will officially recognize Northwind as an independent world. Furthermore you will tell them that I will dedicate my best troops to defend them. What they gain is ownership of a world that is rightfully theirs and the chance to determine their own fate. Davion has lied to them and they no longer need to accept that. You will promise the Highlanders that their troops and their families can live on Northwind as a free people—something denied them under the thumb of the Davions."

"You said that my mission was to neutralize the Highlanders, my lord."

Sun-Tzu smiled slightly before he spoke, savoring the silence like a chessmaster preparing to checkmate. "After making the Highlanders this offer, you will gain their confidence, become one of them. I strongly suspect that Victor Davion will respond with force to retain control of Northwind. You will manage that situation as you deem appropriate, given the scope of your mission."

Sun-Tzu leaned forward on his elbows as he continued. "Two battalions of Death Commandos will arrive in the Northwind system soon after you present my offer to the Highlanders. When the time is right, you will call them in to destroy the Highlanders. The decades of injustice against the Confederation will finally come to an end, and the Federated Commonwealth will pay the cost."

Destroy the Highlanders ... a mission more for an army than one man. Loren did not question the order. He was a Death Commando and the Chancellor was his commander. *I swore an oath to fight to the death for him if necessary to fulfill his will. This is what I've been trained for all my life.*
"The mission is a bold one, Lord."

"Indeed it is, Major."

"I am honored that you entrust it to me, sire, but I am somewhat confused. Surely you have many diplomats or higher-ranking officers in the Capellan military more skilled in such matters. This mission seems to require the subtle skills of an ambassador.

"I am a military man. Neither diplomacy nor deception come naturally to me. This mission seems made up of shades of gray, and I am a man who best understands simple black and white." In the back of his mind Loren could not help but wonder if in reality it was some kind of suicide mission.

Sun-Tzu Liao leaned back slightly in the chair, placing both hands flat on the table. "I have little need or love for career diplomats. The issue of the sovereignty of Northwind is murky at best. My foes would interpret my sending a diplomat to Northwind as too direct a move. As a private citizen carrying a message to your ancestral homeworld, you will be the perfect instrument for achieving my goals.

"Besides, the Northwind Highlanders are a military people. A diplomat would be eaten alive by such warriors. They would not trust him."

The Chancellor's eyes narrowed slightly as he leaned forward. "You are my choice for this mission because of your family history. Your great grandmother, Letha Davis Jaffray, is a hero in the annals of Highlander history, credited with saving an entire regiment. Your grandfather served with distinction as an officer with MacCormack's Fusiliers, did he not?"

The question was obviously rhetorical. Sun-Tzu knew that Loren's family had ties to the Highlanders or he would never have chosen him for the mission. At the mention of his grandfather and the Fusiliers, Loren glanced down at the plaid headband tucked into his waistband. It was all that remained of his grandfather's ceremonial Highlander battle sash. A flood of memories came to life just for an instant. Images of his grandfather, father, and the sound of bagpipes playing in his grandfather's den.

"Of course, sire. My grandfather Corwin Jaffray was a Major in the Fusiliers, but decided not to join the other Highlanders in their so-called Homecoming in 'twenty-eight. Instead he mustered out, choosing to remain loyal to the Capellan Confederation. A part of him was always bitter over the Highlanders' desertion to the Federated Suns. My father was also offered a slot in the Fusiliers, as is the Highlander tradition, but he turned it down to serve your mother as one of the Commandos. I am, for lack of a better word, intimate with the traditions of the Highlanders."

Sun-Tzu nodded sagely. "I know. I also know that, as a man with blood ties to the Highlanders, you will be treated as one of their own, a kindred MechWarrior. You are also a direct link to one of their greatest heroes. The current CO of the unit, Colonel MacLeod, took command of your grandfather's former unit after the Highlanders defected to Northwind. He and the others will accept you on face value, like the proverbial wolf in sheep's clothing. And when the time is right, the wolf will spring forth to slaughter the flock."

"Still, sire, there must be others more qualified. I live to serve you, but I only wish to see the success of such a mission."

"Yes, perhaps there are others, but none that I'll have. There are one hundred eighty-six relatives of the Highlanders still in the Capellan Confederation. Of these, only fifteen have family members still active in the military. I have personally reviewed their files. I want you, Jaffray. You are daring—I saw that today. You don't hesitate to take extraordinary risks and turn certain defeat into victory. You are also a man who understands tactics and strategy."

Again Loren might have protested, but Sun-Tzu held up one glittering hand for silence.

"Most MechWarriors would never have taken on three-to-one odds and survived as you did earlier today. And I read in your service record that during one raid, you killed two of your fellow Commandos who were injured rather than let them be captured. You are undoubtedly the man for this mission, Major Jaffray."

Sun-Tzu leaned forward in his chair, his thin features highlighted in the bunker's yellow lights. "Perhaps it will interest you to know that Colonel Hertzog spent at least thirty minutes trying to dissuade me from offering you a mission. He claimed not to like your 'style' of combat, saying that you rely too much on guile. He did everything he could to convince me that you were not the man that I wanted."

"And that is good?" Loren said.

HIGHLANDER GAMBIT 37

"Yes. I have found that most military men are unwilling to part with good officers and troops. Based on the squirming done by your commanding officer, you must be one of the best warriors I have. And for this mission, I need the best."

Loren felt his heart begin to race with excitement, but he remained formal and deferential. "I appreciate your confidence, Excellency."

"Success is everything. And you will use any means necessary to win it. Understood?"

"Understood, sire. What assets will I have at my disposal?"

"I am sending a gift to the Highlander command staff—it is being loaded into a DropShip as we speak. A JumpShip will also be at your disposal. Sometime after your arrival on Northwind I will send two battalions of Commandos to a pirate jump point in the system. Once the people of Northwind accept my generous offer, Victor Davion will no doubt toss anything he can at the world to regain control of it. That is all I can tell you, Major, except that you will be my sole agent on Northwind. You won't have to contend with interference from anyone wishing to 'assist' you." From this, Loren understood that Sun-Tzu was holding the state security forces of the Maskirovka in check for this undertaking. It added even more gravity to the mission.

"The Death Commandos will begin a combat drop on your orders only, and you alone will have the authority to abort such an action, if necessary." The Chancellor reached into the cuff of his silk sleeve and pulled out a small object. He carefully slid the dark blue diskette across the table toward Loren. "That disk contains the latest intelligence data on the Northwind Highlanders and the planet itself. Profiles of unit commanders, TO&E, and so on. All the codes you need are there as well. Commit them to memory."

Sun-Tzu Liao rose slowly from his chair and looked down at the young officer. "You have not yet said whether you accept this assignment, Major Jaffray."

Loren rose from his chair, once again feeling a slight chill and not knowing from whence it came. "Command and I obey, Chancellor. It is a chance to right a great wrong."

Sun-Tzu's eyes locked with Loren's. More than stern, his

gaze was almost fierce. Loren thought about the stories he'd heard of Sun-Tzu's mother and for a moment he saw Romano Liao's wild eyes peering through her son's. Then the look was gone, the Chancellor's expression as calm and inscrutable as before. "Beware of sentimentality, Major. This mission is much more than it seems and you will be very much alone. Righting wrongs is noble—but it can also be deadly. Such ideals will not preserve you once you enter the camp of our enemies."

"I understand, my lord." Again Loren felt his heart race with excitement.

"Understand this too, then. Your mission is critical to the Capellan Confederation. You will use *any* means necessary to neutralize Northwind and the Highlanders—be it assassination, deceit, or guile. Nor will you hesitate to sacrifice either your life *or even your honor* to achieve our goals. Nothing must divert you from the purpose of the mission. There is no room for failure."

Loren did not know how long he stood there after the door had closed behind his lord.

There is no room for failure, the Chancellor had said, and those parting words echoed in his mind long after Sun-Tzu had gone his way, leaving the young officer to contemplate the strange and twisting path of fate.

4

Kohler Spaceport
Tara, Northwind
Draconis March, Federated Commonwealth
11 September 3057

The limousine pulled up to the edge of the tarmac of the Kohler Spaceport, and the young infantry trooper stepped up smartly to the rear door. He held it open, snapping a salute to the gray-haired man in Highlander dress tartans who stepped out onto the hot tarmac.

Colonel William MacLeod returned the salute as his executive officer followed him out of the limo. Adjusting his battle sash where it draped over his kilt, he lifted his eyes to the early evening sky over Northwind, scanning for some sight of the arriving DropShip.

Major Chastity Mulvaney emerged from the vehicle in similar dress uniform. A worried frown creased her brow and her movements were abrupt, almost stiff.

She too lifted her eyes to the sky overhead, searching for the ship they'd come to meet. "I still have my doubts about this entire arrangement, Colonel."

MacLeod smiled as he turned to look at her. "I did not become the Commanding Officer of the Northwind Highlanders by taking foolish risks, Major. It's true I was caught off guard by the communiqué that Sun-Tzu Liao was sending a messenger and gift to Northwind. And I was even more surprised to find out that it was the grandson of old Ironclad Jaffray. But to refuse such a gift and visitor might do more harm than accepting them."

"Don't you think it's a slap in the face to Victor Davion? He's the one we work for, after all."

MacLeod chuckled. "Let's just say it's a way of keeping open our options. We Highlanders have been mercenaries for centuries. We sell our services, the services of war. I prefer not to insult a potential employer, even when the prospects of employment are remote. Upsetting our beloved Planetary Consul and his aide is merely a side benefit."

"This Loren Jaffray may be related to the Highlanders by blood, but he isn't one of us, Colonel. He's a Death Commando. You know what that means, sir."

MacLeod smiled, letting Mulvaney have her tirade.

"He's a fanatic, a trained terrorist, and he takes orders directly from the Chancellor, who's the only one he's accountable to. You know what kind of jobs the Commandos are assigned—sabotage, assassinations, kidnappings, terrorism—you name it."

MacLeod shook his head in mock amazement. "I never thought I'd see the day when my executive officer was afraid of one man. Besides, one man's terrorist is another man's freedom fighter."

"I'm not afraid of him, sir."

Colonel MacLeod had heard it all before, had been hearing it for days, in fact. He and Mulvaney had discussed at length whether to permit Jaffray's visit. Though he'd come to trust her instincts, in this case MacLeod thought they simply didn't have enough information about either Jaffray or his business on Northwind to deny permission.

"It's too late, Major," he said. "Jaffray's on his way to Northwind, and you know it. We'll treat him with the same respect due any courier of blood relation of the Highlanders."

MacLeod paused and lifted his eyes again to the sky. "And if this laddie thinks he's coming here to do some dirty work for Sun-Tzu, he'll find himself such an 'honored guest' that he's never out of our sight. We'll be keeping a sharp eye on him and if he means to harm the Highlanders we'll find out about it. Keep him close, Major, so our security people can watch his every move."

Their conversation was interrupted as another gleaming limousine pulled up. The small fender flags of the Federated Commonwealth fluttered slightly in the evening breeze as the driver got out and went around to open the rear door for his two passengers. Appearing first was Drake Burns, Federated Commonwealth Planetary Consul of Northwind, complete with flowing cape. He was followed by a shorter man, Drew Catelli, the sight of whom made MacLeod's expression darken slightly.

The taller man strutted arrogantly over to MacLeod, then bowed with more formality than necessary. Behind him the small honor guard band of the Northwind Highlanders had begun to assemble. The Consul threw them a glance, then returned his attention to MacLeod. "This is a most peculiar meeting, Colonel. I assume you have not changed your mind about approving this Liao officer's request to visit Northwind."

MacLeod shook his head. "The message I received indicated that this Loren Jaffray wishes to visit Northwind for personal reasons, Consul Burns. Members of his family were heroes of the Highlander clans and I would not tarnish our traditions by turning him aside merely because of the flag he wears on his lapel. Besides that, he is carrying a message and gift from Sun-Tzu Liao to the Highlanders. It is fully in my rights as the sovereign of this world to grant him access."

"Quite. But you are treating him like a visiting dignitary instead of a trained terrorist," said the shorter man, pointing to the honor guard band.

"That band is not here for Major Jaffray, Colonel Catelli. It is here for me. It is a Highlander tradition to greet visiting kin or dignitaries with bagpipes. We would salute you the same way, as I believe we did when you arrived on Northwind. But unless you have some specific charges or evidence against Jaffray, I'm going to respect his right as a bloodkin of the Highlanders to visit his homeworld." MacLeod was weary of having to defend his decision. Besides the many discussions with Chastity Mulvaney, he'd had to endure several long debates with Burns and Catelli.

Drake Burns cut in impatiently. "You seem irritated this evening, Colonel. I hope we have done nothing to bring on this mood."

MacLeod's face reddened slightly, and he crossed his arms in open defiance. "I had, in all honesty, hoped to settle the Glengarry matter before we met again."

Burns was unshaken by MacLeod's refusal to coat his words in a veneer of diplomacy. "Ah yes, your formal protest over the payment terms for the Glengarry operation. Is that the matter to which you refer, Colonel?"

"You know damn well it is. You hired us to help put down the uprising in Skye and we did our duty. Then when we go to refit, you try to sell us repair parts at three times the going rate. I had to import the supply parts from the Free Worlds League and you refused to pay the bill, despite the clause in our contract guaranteeing reimbursement. As I said in our last meeting, you will not bind the Highlanders to your Federated Commonwealth company store."

"You exaggerate, Colonel. This is nothing more than a minor contract dispute," Burns said, casually checking the cuffs of his shirt to imply how unimportant was the matter.

"The Highlanders will not be absorbed into the FedCom military machine, Consul Burns. That I can assure you." MacLeod was about to say more when they heard the distant rumble of an approaching DropShip. There would be another time to address the issue ... another place ...

The DropShip *Bec de Corbin* shuddered slightly on final approach to the spaceport on the outskirts of Tara, the capital of Northwind. Loren checked his safety belt to make sure it was secure as he crammed his muscular frame into the flight seat. A *Leopard* Class DropShip was spartan at best, and often took a buffeting from turbulent planetary air disturbances because of its smaller size. But Loren Jaffray had been experiencing the bumps and grinds of DropShip landings since the age of fifteen, and had long ago become accustomed to every sound and sensation of one.

Northwind! After a lifetime of hearing about it from his father and grandfather, he felt a wave of excitement rise in him as he watched the surface of the planet looming nearer through the viewport. He knew all about its history, how

Northwind had been settled by colonists from Terra's own Scotland, Ireland, and Wales during the early years of space exploration. Those settlers had taken immediately to Northwind because it reminded them so much of their former homelands.

Centuries later the residents of Northwind, in conjunction with their Capellan sires, had raised the regiments of the Northwind Highlanders at the height of the Star League. In that era the Northwind Highlanders were known as one of the finest military units ever formed. But the Star League collapsed and Northwind was seized by House Davion's Federated Suns. The Highlander regiments retreated into the Capellan Confederation, where they found refuge for more than three centuries, awaiting the day they might return to Northwind. As time passed, the Scots, Irish, and Welsh accents faded with the influx of recruits from across the Inner Sphere. But never lost was the Highlanders' longing for their homeworld. Northwind became like a grail, the dream of it binding them so tightly that even three centuries of war could not break the bond.

The dream came true in 3028, when the Highlanders signed the Northwind Agreement with Hanse Davion and abandoned the Capellan Confederation. The return was known as the Homecoming, but for Loren's grandfather the victory had been a double-edged sword. As a dissenter to the decision, Corwin Jaffray had renounced his commission with the Highlanders. Though Loren was not yet born when the Highlanders returned to Northwind, he wore the memory of it like a scar. It was almost as though he had inherited his grandfather's sorrow at losing both his unit and his chance to return to Northwind.

And now Loren was about to take his own place in the story, picking up where his grandfather had left off. It was not just because he was a Death Commando that Sun-Tzu had selected him for this mission, but because the Chancellor hoped Loren's kinship with the unit would win him the trust of the Highlander command staff. And once Loren opened that chink in their armor, his mission was clear.

Destroy the Northwind Highlanders.

He'd left Krin immediately, spending the last ten days of transit reviewing the most current data on Northwind and its infamous garrison. Perhaps the most important point was the strain that had begun to fray the relations between the Highlanders and the Federated Commonwealth. Perhaps that was why the Highlander commander had approved his visit. Loren had read the text of Sun-Tzu's message to him and could still remember the words: "... Major Jaffray carries with him a message from myself as the ruler of the Capellan Confederation and a gift to the Highlanders from the Capellan people. Please consider him a private courier, with my personal assurances that he comes in the spirit of peace ..."

Perhaps they were curious and interested about what the Chancellor had to say, or perhaps they wished to use him as a pawn against the Federated Commonwealth. Regardless, the Highlanders' response had been diplomatically cordial. Not so the Federated Commonwealth's. The moment the Liao JumpShip entered FedCom Space, they'd had to submit to an inspection that seemed to go far beyond the call of duty.

Loren, meanwhile, had been busy delving deep into the history of William MacLeod, learning that the paths of the MacLeods and the Jaffrays had crossed before. When Loren's grandfather had decided not to join the Homecoming, it was a young Major MacLeod who was promoted to Major Corwin Jaffray's former command. The Chancellor must have known that too, and Loren marveled at how well he had planned this mission.

The ship rumbled as the maneuvering thrusters corrected the ship's flight, adjusting for final approach to the spaceport. The *Bec de Corbin* angled upward to slow its speed and dissipate the heat that had built up on its reentry plates. It jerked slightly as the landing struts lowered, prompting the passenger messaging system to inform Loren to brace for landing.

He looked out over the city that seemed to be rushing toward him and was impressed by its size and myriad twinkling lights. The changing of the city's name had been one of the dozens of topics he'd reviewed during his journey. Tara was the name given it by the Highlanders upon their return, replacing the Davion one of Cromarty City. Though the Davion locals still protested, the name Tara was actually the more venerable, dating back hundreds of years to a time even before the Davions took Northwind from the Capellans. Such was the ongoing debate over Northwind's sovereignty and ownership.

The ship rocked again in a sudden down draft of air and Loren felt the safety belts dig slightly into his shoulder. Looking up, he saw the final-approach warning light come on and felt the *Bec de Corbin* slow slightly. It took an additional ten long and tedious minutes for the ship to finally touch down on the tarmac, bouncing slightly and eventually taxiing to the runway. As it finally came to a total stop, Loren popped the safety belt free and moved to the personnel access hatch. He carefully tucked the book he'd been reading into his briefcase. It had been years since he'd read Machiavelli's *The Prince,* but the sudden thrust into the world of political intrigue had brought it back to mind as the one text that might prepare him for this new kind of warfare.

Loren smiled as he opened the briefcase and took out his small pulse laser pistol, which he strapped around his waist. He snapped the case shut and set the security seal.

Catching sight of his reflection in the hatch window, Loren hurriedly ran his fingers through his hair and also straightened his dark green tie. He wasn't particularly comfortable in his dress uniform, but had decided the warrior garb would make a stronger impression than if he came as a civilian. At first he'd considered removing the Commando death's head insignia from his lapel to avoid infuriating the Davion officials who were bound to meet him, but in the end he left it on. Loren smiled to himself. *Let them see what kind of MechWarrior I am. Let them worry about me.*

Loren had another, deeper reason for leaving the small pin in place. The Northwind Highlanders would have more respect for someone who came as a warrior, proud and fearless, and they would no doubt understand that to wear the insignia was a small symbol of audacity.

The airlock outer hatch cycled with a slight hiss, followed quickly by the inner hatch. Loren did one more quick check of himself as the hatch slid open. His first step down the boarding ramp would put him on territory officially controlled by the Federated Commonwealth. The thought gave him just the slightest shiver. The Liaos and the Davions had been hating each other thoroughly for three centuries of war.

Loren strode down the ramp quickly, his high leather boots tapping smartly. At the foot of the ramp was a handful of people in various uniforms awaiting him in the dim light of the setting Northwind sun. The warm night air was pleasing compared to the recycled atmosphere of the *Bec de Corbin,* but Loren found it harder to breathe at first, being thinner and sweeter-smelling. By the time he reached the end of the ramp he was virtually panting to take in enough air.

Suddenly there came the mournful sound of bagpipes and the beating of drums as the honor guard behind the official greeting party struck up a fast-paced tune. The guard also carried the flags of the Highlander regiments, each held proudly aloft in the fading light. Remembering his grandfather's collection of march music recordings, Loren searched his memory for the name of the tune. It was not long in coming back to him ... *"Scarlet and Green."*

The greeting party was a mixed lot of uniforms and faces. On one flank stood what appeared to be a Davion noble. Dressed in a flowing purple cape and khaki dress suit, the man looked almost disinterested as Loren approached. At his side was a shorter man in similar dress plus formal boots and spurs—the mark of a Federated Commonwealth MechWarrior. This one did not hide his emotions, but glared at Loren, his hostility seeming to increase with each step closer.

In the center of the entourage stood a tall man in a black uniform shirt and dress kilt of blue and green tartan, obviously a Colonel by the stripes on his warrior's sash. His bearded gray face was not unfriendly, but he stood there with fisted hands on his hips, making a formidable impression under the tarmac lights of the spaceport. *MacLeod.* Loren recognized him immediately from his briefing.

At the Colonel's side was a female officer. Like MacLeod she was dressed in a traditional Highlander Stewart tartan, the uniform showing off the trimness of her figure. She also wore high black boots and a studded leather holster. Her gaze was nearly as hostile as the short Davion officer's and her crossed arms sent Loren a clear message about how she felt at meeting him. He noticed a long, brutal scar running down her right arm. Despite her bold body language, Loren found her appealing. Or maybe because of it.

He stopped within arm's reach of the party and gave the older Highlander officer a formal salute.

"Welcome to Northwind, Loren Jaffray," the officer said with great dignity, extending his hand.

"It is a pleasure to be here, sir," Loren answered, returning the firm grip of the man's strong, callused hand.

"Colonel William MacLeod," the officer said proudly. He gestured to the woman at his side. "And this is my executive officer, Major Chastity Mulvaney." Loren made a deep, formal bow.

"A distinct pleasure," he said, rising from his bow.

"Indeed, Major Jaffray. Calling this meeting a pleasure is slightly presumptuous on your part, given the rather unusual nature of your visit." Her tone was curt, almost tart.

Loren let the remark pass like a blow that had missed its mark. "I'm quite pleased to say that I'm not visiting Northwind as a diplomat, Major Mulvaney. I'm a soldier, a MechWarrior like you. I have come here for personal reasons—R and R. The message I carry is for the convenience of Chancellor Liao. It saves him the time and needless delay of sending it through normal channels, not to mention the risk of tampering by Word of Blake or ComStar. The Chancellor also wished to send a gift and believed it most fitting that it be delivered by a kin of one of the Highlander clans."

"What is your unit, Major Jaffray?" Mulvaney asked.

"Loren, please. And I'm with His Excellency's First Death Commandos."

"Tough unit, Major," she said, ignoring the invitation to use his first name. "By Capellan standards, that is."

MacLeod frowned slightly. "Major, need I remind you that Mr. Jaffray is here as a guest of the Highlanders? The Jaffray clan name is one that graced our rolls for centuries." Loren could tell by the exchange of glances that the two officers must have had similar discussions prior to his arrival. He'd known that his visit would cause some tensions, but it wouldn't suit his purposes to have them surfacing so soon.

The taller Davion official chose that moment to step between Loren and Mulvaney, almost totally obstructing Loren's view of the Highlander officers. "To what do we owe this unexpected visit, Major?" the man said in a nasal tone. Loren winced slightly at the heavy whiff of cologne.

"I don't believe we have met," he said.

"Oh, of course not. I'm Drake Burns, Planetary Consul Drake Burns. I represent the interests of the Federated Commonwealth here on Northwind." Burns extended his hand and Jaffray shook it, noting how different it was from the forthright grip of MacLeod. "It is most unusual to have a Capellan MechWarrior visit Northwind. The news took me very much by surprise."

Loren pressed his thumb against the security ID system of his briefcase and pulled out a small packet of papers bearing his verigraph passport and travel papers. He handed them to Burns, who looked them over briefly. Standing behind the Consul, the short Davion officer peered at the paperwork as well. "I am not here on official business with the Federated Commonwealth," Loren said. "My visit is strictly personal."

Burns stared at Loren, his gaze running from head to toe as if searching for some defect. "Personal, eh?" he said, handing back the paperwork and Loren's ID badge. "Your passport seems to be in order, so on behalf of the Archon-Prince I welcome you to Northwind and," he added with emphasis, "to the Federated Commonwealth."

"Thank you, Consul."

The shorter officer next to Burns spoke up. "I think you will agree, Major Jaffray, that it is rare for a man on vacation to bring along his BattleMech. Your flight manifest lists a 'Mech. You must have some unique ways of relaxing."

Loren smiled politely. "The 'Mech is a gift from Chancellor Liao to Colonel MacLeod and the Highlanders. A brand new *Huron Warrior*. It represents the bond that our two peoples once shared. I realize that such presentations are usually accomplished through more formal diplomatic channels, but as I said, the Chancellor decided to take advantage of my visit. I must admit, though, that I had hoped to present the gift in a more private setting." Loren extended his hand to the short man. "We haven't met formally. Your name, sir?"

Burns shook his head in feigned stupidity. "Silly me. Of

course. Permit me to introduce you to my aide de camp, Drew Catelli."

"I'm pleased to meet you, Mr. Catelli."

Catelli gripped Loren's hand tightly, making it obvious that he would be ever so delighted if the handshake were painful for Loren. "Actually, I'm a Colonel, but the Consul and I do not usually stand on such formality. It is a rare experience to receive someone of your background on Northwind, Major." His eyes wandered to Loren's lapel and to the death's head insignia of his unit.

Yes, I'm a real Death Commando. What propaganda have you heard about us? What fears does it arouse in you? Enough to draw you into my trap, I hope. "A Colonel? I thought that the Highlanders garrisoned Northwind alone." Loren had read the intelligence reports, but wanted to hear the "official" version of Catelli's command for himself.

He had hoped the Colonel would offer it, but it was Consul Burns who cut in. "Well, it's a kind of formality. You see, Colonel Catelli commands the Northwind Consul Guards."

"I see. Perhaps we will get a chance to talk shop sometime, sir. I always look forward to learning more of the ways of my fellow MechWarriors." Loren made sure that his tone was properly respectful as he contemplated the shorter officer. Every planet maintained some sort of embassy or consulate, some less formal than others. Having a platoon of infantry for defense of a consulate was not uncommon. According to the information in his briefing, the size of the Consul Guards on Northwind was significantly more. Loren wondered how the Highlanders felt about having a Federated Commonwealth garrison on their world. He made a mental note to find out. Having seen Drew Catelli's icy expression, he knew it was a card he might want to play.

"Chancellor Liao has sent me a 'Mech?" Colonel MacLeod sounded surprised and pleased. The price of a brand new BattleMech was staggering for any ordinary individual, but that wasn't the only thing that made the gift unusual.

"Yes, sir, he has. As a gesture of goodwill between our peoples. There have been differences in the past, but now that Sun-Tzu is Chancellor, he wishes to assure you that the

Capellan Confederation looks forward to better relations with you and your people."

It was obvious from his expression that Colonel MacLeod was impressed by the gift. "Major Jaffray, this is a fine present and I for one would not look a gift horse in the mouth. Thank you, and thanks to your Chancellor."

Consul Burns stepped forward. "On behalf of the Federated Commonwealth, I accept this gift."

Colonel MacLeod also took a step forward. "Forgive me, Consul, but as the planetary leader of Northwind, *I* will accept this gift as the sovereign of the planet." The two men exchanged stern glances.

Burns sneered slightly, biting his lower lip. He was not about to relent so easily. "My Highlander counterpart and I have always differed in defining sovereignty when it comes to Northwind. I understand that you carry a message for Northwind as well, Major Jaffray."

Loren looked at the Consul and at MacLeod, hoping not to become involved in the conflict between them. It was Colonel MacLeod who spared him. "Again, Consul Burns, I believe that the message is for my eyes as the ruler of Northwind. I have the option of passing on that message to you as a courtesy, a courtesy that at this time I am not inclined to extend."

Burns was obviously infuriated but did not want to concede defeat, at least not in front of Jaffray or the others gathered at the spaceport. "Perhaps we can continue the discussion over a few drinks, Colonel. Now that we've completed the formalities, I invite you all to the Consulate for cocktails. It will give us a chance to get to know each other in a less formal setting and perhaps for Colonel MacLeod and I to reach some accord on this issue." Consul Burns looked over at Colonel Catelli, and Loren could not help but notice the officer slowly nod in approval.

"I appreciate the offer, Consul, but it has been a long and bumpy flight. I think I'd like to spend some time with Colonel MacLeod tonight, then perhaps retire. I doubt I'll ever get used to JumpShip travel. It's exhausting, not to mention unnerving."

Drew Catelli stepped in quickly. "When Colonel

MacLeod told us of your pending arrival we made arrangements for you to stay at the Consulate, Major."

The prospect of being surrounded by Davions did not much appeal to Loren. "I appreciate the offer, but I'm not accustomed to such luxury. If Colonel MacLeod wouldn't mind, I'd like to bed down in the Highlanders' BOQ."

Though the request apparently caught him by surprise, MacLeod stepped forward and slapped Loren on the back. "When you said you weren't a diplomat, I wasn't sure. But now you're talking like a real MechWarrior. You'll bunk with my officers while you're here, Major."

Catelli's face flushed red. "It is customary to accept the honor of lodging in the Consulate. To refuse borders on offense."

Chastity Mulvaney stepped into the conversation circle again. "Come now, Colonel. There's no need to turn this into a diplomatic incident. Major Jaffray has come far and brought us gifts. And personally I'm not much for social hobnobbing myself. Great Gaffa knows we've had our share." Loren threw her a look of gratitude.

"And besides," she verbally slapped, "if he's too tired, we shouldn't push him."

Loren bristled. "I would like to assure the Major that while I am not in the mood for formal social affairs, I am more than willing to carry my own weight."

"Excellent, then!" Colonel MacLeod said. "A limousine awaits us. We'll go to The Pub for a few drinks. At least this way I can please two people—Mulvaney and Jaffray." He turned to the two Davion officials with a cheery grin. "As Major Jaffray said, his business is with the Highlanders, and as you both know, The Pub is off limits to anyone not of Highlander blood. Otherwise I'd be happy to have you join us."

Consul Burns bowed, hiding the irritation Colonel Catelli made no attempt to disguise. The shorter man ran his fingers around the tightly twisted ends of his handlebar mustache in a nervous fidgeting manner as his superior responded.

"As always, Colonel MacLeod, the Federated Commonwealth acknowledges the traditions and customs of the Northwind Highlanders," Burns said stiffly.

He turned his gaze back to Loren. "It was a pleasure

52 Blaine Lee Pardoe

meeting you, Major Jaffray. If there is anything that we can do for you during your stay, please let me know."

Loren nodded cordially and followed MacLeod and Mulvaney to their waiting vehicle, but something in the Consul's tone made him think back on the words later that night.

As the hover limo moved away from the tarmac and the Highlander honor guard marched off toward a nearby hangar, the Davion Consul leaned over to his aide de camp. "Interesting fellow."

"More like a potential problem, I'd say," Catelli said coldly.

Burns shrugged his disagreement. "And I'd say you're seeing ghosts in the closet again, Colonel. This is no Capellan general plotting an invasion, but a very junior officer here to meet with his grandfather's former unit. He is seeking his roots. You yourself gave me the intelligence file on the man. His great-grandmother was a hero to these people."

"You forget that he's also a Death Commando, not some ordinary MechWarrior. You know what they are. The Liaos use them for nothing short of state terrorism. They're trained assassins and terrorists."

"And your intelligence file on Jaffray shows none of that in his record."

"That we know of."

"Quite. I apparently place more faith in Federated Commonwealth's intelligence services than you do. Odd, given your own background," Burns returned in a snide tone.

Catelli changed this tack. "What of MacLeod's posturing on the sovereignty issue again, Consul? You bowed down to him on the gift of a BattleMech and this message Jaffray is carrying—whatever it is."

Burns shook his head. "Our Colonel MacLeod and I have been dancing around this issue for several months now. You worry too much. He has won nothing. I would have turned over that 'Mech to him anyway and that message is probably no more than greetings from the Chancellor. What victories MacLeod wins in private meetings like this are lost when he deals with the Federated Commonwealth as a whole. For all

I care, the Highlanders can think whatever they want about the rule of Northwind. Reality is what counts. Reality is that they are part of a greater whole. Period. You must stop fretting so much, Colonel."

"With the increased unrest we're hearing about from the Sarna March, I take all threats seriously, sir. Our visiting Major may be gathering intelligence for a Liao strike against Northwind in retribution for the Highlanders' defection back in 'twenty-eight. Or worse. Remember those reports we went over last week, the ones describing the marked increase in Capellan-based subversive activity. If I were Sun-Tzu Liao, this man's visit would offer the perfect pretext for starting trouble. For all we know, he may be plotting to foment an all-out revolution here on Northwind."

"You can't be serious. Northwind is at least five jumps from the Capellan border. The thought of this fellow leading a rebellion in the name of the Confederation is ludicrous. Why use someone so openly when undercover agents would do the job so much more efficiently?"

"Trust me, Consul. I have more than a passing acquaintance with these kinds of intelligence operations. And I know the Capellans well enough not to trust them. With your permission, I'd like to have this Jaffray followed. To make sure he is what he says he is."

"Indeed," Consul Burns replied. "As you wish, Colonel. Let me know if you learn anything interesting."

Catelli watched as the Davion official walked away. "Yes, sir," he said. "You can be sure of that."

5

The Fort
Tara, Northwind
Draconis March, Federated Commonwealth
11 September 3057

Loren stiffened slightly and looked at his refilled tankard and the rich head of Northwind ale that was slowly collapsing in the warmth of the officer's club. He picked up the drink and looked directly at the commanding officer of the Highlanders. "Colonel, I bring an offer of sorts, a message, to the Highlanders from Chancellor Liao. I ask only that you allow me to present it to your ruling body."

"You came all this way for that, Major?" MacLeod said. "Such a message could have been sent by courier or transmitted by HPG."

"No, sir. Not this message. Chancellor Liao asked that I personally deliver it to you and the Highlander Assembly of Warriors."

"What is the nature of this communication that a personal envoy must deliver it?" MacLeod asked, lifting his own tankard and taking a long cool sip of the reddish ale.

Loren looked around to be sure that no one except Mulvaney and MacLeod could overhear the conversation. He had hoped for a more private meeting place, but the time seemed too ripe. "The Chancellor is concerned about the future of Northwind and the Highlanders. He makes you a proposal in hopes of honoring the spirit of our former alliance."

Mulvaney chuckled slightly. "How touching. Somehow I have a hard time believing that the Chancellor of the Capellan Confederation lies awake nights worrying about the Northwind Highlanders."

"Perhaps you're right, but all I know is that Chancellor Liao heard of my petition to travel to Northwind and decided to use it as an opportunity to open the lines of communication with the Highlanders. That is all that he told me."

MacLeod looked even more incredulous. "Loren, forgive me, but since the day we left the Confederation thirty years ago there's been little love lost between House Liao and the Highlanders."

MacLeod looked away, his expression saddening for a moment. "The Homecoming was a great moment for our people, but it cost the Capellans both lives and worlds. I'm good, damned good, but not good enough to change the past, Major."

"That's true, Colonel, but it's also the past. Sun-Tzu Liao is not his mother."

"How do we know what you're telling us is the truth?" Mulvaney demanded sharply. "You arrive here on Northwind and we're to believe that suddenly, after decades of animosity, the Capellans want to be our friends? What do you take us for?"

Loren shook his head. "There isn't anything I can do to prove that I'm telling the truth, Major, and besides, neither of us can really know what's going on in the mind of the Chancellor. I can only repeat that he wishes me to deliver a proposal to your Assembly of Warriors. The decision is for them to make, not you, Major Mulvaney."

Colonel MacLeod shook his head. "The Assembly of Warriors needs a quorum to meet, Major, and we don't have one now. The other three Highlander regiments are either on Ozawa or posted along the Clan border. The Assembly of Warriors won't meet again until the Fusiliers rotate here from Ozawa toward the end of next month."

Loren felt his heart skip a beat. Had he come all this way to fail in his mission within an hour of landing on Northwind? *No. There had to be another way—there was al-*

ways another way. He tried to remember anything he could, either from his briefings about Northwind or from memories of his grandfather. There had to be some way to fulfill his mission. Then it came it him, some history and hope, and in a way that he knew MacLeod would understand.

"My grandfather told me of a special gathering the Highlanders used to call in times of emergency. I believe it was called the Cabel—a Warrior's Cabel."

Mulvaney cut in. "We *used* to call Cabels, Major. That was before the formation of the Assembly of Warriors. Now that we have the Assembly I'm not even sure anyone *has* the authority to call a Cabel. Such conclaves were only called by the Commanding Officer in times of need when a formal base camp had been established."

Loren was not about to give up. "Maybe it's just that there's been no reason to call one. Now that the base camp is once again Northwind you do have the authority to call a Cabel. And as for the need, you'll have to take my word."

"You're right, Jaffray. Technically, at least," MacLeod said. "We haven't needed a Cabel in years. But, then again, we've never had half our regiments so far from Northwind. Even if we did call a Cabel, the vote is non-binding. The most you might hope for is that the Warrior Cabel will agree with you and vote to recall the Assembly."

Loren nodded with excitement. "Exactly, sir. At least it will be a body of Highlanders hearing the Chancellor's proposal."

Mulvaney shook her head. "You can't be seriously considering listening to him, Colonel. He's an outsider. He has no right to ask you to summon a Warrior's Cabel."

Loren caught her eye and held it. "What's your problem, Mulvaney? Ever since I stepped off the DropShip you've been acting like I've got the plague. Have I offended you somehow? If so, I'm sorry, but if I didn't, get off my back."

Mulvaney squared off in front of him, her muscles tensing and a flush rising in her face. "Your presence here *does* offend me. Major, I worked hard to become a member of MacLeod's Regiment, even harder to be an officer. In you walk, two generations removed from even knowing a true Highlander personally, and I get ordered to treat you like an equal. Well, you're not an equal to me, not by a laser shot."

"I'm a MechWarrior just like you," Loren retorted, "and I've ranked as one of the best in the Confederation. And while you're digging those fancy boots into the ground spouting off about your pride, remember one thing—I and my family have faithfully served the Confederation for centuries. And while it may not carry weight with you, my grandfather was a battalion commander in the Highlanders and decorated nine times for bravery under fire. I won't even bore you with a discussion of my great-grandmother and her deeds. You place a lot of weight on history, and I'm here claiming my rights as true-blooded Highlander kin."

Mulvaney sneered in response. " 'Best' for the Confederation may mean something to the rest of the Inner Sphere, but here on Northwind it doesn't mean spit. You want to prove to me that you've got what it takes, Jaffray?"

"Yes. Any time. Any place." *If I can't win her over, I'll defeat her. Whatever is required to fulfill the mission.*

Suddenly MacLeod stepped between them, one hand extended to take the long red tartan sash Plunket was holding out to him. Loren heard the scrape of chairs all around them, the other Highlanders rising from their seats to see what was going on. He wasn't sure what kind of challenge he'd walked into, but he sensed that he would have to win if he was also going to succeed in his mission.

"I know you've got your head full of steam," MacLeod said to Mulvaney as he tied her right wrist with one end of the heavy wool sash. "Try and keep cool. He's a little bigger than you so stay low and you can probably bring him down." The regimental commander then stepped over to Loren and took his right wrist, tying the other end of the sash tightly around it.

"Mulvaney is fast and usually spills her energy quick in a fight. She's a wildcat but loses her steam in a drawn-out match. I warn you though, lad, she's never lost an honor match in the three years she's been in my command," MacLeod said as he checked his handiwork.

Then the Colonel stepped back and Loren saw that he and Mulvaney were about three meters apart and bound to each other at their right wrists. She lowered herself to a crouch, fury in her eyes. Loren looked from her to MacLeod and then to the small gathering of Highlander officers that had begun to form around them.

"Majors Loren Jaffray and Chastity Mulvaney, in the way of true Highlanders, you must settle this question of honor. You will fight until one of you is down for the count of three. You will begin at the sound of the horn. In the eyes of your peers let honor be served!" Mister Pluncket handed a small brass horn to MacLeod. All round them the other Highlander officers, each clad in the various tartan kilts of their clans, made bets on who would win the match. Loren listened for a full minute to the bidding and realized that his odds of winning were being set very low.

Like his opponent he lowered himself to a short stance and held his arms out to prevent her from flanking him. The sash hung between them just above the floor. Loren closed both eyes for a moment and drew a long breath. He was becoming more accustomed to Northwind's thin atmosphere, but it was still going to limit his ability.

He heard Colonel MacLeod blow the horn and in less than a heartbeat Mulvaney was springing into the air like a jaguar leaping for prey. She loomed over him and he thought for a moment that she must have misjudged, jumping too hard. He dropped to his knees and threw himself forward as she landed behind him.

Then suddenly his right arm was yanked behind him as Mulvaney pulled the sash hard and across his back. Loren lost his balance and Mulvaney leaped onto his back with both knees, knocking the wind out of him in one fell blow. His ears rang as he gasped for breath, but Mulvaney did not let up. Seizing more of the sash she pulled again and turned him over on his back as he finally managed to get his breath. Around him he heard cheering and jeering while she straddled his chest and pinned the sash down on both sides of his neck, choking him with her full body weight. His lungs ached for air and he felt his vision begin to tunnel like a drunk's. Sounds also began to fade, except for the pounding of MacLeod's tankard on the bar. Once ... twice ...

In a last desperate effort Loren thrust his legs up and seized either side of Mulvaney's head, scissoring her back and off of him. Gasping for breath he rolled to the side and then up onto his feet. The cheering of the crowd rose as

Mulvaney also came to standing. Loren was still struggling for breath against the dizziness resulting from her assault.

She jumped again, this time feet first, with a flying kick to his waist. Loren pivoted as she flew past, striking her back with both fists. As she landed he pulled the sash hard, throwing her off balance and sending her rolling to the floor. Still full of fury she rose again to face him, this time looking more harried.

Mulvaney threw a wild punch with her tied fist, just catching the corner of Loren's face. Instead of reeling, he jammed his elbow back, catching her in the center of her rib cage. She staggered back slightly under the impact as if fighting for breath. The tables had turned. It was time to strike and strike hard.

In a sweeping move, Loren grabbed the sash halfway and pulled it back with all his body weight. As Mulvaney came rushing straight at him, he rolled down onto his back and extended his legs to catch her at the chest and flip her over him and into the air. Loren continued his somersault, ending it with her body pinned. Dazed by the impact of his landing square on her back, Mulvaney lay there without moving. The three poundings of MacLeod's beer tankard seemed to take a lifetime. When it was done cheers rang from the gathered officers as Loren rolled off Mulvaney and sat watching her struggle to get up. Both MechWarriors were drenched in sweat and Loren's heart wouldn't stop racing. Each drag of air seemed to leave him wanting for more.

It took several minutes for the two of them to finally stand upright. Neither spoke and MacLeod only smiled and ordered more ale. Loren still fought the humid air, but finally able to function, despite the hot pain in his jaw and neck. Mulvaney looked exhausted too.

"A wonderful display, both of you!" MacLeod said. "Now then, Major Jaffray, you've seen a little sample of how we Highlanders settle our disagreements. Instead of letting petty grudges build and fester, we let them out. Perhaps it's the only thing we and the accursed Clans share. But honor has been served."

Colonel MacLeod looked over at Mulvaney. "Major, I believe there is something you owe our visitor."

Mulvaney nodded. She rose to her full height and looked

60   Blaine Lee Pardoe

Loren in the eye. He could still see some of the previous fury, but the outright hatred had faded. "You have proven that you are worthy of your Highlander blood claim. I was wrong about you."

Loren rubbed his neck and felt the skin raw from where the wool sash had burned his flesh. "This sure is one hell of a way to settle disagreements."

"That it is, Major," MacLeod said proudly. "There's been tension between you two since the moment you met. Now it's vented. And more important, no one was killed. This is the way we Highlanders settle conflict."

Loren reached out and took a deep drink of ale. The cool liquid seemed to relax his muscles. "Colonel MacLeod, about my proposition."

"Lad, if you're wondering if this changes my position, banish the thought. If anything, my respect for you just went up a notch or two. I feel a little guilty, though."

"Why is that, sir?"

"I put ten C-bills on Mulvaney to win."

"Who bet for me?"

"I did," came a voice from behind the bar. Loren looked over and saw Mister Pluncket give him a wink. "If there's one thing a bartender can spot it's a winner."

MacLeod put his hand on Loren's shoulder. "You've had a long day of it, lad. Major Mulvaney will take you to your quarters. We'll meet tomorrow and talk about this proposal a little more."

"Yes, sir." Loren let go a long breath of air and turned back to Chastity Mulvaney. "After you, Major." She nodded, combing the hair back out of her eyes with her fingers. Loren followed her outside, wondering about the wisdom of turning down the offer to stay at the Davion embassy. Now he would have to walk with Mulvaney after beating her in a test of honor.

As they crossed the massive courtyard of The Fort, Loren stepped up his pace to come alongside her. "No hard feelings, then, Major?"

She didn't look at him, "No, Major Jaffray, not on the question of honor. I acknowledge the Highlander blood in your veins, but that doesn't change my opinion of you. I'm just not used to getting beat."

"A good MechWarrior never relishes defeat."

"Like I said, this is a new experience for me."

"I hope that at least we can still work together. I have a lot to learn about Northwind and the Highlanders. From what I saw tonight you're the kind of person it would be an honor to call a friend." Loren remembered the fire in her eyes and wondered what might have been if they'd met under other circumstances.

Chastity Mulvaney stopped and turned to look at Loren. Her face as wan and tired. "You don't understand me at all. Do you know why I don't like you, Major? Haven't you figured it out yet?"

"Please, call me Loren. And the answer is no, I have no idea why you dislike me so. As far as I know I've done or said nothing to offend you."

"Major, in my eyes, you're here for only one reason. To harm the Highlanders. And I know it in my gut."

"But Major, I'm—" *How could she possibly know?*

"I know ... I know ... you're here to present your precious Chancellor's proposal. To you maybe that's all it is. But ever since we received your request to visit I've sensed that it could only mean no good."

"That isn't my intention and you know it." *Does she know? Impossible.* Loren deliberately kept his face stiff and emotionless, not revealing his sudden concern. *If I've been betrayed I know what I must do.*

"Oh, I'm sure you're what you seem to be, a MechWarrior and not a diplomatic messenger. Fine. That Loren Jaffray I actually admire. The question I have is, do you even know your real mission? I've read about how you Death Commandos all swear an oath to serve the Chancellor to the death. Maybe you're just a pawn in his hands."

The words stung Loren as deeply as if Mulvaney had stabbed him. Ever since leaving Krin he'd been wondering the same thing. But that couldn't be. He was a trained professional. He'd been chosen because he was the only person who could infiltrate the Highlanders and draw them away from service to Davion. That was all ... it had to be. "I understand what you're saying and I'd be a liar if I didn't tell you that the same question has crossed my mind. Politics is politics, after all, but I'm only a soldier. My intent is clear, and my mission is straightforward."

"I won't debate this with you. I don't care what you think your intentions are, it's their results I'm interested in. You're like the eye of a hurricane that's just blown onto Northwind. The eye of the storm is always calm, the real damage happens all around it.

"But no matter what happens, remember this night and our little test of honor. I know I won't forget it. And *Loren*," she said, stressing his name rather than his rank, "mark my words. At some point you're going to have to choose between being a Capellan MechWarrior or a Highlander kinsman." She gestured to one of the buildings off in the distance. "That's the BOQ. I'll meet you for mess at 0700 hours . . . Major Jaffray."

With that she moved off into the darkness as Loren wondered whether Chastity Mulvaney might know something he didn't.

6

The Fort
Tara, Northwind
Draconis March, Federated Commonwealth
12 September 3057

"I trust you found our mess to your liking," Colonel MacLeod said as he, Loren, and Mulvaney passed down the maze of corridors winding through The Fort's huge interior the next morning.

"There is one constant in all militaries, sir, and that is the food," Loren said. MacLeod chuckled in agreement.

"How's the jaw this morning, Major?" Mulvaney asked.

"I hope as good as your ribs, Major," Loren retorted. He wouldn't admit it, but his jaw was still very sore from the fight the previous night.

MacLeod chuckled softly again at their sparring. "Now then, Major Jaffray, you mentioned that the Chancellor has sent me a gift."

"Yes, sir. A new *Huron Warrior*. A BattleMech right off of the assembly line."

"Splendid! What do you say we take her out for a trial run?"

"Yes, sir. She's prepped and ready at the spaceport. Unfortunately I have no 'Mech myself." Loren's disappointment was genuine. Since the first day he'd piloted a BattleMech, his pleasure in it had never paled. For him it was a way to relax, despite the fact that some of his most dangerous and deadly moments had taken place in the cockpit of a BattleMech. Piloting a 'Mech gave him a feeling of oneness with himself that he not only missed, but craved.

"Not a problem. I usually pilot a *Gallowglas*. You take her while I check out exactly what a *Huron Warrior* can do."

Loren nodded. He'd operated a *Gallowglas* once before. Similar to a *Griffin* in its humanoid appearance, it was equally good at mauling an opposing 'Mech.

"I'll arrange for you to use the Southern Training Range, sir," Mulvaney said.

"Excellent. Why don't you join us?"

Mulvaney shook her head. "If you'll excuse me, there are a few other matters I need to take care of this morning." Her cold gaze told Loren that she still had not forgiven him for her defeat at The Pub.

"Too bad," Loren added. "If you're half as good in a cockpit as you are in a brawl I'm sure you'd prove a true challenge."

Mulvaney squinted slightly. "Major Jaffray, I assure you that I am much better at piloting a BattleMech than I am at fisticuffs. Pray that you are never on the receiving end of that set of skills, sir." With that she turned on her heel and started down an intersecting passage, while MacLeod and Loren continued on toward the massive 'Mech bays at the far end of The Fort.

An hour later MacLeod and Loren had walked their massive war machines out to the staging area of the Highlanders' Southern Training Range. Around them the rolling hills were carpeted with deep, lush grass that rippled in the breeze, and in the distance were the famous moors of Tara.

BattleMechs were the pinnacle of military technology and had been so for the past six hundred years. Standing upwards of ten meters tall Loren's *Gallowglas* could top sixty-five kph at a full run and even had the ability of limited flight, with a jump capacity of ninety meters. MacLeod's new *Huron Warrior* could, at a full run, move at more than eighty kph.

Armed with particle projection cannons, pulse lasers, short and long-range missiles, and a wide range of ECM, a

'Mech could wield staggering firepower—enough to level a city single-handedly. They also had maneuverability. No tank had ever jumped up and down on another tank. Nor had any mere tank ever reached out and ripped another one apart with its massive hands.

The comm set in his neurohelmet sparked to life as Loren adjusted his helmet settings. "Comm check, Major Jaffray," boomed the voice of MacLeod.

"Verified and operational. What is the run, Colonel?" Loren asked as he adjusted the neurohelmet's sensor tabs for better contact. Good skin contact was important, and Loren, like most of his modern breed of knight, shaved the small sensor contact points on his scalp to ensure the connections.

"We make a run through the lowland moors and up the hill on the other side. Dummy tanks and 'Mechs are positioned along the way. You see them, you shoot them. The computers on our 'Mechs are running the standard training software, which will simulate actual damage. I'm sure you're used to this kind of thing."

"After you, sir."

"Aye, lad," came back the response. The faster *Huron Warrior* leaped into action, trotting ahead of the *Gallowglas*. Loren punched his foot pedals and throttled the *Gallowglas* forward. The 'Mech's massive gyro purred to life at the sudden start-up and he concentrated on adjusting it. The feedback of his own brainwaves ran from the neurohelmet to the gyro's controls, compensating for the movement and balance changes. He followed MacLeod down the hillside, scanning his flanks and wondering when the simulated attacks would begin.

Chastity Mulvaney made her way down the narrow cobblestone street, carefully examining every pedestrian she passed. The morning sun poked occasionally between the tall buildings and down onto the streets, offering small spots of warmth as she walked. Though it was true the meet she was headed for did not violate any specific orders, she couldn't help wondering if she were betraying her trust. Spotting the small cafe, she crossed the street and went in. Except for the waitress at the counter and the lone patron in a rear booth, the place was empty. Mulvaney walked back to the booth and sat down across from its occupant.

"I'm pleased you could come," Drew Catelli said as he took a sip from what was apparently a glass of ice water. "I apologize for the earliness of the hour, but I thought the two of us might have something of mutual concern to discuss."

Mulvaney stared at him for a long moment. She had met with Catelli in an official capacity many times in the past, but this was their first private meeting. She, like MacLeod, had more respect for him than for his superior, the Davion consul. Burns was all pomp and circumstance, but Catelli was a warrior. That alone gave him more in common with the Highlanders than his politically appointed superior. "I want you to know that I only agreed because you mentioned having some information that might be of interest to me and to the Highlander Command."

"Yes, indeed I do," Catelli said, opening his leather day case and pulling out a small sheet of paper. Mulvaney could not see what was on the printout, which Catelli proceeded to study intently. "As you may be aware, there has been an upsurge of civil unrest in the Sarna March. We have had reports of terrorist activity on several worlds, activity that looks suspiciously like the work of outside agitators. We suspect that Sun-Tzu Liao is either funding or directing these guerrilla movements."

"I see." Mulvaney was aware of the increasing tensions in the Sarna March, but she thought it better to offer no comment and wait to see what Catelli had to say. After conquering the Capellan worlds that now formed the Sarna March, Hanse Davion had used his wife Melissa to win the loyalty of those planetary populations. Melissa had taken the task to heart and been enormously popular. Now that she was gone Prince Victor was likely to have his hands full with what had never stopped being essentially Liao worlds. The trouble in the nearby Skye March had still not completely died down either, even after Glengarry. That was partly because Victor had named the pro-Davion David Sandoval to replace the rebellious Richard Steiner as military commander of the region. Steiner had been transferred to Tharkad, effectively kicked upstairs. That had bolstered Victor's power in the

Skye region, but had done nothing to win him more support in that troubled sector of his realm.

"Yes, I'm sure you do. Now perhaps you understand my concern regarding our recent arrival on Northwind, this Major Jaffray?"

"Do you think Liao might have sent him here to stir up similar trouble between the locals and the Highlanders?"

"I'm not accusing him of anything—yet. But I'm curious about why he has come to Northwind to meet directly with the senior officer of the Highlanders. I'm also curious as to why he, a member of a blatantly terrorist unit, the Death Commandos, has been sent here. I don't buy this charade of a vacation anymore than you do. I must say, Major Mulvaney, that you've never struck me as someone likely to take such a man so blindly into your house."

"For what it's worth, I don't believe that Loren Jaffray is a terrorist, Colonel. He'd never have come to Northwind so openly if he was."

"So you trust him, eh?"

Mulvaney shook her head and her forehead wrinkled. "No, I don't trust him. I merely said I don't think he's a terrorist. I'm not sure why he's here, but I don't believe his story of visiting the land of his forefathers either."

"So why *is* he here, Major? Enlighten me."

She drew in a long, tight breath. "You're asking me to violate confidences, Colonel."

"What I'm asking you to do is preserve or even save the Northwind Highlanders from possible harm. What loyalties you honor in the process is something only you can decide, but I know that your first loyalty is to the Highlanders—not to some outsider sent here to cause trouble."

"I told you I'm not totally convinced that Jaffray is here to intentionally create trouble. I may not trust him totally, but as yet he's done nothing to indicate that he's deliberately out to hurt my people. Colonel MacLeod says we're to watch him like hawks. So let's just say that's what I'm doing—for now. That's the reason the Colonel decided to let him stay in our barracks, which he had rigged up with cameras and microphones so we could watch him."

"The problem is that you aren't sure," Catelli said, then held up a hand when Mulvaney opened her mouth to speak.

"Wait, Major. I'm here to ask you to think something over very carefully. The biggest question you face is whether you're willing to endanger the Highlanders' relationship with the Federated Commonwealth. Will you risk the lives of your men and women to the good will of this total stranger . . . a man whose ties to the Highlanders exist not in blood but on paper?"

Mulvaney paused and considered the question carefully. Was she violating the trust of Colonel MacLeod simply by talking to Catelli? And what did she really owe Loren Jaffray in the way of confidentiality? Besides, he hadn't really told her that much in the first place. All he'd said was that he carried a message from Sun-Tzu Liao for the Highlander Command. Surely, to reveal that information could not cause any harm or give away anything that Catelli had not already heard at the spaceport.

"All he's said is that he has a message to the Northwind Highlanders from the Capellan Chancellor."

Now that Mulvaney was finally opening up, Catelli moved in quickly. "We already know that, Major. What is this message that it's so important?"

Mulvaney shrugged. "He hasn't said, yet. All he's told us is that it's important enough for the Assembly of Warriors to hear."

Catelli's expression grew more serious. "That's all?"

"He also requested that we call a Cabel of the Highlanders present when he found out that we didn't have a quorum for an Assembly with so many of our people offworld. That's all he's said. I'm guessing that the Capellans may want to offer us a contract. Obviously not something we could accept."

"What are his plans for the next few days?"

"Jaffray's going to drill with the Colonel, then get a formal tour of the city later on. Colonel MacLeod has a deep respect for Jaffray's family, and from what I can see, our visitor is playing on his sentimentality. But the Colonel insists he's keeping Jaffray close in case he *is* some sort of threat."

"Do you think Colonel MacLeod might be influenced by Jaffray?"

"Influenced is a strong word. The Colonel has spoken to me a great deal about his respect for Loren's grandfather and his leadership in the Highlanders. But no matter how much store he puts in history and tradition William MacLeod would never do anything that might endanger the Highlanders. He's a crafty man. Despite my protests, I think he's using this time and opportunity to size Loren Jaffray up."

"You've been most helpful, Major," Catelli said as he slid out of his seat and laid a C-Bill on the table as a tip. "I'd advise you to keep your eye on our mutual friend. Men like Jaffray are often not what they seem. Meanwhile I'll put some of my own assets to work finding out if he *is* an agent. As always, your loyalty to the Federated Commonwealth is appreciated." With a nod Catelli turned and walked out of the small cafe.

Chastity Mulvaney didn't watch him go. Her thoughts were too busy circling around and around the questions that had troubled her since the moment she'd first heard the name of Loren Jaffray.

7

Peace Park
Tara, Northwind
Draconis March, Federated Commonwealth
17 September 3057

"I wanted to come here to talk, Loren"—MacLeod waved one hand in front of them as they walked—"to our Peace Park. It's one of the oldest parks in the Inner Sphere. The First Lord himself dedicated it in 2657. It was undamaged even after House Davion drove the Highlanders from Northwind three hundred years ago." The point was not lost on Loren. The Succession Wars had consumed entire cities and left virtually no part of the Inner Sphere untouched. To see a bit of the former Star League's glory preserved on Northwind only added to the mystique and allure of the world.

"It's quite beautiful, sir."

"Calming too. I come here when I need to do any serious thinking. To stand among the immortals here in the park and think about history and my people's place in it. That's why I chose this place to discuss your Chancellor's proposal to the Cabel. And to hear your thoughts on Thomas Marik's declaration of war."

"It surprised me as much as anyone, Colonel," Loren said, and that much was true. Last night he'd watched Marik's broadcast, followed by the startling news that both Marik and Liao troops were striking at worlds in and around the Sarna March. "Who'd have expected Victor Davion to deceive Thomas about the death of his son and put a double in the boy's place?"

MacLeod grunted expressively. "Plenty of people wouldn't put it past him. The Prince doesn't seem bound by anything but his own desire for power. Look what he's done to the Highlanders—trying to play us for fools ever since Glengarry. Neither contracts nor promises nor honor seem to mean anything to him."

Loren stopped in front of one of the gleaming white marble statues. The name etched on the base of the monument was that of a General Benjamin Jenkins Novak of the Star League Defense Force. He studied the stern but noble expression on the face of the statue while he spoke.

"Then I'd say the Chancellor picked just the right moment to send me here. The offer he sends you would right any wrongs that have been done you."

"I'm listening, lad."

Loren saw no reason to mince words. "The Highlanders have been waiting a long time to own Northwind free and clear, and the Chancellor understands what it would mean to your people. What he sends you is an offer to support a drive for an independent Northwind. Not just Capellan support, but that of House Marik as well."

"Do you have any idea what you're saying, Jaffray?"

"I do, sir. For two centuries House Liao was unable to fulfill its promise to return Northwind to your people—our people. Now Sun-Tzu is willing to support the Highlanders in a bid for freedom."

"My people will not simply exchange one warlord for another. If your Chancellor thinks that we will acknowledge him as liege lord over Victor Davion, it's a waste of time to even present the proposal."

"No sir, that isn't a condition at all. Sun-Tzu will support a Highlander push for total independence for Northwind, with no strings attached. If you accept his offer he will officially recognize Northwind as an independent world. He is certain that he can also guarantee recognition by Thomas Marik as well."

MacLeod also contemplated the general's stone face for a

moment. "I'm sure Sun-Tzu knows that Victor Davion won't sit back and let Northwind slip through his fingers. Especially not now, with an invasion on his hands."

"The Chancellor asks me to inform you that he would back you with force, if necessary. And Marik said it himself on the broadcast—he'll support all those wanting to liberate themselves from the Davion yoke, including worlds in the Sarna March."

"And what does the Capellan Confederation get out of the 'liberation' of Northwind?"

Loren knew that whatever he said now would either seal or destroy his credibility. "You have every right to be skeptical, sir, but I assure you that the Chancellor has no intention of placing a garrison here or imposing distant rule. What the Confederation gets is the fulfillment of a centuries-old obligation and a new ally."

"And ...," MacLeod prodded.

"And while the Chancellor would never say so directly, he would no doubt enjoy making Prince Victor Davion squirm while depriving him of one of his most elite merc units and one of his most key worlds."

MacLeod shaded his eyes as he looked back to Loren. "Your timing is better than you imagine, Loren. There have been a number of points of contention between the Federated Commonwealth and the Highlanders. Drake Burns calls them 'issues of sovereignty,' but whatever you name it, it's not a game I like being forced to play. We are mercenaries, but our so-called liege lord hasn't been too good at holding up his end of agreement. Payments have been late and repair part prices have been jacked so high that it's nearly impossible for us to fulfill our financial obligations. We're still owed for our work in helping clean up on Glengarry last year. But no matter how much I protest, I might as well be talking to a stone wall.

"We served House Davion in the War of 'Thirty-nine and now our regiments stand guard on the FedCom's Clan borders. But it looks to me like Victor Davion is trying to break our backs, slowly drive us to bankruptcy, perhaps hoping to weaken us and eventually absorb us into his own House military."

"Your relations with House Davion are your own affair,

Colonel, but even in my short time here I've observed the strain. The conflict over who rules Northwind was obvious between you and Consul Burns at the spaceport. There's also the question of this Colonel Catelli and his 'Consul Guards.' How many troops does he have under him, sir?"

"A heavily reinforced company of 'Mechs and a battalion of infantry and conventional armor."

Loren shook his head. "Where I come from that amounts to a garrison force, Colonel. Why would Victor Davion place a battalion of troops here when he already has a regiment of the finest troops in the Inner Sphere as the standard garrison?"

"My staff and I have had this discussion a dozen times, Major Jaffray. But you tell me, why would he?"

"I'd say it's the first step in the Federated Commonwealth trying to take over your regiments. Davion doesn't trust you totally and so he sends troops here to make sure you stay in line. Over time his people gradually usurp your authority and exert greater and greater Davion control. Eventually the Highlanders become no more than a local militia."

"Unfortunately that's been my analysis of the situation as well. Mulvaney and several other younger officers may have fallen for the line Burns and Catelli have been feeding them, but I see right through it. And so do Colonels Senn, Cochraine, and Stirling. It's also interesting that Davion didn't bother to send the troops until the other three Highlander regiments were all off-world. They call it a coincidence. But we see through the charade."

"And then there's the Clan threat, sir," Loren added.

"Yes, the Clans." The mention of the invaders and the swath of damage they had cut into the heart of the Inner Sphere was enough to chill the heart of even the most confident MechWarrior. Using highly advanced, sophisticated technology, the genetically bred warriors of the Clans would have swallowed the Inner Sphere whole if not for the stalling action of ComStar on the planet Tukayyid. But the ferocious Clans still hovered like a plague on the borders of the Federated Commonwealth and the Draconis Combine, waiting for the Treaty of Tukayyid to expire—or a chance to break it.

"Our current contract calls for us to garrison Northwind

74　Blaine Lee Pardoe

and Ozawa here in the Draconis March as well as worlds on the Lyran/Clan border. I'm sick of seeing Highlanders posted on the Clan front while able F-C troops are assigned to worlds six jumps from any threat."

"So, Colonel, will you support calling a Cabel to hear the Chancellor's initiative?"

MacLeod crossed his arms across his chest, but did not speak for several moments. "Not all Highlanders feel the way I do, Major. A good number of our people are very pro-Davion, mostly those who were born and raised here, second generation. After Hanse Davion allowed us to return to Northwind, they thought he could do no wrong."

"Hanse Davion is dead. And no matter how anyone cuts it, Victor Davion is not his father."

MacLeod chuckled slightly. "True enough. But what I'm trying to say is that even some of my top officers, Mulvaney included, are fiercely loyal to the Davions. There will be resistance, especially with this war breaking out."

"But the Highlanders are no longer alone, Colonel. The Capellan Confederation and the Free Worlds League will stand with you. You'll support the initiative, won't you, sir?"

"Yes, Loren Jaffray. I will call a Cabel. We'll discuss the proposal and vote on whether to convene the Assembly of Warriors." MacLeod was just reaching out to shake Loren's hand when suddenly he was knocked off his feet and thrown backward, smashing into the base of the statue.

A spray of blood spattered the gleaming white marble as MacLeod slid down against it, smearing the base of the statue with a bright red stain. Loren leaped forward into a crouch, grabbing MacLeod under the armpits and dragging him around to the other side of the statue.

"What happened?" MacLeod gasped, grabbing at the bloody spot on his right arm. Loren pulled the Colonel's hand away and saw that the flesh had been torn over a fist-sized area. Telltale needle-like shreds poked up from the wound. "Needler fire! Damn!" A needler pistol was a fearsome weapon that sprayed out a blast of plastic needles at deadly velocities. Loren looked across the trail and saw nothing but thick underbrush across the path. "Hold the wound tight, sir," he said, reaching for the laser pistol in the holster at his waist.

Loren's mind was on fire. The Highlander's CO was wounded, perhaps dying at his feet. He could finish him off right now and make it look like the work of an assassin. *No, I need this man. Keeping him alive is my best chance at destroying all the Highlander regiments.*

MacLeod took out a small communicator from one of his pockets and painfully pressed the activation stud. "This is MacLeod! Condition Green. Peace Park!" Then he dropped the device as a spasm of pain wracked his arm and blood seeped through his fingers. Loren heard voices respond on the communicator but did not really listen. Instead he concentrated on spotting the assassin in the surrounding brush. If he'd been the shooter, he'd be moving to flank to get a better field of fire. Going with that hunch he spied a rustling in a spot where he'd have taken position in the shade of a massive elm.

The next moment a section of leaves suddenly disintegrated as another volley of deadly needles sprayed the base of the statue near his leg. The all too familiar warmth running up his thigh told him he'd been hit. Loren ignored the wound and went flat on the grass, firing at the area where the rustling had occurred. Ten bursts of laser bolts shot out of the pistol and into the growth.

Then a man bolted from the bushes and ran wildly down the trail. Loren fired after him but failed to hit as the figure vanished from his line of sight. Glancing back, he saw that MacLeod had lost a great deal of blood and was beginning to look almost gray. The Colonel was still conscious as Loren crawled back to him, his leg red-hot with pain.

"Did you get him, lad?" MacLeod asked between gasps.

Loren shook his head and looked down at his own painful wound. A half dozen splinter-needles had passed through the side of his leg, and blood was pouring from the wound. He pressed a hand tightly over the spot and leaned against the base of the statue. The wound stung even more as he held his hand against it, telling him that some of the needle fragments were still lodged in place. "He got away, sir."

"Damn. Help better be coming soon," MacLeod said, grabbing the communicator and signaling again. Loren swept the area visually, looking for anything out of the ordinary. There was no sign of the assassin and no indication of a follow-up attack.

"I'm trained in this kind of work, sir. Whoever's behind this is a professional. They had us in an open-fire zone with a well-marked escape route." *Somebody is playing for keeps, either from within the Highlanders or sent by Victor Davion. We were lucky this time. Next time we might not be.*

Overhead he heard the thunderous rumble of a VTOL moving into position. Looking up, he saw that the craft showed the insignia of the Northwind Highlanders, the planet topped by a plaid tam-o'-shanter. They would live, but both would be in pain for a while, especially MacLeod.

"What do you think, Loren? Was he out for you or me?" MacLeod asked as the infantry deployed around them. A medic moved to the Colonel and began to assess the damage.

"Maybe both," Loren said as he felt the first sedative enter his bloodstream. He looked up at the regal white statue of the Star League general towering over them, seeming to gaze beyond them in the direction from which the shots had come. It made Loren wonder if the leaders of the Inner Sphere ever learned from the mistakes of their past or if they only sought to repeat them.

8

The Fort
Tara, Northwind
Draconis March, Federated Commonwealth
18 September 3057

"Have you recovered any evidence from the scene yet?" Loren asked Mulvaney as he watched the last of the auto-bandage wrap being taped to his thigh, its thin computerized pack monitoring the wound and providing the pain-killer medication as needed. The passing of twenty-four hours had taken the edge off Loren's adrenaline rush, but not the pain.

"Our troops sealed off the park, but the assassin vanished into thin air. Hell, we didn't find so much as a boot print. As a precaution, I've ordered regimental security to yellow status in all our garrisons. We may also need to increase base security."

"Good thinking," MacLeod said.

"The big question now is which one of you was the target?" Mulvaney said coldly, turning to Loren. "That wound of yours is only a nick."

Loren shrugged, not bothering to point out that the needler had done a good job of tearing flesh and muscle tissue. "Your guess is as good as mine. With a needler rifle for a weapon he could have been trying for both of us. But I haven't been on Northwind long enough to win enemies."

"Don't be too sure," MacLeod put in. "There are a lot of

people, some Highlanders included, who might take offense at a Capellan officer among our ranks. Especially at a time like this. The Federated Commonwealth and the Capellans are at war just a jump or two away from here. But no member of my regiment would ever commit such a dishonorable act—that's not the way we handle it in the Highlanders. And damned if I know why anyone would go after me personally unless it was some Skye fanatic out for revenge."

He let the doctor finish adjusting the bandage over his wound, and waited till the man had walked away before speaking again. "Now, then, Major, let's hear what else has been going on in the midst of all this excitement. Status report." MacLeod rubbed the wound on his arm and looked over at Mulvaney.

She held out a printout. "I was going to hold this until you were released from sickbay, but it's pretty hot. It was in the latest dispatch dump from ComStar. Came in twenty minutes ago."

Colonel MacLeod looked over the printout and his face wrinkled in amazement. "I'll be damned!" he murmured.

"What is it, Colonel?" Loren asked.

"Regimental business," Mulvaney answered curtly.

The Colonel ignored her. "A communication from Katrina Steiner of the Lyran Commonwealth." He read the sheet verbatim. "Per my direct order, all garrison forces of the Northwind Highlanders in the former space known as the Lyran sector of the Federated Commonwealth are officially relieved of duty and ordered to return to Northwind as soon as possible. As all troops within Lyran space are under the command of the Lyran Commonwealth State Command, I personally relieve them of their posts. The current state of civil unrest does not involve the Northwind Highlanders and I have no desire to see them involved or otherwise at risk.

"I further offer the good men and women of Northwind the protection of the Lyran Alliance, should they need to defend their interests. Good luck and godspeed. Katrina Steiner."

"Lyran Alliance?" Loren said. "What's that?"

"Katrina went on the holo and condemned Prince Victor for attempting to replace Thomas Marik's son with a double. She declared a state of crisis and said she was withdrawing from the Federated Commonwealth to keep the Lyrans out of the war."

"So she's leaving her brother high and dry," Loren said.

MacLeod nodded. "It's nothing short of civil war. Victor Davion's not going to give up the most powerful state the Inner Sphere has ever seen without a fight."

"We haven't heard any official response yet, but Katrina's ordering our troops out of her space so that they can't be used against her in a war with Victor."

Loren couldn't help but smile at the fix this left Victor Davion in. "This will make the little uprising on Glengarry look like a raid. Glengarry was just the beginning."

"Prince Victor Steiner-Davion is our liege lord, Major Jaffray. I don't know how it's done in your Capellan Confederation, but the Federated Commonwealth is a bit more organized. This upstart Katrina hasn't got the authority to order us around. And even it she thinks she can, we don't have to obey those orders," Mulvaney said firmly.

"I beg to differ, Major," MacLeod said. "I'd say that our young Ms. Steiner has done her homework rather well. All units in the Lyran State Command take their field orders from Tharkad. Her brother cannot issue countermanding orders until the units enter the Federated Suns Command. Pretty craft young woman, I'd say." MacLeod didn't disguise his admiration, and Loren shared it. It was a bold action on the part of Katrina Steiner. And as any warrior knew, it was boldness that separated the dead from the living.

"What will you do, Colonel?" Loren asked.

"Right now, we get on over to the War Room. I want to review our current roster and get some messages out to the regiments in the field. This order changes things a great deal."

"Someone tried to kill you within the past twenty-four hours and the assassin is still on the loose," Mulvaney protested. "With all due respect, sir, you should rest some more. I can handle the duty assignments and whatever orders you may have."

MacLeod slipped off the table and onto his feet. It was true that he looked drained and was obviously in pain despite the painkillers. "Major," he said, "I know my duty as well as you. I'm not just a regimental commander, but CO of all the Highlander units, here and abroad. This is no time for me to sit around twiddling my thumbs. Even if the bastard had shot off my arm I'd still be going to the War Room." He took a firm step toward the door and looked back at the two Majors. "Jaffray, you're with us."

"Sir?" Loren couldn't believe what he was hearing. As a member of the Capellan Armed Forces, his presence would be unusual, to say the least.

MacLeod turned and faced him with the same look he'd given Mulvaney only moments before. "No lip out of you now, lad. I want you in Operations with Mulvaney and me, for now anyway."

"Sir!" Chastity protested. She cast an angry look at Loren, then back at Colonel MacLeod.

"Major, before you hit me with a hurricane of arguments and quotes from operations manuals, let me just tell you this. Jaffray here just saved my hide, and in anybody's book that counts for quite a bit. Besides that, he's a seasoned officer in an elite military unit. He might just be able to offer us some help."

"This is most unusual, sir. He's a *Capellan* officer." Mulvaney didn't use the word "enemy," but the undertone was clear.

"Well, I'm not intending to let him walk out of there with any military secrets," MacLeod said, turning toward the door again. "And besides, that's an order." The last words were spoken in a much sterner tone.

Loren felt his heart begin to pound slightly at the thought. There was more on his mind than the chance to see the inner workings of the Highlanders' regimental command structure. War was breaking out in the Inner Sphere, and he'd spent his life training in the art of war. Now he found himself separated from his unit.

What bothered him for a fleeting moment was that he did not miss the Death Commandos. He should be longing to return to his unit right now—it was the very nature of his training. But instead he felt an uneasy comfort being with MacLeod and even Mulvaney. The Northwind Highlanders had begun to accept him as one of their own. It was a feeling of family that he'd not felt since the death of his grandfather. Losing the old man had pained him deeply, but suddenly on

Northwind, it was almost as if his grandfather was still with him, temporarily overshadowing any thoughts of the Commandos. A twinge of guilt nagged at him with each limping footfall.

He looked down at his lapel and saw the black death's head of the Death Commandos looking back at him, almost seeming to grin. The Highlanders had a rich history, but he had something too—his mission. No matter what, he must never forget the real reason he had come to Northwind.

9

The Fort
Tara, Northwind
Draconis March, Federated Commonwealth
18 September 3057

The Highlander War Room was located deep in the heart of The Fort. Four different sets of guards, each dressed in pristine Highlander formal uniforms, were assigned to various checkpoints along the final passage leading to it. Loren noticed that the walls in this area were heavily reinforced concrete with thick ferro-steel plates embedded for additional support. After passing the final checkpoint he was convinced that the War Room could probably survive a direct nuclear strike if such weapons were ever employed in war again.

He had a difficult time keeping up with the others, the inflatable auto-bandage and sedatives throwing a slight gait into his walk. He knew Mulvaney was furious, but he couldn't help thinking that if their roles were reversed he'd be even more suspicious and protective of his lord and his unit.

At the last set of doors Mulvaney signed them in on a sheet outside a bulletproof security station. The massive chromed doors looked more like a bank vault than the entrance to the command and communications hub of the Highlander regiments. Loren followed the two Highlanders in and heard the doors shut behind him with a deep echoing thud.

The War Room was essentially a fixed command and communications facility. When a regiment was in the field, it used a much smaller mobile command and control facility. But on a stationary assignment like Northwind the larger War Room-type center was the best possible arrangement. Numerous computer-generated map displays lined the walls, and in the room's center were several chairs with built-in armrest controls surrounded by a massive array of computer and communications terminals. Loren saw at least a dozen officers in the dimly lit room, each wearing remote microphone/headsets. As soon as they saw Colonel MacLeod, every bit of furious activity stopped and the officers snapped to attention. MacLeod's injured arm prevented a quick reply, but his nod seemed to be enough.

Loren guessed that MacLeod was permitting him to see the War Room out of pride. Such a place did not offer up great secrets but instead revealed a unit's degree of organization, and what Loren saw in the Highlander Ops Room was impressive. It wasn't the first regimental command center he'd ever seen, and from intelligence reports he'd read on those of Wolf's Dragoons, the Kell Hounds, and the Gray Death Legion, this one ranked in the same elite class. The communications terminals were inter-networked to provide data-sharing on command. The position of the three raised rotatable central seats was optimal to allow the commanding officer and his key staff full view of the entire room and most of the terminal screens. Like the CIC of a combat War-Ship, the room was designed to feed information quickly to the commanding officer. From one spot, a single person and staff could coordinate the activities of all four regiments of the Northwind Highlanders as well as the defense of the planet itself.

MacLeod checked the armrest controls of the largest of the three command seats, then turned to his executive officer. "Run through today's rotation, Major."

"The First Kearny has two battalions of Chahar and one on Sargasso," she said, pointing a hand-held control at one of the computer-controlled wall maps. Two planets along the Clan Occupation Zone map lit up. "Second Kearny is assigned to Hood IV, Newton Square, Arluna, and two companies on Barcelona."

MacLeod watched the map knowingly. "That leaves us with Stirling's Fusiliers on Ozawa, and they're due to rotate back home in a few weeks." The planet Ozawa lit up on the star map as he spoke. Like Northwind, Ozawa sat in the Draconis March. But it did not take a military specialist to comprehend the significance of the other planets mentioned, each in the Lyran sector of the Federated Commonwealth, each located along the border of the Clan Occupation Zone. Should the Clans decide to break the truce and renew their invasion, the Northwind Highlanders were poised to bear the brunt of such an offensive.

"That's correct, sir."

"Suddenly I feel very lonely here," MacLeod said softly, almost to himself. There were hundreds of light years separating the rest of the Highlanders and MacLeod's Regiment on Northwind. Ozawa was nearby, but the other farflung regiments were at least fifteen jumps away by the best possible scenario.

"Lieutenant Gomez," MacLeod barked, looking away from the map. Despite his injury, he seemed to be in his element, in command of his regiment and his forces.

A tall red-haired Highlander stepped forward at crisp attention. "Yes, sir!"

"Open the communications line with ComStar and download any transmissions in the queue."

"Yes, sir." Gomez dropped into one of the three center seats and began to hammer furiously at the keyboard.

Loren peered over her shoulder and then back at Mulvaney. "You have a direct line to the ComStar HPG?"

Mulvaney sat down next to Gomez and began typing as well. "Direct line is a misnomer. We have the capability to batch our transmissions and dump them on a direct line with the ComStar HPG station in the city. We pay a dear price to the Federated Commonwealth for batch updates to our comm center here, but it gives us the next best thing to a direct on-line hookup with the regiments."

"Impressive," Loren said. The hyperpulse generator network was the backbone of all interstellar communications, and having a direct tap to an HPG was rare for a military unit.

"Paint me a picture, Gomez," Mulvaney said as she surveyed her own terminal.

"I have order confirmations from all units in the Lyran Command," the Lieutenant replied. After several slower deliberate keystrokes, Gomez smiled in satisfaction. "We're linked and loading, sir."

MacLeod crowded over Mulvaney's shoulder while carefully pulling a small black case containing wireframe reading glasses from his pocket. Placing them on the end of his nose he squinted down at the monitor.

The electronic maps cast an eerie glow over the War Room's occupants. Some of them were clearly marked "Northwind," while others showed different planets. The icons on the screen were semi-familiar, the markings of military units. The small oval icons of the Highlanders were easily recognizable by the sword against a bright red and blue tartan plaid. The bright colors of the various terrains made the maps look more like some kind of abstract painting than intelligence tools. Loren was all the more impressed. From this one place Colonel MacLeod had his finger on the pulse of four regiments of the Highlanders.

"Well, Ms. Steiner was most efficient," MacLeod said. "She sent the same message to every garrison we have in the Lyran State Command. Our people have already acknowledged her order and are waiting for some word from me."

"Sir," Mulvaney said, looking up from her monitor. "They're all waiting for you to issue the order. Either go or no-go."

MacLeod nodded, once again rubbing his bandaged arm. "I know, lass."

The Colonel's face was a study in deep thought as he gazed into Mulvaney's screen. Then he stood up straight and carefully lifted off the reading glasses, returning them to his case and then to his breast pocket.

"What will you do, Colonel?"

"Good question, Major Jaffray. My gut reaction is to acknowledge Katrina's order and pull my people home."

"Sir," Mulvaney interjected. "Our liege lord is not this

renegade Katrina but Prince Victor Steiner-Davion. To acknowledge this order would be an act of betrayal."

"Has Victor Davion issued a countermand to her order?" Loren asked

"No, but that's not the point, Jaffray, and you know it. The minute we treat her order as valid it means we're going head to head with the Federated Commonwealth."

She turned back to MacLeod. "Sir, if you acknowledge the order, it's a direct action against the Federated Commonwealth."

"There is no Federated Commonwealth anymore," Loren couldn't resist interjecting. "At least not for much longer."

"Major Jaffray, this is a matter internal to the Highlanders and no concern of yours," she shot back. Loren fully expected MacLeod to ask him to leave, given the messages that had just arrived.

But when MacLeod spoke up, his words came as a surprise. "This is a sensitive time for our unit, but I see no danger in having Major Jaffray here. He hasn't seen or heard anything that won't be public knowledge across the whole Inner Sphere in the next twenty-four hours."

"I understand, Colonel. I was merely attempting to keep us focused," Mulvaney said flatly, giving Loren the full bore of her stare.

MacLeod looked over at the tall communications officer. "Lieutenant Gomez, send the following message to ComStar for transmission to Colonels Stirling, Cochraine, and Senn. Have it transmitted Alpha Priority and encrypted under my private security code. Send a straight copy to Lyran Command."

"Ready, sir," Gomez said, her fingers poised above the keyboard. Loren felt the tension in the room rise to an almost unbearable pitch. Colonel MacLeod took a brief glance at the printout Mulvaney had given him earlier, drew a deep breath, and began.

"Per direct Command Order 2546 Lyran Commonwealth State Command, all units of the Northwind Highlanders are hereby ordered to return to Northwind immediately. No engagement of civilians is permitted except in self-defense. Evacuation will take place no less than eight days from acknowledgment of this transmission. All travel routes to

Northwind are to be classified with today's cipher and all unit commanders notified that their priority is to return to Northwind intact."

He looked over at Mulvaney. "I understand your concerns, Major. But Cat Stirling is only a jump or so away in case things heat up with our so-called friends in the Federated Commonwealth."

MacLeod ran the tips of his fingers over his bushy salt and pepper eyebrows. "Order all regiments to stage three security alert. All leaves canceled and all off-duty troops pulled back to their units."

"Yes, sir." Gomez replied. Her fingers were already halfway through the orders even before she acknowledged the command.

The senior Highlander officer turned to Mulvaney. "Major Mulvaney, I want the Caithness Woods sealed and secured by our troops at 2000 hours the day after tomorrow. Invite all off-rotation personnel to a Warriors Cabel there at that time. Deliver the messages personally, no transmissions or written orders."

"Sir?"

"Major Jaffray has been tasked by Chancellor Sun-Tzu Liao to deliver us a message and I've decided to let him do it. Besides, I need to speak with my people and this is the best way. No misunderstandings. I want them to hear it directly from me."

"I'll obey, Colonel, but the timing may not be right. Perhaps it would be better to make no decision until we have a better understanding of the current situation." It was obvious by the slight bounce in her stance that Mulvaney was both excited and angry.

"I've made the decision and sent out the orders, Major." MacLeod looked around and saw the other officers intently watching him and his executive officer. "Let's take your concerns off line," he said calmly, pointing to a door near the far corner of the room.

MacLeod turned to Jaffray. "I'll leave you in the hands of Lieutenant Gomez, Major Jaffray. She can show you more of how our TO&E is compiled. I think you'll find it impressive."

Loren nodded obligingly and turned to Gomez at her terminal while the Colonel and Mulvaney left the room.

MacLeod led Mulvaney to the doorway of a small conference room holding a table and six chairs. The room was painted dark green and the waist-high wainscoting of the walls was a deep mahogany that seemed to add an air of seriousness to the room. Hung in two glass cases mounted into the walls were pieces of armor plating from a BattleMech. Each was scored with weapons hits and bore the autographs of numerous warriors. Mementos of the Highlanders' past.

Mulvaney did not wait for MacLeod begin, but began talking the moment the door closed. "Sir, I am not disobeying your orders, I am just questioning them. We have a duty to defend the Federated Commonwealth. This order from Katrina Steiner means civil war. We shouldn't be pulling our units out but ordering them into action. Remember what happened on Glengarry? We were called in to suppress a minor rebellion. A lot of good men and women died in that effort. This is the same kind of scenario on a much grander scale. Act now to support Victor and we might be able to prevent more loss of life in the future."

MacLeod rubbed his wounded arm as he gazed at Mulvaney. "I know how you feel about this, Major, but this fight is not ours, not yet anyway. My decision stands. The Northwind Highlanders are coming home."

"You do know that as soon as the Federated Suns State Command gets wind of this they'll issue countermanding orders," she returned.

"Let them," MacLeod said calmly.

"What will you do when those orders come, sir?"

MacLeod's steely gray eyes were unblinking in their resolve. "I'm a Highlander. I'll stand my ground. As will you, Major."

"Colonel, Victor Davion won't take kindly to what you're doing, whether it's legal or not. He'll see it as a threat."

"Like I said, Major, I know that the Federated Suns Command will countermand my orders, either directly or to the regiments that are incoming. Our people will ignore those orders and I will be forced into a confrontation with my Davion superiors."

"Field Marshal Hasek-Davion will never stand for this kind of insubordination," Mulvaney pressed. "They might even send troops and 'Mechs to enforce their orders. Even if we stay out of one fight, you're very likely bringing another one right here to our doorstep—sir."

MacLeod put his hands on his hips and shrugged carelessly. "You're right, Chastity, it's entirely possible. But with an invasion on their hands the Davions won't have the manpower to waste on us right now."

"Sir!" Mulvaney seemed shocked by his casual attitude. "What if you're wrong and the Davions come after us? We only have one regiment here on Northwind. We could be outgunned and outmatched."

"I know that, Major. I didn't make the decision lightly. But don't forget. Cat Stirling and the Fusiliers can get here in plenty of time if we need them. And even if Victor Davion throws his best at us, he'll have one hell of a fight on his hands."

10

The Fort
Tara, Northwind
Draconis March, Federated Commonwealth
19 September 3057

Loren's night had been a peaceful one thanks to the painkillers provided by the regimental doctors and the autobandage. The synthetic skin covering his wound made rolling over in his sleep or touching the wound tolerable, but the war news they'd been hearing might make other aspects of his stay on Northwind less manageable. Even as Marik had been making his declaration of war on the holo the other day, both Free Worlds and Capellan forces had been poised to strike at planets lost to the Davions in the Fourth Succession War. And they were catching those planets by surprise. Either Victor Davion was undefended because of troops diverted to garrisons along the Clan border or something had gone seriously wrong with his intelligence on troop movements. Anti-Davion riots and rebellions had also broken out all over the Sarna March.

The invasion must have been part of the reason the Chancellor had sent Loren to Northwind, but he wondered if the war might not turn the Highlanders against him after all. He mustn't fail, but could he still win?

The mess was small and most of the officers seemed to keep to their own little groups, just as in any mess Loren had ever seen. Going through the line he took a serving of toast and gravy. Two brown protein bars and a strong cup of coffee topped off the meal. It offered little appeal, but some of the field rations Loren had endured made the current tray of food seem like a rich banquet. He had just sat down to eat when he heard a step behind him.

"You're the one I heard about. You're that Capellan with Highlander blood. Kin to Letha Jaffray," came a man's voice he didn't recognize. Loren continued to slowly chew his food for a few minutes, then just as slowly began to turn. From the man's tone he could easily be facing a hostile situation. The officer was a lieutenant by rank, young, fair-haired, and well built. He wore a MechWarrior's jumpsuit and from what Loren knew of Highlander regalia, his badges indicated that he had taken down five 'Mechs in his career. Impressive, considering the man's youth.

"Yes, I'm Major Loren Jaffray," he said calmly.

"Word is," the man said, crossing his arms, "that you were with the old man when he took a round the other day."

Loren nodded very slowly, carefully turning his chair so he could look the lieutenant in the face. There was no sign of gun or blade, but if things took a violent turn Loren knew he could bring this fellow down in one springing attack to the midsection. "That's right."

"And I heard you saved his life," the Highlander said, extending his right hand and breaking into a wide smile. "Pleased to meet you, Major Jaffray. I'm Jake Fuller, Regimental Command Company, Security Lance."

"Same here," Loren said, rising to his feet and shaking the man's hand. "And for the record I didn't do anything but fire a few shots off into the bushes."

"Word is you also bested old Ironheart at The Pub too. That makes you one tough hunk of MechWarrior in my book."

Loren shrugged. "Old Ironheart, eh?"

"Is it true you actually beat her in an honor test?"

Loren smiled and couldn't help a small boast. "I did defeat her in a one-on-one. I didn't know her nickname, though."

"It's not what you might think, Major. She's a tough SOB of an executive officer. She's also one of the best

MechWarriors any of us have ever seen or served with. Most of the younger officers would follow her into hell. Those of us who've fought beside her already have on more than one occasion. We started that nickname after what happened on Clermont three years ago. That was a nasty fight, let me tell you."

Loren was curious and interested. "What happened?"

"MacLeod's Regiment was on garrison on Clermont when the Steel Vipers decided to stage a little raid. Those Clan warriors are a tough group of hombres. And those OmniMechs are the best fighting hardware I've ever seen. You Capellans are lucky they haven't hit the Confederation—yet.

"Well, the Major waded right into the middle of a bunch of their Elementals. She must've had a dozen on her but she just kept on blazing away at the Omnis. She took out two all by herself before those armored Toads cut through her cockpit and opened fire on her."

"I had no idea," Loren said. It was true the Capellan Confederation had yet to meet the Clans, but Loren had heard enough stories about how skilled and deadly they were. To survive Clan combat was no small feat.

"You must have noticed those scars on her arm. One of their shots hit her chest and did a number on her heart. She was in the field hospital for a month and they had to outfit her ticker with some artificial parts. After that we started calling her Old Ironheart ... of course never to her face."

Loren cringed at the thought of being attacked by one of the heavily armored Elementals the Inner Sphere warriors had nicknamed Toads. The mental image of one of those armored infantrymen punching through a cockpit and attacking a MechWarrior was chilling. He thought back to the night he and Mulvaney had fought, also remembering her comments afterward.

"I'm a little surprised," he said.

"Why's that, Major?"

"Mulvaney told me she'd never lost a fight."

Lieutenant Fuller's face became more serious. "She didn't until you took her on."

"But you said the Elemental—"

"I said he shot her up, and pretty bad. He might have finished her off too, but she hit the eject button just before going unconscious. When she punched out, the ejection blast cut that Viper Elemental in half. She landed near a full Star of Clan Omnis and was just about dead when the old man ordered my lance into it. He personally pried her out of her cockpit and carried her to the hospital. We dug in and gave him cover. He took plenty of risks that day."

"From what I've seen, your Colonel is one hell of an officer," Loren said.

"You don't know the half of it. His daughter was in the regiment too and was killed the day before by the Vipers. Most men would have pulled back out of grief. Not the old man. He pushed us on." Fuller's eyes narrowed in thought. "When he pulled the Major out of her seat every man in the regiment knew he'd have done the same for any one of us."

Loren understood that kind of loyalty, but it was different with the Highlanders. The look in Fuller's eyes and the tone of his voice said that he'd be willing to face the same battle, the same risks all over again. It was an invisible bond that held the Northwind Highlanders together, strong yet incredibly flexible.

He was about to ask Fuller for more details on the battle and Mulvaney when an officer burst into the mess hall and ran toward them. He recognized her as the lanky Lieutenant Gomez from the War Room. She stepped up and stood facing Jaffray squarely, almost staring him down. "Sorry to interrupt."

"Lieutenant Gomez, right?"

"Affirmative, sir," she replied coolly. "Colonel MacLeod regrets that he cannot meet you for breakfast, sir."

"Problems, Lieutenant?"

"The Colonel wants you to join him in his office," she said smartly. "Immediately, sir."

Loren didn't know what to make of this summons, but he showed no visible concern. Instead he gave Fuller a comradely clap on the back by way of goodbye. By time he turned around again, the long-legged Gomez was already halfway across the mess hall.

Colonel MacLeod's office was surprisingly small and tucked away in an inauspicious corner of the massive Fort.

Loren would have expected something more to match the stature of MacLeod's command, but the small room was furnished with a desk of light oak and seating for four or five others around it. On the wall, mounted in a large frame, was a set of bagpipes. Seated behind the desk was the Colonel, with Mulvaney seated across from him. Gomez remained outside, closing the door once Loren was in.

"Good morning, sir, Major," Loren said as he looked first at MacLeod and then Mulvaney. He also took in the scar jutting out from under the short sleeve of her uniform. *Ironheart.* The name suited her in more ways than one, Loren decided. Chastity Mulvaney was the one island of resistance.

"Sorry I missed our meal, Major. I take it you're recovering well?" MacLeod said, motioning to the chair next to his executive officer.

"Yes, sir, and you?"

"Physically I'm fine, but there are some other issues I need to address and I wanted you to be here."

"Against my advice," Mulvaney added.

MacLeod removed his wireframe eyeglasses as he shot Mulvaney a stern look.

As he usually tried to do, Loren ignored the comment. "What seems to be the problem, sir?"

"Consul Burns and Colonel Catelli want to pay me a visit this morning. Given the urgency of their message, I can only assume that the Federated Suns Command is responding to the orders from Katrina Steiner.

"Plainly put, Major, this is going to be a hot meeting. The Consul believes you're to blame, that you're the one who's pushed me into a rash action against the Federated Commonwealth. You and I know that isn't true, but my Davion counterpart seems to think you could be the next Amaris. I want you here when I shove the whole thing back down his throat."

Loren felt uneasy. He'd known before ever arriving on Northwind that his visit would generate tremendous tensions between the Highlanders and their employer. In a straight-up fight on the battlefield, that would be fine. But this was something different—a diplomatic battle. And, like it or not, he was now being drawn into the front lines.

"Sir, I ask again, please reconsider," Mulvaney said.

"We've already spent the whole last hour hashing over this, Major. I appreciate your fulfilling your duties as my executive officer, but now you're pushing too hard. My orders to the regiments at large stand, and you will obey them as well."

"Understood, sir." Mulvaney's voice was almost contrite.

There was a soft knock at the door and the three officers stood. Loren looked over at Colonel MacLeod, who was stroking his beard in thought. He couldn't help but admire the man's quiet dignity, his command of the situation. *He's letting them stew outside for a minute, wondering and worrying. Nice touch.* Finally the Colonel nodded and Loren opened the door.

David Planetary Consul Burns stepped into the room first, his regal purple cape billowing behind him. His gait was so prim and proper that he seemed out of place on Northwind, and even more so among the rough and ready Highlanders.

Probably just another political appointment, Loren thought. *Nothing to do with skill or honor to the state as in the Confederation; simply a debt owed to some baron or duke.*

Burns affected the same arrogant pose as last time while his aide de camp followed him in. The short, brooding Catelli entered with short stiff steps, then dropped into a parade rest pose in a blatant lack of respect for Colonel MacLeod.

"Consul Burns," MacLeod gestured toward a chair. Burns pivoted quickly and dropped into a chair, fluffing his cape behind him as he sat. Colonel Catelli took a seat next to Loren.

"What can I do for you today, Consul?" MacLeod said, resting his arms on the desk top.

Burns began with a smug tone. "I've come on a matter of great importance to the Federated Commonwealth, Colonel. But this is a matter for the Highlanders. I don't think it involves your visitor at all." He didn't bother to even look at Loren.

"I take it by your tone that Major Jaffray's presence here causes you some discomfort."

Burns nodded slowly as he spoke. "Yes. Considering that

both Marik *and* Liao have begun to invade the Federated Commonwealth. I find having a Liao here bordering on treasonous."

MacLeod smiled in response. "Then I will exercise my right as the CO of the Highlanders. I want him to remain. This man saved my life, and was injured doing so. There's nothing that you can say that he can't hear."

"Indeed." Burns stared down his nose at Loren as if he were a street beggar, or worse. "Once again I find myself bowing to your whims, Colonel. It has come to my attention that yesterday you received an order to withdraw your regiments from the Lyran sector of the Federated Commonwealth. An order, I might add, that you have decided to obey, according to my sources. Do you acknowledge these facts?"

"Acknowledged," MacLeod replied flatly. There was no effort to explain his actions, simply the bare fact.

"You understand," Burns pressed on, "that such an order has no validity in the eyes of the Federated Commonwealth High Command. As such I come to present you with an order directly from the Grand Marshal of the Armies, Morgan Hasek-Davion." Burns handed MacLeod a sealed envelope, which the Colonel immediately tore open and began to read. "I think you'll find everything in order," Burns went on. "You are to disregard the order from the Lyran Command and command all your offworld regiments to return immediately to their posts."

"Thank you," Colonel MacLeod replied, carefully folding the single sheet into a tiny square. "But I'm afraid I will have to ignore the Marshal's order. The Northwind Highlanders are coming home."

Consul Burns' face flushed deep red and his voice seemed to quiver slightly. "Colonel MacLeod, that order was endorsed by Prince Victor Davion, your liege lord. You will obey it."

"No, sir, I will not. When my troops are in the Lyran State Command they take their orders from Tharkad and as such, the other stands."

Colonel Catelli leaned forward, resting his elbows on the desk as he spoke. "The Federated Commonwealth is currently under attack by both the Free Worlds League and the

Capellan Confederation. Not to mention the continuing threat of the Clans along a full sector of our border."

MacLeod's stone face did not waver or show any emotion. "Gentlemen, I appreciate your position, but I will not order those regiments back to their garrisons. We've already faced off against the Clans on several occasions and lost good men and women to them. We did what we had to in the name of the Federated Commonwealth. But this time I obey Tharkad."

Burns leaned across the desk as well. "No matter what you and your fellow regimental commanders wish to think, the universe does not center on Northwind. You have a contractual obligation to Prince Victor Steiner-Davion and if you do not wish to fulfill it, perhaps we can find someone who can."

For the first time since the meeting began, anger flashed over the face of William MacLeod. His nostrils flared and his thick eyebrows drew together until they merged. "As far as I and my troops are concerned, the universe *does* center on Northwind. And as for my obligations to the throne, need I remind you that more than four hundred Highlanders died during the Fourth Succession War in the name of Hanse Davion? Another five hundred men and women from our ranks met their end during the War of 'Thirty-nine. In the recent defense of the Clan border we've lost dozens of other fine troopers. I'd say the Highlanders have done our bit for king and country."

Catelli's temper rose as well. "You are disobeying direct orders, Colonel MacLeod."

"No, I am not, Colonel. My regiments are commanded from the Lyran State Command. I am simply disregarding your new orders."

"You are defying your liege lord."

"I am serving the interests of my people and those under my command. I consider that an obligation of a higher calling. Princes and lords will come and go, but the Highlanders have always been."

"You may put whatever interpretation you want on it, Colonel, but this is a violation of orders and will not be tolerated." Burns slapped his hand on the desktop. "Do you realize the implications of your actions, sir?"

MacLeod placed both hands on the desk and leaned forward slightly. "Aye, Consul, I do. You want me to behave as though the Northwind Highlanders are nothing more than an element of the Federated Commonwealth's Armed Forces. Well, let me tell you a few things. First of all, the Federated Commonwealth failed to honor its contractual obligations after we helped clean up the Skye rebellion on Glengarry. Now comes this attempt to make us a toy unit to be tossed back and forth between Victor and his sister. In reality we are a separate entity, an independent people. If I follow your orders, the Highlanders are no more than a cog in your war machine. We are much more than that, Consul Burns ... Colonel." MacLeod made sure to look each one in the eye as he spoke their names.

Burns was beginning to tremble in anger. "I have bowed to the traditions and customs of you and your precious Highlanders on numerous occasions, MacLeod. Need I remind you, sir, that Northwind is not an independent world but a member of the Federated Commonwealth? Hanse Davion, rest his soul, allowed you to return to Northwind, but this planet is still a part of our holdings. You are merely tenants on this world."

MacLeod's eyes narrowed, but he kept his voice cool and deadly. "Burns, let me assure you that the Northwind Highlanders are not content to be mere 'tenants' of Northwind. It is rightfully ours and we mean to defend our right to it, to the last man or woman if necessary. I suggest that you not try our will in this matter, because this is no idle threat." There was a long pause after he spoke.

It was Catelli who broke the silence, his tone conciliatory. "I cannot help but wonder if you are being misled, Colonel." The man shot a quick glance at Loren.

"Colonel Catelli," MacLeod replied. "I resent your implication. This man saved my life yesterday at risk to his own."

"I heard about the unfortunate incident, Colonel. But even you must admit that the attempt might have had something to do with the war going on."

"For all we know the assassin was a Davion supporter who wanted to remove the Colonel as a point of resistance," Loren interjected.

Colonel Catelli's eyes flared. "Or it could have been a

Capellan attempting to stir up trouble here on Northwind as Sun-Tzu Liao has been doing on so many other worlds."

MacLeod held up his hands for silence. "We don't know who fired on us, Colonel. But it does not change my decision either way. The regiments are coming home, period."

Consul Burns rose halfway from his seat, leaning forward with both hands on the desk. "And you realize that the Prince is well within his rights to enforce the orders you are disobeying?"

MacLeod slowly stood to his full height. His rising made Jaffray, Catelli, and Mulvaney also rise to their feet. "If his Highness wants to enforce his will on Northwind and the Highlanders, Consul, I suggest you tell him that he's welcome to try. Hell, let him come here personally if he wants. But mark my words, it would be a grave mistake on his part." He gestured to the door behind Burns. "Thank you for your time and concern, gentlemen."

Burns and Catelli started out the door, but the smaller man stopped and turned back. "Don't let it end this way, Colonel."

MacLeod chuckled slightly. "I was just about to say the same thing to you, Colonel Catelli."

Once they were safely back in the limousine Drew Catelli turned to the man who was officially his superior. "That didn't go well at all, Consul. Matters are now much worse than when we started."

"That is an understatement, Colonel. Neither the Grand Marshal nor the Prince will be pleased."

"I think there may be a way to force MacLeod's hand and possibly put an end to this entire debate. My intelligence sources tell me that the Third Royal Guards RCT is currently being reassigned to the Lyran sector and is passing within jump distance. We could request they be diverted to Northwind to secure the planet. Otherwise, if we wait too long, all four regiments of the Highlanders will be dug in."

"Interesting idea," Burns said, obviously pondering the thought. "Won't their arrival spark protest from the Highlanders?"

"Some of their officers are not as bullheaded as MacLeod, and are totally loyal to Davion. The Third Royals combined with the Consul Guards would be more than a match for MacLeod's Regiment if he decides to fight it out with us. Besides, you know these Highlanders. The only thing they understand or respect is brute force. Bringing the Third Royals here would guarantee that MacLeod takes you seriously."

"It is very risky, Colonel. The Highlanders are a proud people. We could be forcing a bad decision on their part. And don't forget this confounded Jaffray, who seems to be MacLeod's favorite pet."

"Sir, I have several of my men conducting an investigation into the assassination attempt. Our preliminary reports show that it might indeed have been Capellan-sponsored or backed. If we could prove that, Jaffray would no longer be sitting in on our meetings and adding fuel to an already growing fire."

"Are you sure about that?"

Catelli smiled slyly. "I assure you, sir, that before I am done I will have proof of a Capellan link to the attempt." *And if not, then I'll just have to manufacture the evidence I need.*

Burns leaned back and smiled complacently. "Stay on top of it, Colonel. I want this to end peacefully if at all possible. But in case matters get out of hand, I will issue a formal request for the Third Royals to be diverted to Northwind."

Catelli also settled back in his seat. Matters were proceeding according to his plan. Soon, Northwind would be his domain and the Northwind Highlanders a mere footnote in history. There would be no need for men like Burns once he proved his skill and acumen to his superiors. Northwind was merely a stepping stone onto even greater things. And to hell with what it might cost anyone else.

11

The Fort
Tara, Northwind
Draconis March, Federated Commonwealth
21 September 3057

Loren spent much of the next few days after the confrontation with the Davion Consul inside the walls of The Fort. His requests to see Colonel MacLeod were met with a flat response that the Colonel was meeting with officers or busy in the War Room. Loren used the time to continue healing from the attack and following the war news. The Capellans had already launched a number of successful attacks, easily taking the targeted worlds. On other planets in the Sarna March local revolutions were doing the job for them. Perhaps the greatest victory had been a symbolic one, the recapture of the planet Liao from the Davions.

Loren also spent one afternoon simply walking through the massive complex of The Fort. Many of the halls and offices were open to the general public, while other, more sensitive areas were under constant guard and inaccessible.

The structure of the complex was remarkable in many respects. It was not just a hub of military operations, but also the center of the Northwind government and the spiritual focus of the Highlanders. The Assembly of Warriors met in a specially built hall within The Fort itself. Various other government agencies met in the sub-assembly buildings outside the massive walls of The Fort, but on Northwind it was the Assembly of Warriors that carried the most weight and authority.

Though the sub-assemblies were subordinate to the Assembly of Warriors, Loren learned that both Fort and sub-assemblies were connected by a web of tunnels deep beneath the streets of Tara. The arrangement seemed like an apt symbol of the way the Highlanders were intertwined with Northwind and how intricately The Fort was woven into the city's infrastructure.

One of the places he found most interesting was the Highlanders' own museum. It was filled with a collection of artifacts the unit had accumulated in the course of its history, which stretched back for centuries. Perhaps the most impressive piece was the large fist of a *Highlander* 'Mech. Sealed in an airtight case, it had belonged to a lance of Northwind Highlander 'Mechs assigned to the famous Black Watch Regiment. During the height of the Star League the Black Watch had served as bodyguards to the League's Star Lord. When the League collapsed, the Black Watch was also one of the many units destroyed. Loren looked at the defiant fist for nearly an hour, studying it and thinking about the history behind the artifact.

The most unnerving display was a diorama depicting Major Letha Jeffray's holding action in the battle for Goodna decades before. She and her battalion command company had held off an entire regiment of Free Worlds League troops in a narrow mountain pass, buying enough time for over a regiment's worth of Highlanders to escape. Looking at the model representation, Loren felt a shiver, a touch with his past—a past shared by the Highlanders.

As a Death Commando his existence was dedicated to the service of the Chancellor. The fact that he had risked his life many times in the name of his lord had given Loren a sense of purpose, a feeling that his life was full, complete. Mulvaney had called him a terrorist, but Loren considered himself a MechWarrior like any other. Terrorism was a word used by the enemies of the Liao. But for Loren any acts he committed as a Death Commando were simply those of a true patriot.

His tour of the Fort disturbed that feeling. It made him realize that the Highlanders had something he lacked, a rich and living history. By blood it was history that he was a part of, and for the first time in his life Loren almost questioned the sense of duty that gave his life meaning. But he shook off these doubts, vowing to strengthen his resolve and his efforts to accomplish his mission on Northwind.

That morning was spent in the company of Lieutenant Gomez. The tall lithe communications officer had been assigned to accompany him on a tour of Tara proper. They rode in a small two-seater military hover car that she drove wildly, dodging and weaving through traffic. Loren had enjoyed the tour despite the fact that the Lieutenant was decidedly unfriendly. Her coolness was different than Mulvaney's. With the Lieutenant it seemed to be total disinterest, while for Mulvaney it was a way of controlling conflicting emotions. He had spent half the day drinking in the sights of the city, the other half trying to get Gomez to talk to him. After three hours he mentally surrendered and gave himself to simply enjoying Tara and its splendor.

The city was nestled in the foothills of the Rockspire Mountains. Though tall and jagged, the peaks were often invisible in the mornings because of a dense fog that hung over Tara. They were like massive natural guardians, silent, sometimes hidden, yet ever-present. In the bright afternoon sun the peaks were stunning. Loren and Gomez took one of the public tours by helium dirigible, from which they further contemplated the setting. It was easy to understand why Northwind's Scots and English founders had built Tara here; the natural protection offered by the mountains gave a powerful sense of calm and security.

Running down from the mountains was the Grand Thames River. Ages ago the original settlers of Northwind had channeled the river through a maze of concrete through the heart of the city. Dotting the river were impressive structures such as the ComStar HPG and the centuries-old Star League Institute of Arts. The latter, with its impressive granite slab construction and sleek black marble highlighting, was by far the most beautiful that Loren had ever seen. In the past three centuries of almost continuous war, the fact that the building and its contents had survived intact apparently made it almost a religious site in the eyes of art historians.

104 Blaine Lee Pardoe

Lieutenant Gomez ended the tour at The Pub, where Loren was surprised to see Major Mulvaney, apparently waiting for him. She carried a small package wrapped in brown paper under her arm. Thanking his guide, he climbed out of the hover car and strode up to the Major.

He nodded in greeting. "Good day, Major."

'I'm here for the Colonel. He regrets that he has not been available in the past few days, but matters of pressing urgency have kept us both busy. I was sent here to entertain you for lunch, if you so desire." Her tone indicated that the task was, in reality, much more akin to a duty. Loren would have preferred it otherwise, but with Mulvaney he knew better. If she had any interest in him, it was more the way a mother wolf might view an intruder into her den of cubs.

"I appreciate the offer," Loren said, holding open the door for her. She went in without comment and Loren followed. They made their way through the darkness of The Pub to a small booth in the back. Grinning broadly, Mr. Pluncket limped over to their table.

"This is a pleasant surprise," he said, placing napkins and settings on the table.

"Why do you say that?" Mulvaney snapped.

"No reason," Pluncket replied. "It's just that the word running through the regiment is that the winds blow cold between you two. Apparently my sources are not as reliable as I thought."

Mulvaney shook her head. "We're not here together—I mean we are together, but aren't here with each other." She was obviously frustrated. "Damn it, Pluncket. You know what I mean."

The seemingly ageless barkeep ignored the comment. "The entire regiment is astir over the Warrior's Cabel tonight."

"Mister Pluncket, if you're probing for some scoop on what the Colonel will say, you're sniffing around the wrong person," Mulvaney said, casting an eye at Jaffray. "Though our visitor here has some of the inside story. Isn't that right, Major?"

Loren shrugged. He was not about to tip his hand. "What do you recommend for lunch?" he asked.

"The cook makes a mean long grass steer sandwich."

"I'll take one and a Northwind Red, then."

Plhunket nodded and looked at Mulvaney. "I'll have the stew, Mr. Pluncket, and some ale as well." As the older man limped back toward the bar, Loren turned his attention back to Mulvaney. "Are things well?"

She spoke in a soft tone to prevent anyone from overhearing. "'Well'? That is a relative word. We're losing in the Sarna March, but I'll give you this much, you were right about this being the start of a civil war. One of the reasons the Davion troops haven't been able to put up a good showing is that many of the Prince's JumpShips had been reassigned to the Lyran sector and now Katrina won't give them back. How can he get troops where he needs them without JumpShips?"

"I won't be proud if I'm right, Major."

"Really? I'm surprised. I would expect that a famed Death Commando like yourself would be happy to see a foe consumed in civil war."

Loren chose to ignore the heavy sarcasm. "It's true that the Capellans and the Davions have long been enemies. But remember, I am a MechWarrior. Part of me is happy to see the Federated Commonwealth falling apart, but I'd like to be part of its demise."

"We have little in common, Major Jaffray."

"We're more alike than you'd ever admit. Both of us place a value on honor. I would give honor to the Davions with a fight to the end."

Mulvaney leaned across the table, her whisper barely audible. "Consul Burns has visited The Fort no less than three times demanding to see the Colonel, but MacLeod won't meet with him. It's going to get worse now that word is out across the whole damned Inner Sphere that the First and Second Kearny are on their way back home. The local governments are up in arms, being so close to the Clan border. Katrina Steiner has promised replacements, so their anger will probably be short-lived, but it's safe to say that our image has been tarnished in a number of circles."

Loren drew a long breath and shook his head. "I'd say the Highlanders' reputation was already tarnished after they deserted the Capellan Confederation. Millions died because of it."

Mulvaney's temper flared at the comment. "And you blame me for that, Loren?"

"No, but I imagine you blame me for all that is happening now."

She shook her head. "For whatever it's worth, I don't. It's just that you're stirring the pot. Telling the Colonel what he wants to hear, helping him reach a decision that could spell the end for us all."

"You're so damn bitter," Loren said, shaking his head. Mulvaney never hid the contempt she had for him, yet there was something in her anger, a fierceness of sorts, that drew him to her.

"I'll give you bitter. You've only been on Northwind for a handful of days. I was born and raised here. My family served in the First Kearny Highlanders for six generations. To you this place is a tourist attraction, a place you've read or heard about. To me it's home and these people"—she gestured to the other patrons in the bar—"are my kin. They're my brothers and sisters. Your coming here puts all that at risk. You've managed to start a lot of people questioning their loyalties."

Loren could never tell her how happy he was to hear those words. "You're partly right, Chastity. When I first came here, Northwind was just a place to me. Now that I've gotten to know you Highlanders I've learned something. You're my people as well, no matter how much I resist it. Everyone has treated me as an equal—present company excluded, that is.

"I know I'm not a Highlander, but I'm starting to *feel* like one. I told you before that I intended no harm in coming here. Now I understand why I was sent and why the timing of this mission is so important.

"True, my father and I didn't serve in the regiments, but we *never* forgot where we came from. This has become my home too now." Loren had lowered his voice, but he filled his words with intense conviction. And watched her reaction carefully. *Mulvaney is my chief opponent in the Highlander ranks. If I can win her over, my chances of success increase dramatically. The only problem now is that I'm starting to believe my own words too much.*

"I believe you," she said simply.

"What did you say?"

"I believe you, *Loren*," her use of his first name was calming. "I believe your words, but I still don't trust you. Too much has happened since your arrival for it all to be a coincidence. And no matter what, I won't sit back and let anyone threaten my way of life."

"Chastity, with all that's been going on, well, we're both under a lot of pressure." Loren rubbed his thigh where he'd taken the needler hit several days before.

"It's not just the pressure, Loren. I'm used to pressure. As a commander, I've known plenty of it." She was frowning in distress, and Loren noticed for the first time the dark rings under her eyes.

"Chastity, the Cabel tonight. What will happen?"

"MacLeod will let the troops know the truth about what's happening between us and the Davions. He will call for us to rally around him in his decision. Most of the officers and warriors will follow his lead. I'm sure he'll also present Sun-Tzu's offer to the Highlanders."

"And you?" Loren couldn't help wanting her on his side, whether she knew his true motives or not. The idea of Chastity as his enemy pained him.

"I disagree with the Colonel ... and with you, for that matter. My family and the Highlanders have benefited a great deal from our relationship with House Davion. I would honor that bond."

"And if the rest of the Highlanders vote to side with MacLeod?"

Chastity looked into his eyes. "I'm not sure, Loren," she said, then abruptly stood up. "My emotions seem to be getting the better of me, Major. Perhaps the Colonel was mistaken in asking me to meet you here today. I apologize." She reached down to where she'd been sitting and pulled out the package wrapped in brown paper. "This is for you."

"Chastity ..." Loren began, but he couldn't think of any words to make her stay. "Don't go, not this way."

She ignored his plea. "Colonel MacLeod sends these to you so you'll blend in better tonight. Until then." Executing a perfect about-face, Chastity Mulvaney turned and strode out of The Pub, leaving Loren sitting alone in the booth. He hadn't known what to say, but even if he had, things were happening too fast all around them. Events that would only separate him from her, not bring them closer together.

Loren tore open the brown paper. Inside was a garment of red and blue plaid with a thin line of green in the design. He recognized it as the Jaffray clan's own tartan. A dress kilt. Also inside was a black formal shirt and a war sash. A full dress uniform for MacLeod's Regiment.

He held the uniform in front of him, then carefully folded it up. A chill ran down his spine. Now, for the first time in nearly three decades, a Jaffray would once again wear the uniform of a Northwind Highlander. Loren knew that if his grandfather were alive, he'd be bursting with pride. He also knew that the Chancellor would be equally pleased that Loren had managed to infiltrate the Highlanders according to plan. The same emotion, but light years apart. Somewhere, alone, in the middle, Loren Jaffray sat contemplating the gravity of his mission. The Highlanders must be destroyed. For him, there was no choice but to obey.

Mister Plunckett limped over to the table and set Loren's food and drink in front of him. "Don't worry, lad. She's got it for you in a big way."

"What do you mean?" There'd never been any doubt that she had it in for him.

"As if you didn't know, laddie. She's got that look women get when they have a soft spot for a man. I've seen it when the lass looks at you. She may yell and fight like you're the demon incarnate, but inside she sees something she likes. If you're smart, laddie, you willna let her go."

Loren looked at the man and shook his head. "I wish I had your faith."

= 12 =

Caithness Woods
Northwind
Draconis March, Federated Commonwealth
21 September 3057

The trip to the Caithness Woods southwest of Tara was one that Loren found somewhat uncomfortable. He and several other Highlander officers all wearing dress uniforms boarded a hover truck that stopped for them at the BOQ. Loren was surprised that his Highlander uniform fit so well, except that the natural wool of the black shirt made his chest itch almost unbearably. The other big problem was where to place his rank badge and Death Commando insignia. He would not have felt dressed without them, and had finally decided to pin them to his tartan sash. It seemed a good solution, a way of fulfilling his oath to the Chancellor while also showing respect to MacLeod and his grandfather's memory.

Sitting next to him on the bench in the back of the truck was Lieutenant Jake Fuller, whose perpetual enthusiasm reminded Loren of his own early years as a warrior. Though a vehicle like this was most often used to ferry infantry to and from the battlefield, tonight the mood was more festive. Fuller introduced Loren to several other Highlander officers as the truck made its way out of town and eventually into the woods. Most of the others had either heard of Loren or seen him fight the honor match with Mulvaney in The Pub.

110   Blaine Lee Pardoe

Some greeted him warmly. Others—maybe those who'd lost money on the contest—simply nodded.

Caithness Woods was in the rolling hills near the training range where Loren and MacLeod had gone for their 'Mech drill. From what was visible, the woods were neither heavy nor deep, probably covering only a few dozen acres. A bright light rose from the hills deep in the center of the woods and the air rang with voices and music. As Loren and the others climbed down from the hover truck he saw several infantrymen carrying pulse laser rifles and outfitted for night operations. They carefully surveyed each warrior climbing out of the truck, and two of them were using night-vision gear to scan the nearby countryside.

As a military man himself, Loren understood why MacLeod had selected the Caithness Woods as a meeting place. From what he could tell by the light of the moon the cluster of trees was isolated, with the rolling hills providing natural protection from security devices. The open fields surrounding the woods made undetected approach nearly impossible, even in the darkness of night.

Loren followed Jake Fuller and the other officers into the woods, the underbrush snapping against his bare legs and scratching his skin. A kilt wasn't much of an advantage in such an environment, but was otherwise surprisingly comfortable. Slowly the line of officers snaked into the thick of the Caithness Woods, heading toward the light that seemed to rise from the center of the small forest.

As they crested one of the steep hills Loren saw the gathering of Highlanders. Nearly four hundred men and women of all ranks and standings were assembled around a roaring bonfire, their faces illumined by the blazing flames. Many were drinking, but Loren did not see the concealed source of the ale.

The music he'd heard was clearer as they topped the hill. The Regimental Honor Guard was present, bagpipes, flutes, and drums blaring their rendition of *"Hielan Laddie"* out into the night. Around the fire nearly a dozen of the regimental dancers, mostly female, jigged to the rhythm and blare of the bagpipes. He had heard that the regimental dancers of the Highlanders were not just for entertainment but were trained medics who accompanied their kin into combat. The almost festive scene was compelling, and Loren felt a twinge of guilt. These were the same happy men and women who, if his mission was successful, would be dead or broken.

Watchful of his step, Loren followed Lieutenant Fuller down near the bonfire. The warmth and brightness of the flames sharpened the contrast with the surrounding dark. He looked around and recognized the faces of several other men and women he'd met in the past week. He wondered how they would react when the Chancellor's proposal was presented. *Would the Highlanders accept? Or would they toss him into the bonfire? Was the Cabel really now a moot point, considering the actions of Colonel MacLeod in the past forty-eight hours?*

Loren looked for Colonel MacLeod and spotted him near the top of one of the hills ringing the bonfire. In the flickering firelight the CO of the Highlanders seemed younger. The gray hairs that stood out by day, even from a distance, disappeared by night. Gone too were the worry lines and wrinkles of a seasoned regimental officer. Instead what Loren saw was a powerful and dominating man, a consummate leader of his people. Colonel MacLeod spotted Loren and motioned him to come forward. Making his way past the line of dancers, Loren waded through the crowd.

Loren stood only a few steps from the Colonel, but was half a body length shorter thanks to the steep slope of the surrounding hill. MacLeod gazed toward the bonfire and the regimental dancers swaying against the flames. "Impressive, isn't it, Major?"

It was more than impressive to Loren, it was stirring. A line of Highlanders came out of the darkness carrying large pole-like logs, holding them on end. The jubilation and merriment seemed to stop as the procession came into view. Like a long line of funeral mourners they encircled the bonfire, logs upright. The effect was almost hypnotic. The dancing and music slowly dissipated and soon the only sound was the crackling of the bonfire. Loren turned back to MacLeod. "What are those?"

"The Cabers, lad."

Loren watched as one of the men holding a large log stepped from the ranks and came up before him. "They are the past. I had our craftsmen prepare yours." MacLeod made a sweeping gesture toward the log. Loren was unsure what to do, but followed his instincts and the actions of the others. He stepped forward and the younger man handed him the massive caber. He glanced back at MacLeod, but the Highlander CO was again staring off into the fire.

Loren walked forward to the roaring flames. The heart from the fire seemed to keep him focused as he joined the ranks of those in the long line. He moved nearly without thought, almost like being in a trance. He looked at his right and left and saw the stern resolve on the faces of the other troops. On his own caber was the name "Jaffray" burned in by laser. Under it was several smaller words that were difficult to read with the glare of the light in front of him. Turning slightly so that the firelight would illuminate the log he read the words silently: Brighton, Calloway VI, Lopez, and Ningpo.

The names were familiar to him as worlds of the Inner Sphere. His grandfather had talked a great deal about those planets, places where his ancestors had died fighting in the Northwind Highlanders. Looking over his right shoulder Loren saw that the man next to him had a different lineage under his family name of Campbell. On the other side a woman bore the caber bearing the family name Drewkovich.

The bonfire's crackle was broken by the slow, almost heart-like beating of drums. Loren stiffened slightly as the caber dug into his hands. He hugged the massive log against him, ignoring its weight. It was as if they were joined as one. Behind him he heard Mulvaney's voice bark into the night.

"Honors ... 'hut!" Loren could not see the other Highlanders, but heard them snap to attention.

"Brothers and sisters," boomed the voice of William MacLeod to his kindred. "I welcome you all to this most time-honored event in Highlander lore, the Warrior's Cabel. One has not been called in years, but times have changed and the need is great. We begin in the past, with who we are. Let us never forget those who have died for our people. Let us honor the Eternal Roll of the Clans of the Northwind Highlanders!"

The drums suddenly stopped and a lone bagpipe's mournful tones cut into the Northwind night. The sounds of "Amazing Grace" rang upward as Chastity Mulvaney began to call the names aloud. "Wayne, Buchanan, Burke, Jacobsin, MacDougall . . ."

The bonfire flamed anew with the reading of each name. As each clan name rang out in the night, the honor bearer tossed the huge caber into the raging fire. The impact of the cabers stirred the embers, sending sparks flurrying into the night sky. The heat of the flames seemed to reach through Loren's pole to warm his chest and face, burning into and beyond him. He listened carefully for a full ten minutes until he alone was holding the last caber. Finally, Mulvaney called out the name of his clan into the night, "Jaffray!"

With every bit of his strength Loren lifted his arms upward, sending the caber into the air and down into the roaring fire. The log disappeared for a moment as it crashed down, half in and half out of the raging fire . . . a poor toss by the standards of the others before him. Loren's arms hung like dead weights and his face was bathed in the heat of the cascading fire. He was embarrassed by his poor showing, but no one else seemed to notice. The pipe player finished her chorus and the music died away.

Loren felt empty for a moment as he looked into the flames. *I have never had a history. My only real family was my grandfather. Now I find that I'm part of a greater family, one welcoming me with open arms.*

A family that I must destroy.

Colonel MacLeod's voice shattered the night air as Loren stepped back among the other honor bearers. "At ease, fellow warriors. A Northwind Highlander is bound by honor and lives in the past and present. Such is our way. We are here as equals and I ask you to say what is in your hearts.

"Tonight I speak to you of a great need for this Cabel. We face a time of decision and a time of danger. Some of you have served me for years and I wanted you to know what we are up against. To those of you who have just begun your careers you are about to witness what separates us from the rest of the Inner Sphere.

"First I speak to you of our common danger. Most of you have heard of a civil war that is brewing between the Steiners and the Davions. I have received orders for our sister regiments to return to Northwind. I have honored those orders. Our Davion liege lord has, however, issued counter orders for our troops to remain where they are. Tensions are high between us and the Davions and are bound to get worse because I intend to stand on my original orders.

"This is not just an issue of mere orders, but one of sovereignty—our sovereignty. For us to reverse our stand and send the troops back would be a mark that our kind could never bear. Our sister regiments will return to their homeland!" Murmurs rose from among the rank and file of Highlanders. The words were muffled, but Loren could tell there was strong feeling on both sides of the debate.

"On this matter I am not concerned about whether or not you agree. I am the commanding officer of all regiments abroad and the personal CO of this regiment. My orders stand and are not open to debate. But all of you must realize the implications of this course. On one hand, the Davions have, until recently, been a fair employer and have turned this world over to us to administer. Our current contract calls for us to garrison worlds on the Clan border, not to fight in a civil war.

"There is honor in fighting the Clans because they want to enslave us, but a civil war is another kind of fight—a struggle over politics, not survival. Such is not fit duty for the Highlanders. It simply is not worthy of us. And I will not send my people to die over something that has no meaning to us. We are an independent people, with hundreds of years of history and tradition. We're not the lackeys of any House Lord, including any Davion. Northwind is our home, *not* the Federated Commonwealth. It is time for us to look to our own interests.

"We must face the truth, that Northwind is not truly ours. The Davions treat us like mere caretakers, mere *tenants*. Katrina Steiner has given permission for our units to return home. Obeying Victor Davion's orders would only bring us one step closer to becoming absorbed into his army. We are not part of the Davion clan but stand on our own, as we have since the days of the Star League. It is our way.

"But taking that stand will surely bring down on us the wrath of Victor Davion. He will never sit back while we openly defy orders. That is why I must cancel all leaves and hereby order the unit to security status blue until further notice. All Highlander families should remain sequestered, and our Tara garrison will set up checkpoints into and out of the city. Aerospace lances are on full standby. Watch yourselves. Many on Northwind are more loyal to the Federated Commonwealth than to us. Trusted friends may turn out to be bitter enemies. If we are fortunate, perhaps we can work out a compromise with Davion. Otherwise we may find ourselves facing serious repercussions." Loren heard the words and knew the risks that the Highlanders were facing. Their onetime benefactor might rise against them with a vengeance.

"And now I bring before you another matter. Many of you have already met or heard of our Capellan visitor, Major Loren Jaffray. Major Jaffray has traveled far for a chance to visit the homeworld of his family, but that has not been the only purpose of his presence here. He has come bearing an offer, one I ask you all to hear and consider." Colonel MacLeod looked down at Loren and gestured to him. Facing the gathering on the hillside, Loren felt hundreds of eyes boring into and through him as MacLeod continued.

"This Cabel cannot decide on his initiative. We can, however, vote to recall the Assembly of Warriors to discuss and debate the matter. Tonight you must ask yourselves only this: Is this offer worth reviewing and debating?" Colonel MacLeod turned and nodded to Loren, a broad smile on his face.

Loren had been practicing his short speech over and over in the past few days, yet his stomach clenched and his palms became warm and wet with the knowledge that he would not get another chance. Failure to persuade the Cabel to recall the Assembly of Warriors would doom his mission and disgrace him in the eyes of the Chancellor. As a MechWarrior he had faced death hundreds of times, yet he was suddenly nervous about speaking to this gathering of MacLeod's Regiment.

"As the Colonel mentioned, I did not come to tour Northwind, but rather to offer you all a chance at true freedom.

"Chancellor Sun-Tzu Liao sent me here to make you a proposal. I bear it not as a diplomat but as a fellow warrior with blood ties to you. My grandfather served as an officer

116 Blaine Lee Pardoe

in the Highlanders and was recognized for his bravery and heroism. For centuries House Liao was the protector of the Northwind Highlanders. We attempted to fulfill our commitment to return Northwind to the Highlanders as an independent planet. Fate intervened, and through an unfortunate twist of fate, we split as a people ... our promise unfulfilled.

"Until now.

"If the Northwind Highlanders truly desire independence, the Chancellor and the people of the Capellan Confederation are willing to assist. Rather than serve Victor Davion as an overlord, you could be an independent people, free to fight your own battles—or not to, if that is your choice.

"Should you accept this offer, the Chancellor vows to recognize Northwind as a free world under your rule. He also assures me that the Free Worlds League will also honor that pledge. Any attempt to violate that rule would be opposed, both diplomatically and militarily by the Confederation.

"This would fulfill our promise made centuries ago. It would guarantee freedom—*real* freedom. And if the Federated Commonwealth decides to enforce its misguided will over you as a people, the Chancellor is willing to commit troops to protect the freedom of the Highlanders."

A hush had fallen over the crowd, but Loren could not read the silence. Had he failed?

Then a man's voice rose from the hillside. "Colonel, where do you stand on this?"

MacLeod rested his hands on his waist, poised and proper. The light of the bonfire made the silver in his hair and beard shimmer in the night. "I was a Highlander officer when we first returned here. At the time the decision was right. Now I stand here like you, wondering what I want. It seems to me that this is not a vote for us here and now. As Jaffray said, it is a vote for the future. The risks are great and we will almost certainly be drawn into a conflict.

"It would be a sin for me to sit back while we become absorbed by the Federated Commonwealth, no longer free to control our destiny. The risks for all of us are great, perhaps greater than any of us can imagine. But we are always Highlanders. There is nothing that can take that from us. I endorse this initiative—no—I embrace it."

A female spoke up from the ranks on the hills. "Isn't it a dead issue, Colonel? With the regiments coming home, this vote has no weight."

"Not true. This vote and the call to the Assembly of Warriors will add legal credibility to our decision. It is not a moot point, but an issue that all Highlanders must consider, not just those of my regiment."

Another man's voice spoke up. "And you, Mulvaney? Where do you stand?" All eyes turned to Chastity Mulvaney standing next to MacLeod. She blinked, looking startled.

"Since my earliest childhood I've been hearing about our relationship with House Davion," she began slowly. "I don't see the advantage of our so-called independence. We would become the prey of every House leader wanting to establish him or herself as our new ruler."

Lieutenant Gomez stepped forward into the light of the bonfire. "I stand for independence," she said firmly. Loren was shocked, based on the cold-shoulder treatment she'd given him earlier. "I don't want to see us end up like the Eridani Light Horse." Her mention of the celebrated mercenary unit struck a chord with the Highlanders. The Eridani was one of the other few Inner Sphere units that dated back to the Star League. Though it was still officially listed as a mercenary unit, for all intents and purposes the Eridani were just another unit in the Armed Forces of the Federated Commonwealth.

"How can we, one world, survive on our own? We have to keep ties to Davion or we'll die," came another warrior's voice from the darkened hillside.

Loren looked up in his direction. "Northwind does not rely on imports from other worlds for commerce. You have your own crops, industries, and economy. And there can be no threat to your independence once all the Highlander regiments are back home."

Another man stepped out. "How do we know this isn't some trick on the part of House Liao? I want sovereignty, but I won't change one petty dictator for another. Will we be facing a garrison force of Capellan troops on Northwind, like those blasted Consul Guards we have now?"

Loren took a step down the steep hill in the direction of

the man. "Northwind will be your world, free and clear. Should you need help in defending her, the Chancellor will gladly send troops. There will be no garrison force. No 'Consul Guards.' This is not an exchange of leadership. You—the Northwind Highlanders—will be the sole rulers of this planet. This is a simple matter of independence."

There was a full minute of discussion in the darkness and flickering shadows of the Caithness Woods. Finally MacLeod spoke up again, this time his voice more somber and deep. "This debate could go on 'til the wee hours of the dawn. But we have duties to perform. We cannot settle this here, but we can decide whether it is worthy of consideration by our Assembly of Warriors. Step forward, into the light." He gestured toward the bonfire that now roared even higher into the night sky as the cabers continued to burn brightly. "Those in favor of recalling the Assembly to debate and settle this issue, lift up your hands . . ."

Loren watched as more than two-thirds of the Highlanders of MacLeod's Regiment raised their hands toward the night sky. He took note of their faces, proud and strong.

"Opposed?" called the Colonel.

The remaining troopers' hands rose with just as much vigor. These tended to be the younger MechWarriors and troops. Loren looked around at the fire and then back up the hill. With a start, he recognized Mulvaney holding her hand up with the dissenters. She looked at him with a face flushed with emotion, almost as if the voting was painful.

"And so it is done. I thank you all for your help. Let us never forget our past as we go boldly toward our future!" And with those words the Warrior's Cabel came to a close. The Regimental Honor Guard began playing *"Scotland Forever"* as the Highlanders gradually withdrew from the hill and back into the night.

Loren remained staring into the flames of the bonfire. He had been successful in presenting the Chancellor's initiative, but it felt like an empty victory. Especially with the image of Mulvaney voting against him. He watched the flames for several minutes, lost in their heat and light, hoping to purge his feelings of guilt. He had promised his grandfather's people the true fulfillment of their dream, their homeworld truly turned over to them. In reality, his mission was to wipe them out. He knew the Death Commandos and their tactics. They would stop at nothing. And he, Loren Jaffray, would be the instrument of that death and destruction.

13

Federated Commonwealth Consulate
Tara, Northwind
Draconis March, Federated Commonwealth
22 September 3057

"Consul Burns," Catelli began softly as he entered the office of his superior. "We have a problem."

Burns sat back in his chair studying his manicured fingernails, not even looking up at his attaché. "Colonel Catelli, just once I would like you to enter this office with something other than a problem."

Catelli's eyes narrowed slightly at the comment. He saw Burns as a weak, pompous bureaucrat. *Perhaps if you had the courage that the creator gave a sand flea you'd understand my importance here,* he thought, but merely smiled back. "I apologize, sir. However, you must see these flash communiqués from the Federated Suns Command."

He laid a single-page printout across the dark mahogany desk. Drake Burns let it sit there for a few seconds before finally turning his attention to the message. As if bored with the entire conversation, he sighed deeply and began to read. In a matter of seconds his eyes widened in disbelief.

"Have you read this?" he demanded.

"Indeed I have, sir."

"Do you know what this means? Callnath and Denebola.

Wasat. Van Diemen, Marcus, and Talitha have all but fallen and this is only the first wave."

Catelli nodded. "The Capellan troops have been hitting us hard too, plus the terrorist actions on many worlds throughout the Sarna March, apparently sponsored by Liao. Uprisings on Nanking resulted in the assassination of the planetary governor and his staff. On Gan Singh the First RCT's command staff was killed when terrorists stormed their command bunker and set off explosives. It was a suicide attack, but it left an entire regiment without any sort of command structure." Burns crumpled the thin sheaf in one hand and tossed it angrily onto his desk.

"I'm afraid that's not all, Consul." Catelli secretly reveled in the terror on Burns' face. It was a sign of weakness, a weakness that he could control and manipulate at will.

"My own operatives tell me that MacLeod's Regiment met covertly in the Caithness Woods last evening."

"In the woods? Why in the name of the Prince would they meet there?"

"From what my agents tell me it was a ritual ceremony of some sort. Bonfire, bagpipes, the whole ball of wax. Perhaps they were trying to evade our bugging devices in The Fort. Regardless, they apparently met to discuss severing their agreement with the Federated Commonwealth regarding Northwind."

"What do you mean?"

"This Major Jaffray allegedly met with the Highlanders to incite them to rebel against our rightful rule of Northwind. He has encouraged them to rise up and fight us."

"You must be joking."

"I wish I were, Consul. But our Capellan visitor went so far as to offer them the help of the Confederation in fighting us. It's all part of the wave of rebellions and terrorist activity incited by Liao's black ops agents. I don't want to add to your displeasure, but we've received several tips that Major Jaffray may also have been behind the assassination attempt on Colonel MacLeod."

"What are your sources? Are they reliable?"

"They're anonymous, Consul, but come from intelligence sources that have proved reliable in the past."

"But Major Jaffray was also wounded in the attack, wasn't he?"

"A minor wound, sir, apparently intended to draw suspicion away from him."

The news obviously shook Drew Burns even harder than Colonel Catelli had hoped. The diplomat took out his handkerchief and wiped the beads of sweat that had formed on his brow. "Blast it! I've got assassins running free, Colonel MacLeod defying direct orders from Command, a Capellan inciting rebellion, and war breaking out all around us. Colonel Catelli, I'm open to any suggestions you might have to help me resolve all of this."

Catelli clasped his hands behind his back, and tried to keep from laughing out loud. *Just as I hoped. It was almost too easy. One day this office, that desk, this world will be mine. Given the right information at the right time, Burns will beg me to take control.* "Not all the news is bad, Consul. Rumors in the pipeline say that the Third Royals RCT are on their way to help us."

"An action that would only further fan the flames."

"Sir, there are a few things we can do to keep the Highlanders in their proper place."

"Speak, Colonel." Burns seemed on the verge of despair.

"To start with, you must send a message to the High Command, asking them to formally relieve Colonel MacLeod of his command of the Highlanders."

Burns rubbed his wrinkling brow. "Even if I could get such an order there's no guarantee whatsoever that MacLeod would obey it. One thing is for sure, William MacLeod is a fighter. He won't back down."

"Then that's his mistake. Next, we can cut off the Highlanders' intelligence information flow from the Federated Commonwealth. This will leave them ignorant of the events elsewhere and might slow down any rebellious activity."

"They'll still be able to make use of ComStar's commercial network, Colonel."

"I know, Consul, but without access to our intelligence network, they'll have to piece together whatever they can from news reports and their own very limited set of contacts. If they seek aid from any 'exterior' sources it will be slow in coming."

"So you blind them," Burns said. "They still have a regiment based on this continent, most of it in and around Tara. No matter what we think of them personally, the Northwind Highlanders are one of the toughest mercenary units ever formed in the Inner Sphere."

Catelli straightened up crisply. "As the commander of the Consul Guards I have mustered my troops to a camp just outside Tara in case anyone makes a move against either of us, sir. I have already made contacts with some of the loyal Davion factions in the civilian population. Beginning today we will show the Highlanders our resolve to retain Northwind as a part of the Federated Commonwealth. These groups will stage formal protests in the streets and attempt to keep up the pressure on MacLeod and his troops. What the Highlanders will see is a population that wants to remain loyal to Victor Davion."

"Excellent. But what about this Jaffray?"

Catelli nodded slowly. "Yes, our distinguished visitor from the Capellan Confederation. I have given this matter a great deal of thought, and now, with the Capellans invading Federated Commonwealth worlds, I think you'll agree that his status is in question. For one thing, there are the tips I've received implicating him in the assassination attempt against MacLeod. On top of that he attempts to incite outright rebellion at that Cabel meeting last night. I suggest that we arrest this troublemaker and send him to New Avalon."

"Won't that only push MacLeod and his people even closer to rebellion?" Burns was obviously worried about the consequences of his actions, but never looked at the big, strategic picture. For that he had always relied on Catelli.

"Not if we sell it to him and the other Highlanders properly, sir. If we take action against MacLeod's alleged assassin it might win the Highlanders over to our side. This Jaffray hasn't been here long enough to become really thick with the Highlanders. After all, he's an outsider and they're a very close-knit people." What Catelli didn't reveal was that his sources were reporting that MacLeod and Jaffray had apparently become friends. Rather than cementing the mercenaries' relationship with Consul Burns, an attack on Jaffray would only further strain relations between the Highlanders and Burns. A confrontation at this time could easily lead to outright rebellion. And that would open the door for Catelli. Then, and only then, would he be in a position to seize power.

Burns placed his elbows on the table and leaned forward, grinding his eye sockets into the palms of his hands. He had always viewed Northwind as an easy posting for a career diplomat. Now it was becoming a powder keg and he felt powerless to stop the fuse from firing. "We seem to be drawn into a conflict with no hope of winning."

Catelli watched the Consul struggle with his doubts. "I have several agents already infiltrating the Highlander ranks. They tell me that many of the troops and key officers do not endorse disbanding our agreement with them. If anything they believe that the Davions are their best hope for the future."

"Are they willing to stand against their commanding officer if need be?"

"A man that you are going to strip of his post and responsibilities? I don't think that all of them will fall into line, but when a true conflict occurs, the majority of the Highlanders will side with us. Any thoughts of rebellion will be quashed and you, Consul, will be seen as the man who saved Northwind." Burns was a pompous fool and Catelli would play on that as he continued weaving his web.

Consul Burns looked up, eyes red and uncommonly tired for that hour of the morning. "Colonel, how can we take custody of Major Jaffray? He's in The Fort, surrounded by a full regiment of their best troops and BattleMechs. If MacLeod's Regiment doesn't want to give him up there's little we can do about it."

"I've been on Northwind a while, as have you, sir. We both know that the one thing the Highlanders respect is force. They are mercenaries who respect a strong showing. You were never in the military, but I understand these people.

"We'll move the Consul Guards to the spaceport and establish ourselves there. You will issue a demand that the Highlanders meet us there to turn over the spy Jaffray. They'll see us out in full force, they'll show in force, and turn him over. If anything, they'll respect us even more."

If his plan was going to work, Catelli had to get the Highlanders to the spaceport to face off against the outnumbered Consul Guards. If an incident could be provoked or even manipulated, the Federated Commonwealth would have every right to claim control over Northwind and absorb the Highlanders once and for all. He had already set in motion the events to create that incident. Now all that was required was the proper stage, something that only the Consul could provide him.

"What if they won't turn him over?"

Catelli shrugged, then shook his head. "Sir, if you were commander of the Highlanders, would you risk an all-out confrontation with the rightful government over a man you have only known for a few days? Would you place your entire world in jeopardy for such a man? A man who came sowing the seeds of dissent while his own government launched an invasion against your rightful lord. No, of course you wouldn't and neither would I.

"But to answer your question, if they resist, we will defend our right to apprehend this Major Jaffray."

"Perhaps we should wait," the Consul said. "We could send a message to New Avalon and ask them for a course of action."

Catelli had expected Burns to say just that and was already prepared. "Sir, we cannot wait. The Federated Commonwealth is under attack from both Marik and Liao. Perhaps Northwind is next on their list. We cannot sit idly by waiting to hear the opinion of someone who doesn't understand the true situation here, who doesn't know the Highlanders or the pro-Davion sentiments of the people of this world. Remember, the other Highlander regiments are on their way home. To delay could spell disaster."

Burns looked off to the side of his desk where a globe of Northwind sat. He spun the globe as he pondered the plan. The continents and seas spun by. First, the massive green and brown of New Lanark, where Tara was located. Then the small islands of Argyle and the Falkirk Sea and the tiny continent of Halidon passed more slowly as the spinning globe gradually came to rest. The Consul watched the globe spin, as though it could provide him some solace for the decision he was being pressured to make.

"Very well, Colonel. Your words have merit. Prepare the

messages and orders for my signature and contact the Federated Suns High Command to request that they relieve MacLeod of his command."

"Very good, sir." Catelli bowed slightly, then turned to leave the room. *History will remember me kindly even should this go awry. And if it succeeds, praise will follow the name of Drew Catelli forever.*

14

Tara, Northwind
Draconis March, Federated Commonwealth
22 September 3057

Loren's *Gallowglas* moved cautiously toward the entrance into the box canyon. He sensors told him that Lieutenant Fuller's *War Dog* was in this area, but if Fuller had gone into the tight confines of the canyon Loren could no longer detect him. That meant that either he was not there or was hiding behind a rock formation strong enough to block the sensor sweeps. Switching to his secondary monitor to look for heat signatures. Loren saw that a 'Mech had entered the light pass of the canyon. He scanned then for magnetic distortion, hoping that the fusion reaction of Fuller's 'Mech might be emitting enough to be picked up. He got lucky. Near the back wall of the canyon he detected a faint glow behind a huge stone outcropping. If Fuller was in the canyon, it was there.

Loren pondered the approach. If he went straight in, Fuller could pummel him at long range with his *War Dog*'s deadly Gauss rifle. And with the ECM suite the 'Mech carried, it was going to be difficult to engage except at short range, which meant that Loren would take some serious damage. Unless he approached from another way . . .

Loren grabbed the throttle and thumbed his jump jets. The *Gallowglas* shot high into the air over the pass and drew

128 Blaine Lee Pardoe

closer to the rock formation. His sensors squawked to life as Fuller's *War Dog* stepped out into the open, its right-arm Gauss rifle tracking the airborne movements of the *Gallowglas*. Loren lowered his large lasers and PPC, managing to get off his shots before the *War Dog* fired. Suddenly his primary and secondary screens went totally blank, followed by the extinguishing of all the control lights in his cockpit. *Cockpit hit? Did I lose power from only one hit?* Loren reached over and attempted to throw the auxiliary power switch, but there was still no life in the cockpit.

The next thing he knew the simulator cockpit hatch was opening from the outside, flooding the interior darkness with the white light of the Highlander's Training Center. Someone must have cut off the simulator program. Too bad, Loren thought. It was one of the best he'd ever seen. Almost as good as the Commandos'. Chastity Mulvaney's face appeared at the open hatchway as Loren unwound his body from the seat, then climbed out. He saw Lieutenant Fuller also emerging from his simulator.

Loren had now spent almost two full weeks living in the midst of the Highlanders. Jake Fuller had become a close companion, but Jaffray saw through it. Yes, they got along well enough to practice in the 'Mech simulators for two hours a day, but he suspected that Fuller's main task was keeping an eye on him. It could only be on MacLeod's orders, but that was to be expected, no matter how much confidence the Highlander CO showed Loren in public.

"You need to report to your ops officer right away for a staff officer briefing, Lieutenant," Mulvaney told Fuller, then turned to Loren. "The Colonel wants to talk with you," she said curtly.

Fuller waved from across the room and Loren returned the salute. "Is there a problem, Major?"

"That would be a gross understatement," she said, leading him out of the room and into the hall.

"What do you mean?"

She stopped in the mid-stride and turned to him. Waving a finger at Loren the whole time, she spoke in a voice that was angry but not loud. "You knew all along, didn't you? Knew all along that the invasion was coming and just led us into your little web. I've been right about you from the start."

"I knew as much as you did, and that's all," Loren said, which, technically, was true. But Loren also knew that it was only a matter of time before the Davion Consul and his attaché called for his removal—or worse. He suddenly felt very alone on Northwind.

"I don't know if you're lying or telling the truth," Mulvaney said. "But if you *are* lying, you'd better know this. No one is going to harm the Highlanders. Not you, not the entire Capellan Confederation. I'll die before I see that happen."

Loren looked deeply into her eyes. "At the Warriors Cabel," he said. "I saw how you voted."

"Don't get me wrong," she said sharply. "I follow orders, but only to a point. Right now I'm torn as to how to fulfill those orders. As a Highlander, I have one set of responsibilities. As a loyal subject of the Federated Commonwealth I have another. So far I have not had to choose between the two. That may change."

Loren understood conflicting loyalties. A part of him wanted to be with his unit, especially with a war going on. He had trained his whole life for war, and now when it finally came he was off light years away from his unit playing diplomat.

Then again, the Highlanders had treated him as more than an equal, as a member of their family. It was a kind of military existence he'd never witnessed before, but now he understood why his grandfather had remained so attached to his memories of the Highlanders. In the Capellan Armed Forces everything was cold and impersonal. Here there was camaraderie, trust, a oneness with each other. An invisible bond that held the men and women together. It was silent and unseen, yet unbreakable.

Without further discussion, Loren and Mulvaney continued down a familiar passage leading to the office of Colonel MacLeod. Loren followed Mulvaney in and she closed the door behind them. The Colonel motioned to the seats in front of his desk.

MacLeod seemed tired and Loren could tell that the stress of the last few days was beginning to take its toll. The Colonel shuffled through the pile of papers on his desk and pulled out a formal letter.

"This was delivered from the Davion Consulate this morning. It's signed by Consul Burns, but I can see the hand of Colonel Catelli all over it."

"Orders, sir?" Mulvaney asked.

"More than that, I'm afraid. It's a demand." The Colonel held the sheet up and looked through his reading glasses at the text. "By order of Planetary Consul Drake Burns and the Federated Commonwealth, Major Loren Jaffray of the Capellan Armed Forces is to be remanded to the custody and direct supervision of the Northwind Consul Guards. Major Jaffray is charged with inciting civil disorder and involvement in the assassination attempt on Colonel William MacLeod!"

"What!" Loren shot to his feet. "I had nothing to do with it, Colonel. Damnation! They fired on me too." Loren's wound was healing well, but mention of the attack brought back a wincing memory of the pain. "If I was going to have you killed, I could have found hundreds of other opportunities. None would have been this obvious."

"At ease, Major."

Loren regained his composure. He looked over at Mulvaney, but her eyes were fixed on her commanding officer. "Yes, sir," he replied, returning to his seat.

"What happens if we don't turn him over, sir?" Mulvaney asked, surprising Loren slightly.

"According to this, Catelli is bringing his Consul Guards to the spaceport tomorrow at noon. They want us to hand over Loren at that time, and if we don't they'll execute a search of Tara, building by building, street by street."

Loren knew the implications of such a search. Using 'Mechs and tanks to try to find a single man could take days and cause incredible damage. The sight of Davion infantry ripping up Highlander family homes looking for him was not a burden that he wanted to carry ... not after the way the Highlanders had treated him. "Colonel ... Major. I want you to know that I am not guilty of any acts against the Northwind Highlanders. This 'civil disorder' the Consul mentioned is my presenting the Liao initiative at the Cabel.

I have not done anything to warrant the revoking of my freedom."

The remark was a coy one on his part and Loren knew it. He had managed in a short period of time to infiltrate the Highlanders and nurtured the seeds of rebellion. Now the Davions were playing into his hands by making him personally an issue. This would bring the issue of sovereignty into question. If MacLeod let him be turned over, he would look weak to his own people. If he stood firm, it drove a wedge between the Northwind Highlanders and House Davion. Loren was willing to take the risk. It was why he had come to Northwind in the first place.

"Lad, we know that," MacLeod said, taking off his reading glasses and putting them on the table.

"Sir, I can't let Catelli and his cronies tear the city of Tara apart in my name. I'll surrender peacefully to them." Loren knew that with a war going on between what was left of the Federated Commonwealth and the Confederation he would be made a public spectacle. There would be a show trial, a drumhead. He would be found guilty regardless of the real evidence.

But *offering* to surrender was a gesture he had to make. The honor of his grandfather had something to do with it, but in reality he knew that Colonel MacLeod would not allow him to go in such a manner. To do so would violate the elder Highlander's own code of honor. The offer would be a sincere one, but he was also playing a strong hunch that he would not have to face the wrath of Colonel Catelli or Consul Burns.

MacLeod smiled thinly and leaned back in his deep leather chair. "No Major, I won't allow it. You've done nothing wrong. This isn't about you, this is about the Northwind Highlanders and our right to independence."

Loren thought about how easily he had read MacLeod. How easily an apparent show of honor had won his trust. *In the end it will be his undoing.*

Mulvaney leaned forward. "What do you proposed we do, Colonel? These are direct commands from our liege lord's representative. To disobey that order would be to break our agreement with the Archon Prince. There must be some sort of diplomatic way to resolve this."

"The day that I bow to Drake Burns or Drew Catelli is the day I am no longer fit to command. Diplomacy has no place in this. We are not dealing simply with diplomatic gestures, we are dealing in politics and power. Whatever I do, Catelli and Burns will keep trying to find a chink in our armor. I can't even contact Cat Stirling because Catelli has ordered ComStar to sever the Fort's direct link with the HPG. Now we no longer get military intel, but have to rely on commercial communications. They won't be satisfied until the Highlanders are broken and scattered to the four winds. No, we will not fulfill their demand. This charade as to who rules Northwind ends tomorrow at noon."

The look on MacLeod's face changed then, going dark, becoming a warrior's expression. Loren knew the look well, having encountered it in many a battle. The determination was not just evident but seemingly cast in stone.

15

Kohler Spaceport
Tara, Northwind
Draconis March, Federated Commonwealth
23 September 3057

The BattleMech storage bay was lit only by a few dim yellow night lights and was empty except for the black-clad agent and the 'Mechs. The war machines stood silent in the darkness, like three-story statues guarding a long-lost temple, mute witnesses to his actions throughout the night. Each BattleMech was flanked by a gantry and quick access ladder. The man moved up the ladder quickly, careful not to make any sounds. His dark suit was designed to eliminate his thermal image from the sensors installed in the bay, but could do nothing to mute the sounds he made. The small devices he had planted on the windows would blind the motion sensors as well. There were many guards outside the building but only two inside and he had managed to avoid them for the better part of two hours as he did his work.

The man climbed the *Shadow Hawk*'s gantry and pulled at the cockpit hatch. There was a dull echo as the hatch opened and for a moment he paused to see if the sound had attracted any attention. Satisfied, he slid into the cockpit and removed his night-vision goggles. No longer fearing the thermal sensors, he felt free to go about his work of sabotage.

Disabling a BattleMech could be done quickly by an expert, but that was not his mission. His superior had given him specific instructions, which he'd been following closely throughout the wee hours of the morning. This would be the last one he could get to before the change of patrols and the arrival of the Highlander techs and engineers. He reached into the breast pocket of the black turtleneck and pulled out the instrument of his sabotage—a laser diskette.

Sitting in the command couch the man activated the *Shadow Hawk*'s computer, as he had done many times before that night. Then he carefully activated the BattleMech's DI, or Diagnostic Interpreter, computer system. Most people thought that the battle computer was a 'Mech's main system, but technicians and engineers knew better. The battle computer was merely a slave to the DI system.

The DI computer was the brains of the BattleMech. It controlled movement, jumping, and virtually all sensor-data interpretation. He booted it into engineering/diagnostic mode and slid the six-centimeter diskette into the feed slot. Using the small keypad in the cockpit he accessed the disk and watched with glee as the numbers and words flashed across the secondary monitor. The program loaded itself into memory, becoming stored in the battle computer's communications sub-system. There it would wait until the proper coded transmission was received. If all went as planned there would be no evidence left intact of the crime.

It took a full three minutes for the program to load. Every half minute the man looked out the hatch to see if any guards had arrived. He was most worried because of the audible beeping that came from the DI computer as it finished loading and concealing the program. It was far too soft for anyone to hear outside the cockpit, but he did not like the risks. He carefully removed the diskette and secured it in his pocket, then shut off the system.

This plan would work. He had failed before to kill the Capellan. But this time he would redeem himself with a grand success. He personally would deliver the death blow to the Northwind Highlanders and restore himself to the Colonel's good graces.

Like a black python, the agent slid down the gantry ladder to the floor of the 'Mech bay. Working his way along the massive 'Mech doors, he found the one he'd jimmied to break in. He would singlehandedly end the betrayal of the Highlanders. One man against an entire BattleMech regiment, and he would be the victor. All that was left was the confrontation and the signal. Then it would all be over.

"So you're joining us in this little stroll, eh?" Jake Fuller said as he and Loren walked through The Fort to the 'Mech bay.

"Colonel MacLeod asked me to attend the final briefing. I was hoping to get assigned to a BattleMech if we do square off against the Consul Guards." Loren knew the chances of the Highlanders assigning him a BattleMech were thin at this time. He had won MacLeod's trust, but was still not a true Highlander in their eyes. He felt naked somehow, a MechWarrior without his weapon.

"We have spare 'Mechs, but with the current situation, I doubt you'd want to become a target in one. If things get hot, the odds are pretty high that you'd be the center of this fire storm."

The thought didn't bother Loren. He'd already faced death so many times in his career. He was more concerned that if he wasn't present matters might actually defuse. It was critical to the success of his mission that the Davions go head to head with the Northwind Highlanders.

"I only hope that I'm there to see the Highlanders in action," he said softly. "It would be fitting that a Jaffray once again fight alongside Highlander kin." Loren wondered what part of his words were truth and what part was simply the script he needed to fulfill his mission.

Reports had filtered in all morning of the Consul Guards gathering on the tarmac of Kohler Spaceport at the far edge of Tara. Davion protesters had also been lining the public entrances to The Fort. Loren had not gone out to see them, but Fuller had told him that some of the protesters were carrying signs calling for his arrest. Colonel MacLeod was burned in effigy, and Loren had heard two other MechWarriors describe the burning of the Highlander and the Capellan banners.

The mission briefing was equally tense. Loren overheard several officers discussing whether he should simply be turned over. Among them were people who had voted against the Chancellor's initiative. Colonel MacLeod knew the sentiments of his troops, but told them they must overcome their desire for vengeance. They had a mission to accomplish and orders to fulfill.

The mission itself was not easy. With the Consul Guards in positions all around the spaceport, the Highlanders would try to surround them, interposing themselves between the Davions and the city, cutting off any escape route except through the wild country to the south. MacLeod would deliver his formal reply to Consul Burns' demand in person, then would order the Consul Guards out of Tara. And he was willing to back it up with force.

The rules of engagement were clear as well. If the Highlanders were fired upon they were to return fire, but only against enemy forces engaged in hostile actions. MacLeod had made it clear that restraint was to be the governing force. The last thing anyone wanted, especially the Highlander CO, was for someone to trigger an all out-war between the Northwind Highlanders and the Federated Commonwealth. Everyone knew that this was as hot as it could get without a formal declaration of war.

Loren watched the faces of the officers and again felt a twinge of guilt. The Highlanders were some of the best warriors in the Inner Sphere, and, by his mere presence, he was drawing them into a conflict with the Federated Commonwealth. If his mission was successful, many, if not all, of these people were going to die. And he, Loren Jaffray, would be responsible. He was no longer sure how he felt about that.

Chastity Mulvaney had just come into the briefing room. Like the rest she had donned a cooling vest and was carrying her neurohelmet under one arm. She looked tense, the muscles of her face held tight and her teeth gritted together. She walked over to several of the other command company members and handed them orders. Then she strode up to Loren.

"Major Jaffray, I assume, by the way you're dressed, that you've *not* gotten your orders?"

Loren shook his head. "No, Major."

"Very well, then. Colonel MacLeod has asked that you take the jumpseat of his *Huron Warrior*. He wanted you assigned your own 'Mech, but I convinced him that considering your status as a Capellan, it would be best if you only rode shotgun." Some 'Mechs, like this variant of the *Huron Warrior*, had cramped little fold-down seats behind the pilot's command couch. They did not have controls themselves and were risky at best for the rider. *At least I'll be there*, Loren told himself.

"You opposed my being assigned a 'Mech?" Loren didn't try to disguise his irritation.

Mulvaney smiled slightly, seeing that she had managed to get to him. "Yes, Major, you have your assignment. If you don't want it you can remain here at The Fort with the other noncombatants."

This is not the time to fight her. Best to cut my losses. "Yes, sir," he replied. In this situation Mulvaney was his superior.

Mulvaney raised her voice so that all the lance commanders could hear her. "Listen up, you dunderheads! This is the final intel briefing before we set out. Our scouts report civilian mobs at the west gate so we'll be using the north gate for departure.

"Maps should already be unloaded in your battle computers. Review them. The Consul Guards are deployed along the south edge of the spaceport near the open fields. Our reports show they have a full lance of light hovercraft that we didn't even know existed. Command Company is going to take the center, with First Strike Company on the right flank with Second Assault Company on the left. Behind us is Second Battalion's First Gurkhas. The First Border Armored Cavalry is on the right flank and will form a rear guard if we need it. Any questions?"

Captain Sullivan of the First Strike Company was the only one who spoke up. "What's the temperature of our Davion hosts, Major?"

"Tensions are high, people," Mulvaney said. "Repeat, tensions are high. Local news has been playing it up that we're renegades and they're doing a pretty good job of keeping the Davion natives whipped up. We're not looking for a fight, but we may get one. Keep your heads clear, check your connects, and don't think that just because this is Northwind there isn't any danger. Colonel MacLeod's calling the shots and we do it his way and by the numbers."

She looked around and made sure that her message had sunk in. "All right then, Highlanders. Mount 'em!" Mulvaney led the way, with the rest filing out behind her and to their respective 'Mechs.

It took a full twenty minutes for Loren to reach MacLeod's *Huron Warrior*, but a lot less to climb up the footholds to the cockpit, where the Colonel was already in the pilot's seat. He motioned Jaffray to the tiny rear jumpseat, which was a tight fit, high and behind the pilot. Loren found it equipped with a duplicate secondary monitor and controls and communications gear. The stiffness of the light cooling vest made the tiny seat feel even more uncomfortable.

"Run through the pre-operations checklist, laddie," the Colonel said as he began to power up the 'Mech. The BattleMech's computer systems ran through their start-up boot procedure and Loren downloaded the map data. Then he pulled up the battle computer and did a full review of the terrain. The streets leading to Kohler Spaceport were narrow urban passes except for the main thoroughfare that the Regimental Command Company was going to take. The 'Mech's DI computer showed that two of the armor plates on the rear leg had bad sensor-feed connections and would eventually need replacing, but there was nothing that would impede combat.

"I appreciate the opportunity to ride as your second, sir," Loren said as he finished his on-screen checklist.

"It's good having you close by, Loren. The chance to pilot with a Jaffray in combat is something that these old bones have been looking forward to for decades. I like to think that you'll bring us the same luck as your grandsires."

MacLeod carefully piloted the *Huron Warrior* out of the bay and formed ranks with the rest of Regimental Command Company. They were not deploying to the spaceport as in a normal military operation. Instead they would march in a two-abreast column formation to meet with the Consul Guards. According to MacLeod there was no point in provoking matters further. He would do enough of that himself with his reply.

The formation passed out of the north gate of The Fort, which was more tunnel than gate. Wide enough for two 'Mechs to pass side by side, the tunnel ran through the massive granite wall and out to the street. MacLeod's regimental march to the spaceport was quiet, with none of the usual chatter Loren would have expected coming over the commline. *They're as professional and disciplined as any Death Commando unit. They're facing death but no one expresses fear.*

The spaceport was essentially a large open tarmac that stretched out for two kilometers square. The ferrocrete was designed to withstand the heat and weight of the massive DropShips that landed there. Liquid hydrogen bunkers were kept kilometers away, their fuel piped in deep under the tarmac. What made most spaceports like Kohler functional were the supporting buildings and transport systems. Less then ten years old, this was one of the most modern that Loren had seen.

What made it different was the formation of BattleMechs and tanks out in the middle of the tarmac. A full company of twelve 'Mechs stood in single file squarely facing the Highlander Command Company. Surrounding them were two full companies' worth of armored vehicles and supporting infantry. The Northwind Consul Guards stood silently as MacLeod in the *Huron Warrior* led his forces into position.

As the Command Company stopped a mere two hundred meters from the Consul Guards, Mulvaney opened up a communications channel and ordered the lances to deploy in a square against the Davions. Loren did several quick short-range sensor sweeps from his jumpseat's system and confirmed that the other Highlander flanking forces were moving into position at the far edges of the spaceport, should they be needed. The time had come, high noon. The time of Colonel MacLeod's response to Burns' ultimatum.

"Colonel William MacLeod of the Northwind Highlanders, by decree of Northwind Planetary Consul Drake Burns of the Federated Commonwealth, I demand that you turn over the spy and saboteur Major Loren Jaffray." The message was beamed on a wide band so that all the Highlanders and Consul Guards could hear.

MacLeod waited several seconds to respond. "Colonel

Catelli, I implore you to withdraw your Guards and stand down."

"I'm afraid that you do not give the orders here, Colonel. I say again, turn over Major Jaffray." The smugness in Catelli's voice was obvious.

"Why isn't the Consul here himself?" MacLeod returned. "Doesn't he have the stomach to face the Northwind Highlanders like a man? Or is it you who is behind all this, Catelli?"

"I speak for the Consul in this matter, Colonel. Turn over Jaffray or face the consequences."

"I refuse."

"Colonel MacLeod, I have uncovered evidence implicating your guest in several suspicious activities, the least of which is the attempt on your life. The Capellan Confederation has recently begun a major invasion of the Federated Commonwealth. They are enemies of the state. His travel papers and passport have been rescinded and he is to be turned over to my custody."

"Do you think that I'm an idiot, Catelli?" fired back MacLeod. "Turning him over to you would be his death. And as for enemies, the Capellan Confederation has not attacked Northwind or any Highlander units. Just because they are your enemies does not mean they are ours. Your battle with them is an internal affair."

"He is a spy."

"He is our honored guest."

"Colonel, we intend to transport Loren Jaffray to New Avalon."

"He will remain with my regiment and if you attempt to take him you will be met by force."

"Your answer stands then, Colonel MacLeod?"

"Yes, it does."

Loren felt perspiration form on his body despite the efforts of his lightweight cooling vest. The *Huron Warrior*'s cockpit was no hotter than before, but the tension level was definitely higher. He expected Catelli to order a full attack next, but MacLeod did not seem either tense or fearful. His fingers simply drummed the environmental control access panel as if he were bored.

"I had hoped it would not come to this, Colonel," said

Catelli in a low, menacing tone. "By order of Field Marshal Morgan Hasek-Davion, I hereby relieve you of command of the Northwind Highlanders and the troops known as MacLeod's Regiment therein. The duty falls to your second in command, Major Chastity Mulvaney, who is ordered to report to me."

Suddenly Loren wondered if it would be MacLeod who ordered an attack rather than Catelli. What shocked Loren and probably most of the Davion Consul Guards was MacLeod's response. Over the wide communications band came the sound of laughter. A roaring guffaw that was impossible for a man to fake. It went on for nearly half a minute before MacLeod issued his more formal reply.

"Colonel Catelli, who are you to say who can and cannot serve as the commanding officer of the Northwind Highlanders, let alone my regiment?"

"I have been granted the authority by the Federated Suns Command. As such I ask you to step aside, Mister MacLeod." His use of a civilian title was not lost on Loren or the other members of the Command Company.

MacLeod's voice changed to a much sterner and formal tone. "I do not acknowledge your right or the right of the Federated Commonwealth to interfere in the internal affairs of the Northwind Highlanders. You have no authority over me or my troops."

"Very well, *Colonel* Mulvaney, as the acting CO of this regiment, I order you to turn over the spy Loren Jaffray."

Loren looked at his and MacLeod's short-range scanner and listened intensely to his own headset communicator for Mulvaney's response. How she would respond was a total mystery. Loren saw a flicker on the *Warrior*'s communications console, an incoming transmission of only a few characters. It was not jamming, but a deliberate message of some sort. Before he could react, Mulvaney began her reply.

"Colonel Catelli, I—" Her response was cut off by the squawk of warning sirens and short-range sensors in the cockpits of every 'Mech on the tarmac. *Incoming fire!* The sensors told Loren that the 'Mech was under fire, but he did not feel the usual impact of shells or lasers. Rather than question the sensors, he braced himself for a wave of impacts from the assault. Glancing across the field in that first instant of the battle he saw nothing. No missile air-trails, no glare of lasers. No lightning bursts of PPC fire. No smoke. *Nothing!* Yet the *Huron Warrior* shook several times as if it were taking hits, and from what he saw on the secondary display, the 'Mech seemed to be taking damage.

Jaffray told himself that it had to be a mistake, but MacLeod reacted immediately to the sensor data. Loren, not wired to the BattleMech's DI system with a neurohelmet, was reacting more as a man not tainted by the false images. The *Huron Warrior*'s sensors told him the Highlanders were under attack, but his own eyes told him differently.

Loren twisted in his seat as MacLeod drove the *Huron Warrior* hard to the right and broke from the ranks. The sensors were screaming that they were being fired upon. All around him he saw both Highlanders and Consul Guards breaking formation to turn and open fire.

Loren punched up the regimental command company's communications frequency and monitored the activity. He felt frustrated, like a man blindfolded. Without a 'Mech of his own to pilot, he was limited to being a spectator—a spectator who saw that the scene unfolding was a false one. As the lead 'Mech, MacLeod had just taken the *Huron Warrior* a step forward when his sensors registered an autocannon hit to the right torso. There was no explosion, only a slight buffeting of the 'Mech as it stepped. From his high jumpseat Loren saw the cockpit's primary screen. Though he had not seen anything incoming, it showed a pair of short-range missiles streaking past them to hit a Highlander *Warhammer* that was falling back in the ranks behind him. What struck him was that the sensors did not paint the missiles as targets.

No explosions, no signs of damage, yet their computer indicated they were under attack. *Where was the impact of those first shots? Why hadn't he seen any missiles or laser fire?* The *Huron Warrior*'s computer told one story, but Loren's own senses told him another. He stared at the secondary screen and suddenly remembered the comm signal just prior to the attack. Some sort of coded command had been transmitted to the *Huron Warrior* and to all the other 'Mechs, Davion and Highlanders alike. It was a short code and looked like it read directly into the DI computer. *Why would somebody transmit to every 'Mech in the line unless . . .*

With his right hand Loren reached over and hit the command channel control on the communications control board. "Colonel, we have a problem here."

"This isn't the time for chatter, Major," MacLeod said, leveling the massive Gauss rifle for a shot across the shimmering black tarmac of the spaceport.

"Colonel, this isn't right. A transmission was sent to all our 'Mechs. This whole attack is some sort of program running in our battle computers."

MacLeod targeted the rifle and fired. The *Huron Warrior* recoiled as the shot went off. "What are you saying, lad?"

"We have to stop this, Colonel. It's a mistake. I don't know how, but we have to stop this now!"

16

Kohler Spaceport
Tara, Northwind
Draconis Combine, Federated Commonwealth
23 September 3057

"It's a trick!" Loren shouted. "We've got to stop!"

The *Huron Warrior* strained and almost slipped on the ferrocrete tarmac as MacLeod ceased cutting to the right flank and fell back slightly. A barrage of autocannon shells, real shells this time, followed the 'Mech's movements, only grazing the left arm of the *Warrior* before losing their weapons lock. The impact tugged at the arm, sending a spray of destroyed armor plating to the rear.

"Are you sure?" MacLeod asked.

"It's a trick, Colonel," Loren repeated desperately, knowing that the false attacks were now being replaced by real ammunition, lasers, missiles, and cannon fire. Both sides were being sucked into fighting a battle they thought the other had started.

MacLeod pulled up the same data Loren had on the cockpit's secondary monitor. He reviewed the strange signal and the flight telemetry data from the missiles and weapons being fired.

"Damn Catelli!" MacLeod hissed, then opened a communications channel to all forces fighting across the open spaceport. "This is Colonel MacLeod, command code Alpha

Tango Five. All Highlanders cease fire. Repeat, hold your fire. Pull back one hundred meters and regroup."

"Colonel, sir?" came the familiar voice of Chastity Mulvaney.

"Major, this is no game. All troops disengage. This whole bloody attack is some sort of Davion trick. I'll not be a party to starting a war. Check your communications system and you'll see that something is running in your 'Mech's computers that makes you *think* we're under attack."

There was as long pause. Mulvaney's response was short and direct. "Damn!"

A Highlander *Crab* only a few meters away kept firing as it moved slowly backward. MacLeod sidestepped the *Huron Warrior* and to Loren's surprise struck the cockpit of the *Crab* with the *Warrior*'s damaged left arm. The impact did no damage but reinforced his orders. The *Crab* ceased its attack and fell back. Despite the sudden change of tactics, the Consul Guards continued to press their assault.

Loren checked the sensors and saw that Mulvaney was moving her own 'Mech in between a few Strike Company hold-outs who seemed unwilling to break off. From what Loren was able to read, her 'Mech was literally stepping into the line of fire between the Consul Guards and her own unit to make them disengage. Reluctantly the Highlanders fell back.

The Consul Guards continued to harass and follow them as they retreated to the far end of the spaceport. One wave of short-range missiles covered a Highlander *Locust* like a swarm of deadly bees, stinging madly. The light 'Mech struggled under each warhead's impact, fighting the pull of gravity and death. Somehow the pilot managed to keep his machine standing and moved to the rear. MacLeod signaled to Jaffray as the *Huron Warrior* took a stab from a large laser in the right leg. Jaffray felt a wave of heat rise in the cockpit. His own smaller cooling vest was less effective than MacLeod's, but it helped some in the hot, cramped cockpit. "Find me the communications channel that Catelli's men are using, and find it now."

Loren's fingers danced across the jumpseat's keyboard controls. The sensors probed the compressed microwave signals until the display showed the spider web of signal patterns between the icons representing the Consul Guard BattleMechs. He isolated the signal and passed it to MacLeod's communications controls.

"On-line, Colonel," he said.

Colonel MacLeod opened up a transmission on the Davion channel. Their signal packets were scrambled, but he knew they would hear his because it was not being compressed or secured. "This is Colonel MacLeod of the Highlanders. I have ordered my troops to disengage. This battle is a trick somebody's played on both of us. I request a cease-fire until we can sort this out."

The Consul Guards did not stop firing, however. Missiles raced toward the Highlanders, tearing into both the 'Mechs and the ferrocrete. Crimson blasts of laser fire cut into the armor of several of the Highlander 'Mechs, and Mulvaney's *Marauder II* took two heavy PPC hits. *If the Davions don't break off, MacLeod is going to have to order his people back into the fight. Otherwise the Highlanders will be wiped out. This isn't how I expected my mission to unfold ... not yet anyway.*

The temperature in the *Huron Warrior*'s cockpit dropped another dozen degrees as it dodged a wall of long-range missiles. "Damn it, Catelli, we're holding fire. Order your men to stop!"

Gradually the Consul Guard 'Mechs ceased firing, killing power to their weapons.

Loren sucked in the hot cockpit air and took a long look at the 'Mech's damage indicators. Four heat sinks had been knocked out and any armor left on the *Huron Warrior*'s legs was more myth than reality. Two errant Davion missiles had dug deeply into the 'Mech's lower torso, knocking the fusion reactor slightly out of balance. Thus far they had been lucky, but Loren didn't feel it yet.

The communications channel crackled to life. "What is the meaning of this, MacLeod? First you attack us, then your troops blast apart the spaceport like a pack of vandals. Now you call for a cease fire." Colonel Catelli was obviously infuriated.

"Permission to speak to the forces, Colonel," Loren said.

"It's all yours, Major," MacLeod said as he opened communications again with all the gathered forces.

"We've been tricked into firing on each other. Our sensors detected an attack, but neither side was actually firing."

"What do you mean? The Highlanders fired on us first," came the voice of an anonymous Consul Guard warrior, followed by the babbled affirmation of several others. A clamor of Highlanders simultaneously rebutted with a direct counter claim.

"That's what I'm saying," Loren insisted. "Somebody tampered with our 'Mech computers. They were running some sort of simulator-like program. It's the only explanation. Check your communications logs. You'll see the signature of a coded transmission being sent into our 'Mechs and feeding some program to the DI computer." While speaking, he was still attempting to find the hidden files from his keypad. "But I'll be damned if I can find a trace of it yet. This whole bloody thing was a trick to provoke an incident. Catelli's people were probably tricked into firing at us as well. Either way the Highlanders get framed for attacking the Consul Guards."

"Command Company and all troops go to hot-standby status," said Mulvaney. "Wait for our orders. Colonel, what do you make of this?"

"I see some evidence of what Jaffray is saying," MacLeod answered. "A signal was beamed to my 'Mech via microwave from the Davion 'Mechs. Something in my system got activated."

Loren felt his adrenaline rush slowing down. To one side he saw Fuller's *Shadow Hawk* slowly stagger to its feet. Smoke still trailed from the hits to its back as the light 'Mech hunched over from the loss of support strength. From the looks of it Fuller's 'Mech would be spending several long days in a repair gantry. The cockpit heat dropped enough to make Jaffray reset his cooling vest controls.

"I'll be ... we *have* been tricked," came back Fuller's voice.

"I received some sort of signal, but damned if I know

what it was, Colonel," came another voice Loren did not recognize.

"I see some traces of a transmission here as well," Mulvaney said. "Colonel Catelli, are your forces also picking up the same evidence?"

MacLeod didn't waste any more time trying to find answers among his own ranks. "Colonel Catelli, perhaps you'd like to explain? Are you afraid to fight your battles like a *real* MechWarrior? Is that why you hide behind sabotage?"

Both sides of the brief battle silently faced each other across the spaceport tarmac. From the *Huron Warrior*'s jumpseat Loren surveyed the impact of the brief few minutes of fighting. Several dead or wounded infantry were being removed from the field. Many 'Mechs on both sides were mauled and pitted from missile and laser impacts. Given the ferocity of the battle it looked as if MacLeod and the Security Lance had taken most of the damage. The left-side PPC on young Lieutenant Frutchey's *Warhammer* was battered so badly that it dragged on the ground alongside its battered legs. The SRM pack on its shoulder was totally gone, as was its massive searchlight and most of the shoulder where it had been mounted. The other 'Mech in the lance, a new model *Watchman,* had its rear leg jump jets ripped wide open and its back looked more like a section of potholed road than armor plating.

Colonel Catelli didn't answer for several moments, perhaps waiting for the Highlanders' fury to subside. "How dare you accuse me of stooping to such a ludicrous plan. It's no wonder you've been removed from your position, MacLeod. If you want to accuse somebody of sabotage, I suggest you look to the man I came to apprehend. Your insinuation stings my honor. First, you very nearly lead the Highlanders into a war with the Federated Commonwealth and now you have the gall to claim that it was we who tricked you into firing at us. Now then, surrender Major Jaffray and we will call this matter closed."

"Major Mulvaney, pull your forces back with the rest of the Command Company so we can finish this once and for all," MacLeod ordered. He switched to wide band. "If that little bastard wants a fight, laddies, I say we send him on an express transport to hell."

As if to emphasize his point MacLeod moved the *Huron Warrior* forward toward the Consul Guards. His 'Mech was in no condition for any sort of prolonged or drawn-out fight, and despite the discovery of the subterfuge, the battle was about to be joined again. He kept his sensors focused on the Davion line and walked diagonally toward the Command Company. The Consul Guards were pulling back slightly, but not enough to make a difference if or when the battle erupted.

Loren wondered about Mulvaney. Restraint was not her hallmark. If fighting broke out again she was going to be forced to choose sides.

Not surprisingly, she was the one who broke the communications stalemate. "Colonel MacLeod, we've got to withdraw. This whole confrontation is wrong, ethically and morally." Loren was shocked that she spoke in such a defiant tone over a wide communications channel audible to everyone.

"Not now, Major." MacLeod was leveling the *Huron Warrior*'s massive Gauss rifle at the Davion 'Mechs. Across the tarmac Loren saw Catelli pulling back but obviously preparing to dig in for a battle. *He'd rather press a losing battle than admit his guilt in the sabotage. He's either a calculating genius or an incredible fool.* Outgunned and outclassed, Catelli would not last long. There was no place to hide, no terrain he could use. At best he might be able to flee or eject, but either way this fight was destined to be a short one. That had probably been Catelli's intention all along, Loren thought. Men like Catelli always managed to survive. And either way, the Federated Commonwealth would have a reason to attack Northwind. *He's no fool. He devious and dangerous.*

"Colonel Mulvaney, this is Colonel Catelli. By order of Field Marshal Morgan Hasek-Davion you are in command of the Regiment now. If you are party to this fight you risk all that the Northwind Highlanders have fought for over the centuries."

MacLeod lost his temper. "Blast it, Catelli, shut up! She's a loyal Highlander and I am her superior officer."

"Not anymore. You've been relieved."

"Highlanders, on my mark," MacLeod said in a determined tone. Loren watched as the Colonel precharged and loaded the Gauss rifle and targeted Drew Catelli's cockpit. *Catelli's not giving him any option.* If anything happened, MacLeod apparently wanted the first hit to be square into Catelli's *Atlas*. The heads up display indicated a full weapons lock on the skull-like head of the *Atlas*.

"No!" Mulvaney's voice echoed loudly. Her *Marauder II* broke rank and moved forward. "I can't do this, not this way."

"Major, fall back in line." MacLeod's voice was angry but controlled.

"With all respect, sir, no. Victor Davion is our liege lord, our rightful ruler. Fighting the Consul Guards is wrong, sabotage or not. Disobeying orders from the High Command is wrong. I can't just stand by while all this happens."

Loren heard the strain in her voice, but his eyes remained fixed on the short-range scanner for any sign of activity from across the spaceport. No matter what was unfolding on the communications channel, Loren's training wouldn't let him lose his focus.

Colonel MacLeod must also have sensed her conflict. This time his voice was softer, almost paternal. "We can settle this later, Major. For now, fall in and prepare to follow my command."

"No, sir, I can't. I've been fighting in service to the Davions my entire life. They gave us back our homes, helped us reclaim our birthright. I can't turn my back on that."

"The Regiment is your home. The Highlanders are your home. Major—Chastity, we are more than warriors, we're family."

Mulvaney's voice was firm now, unhesitating. "Yes, and that's why I can't stand by and watch the Highlanders destroyed from within. Our people must survive despite this conflict. This is the way." With that her *Marauder* took several steps toward the Davion line.

Her words were now directed to the Highlanders at large. "I've spoken with many of you who agree with what I'm saying, many of you who voted against the proposal from Liao. Rather than fight here and now, you can join me. We'll fight, but not against the Davions. Let this be our test of honor as a people. Follow me and we will preserve our dignity and commitment." Her *Marauder II* picked up speed as it made its way across the tarmac.

Loren cut in without asking permission to speak. "Mulvaney, Jaffray here. They tricked you into this. They tampered with our computers and deceived us into firing our weapons. You can't trust them."

"All this from a Capellan spy sent to subvert the Highlanders," Catelli said. "Where should the loyalties of true Highlanders lie? With a government at war with the Federated Commonwealth or with your rightful liege lord?"

Loren would have given anything to be piloting his own 'Mech at that moment. *Mulvaney won't fall for such an obvious play on her emotions* ...

But then several other Command Company 'Mechs also stepped forward. A *Griffin,* a *Scarabus,* and a *Goliath* all fell into line behind Mulvaney as she left MacLeod's Highlanders behind. Loren's sensors showed other 'Mechs breaking ranks and moving away as well. In all, just short of a battalion of 'Mechs, tanks, and vehicles moved in a snake-like formation over to the Davion lines.

"Excellent," Catelli hissed over the frequency. "Now the odds are even."

"No!" Mulvaney said. "This is not the time or the place. Attack now and I won't hesitate to order my troops to attack your troops."

"Sir," cut in Fuller. "Your orders, Colonel MacLeod?"

MacLeod lowered his Gauss rifle. "Hold your fire. We don't fire at our own, not like this ... not now. The time will come to settle this matter."

"This is your last chance, MacLeod. Step down, turn Jaffray over to us. End this senseless division of your people," Catelli pressed.

"I suggest, Colonel Catelli, that you and your troops withdraw from this area immediately before I reconsider my position and blast you off the face of this tarmac."

"Cromarty City is more mine than yours, MacLeod. It is a landhold of the Federated Commonwealth and I represent

Prince Victor Steiner-Davion's will here. I won't be run off like a common criminal." Referring to Tara as Cromarty was obviously calculated to irritate MacLeod and the other Highlanders, as was his claim to represent the Prince's will. The statement implied that it was he, not Drake Burns, who was truly calling the shots for the Federated Commonwealth.

But MacLeod was not so easily goaded. "Colonel, the city of Tara is off limits in our dispute. Too many Highlander families are there, not to mention thousands of other civilians and your own government offices and facilities. Any fighting there will make New Delos look like a walk across the moors." It was a saying that had grown up among mercenary units ever since the day the Mariks had attacked the families of another mercenary unit, the famous Wolf's Dragoons. In response, the Dragoons had nearly burned New Delos to a cinder.

Catelli backed down. "You want Tara treated as neutral territory, then?"

"Yes. Destroying any of the city or its innocent civilians will not do either of us any good."

"I concur, but on that point and that alone. Any pursuit by your troops and we will respond in force. You must remove your forces from the city in twelve hours. Otherwise the agreement is off." As Catelli spoke he turned his *Atlas* and began to move away.

"Colonel, shouldn't we pursue?" It was Lieutenant Fuller's voice. "They're headed away and are vulnerable. If we wait they'll organize and prepare a defense. Now is the perfect time to strike."

"Colonel, sir," another voice cut in. Loren recognized it as that of a Captain named Laurie Carey. "We can't take them now, sir. It's not the Highlander way. Not from behind and in the open." Her words were seconded by several others.

MacLeod's voice sounded almost weary. "Mulvaney has chosen her path, and like it or not, I respect her decision. According to what some of us read, our 'Mechs have been tampered with. I won't go into battle not knowing the full extent. For now, we withdraw and regroup. Tomorrow morning we set out in force after them."

"And when we find them next time, sir?" Fuller asked, echoing the question in Loren's own mind.

"When we find them, we take them down. Honor or not, there can be only one leader of the Northwind Highlanders—and I am he."

17

The Fort
Tara, Northwind
Draconis March, Federated Commonwealth
24 September 3057

Loren watched as a squad of techs began to work on MacLeod's *Huron Warrior*, and wondered if the damage could be repaired by the next day. The cockpit monitors had told one kind of story about the damage. To actually view the physical destruction was another. Seeing the ripped and burned armor plates, the severed myomer muscle strands, the deep laser cuts was a lot different than seeing readouts on the secondary screen. Watching the repair crews always reminded Loren of how mortal a warrior was in the cockpit of even a mighty fighting machine like a BattleMech.

The march back to The Fort had been somber and long, with only an eerie silence filling the commlines. A silence that seemed to underscore the feeling of guilt welling up in him, guilt for what had happened to the Highlanders, in more ways than one.

He had not been counting on the defection of Mulvaney and the other Davion sympathizers. Now, because of his presence and actions, the Highlander regiment on the planet was split into two fighting factions. And that's how they would be when the Death Commando unit came to crush them.

Strangely enough, Loren had been impressed with the way MacLeod had honored Mulvaney's decision. For a Death Commando, the Colonel's response was almost alien, but from what Loren knew of the Highlanders, he thought he understood it.

Jake Fuller walked up just as the work crew began repairs on the *Huron Warrior*'s reactor shielding, removing much of the insulation and control circuits. "Looks like the old man and you were lucky to hold that baby together. Another bump there and you'd have been history."

Loren grinned. "The thought never entered my mind."

Fuller grinned back. "The word is that a number of our technical folks have bugged off to join Mulvaney and Catelli."

"We have a saying in the Confederation," Loren said. "Firepower can defeat a foe on the battlefield. Rumors can slay a regiment from within."

"Point taken," Fuller said. "It's just that we're all a little stressed. I for one never expected Mulvaney to break ranks like that." Loren remembered her *Marauder* moving across the tarmac away from MacLeod's Regiment and felt a sense of loss. It had nothing to do with the mission, but everything to do with her leaving.

"How's your *Hawk*?" Loren asked, thinking to change his mood with a change of subject.

"According to the crew she'll be ready to field in eight hours. Frutchey's *'Hammer* is more replacement parts than original and he's a little shook up, but he'll march with the rest of us." Fuller watched as the tech crew literally climbed into the back of the *Huron Warrior* with tools and replacement myomer bundles in hand. "I still can't believe what happened."

"What do you mean?" Loren asked.

"How did you know the attack was fake? Every instrument in my cockpit told me we were under some damn heavy fire. And the 'Mech was rocking with every simulated hit."

Loren grinned. "If I hadn't been riding shotgun with the Colonel I'd never have known either. Without a neurohelmet feeding me the false images. I was relying more on my natural senses. In the end, I guess I played a good hunch."

The casual reply shocked Fuller. "Hunch? You mean you weren't sure?"

Loren turned back from the work on his 'Mech and let go a thin grin. "Yes and no. Looking back, there was a good chance I was dead wrong. Something in my gut told me that none of it made sense. That, and I've had a lot of experience working with synthetic reality programs."

Fuller's jaw dropped open in amazement at Jaffray's frankness. "I can't believe we broke off our entire attack all on the basis of a pure hunch."

"What counts now is that I was right." Loren put a hand on the other man's shoulder. "Listen, I'm not talking down to you. We've both been in battles before. The only difference is that I've seen more than you. If I've learned one thing it's that it's usually better to play a good hunch than sit back and play it safe."

"We would have kicked the Guards' butts."

"Yes. But you'd also have handed Victor Davion a perfect reason to try to disband the Highlanders. Men like Catelli are dangerous. He'd have punched out and made a getaway. People like him always manage to survive; it's all part of the game they play. They understand power but not leadership. He would have twisted the truth to the point where the Highlanders looked like heinous criminals. As outlaws he would've broken you all."

"You talk like he won't do that now anyway."

"Yes and no. Catelli will try to portray the Highlanders as criminals, but the truth of the matter is that you could have crushed him and didn't. The whole Inner Sphere knows the reputation of the Northwind Highlanders. They know that the unit could blast a battalion of 'Consul Guards' to dust in a matter of minutes. The fact that Catelli and his people survived adds credibility to our side of the truth."

"Well, at least we have that," Fuller said. Loren nodded, but in his heart he knew that it was the victors who decided what history would call truth.

Glancing across the 'Mech bay Loren saw a tall slender figure that he recognized as Lieutenant Gomez making her way through the busy repair bay in record time. Within moments she was standing in front of him, flashing a crisp salute. Jaffray returned it, taken off guard by the gesture.

"What can I do for you, Lieutenant?"

"Colonel MacLeod wants to meet with you on the parade field in the mobile HQ."

Loren gestured for Gomez to lead, then fell into step, managing to keep up with her for most of the way over to the parade grounds.

"Did your intel boys and girls have any luck finding traces of whatever it was the Davions had loaded into our 'Mech computers?"

Gomez did not break stride or even turn to face him. "Yes, Major. Apparently it was a variant Ironclad-type virus, triggered by a three-character microwave transmission. According to Captain Dumfries of our Intel platoon, it loaded resident in the DI computers, giving us ghost images of enemy fire and telling the 'Mechs' myomer controls to simulate impacts and damage. Some copies also made their way into a handful of our tanks, but they weren't as sophisticated in simulating combat."

"Did it do any more damage than that?"

"No. About half our Command Company 'Mechs were infected with the virus plus about a third of our other 'Mechs. We're in the process of checking and purging the bug. It looks like a lone individual penetrated our security systems last night. Probably wearing infiltration gear to get by the guards and heat sensors. A re-check of our systems picked him up on only three of our motion detection cameras and even then it was only a faint trace in the dark. Fortunately there is no other evidence of other sabotage."

"We were lucky," Loren said. What he didn't say was that a saboteur could cripple even the most powerful BattleMech if that person had the right tools and the right skills. Just such skills had been part of his own Death Commando training, and been put to use on more than one occasion.

"Yes, sir. And sir—"

"Lieutenant?"

"Thank you, sir." It was obvious that the words were as sincere as they were hard for Gomez to utter.

"Thanks for what?"

"If not for your actions we'd have fallen into Colonel Catelli's trap."

"We're not out of this yet, Lieutenant. But for what it's worth, you're welcome."

18

The Fort
Tara, Northwind
Draconis March, Federated Commonwealth
24 September 3057

The parade grounds had been converted into a staging area for MacLeod's Highlanders. In the center were gathered clusters of hover transports and trucks, while close to a full battalion of BattleMechs stood like perimeter guards at intervals around the grassy field. Larger trucks loaded with supplies were in the process of being checked and re-checked. Several platoons of infantry were busy cleaning and inspecting their weapons while others worked on the various ground tanks and hovercraft being prepared and loaded for an extended campaign. The remaining trimmed-down battalions of 'Mechs stood in perfect line formation being inspected by their pilots and field techs.

MacLeod's Regiment, reorganized to make up for the troops that had followed Mulvaney, now consisted of roughly three short battalions and a mixed battalion of armor and infantry. It was just one of the ways the Colonel had swiftly responded to the situation, but it might not be enough for the coming fight.

Gomez led Loren through a maze of vehicles and troops to the very center of the parade field, where several large vans arrayed with communications dishes and antennas were stationed. Loren knew immediately that this was the core of the regimental field HQ, and he followed the Lieutenant to one of the smaller vehicles. As they opened the door and stepped in, MacLeod greeted them heartily.

"Major!"

"Colonel. You wanted to see me, sir?"

MacLeod beckoned Loren into the van, whose walls were covered from floor to ceiling with computer and communications gear. Three other Highlander officers in field fatigues were working at keyboards and consoles. Gomez immediately took a seat and joined them. MacLeod was standing at an electronic map similar to those in the War Room, this one a table model nearly two meters square.

MacLeod shook Loren's hand firmly. "I need your eyes and mind in this strategy meeting. And, I wanted to thank you personally for what you did out there. Your quick thinking saved us."

Loren nodded. *What you don't know is that I only postponed the inevitable.*

Several other Highlander officers entered through another small doorway, their faces familiar from either the Cabel or Loren's time exploring The Fort. They huddled around the map as MacLeod assumed his station at the controls, all wearing the serious faces of men about to enter battle.

"Gentlemen, for those of you who haven't met him, this is Major Jaffray. I've asked him here for his input." A flurry of hands extended across the table and Loren shook them firmly.

MacLeod activated the map, and the plain white grid came to life in a flood of colors. Along the northern edge was the city of Tara. Running down from the western mountains was a river that flowed across the city and then poured into another, wider estuary just to the east of Tara. The wider river traveled south, then back west into the Rockspire range. Heavy woods, marshes, and other rugged terrain surrounded the city to the south, then gradually thinned out.

"This is Tara and her surrounding terrain. At last report the Davions and Mulvaney were here," MacLeod said. A small red icon appeared on the map in the shape of a fist over a sunburst, symbol of the Federated Commonwealth. It was positioned nearly twelve kilometers southeast of the

Kohler Spaceport heading south toward the wide river. "Given what Catelli was fielding against us and the troops that went with Mulvaney, we estimate them at a heavily reinforced battalion. Over two and a half companies of 'Mechs in mixed weight classes, four lances of ground armor, and six platoons of mechanized infantry."

One of the officers, a short stocky Major whose name tag read "Huff," cut in. "It was a mixed bag of troops that went with Mulvaney, but we've filled out the ranks with the company we had stationed on the Kearny continent. We've completed our reorganization and are ready to go, sir."

MacLeod stroked his beard and nodded. "Good. Now then, the real issue is how we want to deal with this situation. I've got some ideas, but I'd also like to hear yours."

"Sir." One of the Captains, a man named Steed, leaned across the map as he spoke. "Several of us believe that the best approach might be to intercept them before they reach the Tilman River." He pointed to the wider river to the east of Tara. "We can use our aerospace assets to batter and whittle them down without having to commit our ground forces. We hit them before they can get to the river bed and use it like a highway upstream."

MacLeod shook his head. "I was thinking along the same lines at first, but Major Huff and I realized that there's a problem. Our aerospace forces are scattered across the planet and word is just starting to reach them. Many of those lances might have gone over to Mulvaney, but for the time being they've opted to simply stand down at their bases.

"And there's more. Two hours ago the face of this conflict changed, perhaps dramatically. One of our long-range interceptor patrols detected the arrival of JumpShips at our nadir jump point. They've begun to deploy DropShips from there, so we'll need the bulk of our space-fighter assets as combat air patrol in case this force is incoming Davion reinforcements. What I'll be holding back can provide us some support, but not enough to pull off the kind of bombing and strafing you envision, Major."

"How many ships are we looking at, sir?" another Captain asked.

"Unknown at this time. We've transmitted numerous messages, but thus far they've not communicated back. ID scans on their transponders show them as military transports, but not what they're carrying or if they plan to stay around. We have little choice but to assume that they're hostile.

"And we've yet to scour other jump points in the system. I'm afraid that for a while we're going to need our aerospace fighters for possible protection of Northwind if this is some kind of Davion invasion force."

"It might also be a diversionary force, sir," the Captain said. "Especially the way they're just sitting at the jump point right now. It's as if they're trying to bait us into going out there and taking a look. Then they lure off our fighters and hit us from a pirate jump point."

MacLeod nodded agreement. "Very likely it is. But my hands are tied. We've only got limited fighter support to start with and I've got to view any incoming forces as potentially hostile. The Davions have controlled Northwind for three centuries, so chances are they know a number of ways in and out of the system. I have to assume those ships are genuine. If I don't we'd never be able to engage them in time to do any real damage."

"Given that, how do you propose to take on Mulvaney and Catelli?" Huff asked.

MacLeod pressed several control studs at the edge of the electronic map, expanding the viewing area by reducing the size of the image. Loren watched as the city of Tara shrank and more of the surrounding terrain came into view. The dark green area next to the red icon told him that this was the edge of a deep forest. Nearly sixty kilometers south of that was the thick blue streak labeled the Tilman River. It wound along the south edge of the map, eventually cutting back to the dark gray that was the long spine of the Rockspire Mountains to the west.

MacLeod's small laser pointer cast a bright red point of light as he talked. "In thinking about the situation, the first question to answer was where in the hell are Mulvaney and Catelli going? Past the Tilman River and you're into wild country where you won't find a city or town for at least a week's travel. So, they wouldn't continue east because of the limited supplies they're carrying. Everything I saw indicated that Catelli hasn't provided for a protracted campaign against us."

"The Castle then," Huff said flatly.

MacLeod nodded. "It's the only place where they can hope to make a stand and survive. And there are enough parts and supplies there to make it worth their while."

"Excuse me, sir, but what is The Castle?" Loren asked.

A green point of light appeared in the middle of the Tilman River halfway along its westerly route toward the steep valleys of the Rockspires. "The Castle was built by the Star League Defense Forces centuries ago. It's a heavily reinforced bunker complex of tunnels and accesses housed under the waterfalls of the river itself. We use it primarily as a fallback base of operations in the event we ever have to defend Northwind."

"Why didn't you base your operations there instead of The Fort?"

MacLeod stared at the map as he spoke. "Three centuries of war and abuse have left the place in less than good condition."

Major Huff pointed at the green spot of light. "What's really important, Jaffray, is that it's full of supplies, rations, parts, and ammo. With all those tunnel accesses, it will be damn tough to pry them out if Mulvaney and the Davions can get there. She could dig in and plant her butt there in perfect protection."

"What about defense? What do you currently have at The Castle?"

Huff shook his head. "One platoon of infantry. But the platoon leader has sided with Mulvaney."

Studying the map, Loren understood the logic. Using the wide river banks of the Tilman River, Mulvaney and the Davions can and Catelli could move quickly through the forest to the bunker complex. *It's too easy. It's not her style of fighting at all.* "Colonel, if I were Mulvaney, I'd never dig into one spot, no matter how good it is. Don't forget that we outgun them overall and are equipped for a long fight. I think I'd stay on the move, wear us down, only committing to a fight when absolutely necessary. Is there any other place she might try to break for instead?"

MacLeod moved the pointer beam past The Castle and along the river as it snaked west. Then he slid it up across the light green and brown hills and into a pass in the

Rockspires. A press of a control stud and another bright green ball of light appeared similar to that on The Castle. "The only other point she might try for is our training camp in the mountains. We have several other depots and bases on Northwind, but only these two have the kinds of supplies and parts that will do them any good. It's quite a trek, but the area is almost abandoned at this time of the year, with only a small infantry garrison to protect it. The camp has ample parts and supplies to keep their BattleMechs fielded and operational.

"At first I thought that's where she'd head, but it's getting her forces up into the mountains from her current location that would be tricky. On a direct run from Tara, there's a highway that can get you up into the camp within three days. But right now they're heading the other way. Given the terrain they'd have to cross from their current position, it would take them weeks to reach the camp. That's why I ruled it out."

Loren stared at the site and thought hard. From The Castle the trek north along the Tilman River's headwaters to the training camp was short but rugged. In his own career he'd earned a reputation for unorthodox tactics and strategies. Mulvaney had struck him as someone like him. The best bet, the safest move that she could make was the one that Colonel MacLeod anticipated, a break for The Castle. That was exactly why Loren was sure she would not do that at all.

"Sir, if I were Major Mulvaney, I'd continue up the Tilman past The Castle and head for the camp in the mountains instead."

"Why?" Huff countered. "It would take you twice as long to get there and would be tricky as hell to defend. With all due respect to Major Jaffray, I don't think he appreciates the terrain here. No way. She'll break for The Castle and dig in there."

"I wouldn't do that at all if it were you and I fighting, Major Huff," Loren returned.

"Because you'd keep on the move—yes, Jaffray, I heard you before."

"No, Major Huff, I'd do it because you would expect me to."

"Remember," injected a gray-haired Captain. "We're not

just taking on Major Mulvaney, sirs. We're also taking on Catelli: Major Jaffray would have a good point if we were just going after Mulvaney, but Catelli is an old-school Davion. His career has been reduced to leading a band of paltry Consul Guards. If he was worth his salt they'd have kept him in the field commanding troops on the front line."

Loren crossed his arms, not in defense but in deep thought. "The worst thing you can do with an enemy is underestimate him. Catelli holds the rank of Colonel and came very close to getting us to start an all-out war."

This time it was Captain Steed who spoke up. "We're all grateful for your insights, Major Jaffray, but we mustn't forget that now we're fully fielded, outnumbering Mulvaney and Catelli nearly two to one. No matter what direction they go, they don't stand a chance."

MacLeod's face darkened suddenly into a frown and he pounded his fist on the electronic map board. "Listen up and listen good. I think Jaffray's hit on something important, and we don't want to get too cocky about this. We may outnumber them, but history is full of cases where outnumbered troops have managed to pull off victories. Look at how many times units like Snord's Irregulars, the Kell Hounds, the Gray Death, or even the Black Thorns have managed to turn the odds in their favor, been outnumbered and turned sure defeat into victory. I have no desire to add Mulvaney or Catelli to that honor roll."

"Understood, sir." Steed's face was red.

"Good. I think Jaffray's ideas have merit, but at the moment our target is only a few days away from The Castle. Regardless of whether they continue on to the Rockspires, we have to make sure they don't get any troops into that complex."

"Well, then, it's a race," Major Huff said, pointing to the river. "Once they get to those wide river banks they can move pretty rapidly. If we try to send even a company of light 'Mechs through the surrounding forests they'll probably beat us to The Castle. Our best bet is to lock into a pursuit mode and hit their butts as they move along the river."

"My thoughts exactly," MacLeod returned. "I want First Battalion in the lead. Second Battalion will deploy its scout lances to First. The key to this is not to let Mulvaney and

Catelli bog us down once we find them. Hit them and hit them hard. Run right through them. But we don't want to kill any Highlanders if at all possible. Cripple their BattleMechs, knock them senseless, but don't kill them unless it cannot be avoided. If I know the Major, she'll be giving her people the same orders."

Once more, Loren was surprised that this was how MacLeod would deal with rebel troops, but said nothing.

"And the Consul Guards, sir?" the gray-haired Captain asked.

MacLeod leaned forward, his expression stern and angry. "Teach them what it means to fight the Northwind Highlanders." His voice left no doubt in anyone's mind about what he meant. "We deploy in one hour, gentlemen. Major Jaffray, your assistance has been valuable thus far. With war breaking out around us, there's little chance of you linking back up with your Commandos. What would you say to joining us in this?

"Nothing would please me more than having a Jaffray in my ranks again. I've got a place for you with the regimental command's Security Lance if you're interested."

Loren felt a blush rise to his face. This was a moment that his grandfather would have given anything to see, the return of the Jaffray clan to the ranks of his former unit. Now it was happening, but in a way Corwin Jaffray could never have envisioned.

"I would be honored to accept your generous offer, Colonel. But . . ."

"What is it, lad? That you don't have a BattleMech? You can use my *Gallowglas*. She's a fine machine."

No, it wasn't the lack of a 'Mech that bothered him. To leap at the offer would make some of them wonder about him, and Loren knew that. "Sir, I've already overstepped my bounds for this mission. For me to fight with the Highlanders would be a thrill, but my oath is with the Capellan Confederation and to serve the Chancellor. I could be labeled as a defector, traitor, or worse by my own people if I went into combat with you." Loren spoke the words for MacLeod's benefit, not is own. The Chancellor had told him that he must sacrifice even his personal honor to the success of the mission. He knew the Highlanders would never trust him if he didn't raise some objection.

MacLeod grinned and laid one hand on Loren's shoulder. "I doubt that any court in the Inner Sphere will convict you, Major. Any hopes you had of staying out of this fight were destroyed by our esteemed Consul Burns. And, in case you've forgotten, the Capellans have just started a war against the very people you're going to be fighting."

Loren nodded and smiled. The formalities accounted for, it was now time to do what he did best.

MacLeod shut off the electronic map. "The rest of you, good hunting and good luck." With those final words the Highlander officers quickly dispersed to find their 'Mechs and their men and to get the operation underway.

= 19 =

AFFC DropShip **Despiser**, *Pirate Jump Point*
.01326184
Northwind System
Draconis March, Federated Commonwealth
24 September 3057

Marshal Harrison Bradford watched out the viewport of his DropShip, *The Despiser*, as it and the JumpShip to which it was attached emerged at a jump point in the Northwind system. The usual queasiness in his stomach rose and passed quickly as the ship and the rest of the universe materialized around him. *The Despiser* was a smaller DropShip, a *Fury* Class assault transport, primarily a carrier of infantry troops and supplies. It was rare that a man like Harrison Bradford, Marshal of an elite Federated Commonwealth Regimental Combat Team, entered battle riding in with the infantry, but he did not consider himself ordinary. His communications with the Federated Suns Command and with his operative on Northwind, Colonel Catelli, indicated that he would be facing a deadly enemy, the Northwind Highlanders. Such a foe demanded special measures. *We're not going to let this planet fall to Liao.*

The use of a pirate jump point posed a number of risks, but such risks were often necessary. The normal jump points, at the zenith and the nadir of a planetary system, were far outside a planet's gravity wells. Pirate points were much closer to their destination world, but the slightest failure of calculations could mean a possible misjump and the destruction of the ship and everybody on it. This point between Northwind's moon and the planet itself was tricky to navigate, but perfect for getting not just Harrison but his entire fleet onto the surface in record time.

He pressed his wrist communicator. "Marshal Harrison here, Captain Luce."

"Yes, sir," came the voice of *The Despiser*'s captain.

"Begin your scan for the communications satellite. Let me know as soon as you've retrieved the data."

"Incoming now, Marshal. I'll download it to your quarters."

Harrison looked over at the terminal and saw the data file streaming by. He carefully paused the file and read intently. It was, unfortunately, not everything he'd hoped for. Catelli's attempt to embroil the Highlanders in an incident had apparently not gone as planned. All that he'd actually managed to do was splinter the Highlanders. The transmission was eight hours old.

"Captain, disengage from the docking ring and send the JumpShip a transmission. The message is: Lancelot."

"Understood Marshal, code phrase Lancelot. What about the Highlanders' aerospace fighters, sir? I recommend we hold the ship in position until we're sure where they are."

"I've already taken care of their aerospace support, Captain. I'll send you landing coordinates in a few minutes. Your concern is noted, but all you have to do is get us to Northwind in one piece." As *The Despiser* tugged free from its JumpShip and moved toward the massive globe of Northwind, Bradford Harrison smiled knowingly and sat back in his small bunk.

A diversionary force had been sent to the system's nadir jump point with the task of drawing away the bulk of the Highlanders' aerospace fighter defense. While MacLeod's fighters were chasing down the decoy DropShips, Harrison could drop onto Northwind almost undetected. Thus far everything was going as planned. In a matter of hours, MacLeod's forces would be crippled and ready for the kill.

Bradford glanced out of his viewport long enough to see the dull blue flash as the JumpShip leaped between the stars.

Using its lithium batteries to avoid having to recharge, the ship would meet up with the Third Royals RCT, recharge, and return in time for the battle to come.

Loren's new *Gallowglas* was operational and in pristine condition, having been spared the earlier fighting at the spaceport. Painted with splashes of dull gray, green, and brown, the 'Mech showed several burn scars on the armor just under the paint, silent testimony to the damage it had endured under MacLeod. The cockpit was similar to that of other *Gallowglas* types Loren had previously piloted, which would make things easier. *How many battles and fights have you been through?* he wondered, running a hand over the controls.

The other members of the Security Lance had greeted him warmly, especially Jake Fuller. Loren tried to respond in kind, knowing it was important for them. They would need to know him as something more than a voice in their neurohelmets once the fighting began. *If I die, my mission dies with me. I must count on these men and women to make sure I survive.*

Following the path of Catelli and Mulvaney's force was turning out to be relatively simple. Given the number of vehicles and BattleMechs wading into the dense forests, they'd cut an incredible swath in the growth. Scanners were not necessary, but Loren made sure he observed every possible detail as they moved through the fallen brush. He was taking nothing for granted, especially the apparent calm and quiet of the forest.

His neurohelmet beeped softly, indicating an incoming message. Loren tapped on the system. "Major Jaffray, this is Command."

Loren was surprised that the Highlanders did not use formal call-signs. Then he realized that their communications routing system worked on voice identification. It was a sophisticated system that used encoded transmissions and voice identification and probably dated back to the high-tech era of the Star League. Only a unit with a history as long as the Highlanders had the access and expertise to maintain such a system.

"Jaffray here. Go, Command."

"Drop back from formation and link up with base." The "base" referenced was the regimental command center, currently a mobile post nearly three kilometers from the Security Lance's position.

"Affirmative," Loren said and saw a light on the communications systems control that indicated Fuller had acknowledged. Loren pulled back on the throttle and turned the massive *Gallowglas* around. He wasn't sure what was going on, but it had to be important if they wanted him in person.

It took only four minutes to locate the regimental command post, five command vehicles flanked by a full lance of BattleMechs. Loren found a spot to park the *Gallowglas* and quickly climbed down the footholds from the cockpit along the torso and leg of the 'Mech. Several Highlander guards emerged from behind trees, weapons at ready, carefully confirming him personally before letting him near the central command vehicle.

Inside the van Loren found Colonel MacLeod, Major Huff, and another female Captain he recognized from the initial standing around the electronic map. Loren made his way toward them through the somewhat darkened interior.

"Glad you could make it," MacLeod said.

"What's going on, Colonel?"

"Nothing in particular. This is just a routine field ops briefing. Those DropShips we spotted at the nadir jump point are finally starting to move, but at a slow-burn. I've diverted most of our aerospace fighters and sent them on intercept to run combat air patrol, per our plan. Then three hours ago another JumpShip materialized at a pirate point near Northwind."

"What's it carrying?"

It was Major Huff who answered. "A *Fury* Class assault ship."

"An infantry transport? Hell, that's like sending a man with a knife to a gun fight," said the female Captain. Loren remembered her name as Fitzwalther from the Warrior's Cabel. How long ago that night seemed now. Like years, Loren thought.

Huff nodded. "It assumed a quick low orbit and dropped onto Northwind unmolested."

"Where did it drop?"

172 Blaine Lee Pardoe

MacLeod pointed to a spot along the river. "On the banks of the Tilman. One of our few remaining aerolances did a flyby and confirmed it as a Davion ship. It's located just ahead of Catelli and Mulvaney's task force, as if that shocks any of us.

"To be honest I'm not concerned with the ship, but with a bigger question. What if those DropShips we're chasing down at the nadir point are simply decoys? That ship might be only the vanguard of a Davion invasion fleet. Our fighters are already past the pirate point and on their way to the nadir point. Pulling them back is going to cost us time, maybe even cost us the whole battle if Davion is indeed sending reinforcements."

The short female Captain spoke again. "Well, whatever was on that ship, it's just been added to Catelli's force. Even if it was infantry, a hundred troops can still do quite a bit of damage."

"If the nadir fleet is a lure designed to draw off our fighters, we're already too late. To divert our fighters to the pirate point would take too long. And splitting them up would leave both groups too weak to do any damage to any ships they might engage," Huff said. "I think the best course of action is to have them continue on and take those nadir DropShips out."

MacLeod stroked his beard in thought. "What worries me more is that they're using pirate points. If those are Davions, with more on the way, and if they keep using pirate points, they could be on top of us before we could react at all." His worry was one that any regimental garrison commander faced. Usually it took several days to a month for a DropShip to make planetfall from either the zenith or nadir jump points of a system. Using a pirate point, though risky, cut that margin down to a day or even hours. It was a risk that many regimental officers were more than willing to take.

"I'm shocked that the Davions were able to get forces here so quickly," Captain Fitzwalther said. "From the sound of it all hell is breaking loose in the Sarna March."

Loren cocked an eyebrow at the younger officer. "I wouldn't be so shocked by their speed in getting here, Captain. I'd be more worried about what was on that ship in the first place."

"It's a small infantry hauler," Huff said. "Even if modified it could only carry a handful of BattleMechs at most. Like Captain Fitzwalther said, three or four platoons of infantry and support gear can cause damage, but I doubt they could tip the scales of the battle. The odds are still on our side."

"BattleMechs may rule the battlefield, Major Huff, but as we saw just a short while ago, one person can also cause a great deal of damage. I wouldn't write off that ship or its cargo until we know for sure what we're dealing with. And no matter what, I doubt this is the last of the Davion reinforcements coming into the system."

Huff smiled patronizingly. "I appreciate what you did for us back at the spaceport, Major, but now that we're in the field you seem a little timid. Neither Catelli nor Mulvaney have the kind of equipment needed for a prolonged operation. But the Castle does and they're trying to reach the banks of the Tilman to get the speed they need to beat us there, plain and simple. What we're facing here is a unit on the run and this is a race to stop them—period."

Loren smiled back. "I've been called many things in my career, Major Huff, but 'timid' has never been on that list until now. Don't mistake my intentions or comments. I'm simply pointing out that it's best not to make broad-based assumptions. The Northwind Highlanders have a reputation for ferocity. If I were Catelli or a Davion Marshal, I'd be playing for keeps against you. No restraint, only a direct and persistent attack."

Loren knew that his comment regarding the Highlanders' prowess was a gross understatement. *Davion isn't going to let Northwind slip from his grip without a fight. Chancellor Liao knew that and I know it. Whatever is on that ship is meant to give Catelli an edge. Huff can think what he wants. I would play this as if it were a deadly threat.*

20

Southeast of Tara City
Northwind
Draconis March, Federated Commonwealth
24 September 3057

The cockpit of Chastity Mulvaney's *Marauder II* was quiet as she carefully navigated the giant, bird-like 'Mech through the forest. She was tuning out most of the light chatter on the communications channel, concentrating only on maneuvering her BattleMech among the massive trees. It was the motion and the action that kept her going, kept her from having to think too much about all that had happened, kept her from having to consider the gravity of her actions. It was how she always dealt with frustration in her life, by burying herself in her duty.

She was surprisingly calm, despite the calculated risk of joining with Colonel Catelli against her own Highlanders. But she'd seen no other path. Had she remained with MacLeod, Catelli and his Guards would be only a memory right now and the Northwind Highlanders tainted as murderous criminals. Worse yet, the pro-Davion warriors among the Highlanders would have felt betrayed by their own command.

Mulvaney had provided the Davion loyalists in ranks with an honorable way out. Rather than compromise their personal beliefs, they had joined with Prince Victor's representatives on Northwind. Mulvaney's orders to those who'd come with her were simple. This was to be a test of honor on a grand scale. They were not to kill their kinsmen, but to protect the Consul Guards until the matter could be resolved diplomatically once the rest of the Highlander regiments arrived. Mulvaney was certain that Colonel MacLeod understood what she had done. She wondered if Loren Jaffray ever would.

Colonel Catelli had been obviously irritated at her orders, but had not interfered. Instead, he continued to treat her as if she were the new commanding officer of the Northwind Highlanders, using the rank of Colonel every time he spoke her name. But it only annoyed her more with each instance.

She pushed the throttle forward and used the right joystick to turn the *Marauder II* as it walked, using the massive PPC to push aside the thick growth and hanging brush. In three short steps the tree line ended and a flood of light poured down on Mulvaney as she gazed out over the Tilman River. Her viewport filtered the burst of light for the most part, but even the slight increase seemed to warm her slightly. The river itself was nearly a hundred meters across and one-tenth that deep. It was bordered by wide sand banks on either side. It was everything that she and Castelli needed, a wide open expressway.

"Colonel Catelli, this is Mulvaney," she transmitted. "I'm at the river just south of your position. No sign of hostiles." She and her Highlanders had been sent through the forest to the south of Tara to make sure that no one had beaten them to the river banks. As she'd suspected, MacLeod was still a half-day's march behind them. Over time this advantage would erode, but until then it was a classic game of fox and hounds. And for the time being, she was the fox.

"You made good time, Colonel," Catelli said, irritating her with the use of that rank. "Deploy your troops on both sides of the river and begin a gradual advance, per our earlier discussion. I want you personally to fall back to these coordinates and meet with me there." Mulvaney's secondary screen displayed the map coordinates as Catelli transmitted them. She downloaded them onto her long-range readout map.

"Acknowledged," she replied. "Lieutenants O'Leary,

Burke, and Darley, execute Plan Bravo. Darley, you're in command until I get back." She waited a few seconds as her officers acknowledged her orders, then turned and began the ten-kilometer trek to the rendezvous coordinates.

It took nearly twenty minutes for Mulvaney to pilot her *Marauder II* down the Tilman River to where Catelli had ordered. Most of the distance was an easy traverse compared to the dense forest through which she'd been maneuvering the *Marauder* until now. During the last two twisting, turning kilometers of the journey she'd passed several Consul Guard 'Mechs and a number of Guard light tanks. It wasn't just the sight of Colonel Catelli's massive *Atlas* that told her she'd arrived at the coordinates, but the large *Fury* Class DropShip settled on the banks of the river. She quickly dismounted onto the soft sand of the Tilman's shore.

"Good work, Colonel Mulvaney," Catelli called as he and several other officers walked toward her.

"Sir," she said softly, as embarrassed as before to be so addressed. Seeing a flash of stars on the lapel of one of the officers with Catelli, she immediately snapped to attention. The Marshal returned the salute. "At ease."

"Yes, sir," she replied as Catelli and another officer, a young ebony-skinned Major, stepped forward.

"Marshal Bradford, may I present Colonel Chastity Mulvaney of the Northwind Highlanders. Colonel Mulvaney, this is Marshal Harrison Bradford of the Third Royal Guards Regimental Combat Team."

"The pleasure is mine," Bradford said, then turned to one of the officers with him. "And this is Major Daphine Winchester of the First NAIS Cadre." A quick glance down showed Mulvaney that Bradford wore the spurs of a MechWarrior, but that Major Winchester did not. Winchester was either a nonconformist or she was an infantry or armored commander. The New Avalon Institute of Science, the famed NAIS, was the Federated Commonwealth's leading academy. Only the best of the best went there, and they trained in the leading edge of technology. *Even if she's infantry, she's not just another soldier.*

"I wish we could have met under better circumstances, Marshal." She turned to the slender Winchester and said crisply, "Major." The NAIS officer nodded her head once slowly, in full understanding.

Bradford looked over Mulvaney's shoulder at the riverbed where a *Locust* was splashing up the shore. "I had your appointment transmitted to the other Highlander regiments, but they refused to acknowledge it, Colonel Mulvaney."

"I expected that, sir."

Bradford pulled out a long dark cigar and carefully cut off the tip. Then he lit it with an expensive battery-powered laser lighter and took a deep drag, blowing the smoke out through his nose. "You Highlanders are a stubborn bunch, aren't you?"

"Yes sir," Chastity replied. *You don't know the half of it.*

"Well, Colonel Mulvaney, you'll find that I'm pretty stubborn too," he returned, looking into her eyes. "There's a war going on out there and the last thing I want to be doing at this moment is mopping up a rebellious unit, even a unit as famed as the Northwind Highlanders."

"Understood, sir."

"I want to ask you a question face-to-face and I want a straight answer. Will this Colonel MacLeod fight it out with us to the end? If this goes beyond a push-and-shove match, will he be willing to go the distance against us in the field? And before you answer, I want you to know that I'm more than willing to take it that far, especially with Stirling's Fusiliers so near at hand." He drew another long inhale of smoke.

The answer did not require much thought. "Marshal Harrison, I've known Colonel MacLeod for years. His argument is not with you but with how the Federated Commonwealth is treating the Highlanders. I don't think he'll draw our blood intentionally, but both your troops and the Consul Guards will both be fair game in his eyes. And in an even fight, sir, you won't stand a chance." She realized it was a risk being so blunt with the Davion Marshal, but a part of her no longer cared what happened to her personally.

"I see. Well, let me assure you, Colonel Mulvaney, the Federated Commonwealth is able and willing to defend its realm, even from your Highlanders. As we speak, the whole of the Third Royal Guards RCT is staging in orbit over Epsilon Indi, augmented by the rest of the First NAIS Cadre's

Battalion. Colonel MacLeod and his troops don't stand a chance."

"Sir," Catelli put in, "you should know that Colonel Mulvaney's knowledge of the Highlander bases has given us an edge in our efforts to lure MacLeod away from Tara. Together we've come up with some nasty little surprises for his troops as they get closer to us. As a matter of fact the Major has put together a plan that will tie up the rebellious Highlanders under MacLeod for some time." The characterization of Colonel MacLeod's Regiment as "rebellious" bothered Chastity. Who could say, in this situation, which side was the rebel and which the loyalist? The lines had become hopelessly blurred.

Bradford nodded, gesturing with the long cigar as he spoke. "I gathered that from the messages you sent me. You and Mulvaney deserve my deepest thanks. I only wish that this matter was resolved, but we have a lot of work still to do."

"Have you a plan, Marshal?" asked Catelli.

Marshall Harrison put the cigar in his mouth and used the swagger stick he'd been carrying under one armpit to draw a map in the soft wet sand. He sketched out the river and the city of Tara. "I've already taken the precaution of luring away most of MacLeod's aerospace fighters in a chase of a decoy fleet at the system's nadir jump point. But MacLeod's not stupid. He probably knows it's a decoy by now, but he also knows he's got to go after it.

"To begin with we will neutralize MacLeod's ability to communicate with Tara and hence with any other Highlander regiment now heading for Northwind. I need him blind, deaf, and dumb for just a little while, long enough for the next phase of the operation. Once he's cut off from the rest of the Inner Sphere, the attack fleet will enter the system at a pirate jump point and land outside the Tara spaceport. We only need him cut off for a short time, long enough for us to perform an undetected landing. I received word that you're treating Tara as neutral ground and I want you to know that I intend to honor that, Colonel Mulvaney.

"You and your force will continue to lure MacLeod further away from Tara while the Third Royals come up on him from behind as well as prepare a defense against Stirling's

Fusiliers, who are due to rotate back to Northwind in the next three or four weeks." The Marshal drew a line in the sand showing the current position of Catelli and Mulvaney's force and moved it along the Tilman River.

"Once the Fusiliers have been contained, we link up with you and crush whatever is left of MacLeod." To stress his point he slowly ground the swagger stick into the sand where the Highlander force would be.

"I appreciate the fact that you are honoring Tara's neutrality in this fight, sir. There are a lot of Highlander families there, not just those of our regiment but from the others abroad. And thousands of other civilians as well," Mulvaney said coolly.

"Colonel Catelli informed me of your agreement while I was en route and I agree that there's no point in dragging the civilians into all this. But don't get me wrong. If MacLeod or his people violate that agreement Tara will be considered a battle zone. Many loyal Davion citizens live there and I will not stand by and let anyone place their lives at risk. The Third Royals will conduct their landings outside the city and spaceport and will deploy from there."

"How will you contain the Fusiliers?" Mulvaney asked.

"I'm confident that once they see the force we've mustered and hear how MacLeod has taken the law into his own hands, they'll capitulate without a shot, especially with your loyal troops to assist. However, if they don't, I'll have a fully reinforced Regimental Combat Team in place. Trust me, Colonel Mulvaney. I have no intention of fighting Cat Stirling unless absolutely necessary."

"Thank you, sir." So far I trust him, Mulvaney thought, but just how far?

"The key to this operation's success is to blind MacLeod. Cut off his ability to see us coming and that's half the battle."

Catelli grinned broadly. "How do you plan to do that, sir?"

Major Winchester spoke up for the first time. "That's where I come in, Colonel."

Marshal Bradford looked over at Winchester and pointed his swagger stick at her to emphasize his point. "The NAIS folks have a few tricks up their sleeves for us. As a matter of fact, Major, why don't you take Colonel Mulvaney over and show her the new toys you brought with you?"

Winchester gestured to Mulvaney, who followed her towards *The Despiser,* leaving Bradford and Catelli alone. The Marshal drew another deep inhale of cigar smoke, waiting until the two officers had moved out of hearing distance.

"Colonel Catelli, I want you to understand one thing very clearly. I am in charge of this operation. Based on the orders that came from headquarters intelligence, you were under orders to hand me an incident, something to make it look like the Highlanders had attacked the Prince's force on Northwind. That would have made this a quick little operation. Now I've got my troops tied down here with a war raging only a few jumps away. It was my hope that we'd only be here for a week or two. Now, thanks to your failure, it looks like it's going to be a lot longer."

"I'm sorry, sir, but it's that Capellan troublemaker, Loren Jaffray. He guessed what was going on when we tried to sabotage their 'Mechs. His meddling is one of the things that got us into this mess in the first place. At least I was able to splinter the Highlanders."

"And where is Consul Burns?" the Marshal asked.

"Safely in the Consulate back in Tara."

"I met Drake Burns several years ago when his family got him his appointment to Northwind. He's well connected in the FedCom government, but that's about it."

"Yes, Marshal."

"I'm still going to need your help, Colonel Catelli. For me to simply grab Tara is going to cause some political fallout that neither of us needs in our careers at this point. Not to mention that if I march in there without reason every Highlander in the Inner Sphere will come after us. I need you to provide me another 'incident' that will let me take control of Tara."

"Why is the city so important to you, sir?" Catelli asked, then caught himself quickly. "That is, if you don't mind my asking?"

"What I'm telling you does not travel any further than the two of us. I didn't want Mulvaney to hear this, but the truth of the matter is that we anticipate that the other Highlanders will side with MacLeod in this dispute. When Stirling's Fusiliers land they're expected to be hostile and ready for a fight. If I control Tara, I have a plan that will spell their quick destruction. Once we've crushed two of the Highlander regiments, the First and Second Kearny will probably capitulate without a fight. Northwind will be ours."

Catelli listened intensely and nodded. "I assure you, Marshal, that when I'm done, not a person in the Inner Sphere will question your moving in and taking over Tara." *And if I do it right, I can pave the way for my own reign as governor, if not more.*

The Marshal continued to watch as Mulvaney and Winchester finally reached the DropShip. "Do you think she truly trusts us, Colonel?"

"Yes, sir. I do."

"Good. I don't want her to question that. It's vital to this operation that Tara be under my control and that we defeat both MacLeod's Regiment and the Fusiliers. It's your job as our intelligence operative on Northwind to hand me the justification to take control of Tara, no ifs, ands, or buts. Second, I want you to control Mulvaney. The last thing we need is for her to begin questioning us or her loyalties."

Catelli crossed his arms, his smile getting even broader. "Don't worry, sir. I can handle 'Colonel' Mulvaney."

= 21 =

Tilman River Valley
Northwind
Draconis March, Federated Commonwealth
25 September 3057

Loren settled back in the command couch of the *Gallowglas* and shifted his lower body, trying to get comfortable. He was very tired, but hadn't been able to get back to sleep ever since a nightbird or some other nocturnal animal had awakened him by flying or dropping against the viewport of his cockpit. It was 0400 hours, but the frustration over losing sleep had him more awake than tired.

Like many MechWarriors on campaign, Loren preferred to bed down in his 'Mech than in a field tent with the support crews. For him a 'Mech cockpit was a safe cocoon, much safer than a durlon tent on the ground. Most BattleMech cockpits were designed to support long-term operations and the *Gallowglas* was no exception, with an ample freshwater reserve and a command couch that could be semi-reclined. Even if the 'Mech was powered down Loren would be able to start up quickly should the need arise.

But that wasn't likely. He'd already been held back after no less than three strategy sessions. Rather than attempt to reach his lance, Loren had accepted Major Huff's offer of a position near the regimental HQ. It was one of the safest spots in a field regiment, less than sixty meters from the mobile command post.

After reaching the river they'd begun the march southwest with no activity from the downed DropShip, though the ship immediately repulsed several flyby attempts by the handful of Highlander fighters still on Northwind with barrages of long-range missile and PPC fire. A lone infantry DropShip usually wasn't a major threat, but Loren didn't dismiss it so easily. Considering that the fleet at the nadir point was a possible decoy, someone had gone to a great deal of trouble to get this ship smuggled through to Northwind unmolested. Anyone who took such pains was up to something.

He stared through the tinted glass of his viewport into the early morning darkness, in the distance making out the rough shapes of the regimental field HQ's trucks and transports. Their lights had been dimmed and special thermal tarps stretched over the vehicles to help cloak them from infrared scanning. Even the microwave dish on top of the communications van was draped in camouflage webbing. Loren saw several other 'Mechs in the distance, most hidden under the thick cover of the trees.

Thinking about Catelli and Mulvaney, who they'd yet to engage, Loren sat staring blankly through the viewport. Then he reached out to turn on the small secondary monitor that would give him a long-range map of the region. The regimental HQ downloaded information every few minutes to show the latest intelligence on both MacLeod's and the Davion task forces, including their estimated positions. The light from the display cast a greenish glow in the cockpit and only made him feel even more awake. Though MacLeod had sent a few light recon lances out into the night to probe the area ahead of them, they had still not encountered their targets.

Loren had no desire to fight Chastity Mulvaney. He could understand what she had done, now that he'd thought more about it. Rather than see the Highlanders fall prey to infighting, she'd given the pro-Davionists a way to channel their strong emotions. It was a daring move that he respected.

Colonel MacLeod's rules of engagement, on the other hand, were much harder for him to swallow. The Colonel had ordered his people to avoid killing Highlanders who'd gone over to Mulvaney, saying their job was simply to contain and defeat them. That kind of sentimentality had been bred out of Loren by his Commando training. In the same circumstances he'd have crushed Mulvaney back there at the spaceport. Perhaps some things about the Highlanders he would never understand.

Colonel Catelli, on the other hand, was another matter entirely. Loren had sensed that MacLeod's warriors were ready to vent their frustrations by destroying the Consul Guards and their commanding officer. Ever since the landing of the Davion DropShip, rumors had run rampant that a full-scale invasion of Northwind was underway. But from the talk he heard, Loren knew that the Highlanders would meet any Davion troops or 'Mech reinforcements with fierce resistance. It was very likely the Davions were not prepared for the kind of unprecedented opposition the Northwind Highlanders could muster.

He studied the map readout on the screen and pulled up information on the Tilman River from his tactical system. In the darkness of the cockpit he projected the narrow fords and areas that had been classified as rapids. He studied the positioning of The Castle and then extended the view of the map to show the long, north-south spine of the Rockspire Mountains. While MacLeod and Huff continued to believe that Mulvaney would go to ground at The Castle, Loren continued to disagree. He'd read up on The Castle's tactical advantages and knew that the fortress offered incredible defensive capability to anyone who wanted to dig in for a long prolonged fight. But the move was too obvious, the choice of The Castle too logical. Loren was more than ever convinced that Mulvaney would not try to dig in there. *She's a fighter, not a defender. That's her style and she's not about to change now.*

Jaffray shut off the map and rubbed his eyes. *Sleep. Engagement with the Davions is only a dozen hours away at best, and here I sit fighting the one thing I'm going to need most.* He glanced through the viewport again to check the area one more time. Outside his 'Mech the skies over Northwind offered their starry vista. How ironic that he was here, in a Highlander 'Mech, staring up at a Northwind night. His grandfather would have given almost anything to spend just such a night on this soil. Now the grandson that he'd raised almost as his own child was fulfilling his dream. But with a dark twist.

Loren knew that part of the reason he couldn't sleep was because of thoughts about his real reason for being on Northwind. He was to deprive Davion of one of his prize merc units and destroy the very people he was supposed to be helping fight for their independence. These dark thoughts gnawed at the back of his mind. Loren didn't waver from his duty, but it was not easy facing the shadows it cast on his soul.

As he stared out into the forest, Loren saw a faint image, more a movement than a defined shape, shifting in the darkness on the ground near the communications van. At first he barely noticed it, then he sat straight up in the seat and tried to find the shape he'd seen. *Probably nothing more than a sentry on patrol.* Then he saw it again, a shadow in the early dawn gloom, moving near the feet of a nearby *Phoenix Hawk*. He trailed the shape as it moved quickly from bush to bush.

Then his tension level suddenly rose. Why would a sentry be trying to hide in the midst of his own field headquarters? The answer was simple. He wouldn't. *Damn!* Not even taking the time to put on his cooling vest, Loren reached for his neurohelmet and pulled it on. Something was wrong and, thus far, no one had discovered the deadly threat.

"HQ, this is Command Security Four. Security alert at the HQ," he reported tersely as he hit the preheat switch overrides to his fusion reactor. There was not enough time for a controlled startup. If he was going to act quickly he would have to bypass most of the safety formalities.

"Com Sec Four, this is HQ Two. Say again. We aren't showing any problems here," the duty officer said coldly.

"Compound security has been compromised. Enemy infantry in the base!" Loren reached over to his wide-band communications switch. If the headquarters duty officer wasn't going to act, he would sound an all-out alert himself. He tossed the switch, but got no further than that because a series of explosions suddenly lit up the early morning darkness. The shock of the blast shook the *Gallowglas*, and the burst of light, though suppressed by the cockpit glass, made it difficult for his eyes to adjust.

"This is Major Jaffray. Enemy infantry in the headquarters!" he transmitted while watching the fireball rise up into the trees, burning the overhanging branches. The massive blasts had taken out three small trucks and the main communications van. The huge van was gutted in the middle as if a giant creature had taken a bite out of it. Flames and smoke rose from the massive rip and the light from the fires showed a number of big shapes on the ground. The tree branches over the van crackled as the fireball rose.

A message flashed across his primary monitor warning of possible gyro imbalance if he proceeded with a hot start-up of the 'Mech. Loren cleared the error message and pulled all his heat sinks on line at the same time. Ignoring the audible warnings that blared inside his neurohelmet, he ran a short-range scan and saw that the area around him was alive with targets. Slightly larger than humanoid and metallic. Slowly at first, then somewhat faster, he moved the *Gallowglas* forward to the communications van. He was in mid-stride when the mobile HQ van erupted in a deadly blast of explosives. The fireball from the explosion lit up the night and rose upward like a death plume.

MacLeod! Damn! The concussion of the explosion buffeted Loren's 'Mech and he fought a spinning sensation in his head to keep the 'Mech upright. Pieces of the van danced off the legs of the *Gallowglas* as he lurched it to a standing posture. Loren switched on his heads up display and began a sweep of the area. Suddenly in front of him he saw one of the large figures turn and face him. *Power armor!* The attackers were wearing the Inner Sphere equivalent of the Clan's Elemental suits. Infiltrator suits, that's what the inner Sphere Warriors called them. Though carrying less firepower and lacking some of the internal defense capabilities of Clan models, the suits were very deadly at close range. Loren's targeting sights had just lined up with the armored trooper when suddenly the infantryman fired his jump jets and streaked straight at Loren's cockpit.

Unable to get a weapons lock, Jaffray twisted the *Gallowglas* slightly, unsure of how to deal with the new threat. He'd only read about these infantry; Capellan military training did not include power armor or Elemental combat. As the trooper rose in front of him, Loren switched to his weapons joystick and swung an arm at his attacker. The back side of the 'Mech's massive hand struck the armored infantryman in mid-air, sending him flying madly into the trees. The impact barely slowed the momentum of the arm in its sweep.

Across the clearing, under the light of the destroyed field headquarters vehicles, Loren saw three of the power armored infantry fire their twin short-range missiles in unison at a *Phoenix Hawk* as its pilot tried to coax the machine to life. The missiles streaked upward and slammed into the chest and head of the *Hawk,* sending the 'Mech staggering backward from the damage. Flames licked across its torso. A cockpit hit was bad enough, but the pilot had been attempting to power up at the time and the impacts had thrown off his or her balance. The *Phoenix Hawk* lost its fight for survival and staggered backward into the treeline, shattering several trees as it fell.

Without thinking of the damage he was about to unleash, Loren targeted one of the power armored troopers with his sights and triggered the primary target interlock circuit on his weapons joystick. The *Gallowglas* fired both its medium pulse lasers in a torrent at the lone human target. A 'Mech's weapons were designed to take on other BattleMechs or fortified positions. Even with the protection of power armor, there was no chance of survival for a lone individual. The trooper twisted under the barrage and seemed to melt into the ground under the withering hail of death and destruction. Loren was so shocked by the image that he barely noticed the quaking explosions from where the *Phoenix Hawk* had fallen.

A short-range missile raced over the debris of the communications van and slammed into the *Gallowglas*'s right torso. Loren felt the 'Mech vibrate under the impact as he tried in vain to target his attacker. In the distance he saw the darkened outline of an axe-wielding *Scarabus* stagger to life against the power-suited troopers. Its medium and small lasers scarred the night as the 'Mech ran off after a squad of the power infantry, mowing one of the them down as the rest scattered in jump flight. Loren's attention was shattered as

188 Blaine Lee Pardoe

several grenade launchers opened fire on his cockpit from the trees nearby. *They're playing for keeps—and so am I.*

His short-range sensor displays told him that a total of four troopers were firing at him from the trees. Their shots ate at his armor, but what concerned him more was the way they were slowly tracking their shots at the cockpit head of the *Gallowglas*. Loren locked on to the closest pair and fired his medium pulse lasers again. The barrage of red laser bursts tore through the dense leaves and into the trees. Several larger limbs exploded as the hot lasers made them erupt like volcanoes. One of the troopers dropped, either hit or having lost balance. The others continued to fire at Loren with renewed vigor. A rain of machine gun shells danced off his viewport, making him jerk back reflexively.

There was a flash of light from above and Loren saw one of the massive power armored troopers jumping down onto his 'Mech from above and behind. It landed on his forward left shoulder and dug into the 'Mech's head with its massive, claw-like hand. For the first time in a long time Loren felt a wave of panic overtake him. He'd faced death so many times and been trained to ignore the fear, but suddenly, here in this Northwind forest, he thought he might die. Images of what Mulvaney must have faced during her encounter with the armored Clan Elementals rose in his mind. He would not die, not this way, not now.

The problem was that the infiltrator was out of reach. Loren's 'Mech arms and hands were unable to reach the trooper as it meticulously began to rip its way into his cockpit. Loren tried to twist to make the trooper lose his balance, but the infantryman was secure in his position. Time was running out and Loren's mind raced to find a way to remove the infiltrator before his comrades also leaped into the battle.

Just past the infiltrator was the massive shoulder armor extension of the *Gallowglas*. Acting more on instinct than logic Loren quickly raised the 'Mech's right arm. The shoulder plate extension dropped down and slammed into the trooper from behind. If not for his power suit, the trooper would have been crushed. As it was, the impact knocked him from the "neck" of the *Gallowglas* and then to the 'Mech's massive chest and then down to the ground. Loren scanned to fire, but the wily trooper had managed to escape before he could track him. *Next time I'll show him what the bottom of a 'Mech's foot looks like.*

Loren thought of charging the *Gallowglas* into the rest of the power armored troops hidden among the trees. He envisioned swatting and pulling them out of the treetops, but a check of his short-range scanner told him it would be a death trap. Trying to maneuver among those huge old trees would destroy his mobility and he would quickly be swarmed by the infiltrator suits nearby.

There was another way. More brutal, but more effective.

Loren targeted one of the infiltrators just preparing to jump, then triggered a volley from his Tiegart Magnum PPC. The weapon let go its deadly blue bolt of charged energy, which shot into the trees like a wide swath of bright lightning. The shot was off by at least a meter from being a direct hit, but was close enough to destroy the trooper. A secondary arc from the charged particle stream sliced into the infantryman, setting off his ammunition in a series of explosions. Loren ignored the fallen form as it jerked under the blasts like the body of a newly beheaded chicken.

He swept the *Gallowglas*'s targeting sight to the left as two other infiltrators jumped into flight, back and away from Loren. Firing his Sunglow large lasers, he saw one shot go wide. The other, however, seemed to nick one of the troopers in mid-flight. A wave of heat rose into the cockpit and the automatic cooling fans kicked in, pulling the hot air out, but Loren ignored their wailing. The heat severed the trooper's leg at the hip and sent him spinning wildly toward the ground. The other dropped quickly into the distant treeline and disappeared into the night.

Then it was over.

Much as it had begun, the attack ended in a blanket of deadly silence. Loren switched to a long-range scan and surveyed what was left of the regimental headquarters. All five of the primary command and control vehicles that were the heart and soul of the regimental HQ were in flames. Infantry were trying to put out the fires, but it was too late. Survivors were huddled near several of the larger trees. From what Loren saw, there was little or no chance of survival for those who might still be trapped in the vans. In the distance the entire regiment seemed to come to life. There was weapons fire coming from the woods nearby as MacLeod's Regiment tried to stop the power-armored raiders, but it was a futile effort. The damage had been done.

"Command Staff, this is Command One. Fall in on my signal," came a voice Loren was relieved to hear. That of Colonel William MacLeod. Loren locked onto the signal of the transmitting BattleMech nearly a kilometer away from the burning HQ and began to move toward the position of the Highlander commander.

Two platoons of Highlander infantry and several assault BattleMechs ringed the ruins of the command post as Colonel MacLeod and his remaining command staff officers toured. The cool dawn was still pitch black except for the bright spotlights of the security 'Mech aimed in and around the destroyed vehicles. It was almost an hour since the attack, and though the fires were out, most of the Highlanders were shocked that their foe had attacked their command post, achieving almost total surprise.

MacLeod stopped at the remains of the regimental command van and stroked his beard as he stared at it. "Thank the stars I wasn't able to sleep, or they would've gotten me too."

"Our losses were remarkably low," Major Huff reported. "We have twenty-six wounded and twelve dead. Four of our 'Mechs sustained some critical damage, but the other eight suffered only minor damage. From what Dumfries' intelligence boys have been able to verify, nine enemy troops were killed. My guess is that they must've been gunning for you all along in this operation, sir." Huff had been sleeping in a tent a mere twenty meters from the van when it blew up. His short-cropped blond hair was singed and his eyebrows were burned off. He was lucky to be alive.

Loren shook his head. "I don't think the Colonel was their main target. This looks more like an attempt to cut off our communications and command control capability. From the looks of it, I'd say it was pretty damn successful."

"What's the word on Lieutenant Gomez, Major?" MacLeod asked, still staring at the rubble of his command.

Huff looked down. "Pretty iffy, sir. Our medics say she

might lose the leg." Loren had heard that Gomez was one of the handful who'd survived the explosion in the van.

"She's tough as nails. She'll pull through this. Her grandmother was one hell of a MechWarrior and went through a lot worse. It's in her blood to survive."

"Knowing her, she'll be demanding a place in the line even before the painkillers wear off," Huff said.

Colonel MacLeod turned to the small cadre of officers standing around him. "Enough of this little tour. Who hit us and how in the name of the Star League did they get past our security?"

Huff motioned to what Loren thought was a mound of debris from the blast. In the stark glare of the spotlights the image was more shadow than substance. As the entire officer party moved closer he saw the remains of one of the power-suited troopers who'd attacked the post. It was one of those he'd killed with his medium pulse lasers. The armored suit was charred nearly black, with several gaping holes that had totally penetrated the suit. An arm, manipulative claw and all, lay severed next to the victim.

"Captain Dumfries checked out the bodies. They're apparently all part of the First NAIS Training Cadre. From what we can tell from the analysis of their suits, the suits are made of materials that don't show up on active or passive scanners until they are right on top of you. They simply walked into our camp right under our noses."

MacLeod did not lift his eyes from the dead trooper. "Well, it looks like it's finally begun. I was hoping for a more up-front fight, but it's a start at least."

"I'm surprised that Major Mulvaney had anything to do with this kind of attack," one of the support officers said. "This kind of sneaky operation brings her no honor. It's not the way we Highlanders do things." *We. Highlanders.* Loren could almost see the bond as if it were something tangible or physical that he could touch. *Even when on opposite sides of a fight the bond between them is there.*

MacLeod's face seemed to snap to a dark expression of anger. "Chastity Mulvaney would never have anything to do with an assassination attempt. This wasn't a strike against me. This was a perfectly legitimate military action, a midnight raid against regimental communications and command, plain and simple. Quit trying to read more into this than there is. This is a *military* operation, and as much as we want to paint it one way or another, we got beat this time. Remember, she's one of us. Blood of our blood. Highlander kin."

"It could have been worse, sir," Huff said. "According to what I've heard, these NAIS cadres are pretty green."

"Don't get your ego all ready for a field promotion, Major. It's time to update your thinking. These 'green' troops penetrated our security net and knocked out our communications back to Tara or to any vessels in orbit. We're blind and deaf except for the immediate vicinity—for now. And, according to the last reports, we were investigating a possible attack force at a jump point. This strike was simply phase one. The real heavies are sure to come for us pretty damn soon."

Huff looked down. "Understood, sir."

"What about Stirling's Fusiliers?" cut in Captain Fitzwalther. "They're due in-system in a few weeks."

"Yes, but this little raid means we can't tell them what's going on. Cat Stirling is a pretty smart cookie, though. If she plays this by the book she'll take our lack of communications as a warning that not all is calm and peaceful here. That will give her a heads-up, but not much more."

MacLeod's voice took on a deeper, graver tone. "What worries me most is that we don't know what the Davions are up to. Without our long-range communication and planetary satellite-feed relays we won't know when they arrive, where, or how many of them are coming at us."

"Recommendations, sir?" Huff asked.

"We still have battalion-level communications gear. This strike has cut us off until we deploy relays back to Tara. I want you to detail some troops, break out the gear, and have Third Battalion's Signal Platoon start getting us back in contact with the city. It's going to take a few days before we're back up and running, but this is only a temporary setback. What I'm worried about is what they'll be doing while we're blinded. We may be looking at a whole new conflict."

"So what's next, sir? Do we just throw in the towel?" Huff's question was sarcastic at best, just enough to pass MacLeod's scrutiny.

But the words only made the commanding officer of the Northwind Highlanders smile broadly. "Surrender? The Highlanders? Never. Let me answer you with a question. If you were Catelli and had just coordinated an attack designed to cripple our logistics and command control capabilities, what would be the last thing you'd expect us to do?"

There was a long pause, and then it was Loren who broke the silence. "After the damage we just took the last thing anyone would expect is for us to launch some sort of an attack."

"Precisely," MacLeod said and began to outline his operation in the humid near-darkness of the morning under the searchlights of the flanking BattleMechs.

22

Tilman River Valley
Northwind
Draconis March, Federated Commonwealth
29 September 3057

"What were the results of the attack, sir? Do we have any news from Winchester?" Chastity Mulvaney asked.

"According to her preliminary report, the Highlanders' mobile HQ and comm vehicles have been taken permanently out of action," Marshal Bradford told her. "She also reports the Highlanders suffered heavy losses in the raid. Thus far everything is going as I planned." Marshal Bradford's voice was calm despite the implications of what he was saying.

Mulvaney looked out over the river, and felt her heart sink. She couldn't help but feel responsible for those deaths, directly or indirectly. Hadn't she been the one whose information had made the raid possible? Those people were her friends. *Have I made the right choice? God, I hope the Colonel's all right.* Surprisingly she found herself hoping that Loren Jaffray had also managed to survive the attack.

Marshal Bradford smiled thinly and gave Catelli a knowing glance across the small table. "I know what you must be feeling, Colonel Mulvaney."

"Do you, sir?" she said.

"Yes, you're feeling guilty for helping plan a raid on your former comrades. That's a tough one. But you can't give in to those feelings. This is a military operation. The raid was a legitimate military strike. If we hadn't gotten the information from you, we'd have gotten it from someone else. The end result would have been the same."

"That doesn't mean I have to like it," she snapped back.

"I don't want you to be confused on this matter, Colonel Mulvaney. You work for the Federated Commonwealth. There is no room for divided loyalties. You had better get your priorities straight here and now. Your former CO is directly and blatantly defying orders from his superior officer and his liege lord. We are on a mission to cripple and disable MacLeod's Regiment, period."

"I'm more than aware of my priorities," she said coldly.

"As a subordinate officer you had better learn to curb your tongue, Mulvaney. I'm not a Highlander officer and I will be addressed according to my rank and position. Do you understand?"

"Yes, sir. I understand, Marshal," Mulvaney said, regaining her composure. "I am in favor of crippling MacLeod's ability to fight, but I do not approve of assassination attempts on him or his command staff. Such actions will only solidify the resistance of his troops and produce even greater bloodshed for both sides."

Marshal Harrison Bradford leaned forward across the table and looked her straight in the eye. "This was not an attempt on MacLeod's life. This was a military strike. But know this. I will use any and all means at my disposal to enforce the will of Archon Prince Victor Steiner-Davion. This is a military operation, Colonel. We are not here to win favor or to fight some sort of Clanlike test of honor. You and MacLeod may have an understanding about how you want this battle to be waged, but I am not governed by that."

"Yes, sir." Mulvaney was having a hard time with the pressure she was under. It wasn't just that she was now supposed to be the head of one of the Inner Sphere's most important merc units, but that they were involved in a kind of civil war. The strain was a lot more than anything she'd known as an executive officer. Despite the official orders, she did not feel like the commanding officer of the Highlanders, only terribly, desperately alone. She hadn't wanted to leave Colonel MacLeod and the rest of her command.

She'd had no choice. It was a sacrifice. But whatever happened next, Chastity Mulvaney was determined to prevail. Failure was not in her makeup.

"What will you do next, sir?" she asked.

Bradford Harrison smiled, but his flat grin was one of dominance. Mulvaney was his to manipulate and control, for now at least. "That depends on you and what you think MacLeod's next move might be. I'm not going to assume that any of the key command staff were wiped out. Chances are we only managed to knock out their communications capabilities and inflicted some minor losses. So, Colonel Mulvaney, assuming that MacLeod has survived our first strike, how will your former CO respond?"

Mulvaney pondered the question for a moment, thinking about the Colonel and everything he'd ever taught her. "William MacLeod is an emotional man. The attack on the command post must have infuriated him, and now he's also frustrated by his inability to engage us over the past few days. I'd say that right now he's regrouping while preparing to launch a counterstrike. We have some time, but I'd be willing to bet he'll make his move in the next day or so. I can see him sending his troops into an escalated forward advance and catching us on the flats of the river banks. It'll be his lighter recon lances and 'Mechs. The heavies are going to get tied down in the forest, which will work in our favor."

"He'll hit our rear then," Catelli said.

Chastity shook her head. "Not necessarily. He's pretty crafty and likes keeping his opponent off balance. He might send an advance force to strike at the middle of our column. Given the thick forests and the faster rate of travel along the river banks, he may not have an option, though. I'd reinforce the north bank forces and the rear of the columns."

"Excellent. Now then, what I'd like is for us to be in a position to turn back on him and pound his forces when he engages," the Marshal said.

"With all due respect, Marshal, I don't think such a move is prudent. Even with the help of the NAIS power armor we're still outgunned and outnumbered. The river banks are wide, but cut our ability to bring our full force to bear quickly enough. By the time we turn to flank, MacLeod will have disappeared into the forests. And for each minute we're bogged down trying to engage him, he'll be able to bring more of his heavier and slower 'Mech forces to bear. Engaging him directly when he strikes could turn against us too quickly."

"What is the status of his aerospace elements?" Catelli asked.

The Marshal shuffled through the small stack of papers in front of him, scanning for the right report. Finding it, his tight grin broadened. "Last reports have them on their DropShips about a third of the way to the nadir jump point ... well beyond the point of being able to turn back to help MacLeod. I've ordered our decoy DropShips to hold their position to keep the Highlander ships moving away from Northwind."

"Marshal, aren't you worried about the damage those fighters are going to do to your reinforcements?"

The Davion Marshal's grin didn't fail at all. "Plans are in place to make sure that my unit arrives unscathed, Colonel Mulvaney. Don't worry yourself about the details of that operation. You help us deal with MacLeod's Regiment, and I'll worry about getting reinforcements onto Northwind intact.

"Up until now, this has been a conflict that could be written off as an 'incident.' If MacLeod had capitulated after last night, we could have stopped this whole thing. But if MacLeod launches an attack against loyal FedCom troops, it will be interpreted as outright insurrection."

"So what do you think, Mulvaney? Should we simply continue on toward The Castle?" Catelli asked.

This discussion was becoming more and more painful for Mulvaney, with the future of the Highlanders so obviously at stake. "Yes and no," she said slowly. "We need to plan a surprise or two for MacLeod when he shows up. Bloody his nose a little and let him pull back thinking we're in pursuit. If we do it right he'll believe we're falling into his trap. While he thinks we're coming after him, we move at full speed on to The Castle."

"Any ideas about how to slow him down?" Catelli asked.

For the first time since leaving MacLeod's Highlanders, Chastity Mulvaney smiled. "As a matter of fact I do ..."

* * *

198   Blaine Lee Pardoe

Loren pushed the throttle forward as the *Gallowglas* plowed through the forest growth in virtual darkness. He and the rest of the regimental command security lance had volunteered for the duty of fire support for the raid, a duty he didn't mind. It was, after all, much better than slowly slogging his way through the forest to the river bank over the next day. With any luck they'd be flanking Mulvaney's position on the river by the time Major Huff reached his station.

The battle plan that MacLeod and Huff had pulled together was fairly sound considering the limited resources and time that had gone into planning the operation after the raid. Huff was going to move forward with a full company of light and fast-moving medium 'Mechs and strike at the rear of Mulvaney's columns from both banks of the Tilman River. According to the digital readout in his cockpit, the attack would begin in a matter of minutes.

Meanwhile Fuller's lance with Jaffray in tow was going to move further upriver through the forest. Several minutes after the initial engagement, Huff's force would try to lure Mulvaney off to the southeast. As she fell back the Security Lance would strike them square in their flank from the forest. The pincer move would hopefully crush the rear of their column and lure Mulvaney and Catelli's forces into some sort of a pursuit action ... which would lead them into the bulk of MacLeod's Highlanders.

Colonel MacLeod had again emphasized his rules of engagement. They would deal with Catelli's Consul Guards as hostile foes, no quarter given. As for the renegade Highlanders under Mulvaney's command, the rules were different. Killing was to be avoided if at all possible. Restraint was the watchword. In the heat of battle waged by BattleMechs capable of leveling an entire city, it would be impossible to prevent all losses, but MacLeod hoped to prevent as much senseless destruction as possible. It was almost as though he viewed this as a trial of honor for those who had broken ranks.

Loren ran a short-range scan but did not pick up any signs of the river or of the renegade Highlanders. The tactical map told him he was close, but thus far there was no sign of the enemy. No matter. The battle was at hand. He could feel it, smell it, hear it. It was something his grandfather had called "The Sensation"—a combination of a rush of heat and sweat, a tingle in the fingertips, and a dryness in the throat. Yes, the fighting was about to erupt. Loren reached over and ran another scan, this time finally detecting the edge of the riverbank.

"Go, Maroon. Say again, go Maroon!" came a voice over the commline. The code words from Huff's command indicated that he was engaging the rear vanguard of Mulvaney and Catelli's force. Even though the fight was at least four kilometers distant, the signal only confirmed The Sensation. Loren's heart raced faster. Per the plan, he and the rest of the Security Lance halted their advance and turned toward the river. There they were to wait a full five minutes, scanning the forest around them, ready to rush to the river and directly into the flank of Mulvaney's task force.

The pause was enough to bring Loren to the edge of a frenzy. He ran a high-level diagnostic on his *Gallowglas* to make sure the trek through the forest hadn't undone any of the work done by the Highlander techs. The only problems seemed minor. Despite its battleworn appearance, the 'Mech was more than ready to engage.

"Go, Gold. Security Lance Code Gold! Go, Gold!" Lieutenant Fuller's voice boomed. The time had finally come.

The forest was dense and every step toward the river bank required the pilots to use their war machines as gigantic wedges, plowing their way through the trees and thick undergrowth. Loren's short-range scanners picked up several heat images as they neared the river, and the computers identified them as a lance of Galleon light tanks as he closed on the targets. Loren picked up several other confused readings at the maximum range of his sensors, but could not yet determine what they were. It didn't matter at this point. He and the rest of the lance would know soon enough.

The *Gallowglas* broke through the wall of trees and onto the bright sands of the river bed, and it was obvious that the attack was going well. The lance of Galleon tanks was just downriver from Loren's position and moving in a zigzag motion that let them occasionally turn and fire at the advance 'Mechs of Huff's attack force. The light conventional tanks were not the only vehicles moving into view. Five

Pegasus scout hover tanks skimmed across the surface of the Tilman, managing to keep Huff's force from totally overrunning Mulvaney and her Davion allies. Loren could tell that the tanks had not detected his Security Lance as it moved to cut off their retreat.

Then the sensors came alive with magnetic anomaly readings consistent with the containment fields of fusion reactors—'Mech engines. He turned and saw that Mulvaney and Catelli were sending reinforcements after Huff and the Security Lance. Four light and medium 'Mechs were approaching downriver, giving Fuller's Security Lance only a few short minutes to act.

"Concentrate your fire on those hovercraft and the Galleons," came Fuller's voice over the comm channel. "When I give the word we turn and hit those babies. Have at 'em, boys and girls!" Loren leveled his extended-range PPC and blasted at one of the two Pegasus hover tanks moving across to the far side of the river to flank Huff's troops. Ten years ago the hovercraft would have been out of range, but the new modifications to his PPC let Loren hit his target. The brilliant blue energy blast sheared both the hovercraft and the water, sending an explosive spray of steam and boiled-off armor into the air. The impact was so powerful that the course of the Pegasus diverted to the shore line where the craft collided with a tree stump, abruptly slamming it to a drifting halt.

The Davion Pegasus and its sister craft now knew that the Security Lance was there. Fuller's *Shadow Hawk* fired its jump jets and rose to meet the Galleons as they also turned to face the threat of the Security Lance. The Davion tanks and hovercraft could see that it made more sense to take on the four 'Mechs of the Security Lance than fight the full company of Huff's light BattleMechs nipping at their heels.

Loren fired his PPC again, this time feeling the full wash of heat in the cockpit as the weapon discharged. This shot hit the same craft squarely in the side as it turned upriver to face its assailant. There was a brilliant flash of light as the armor exploded off the Pegasus, showering down onto the river. The wounded hovercraft teetered slightly in the middle of its turn as the driver fought to control the craft. *The driver knows the fight is almost over for him,* Loren thought. *Now it's only a question of whether he can survive or not.*

Frutchey and Fuller had accidentally concentrated their fire at the approaching lead Galleon, raining a barrage of laser, missile, and cannon fire down on the small tank. The tank twisted under the explosions as if it were made of wax and been tossed into a cauldron. It exploded, its remains showering onto its sister tanks. The Galleons continued to press onward into the fire of the rest of the Security Lance.

From upriver Loren's sensors told him that the Davion/Mulvaney reinforcements were still closing, but were moving somewhat slower than he would have expected. He leveled his PPC at the Pegasus he'd been battering and targeted it. As the crosshairs locked onto the craft Loren found himself wishing he could somehow spare the crew. This was not a fair fight, a 'Mech against a much lighter hovercraft. Even in a normal tank he would outmass the lighter Consul Guard vehicle and could easily outgun the smaller machine. For the driver and his crew, continuing the attack was suicide. By now the driver's own sensors would be registering the weapons lock of Loren's PPC. If there was a time for him to surrender, it was now.

Still the Pegasus did not flee. Instead the driver did exactly the opposite, accelerating to cut across the river, swinging into a direct intercept with Loren's *Gallowglas*. The move caught Loren off guard, but he knew that couldn't be its intent. He held his fire. *What in the name of the Liao is he up to? I could see one driver and crew seeking a glorious death in a pitched fight, but this is just a raid. And it's not just one, but all of them pushing into us. Why? Unless he knows something we don't ...*

"Trap!" Loren transmitted to every friendly 'Mech that could hear him.

23

Tilman River Valley
Northwind
Draconis March, Federated Commonwealth
29 September 3057

"It's a trap!" Loren hissed. He'd no more than uttered the words when he saw the deep waters of the Tilman open up as a lance of heavy 'Mechs rose out of them.

"Maroon and Gold Leaders, heavies in the river." He fired his PPC at the approaching *Pegasus*, hitting it squarely in the turret. The hover tank vaporized just as it was about to pass the concealed 'Mechs, its magazine of short-range missiles exploding all at once, disemboweling the craft and turning it inside out in a massive ball of fire and black smoke.

The heavy 'Mechs rose out of the water to standing positions and slowly moved forward, opening fire on Frutchey and Fuller with a full spread of missiles and lasers. A renegade Highlander *Mauler* locked onto Loren's *Gallowglas* with a barrage of long-range missiles and a pair of large lasers. The warning siren of the target lock had given Loren barely a moment to react by turning his 'Mech slightly into the incoming wave of fire. Only a handful of the missiles actually hit him, striking the *Gallowglas* in the upper right torso and battering the armor plating there. One of the large laser shots went wide alongside his cockpit, while another dug deeply into his center torso near the fusion reactor.

Loren's 'Mech reeled, stepping to the side and backward at the impact and the recoil of the exploding armor. *They must have used underwater ledges to hide their reactor signatures ... pretty damned tricky.*

The image of the 'Mechs rising from the water stirred Loren more than he knew. He remembered his own trap during the recent exercise on Krin for a moment, then his thoughts turned to his father. The two had never been close. As a Death Commando himself, Loren's father had been absent more than not, leaving the boy's upbringing to his grandfather. He had died in the line of duty when Loren was still a child, and for the rest of his life Loren never forgave his father for not returning. The memory rose now like a ghost from a grave.

His father had died fighting underwater.

Loren throttled his 'Mech to top speed and darted down the river bank toward what was left of the Galleon lance. Being on dry land, he could move his machine at a run, but the 'Mechs wading from the water were still moving slowly against the force of it.

Two PPC shots followed him but missed as he ran. He turned slowly to see exactly what he and the rest of the Security Lance were facing. The ambushing lance consisted of a *Mauler*, a *Caesar*, an *Axman*, and a *Marauder II*. It was the last 'Mech, the one closest to him, that caught Loren's attention. From the paint scheme and the model of the machine he knew both BattleMech and MechWarrior all too well. *Mulvaney!* Her 'Mech's massive PPCs turned toward him. *She's mine!* he exulted, partly from rivalry and partly because he hoped to break the spirit of the Highlander renegades by besting her. Loren did not want to see her dead, merely stopped. For some reason that he could not measure or touch, he wanted Chastity Mulvaney to live and survive.

Loren's communication system barked to life. "Major Jaffray," came the voice over the cockpit speaker. "I lost to you once in a test of honor. Are you read for a reversal of fortune?" Mulvaney's voice filled the small space, cutting through the hot humid air like a stiff breeze. Loren twisted his torso to dodge a pair of SRMs fired from the ambushers, but never lifted his gaze from the *Marauder*'s image. He admired Mulvaney's bravado and couldn't help thinking that she'd have made a superb Death Commando.

"If it's a fight you want, you've got it, lady. Prepare for a repeat of our last match," he said. Rather than simply turning and firing, Loren brought his jump jets on line and tied them to the foot pedal controls. Throttling full forward he leaped the BattleMech upward into the sky over the Tilman River. It was going to be a short jump, but his battle with Mulvaney would be up close and personal. If anybody was going to face Mulvaney in combat he wanted it to be him.

But the jump was only one of the bold actions he was going to have to make. In less than a heartbeat he came up with a plan. One that involved risk, a fight in or around the deep waters of the Tilman River. A chill ran down his spine at the thought. Loren did not like fighting under water. The hardest thing he had ever done was in the training exercise just prior to this mission. But this would be different if it worked. A contest of skills in the water. *I won't end up like him . . . like my father. I won't die the way they said he did.*

Most MechWarriors, when they know that someone is attempting to jump on them, would fire and wait till the last minute to move and throw off their attacker. Loren was surprised when Mulvaney fired her *Marauder*'s jump jets as well. Her 'Mech was still below him as it slowly rose out of the river and into the air. Loren pushed his jets even harder and the heat in the cockpit rose by five degrees. His eyes stung from the sweat inside his neurohelmet as he rose over the *Marauder II*.

Mulvaney was rising slightly, trying to back up to keep Loren in front of her. *I can't fight her using a normal attack. She's too foxy for that. If I want to take her down, I've got to do it in the water. I have to take us both down.* Loren remembered his grandfather the day he had told the young Loren of his father's death. Corwin Jaffray had spoken of his own experiences fighting underwater and that the risks were great. Loren had since learned them firsthand, each time having to face down his fear anew. This time the fear was stronger than ever.

He began the rapid descent at the same time Mulvaney pushed the *Marauder* upward, the two BattleMechs colliding in mid-air over the deep waters of the Tilman River. As soon as they made contact Loren seized the *Marauder II* in a death hug, then cut off his jump jets totally. It was a bold move bordering on suicidal but did succeed in catching Mulvaney off guard. Her jump jets could support one 'Mech but never two. The two massive war machines dropped into the deep waters of the Tilman River with a thundering splash.

The combined impact first with Mulvaney and then the water tossed Loren's body to the limits of the seat restraints in his cockpit. The shoulder buckles dug deeply into his flesh and he thought for a moment that he might have dislocated his shoulder. The bubbling water and rush of mud and dirt outside his 'Mech cut visibility down to less than a meter. He was entwined with Mulvaney and the two of them were still dropping straight down, plunging toward the bottom of the river.

By the time they hit bottom, Mulvaney's *Marauder II* was on top of him, driving the *Gallowglas* like a stake into the deep mud and broken rocks of the river bottom. Warning lights on his secondary monitor told Loren that the landing had ruptured his 'Mech's right leg and that the jump jets there were registering as off-line. *Damn, no quick way out of here even if I was able to get to standing.*

Crushed between the bulk of the *Marauder II* and the river bottom, he tried to check his targeting and tracking systems but found them quirky, going on and off line and unable to get a lock. They'd landed in a deep chasm in the middle of the river, the steep walls around them only eight meters apart and at least twenty meters high. *So that was how Mulvaney and her force had remained hidden so long.* The steep drop-off to the river bottom was more than enough to cloak her forces. From the ledge up above they could simply walk out of the water.

With all his strength Loren worked the throttle, foot pedals, and joysticks of the *Gallowglas,* hoping to roll the *Marauder II* off of him. The temperature in the cockpit was stifling despite the cooling river all around him and he strained against the controls to get his 'Mech free. Mulvaney's bird-like *Marauder* punched wildly trying to stand upright, in the process digging several deep gouges into his torso armor and further entangling the two 'Mechs.

All Loren's efforts to free himself failed. Each time he managed to move, kick, or punch at Mulvaney he took damage himself. *Is this what it was like for my father? Was he trapped like I am now?* And a deeper thought tore at Jaffray as he struggled. *Did he think of me?*

He saw three possibilities. One was to continue this slow grinding wrestle on the river bottom until either he or Mulvaney managed to cripple the other or flood the other's cockpit. The second was to begin firing wildly at the *Marauder* entangled on top of him. His large lasers and medium pulse lasers could hardly miss at point blank range. But Mulvaney would be forced to respond in kind. While her PPCs were too close to use, she still carried more than enough of an arsenal to send him to a watery grave. *She must be having the same thoughts because she's held her fire thus far as well. Neither of us wants to die here.*

No, the first two options were not viable. Most reassuring, Loren felt that for the first time Mulvaney wanted him to live as well. He knew that they were two sides of the same coin, he and Chastity. Together they were honor. Each fulfilled it in their own way. She sought to honor what she believed was the true heritage of the Highlanders. Loren sought to fulfill the honor of succeeding in his mission for the Chancellor.

"Mulvaney, this is Jaffray," he said into his microphone. The audio system crackled from the interference and the powerful magnetic pull of the rock formations nearby.

"I was wondering how long it would take you to call," she replied cockily.

"We're both mired down here. If we work together we can get free."

"Agreed." Her tone of voice was flat. Loren could feel the anger and frustration in that single word.

Best to lower the tension—for now. "My congratulations on your ambush. You won this one." He tried to fill his voice with sincerity, like a knight of old saluting a fellow warrior.

"I can't take all the credit. Marshal Bradford thought this would grind your pursuit to a halt. But enough small talk, Major. We work together to get free, then we settle this like warriors."

Loren ignored her challenge. *Marshal Bradford? That had to be Harrison Bradford, commander of the Third Royals.* Part of being a Death Commando was to study one's foe and Loren knew all the names and postings of the Federated Commonwealth's general officers. "What do we do first?" he asked, adjusting the sensors to compensate for the distortion from the ledge.

"Let's get standing and then go to the surface. I've already spent two hours under water waiting for you to arrive. And I've got to admit I have no desire to see the results of a cockpit hit under these conditions, if you catch my drift."

"I do. I wouldn't look forward to a cockpit rupture down here either, but I assure you it wouldn't be me who took the hit."

"Don't get too bold, Loren. I have no intention of losing to you in combat again. If anyone was to die down here, it would be you."

Loren bit his lower lip. *Perhaps this is how my father perished. Maybe it's better to battle to the end than cooperate with a foe, no matter what the risks.* He wanted to tell her off, rebut her challenge, but knew it would not end the matter. There was never merit in pressing a bad position, and she did outgun him considerably. *This is not how it's going to end, not for this Jaffray.* "Let's can this macho crapola. We work together for now. If you want to settle this, let's do it on the surface where the odds are even."

"Fine. You stay still and I'll direct," Mulvaney replied. Her *Marauder* stirred up the mud and muck on the river bottom as she strained to rise, this time not having to fight resistance from Loren's *Gallowglas*.

"Raise your right arm at the shoulder, keep the elbow straight," she ordered. Loren complied and heard a scraping as her left arm pulled free from behind his 'Mech's back. "Now lift your right leg slightly and move it to the outside at the knee." Again Loren complied silently and Mulvaney's 'Mech finally rose to its feet, though it was nearly impossible to see.

Loren once again began the struggle to get the *Gallowglas* upright, and found the effort much less strenuous without Mulvaney crashed on top of him. His 'Mech also rose to its feet and faced her. In the dim light and the swirling mud of the current the *Marauder II* looked like some sort of mythical sea monster. It was perfectly framed by the high walls of the deep chasm into which they'd plunged.

Loren's secondary sensors flared bright red warnings as he squared off against her. Power readings showed energy being charged to her PPCs. She was not waiting to reach the surface. She was going to fire any moment. He reached up to charge his medium pulse lasers, praying that they would cycle before she fired. Then he began to throttle the *Gallowglas* back, fighting the dark unseen current. *At this range her PPCs will be useless unless she kills the field inhibitors.* He'd let her get the upper hand, but it was too late to regret the mistake.

"You caused all of this, just as I knew you would." She lifted her massive PPCs, aimed and fired them at the high chasm walls. Loren struggled to turn the *Gallowglas* so he could move out of the chasm. Again, too late. Chastity triggered the weapons, sending azure beams stabbing into the walls of the underwater chasm. The water in the particle stream vaporized in a wave of hot jetting steam and bubbles that rocked Jaffray in his seat and battered the *Gallowglas* as it continued to fight the current. Two milliseconds later the rocks exploded on both sides of Loren's 'Mech, sending boulders and close to a ton of debris down onto his machine. He tried to move but found himself tightly wedged in. It would take several precious minutes to get free. In the meantime he was a perfect target.

"Damn it, Chastity! What in the name of hell are you doing?" Determined not to go down without a fight, Loren raised his PPC and locked his crosshairs onto Mulvaney as she back away. *Too close!* He fired but the shot went wide. The charged particles hitting the cool water lit up the river bottom like the noonday sun. But only for an instant. A heartbeat passed and blackness surrounded him once more.

"This will have to end now. A matter on the surface requires my attention," Mulvaney said coldly. "You can die here and put an end to your line now, or you can try and follow me. Either way, you'll never be a Highlander ... not as long as I live."

Her message ended in a deadening hiss of static as she started the climb out of the deep underwater valley toward the surface. Loren barely heard her last words. "I want you to know that I could finish you once and for all right now. So, consider this repayment for our fight at The Pub, Jaffray. Next time you choose the place and I'll choose the time. But know this, I can and have beaten you."

"Mulvaney!" Loren cried, but she was already gone. He scanned the bottom of the river and located a way up, a slow and audacious climb. It took a fully twenty minutes for Loren to finally get his *Gallowglas* to the surface of the Tilman. All during the climb Loren ruminated over what had just occurred far beneath the surface of the Tilman. What he'd thought was going to be a life and death struggle had turned out to be nothing of the sort. Mulvaney had simply toyed with him to prove that she could.

Reaching the surface he looked around at what was left of the battle zone. The renegade Highlander *Mauler* stood knee-deep in the river, bent over at a right angle like a broken toy soldier. The 'Mech's arm lasers were gone and its torso was horribly battered. The pilot was still alive, slowly climbing down the leg ladder into the arms of Huff's infantry. The rest of MacLeod's forces were fanned out all across the Tilman, but the fighting was long over. Fuller's Security Lance was hard to find, but Loren spotted it through the cloud of smoke that had been three Galleon and two Pegasus vehicles.

"Command Security Four reporting," Loren transmitted as he and the *Gallowglas* made their way toward his lancemates. Moving forward he saw that the whole lance had taken damage. Some, like Frutchey, had apparently suffered more than others. But all he could think was, *I did it. Where my father failed, I survived. This time at least, history did not repeat itself.*

"Where in the name of Aleksandr Kerensky have you been?" Lieutenant Fuller demanded, as much from concern as irritation.

"Mulvaney and I had an encounter at the bottom of the river. She left me pinned down there. What happened up here?"

"The Consul Guard reinforcements did some heavy damage after you left. We pulled into the clearing with Huff's force, and discovered it was mined. Huff's 'Mech has all but lost its right leg, and two of his lance lost their 'Mechs. Mulvaney crawled out of the river and caught us off guard. Hell, we thought you were dead. She arrived just in time to lead them out of here. I wanted to pursue, but Major Huff said that without intelligence feed from our satellites we'd be risking running into another ambush."

"Damnation," Loren said as he looked around at the battered hulks in the clearing where the mines of Mulvaney's trap had been set. Both were light 'Mechs, but everything from the waist down was missing. The mines were a good trick on her part. Destroy the BattleMechs but let the MechWarriors live. She had honored her code and word.

"You were gone for some time," Fuller asked slowly. "What happened?"

"We 'negotiated.' She let me know that she could beat me if she wanted to," Loren said slowly.

"Let me make sure that my gyro's still balanced. You two collide in mid-air in the middle of an ambush, drop to the bottom of a river while a battle rages above you, and you talk?"

"Yes."

"What did she say?"

"She said that the next time I could call the shots." *And she's right. Next time we meet it will be on my terms.* "And something else. She mentioned a name."

"What name?"

"Marshal Bradford. And unless something has changed in the past few days, that means we're facing the veteran forces of Victor Davion's Third Royals Regimental Combat Team as well as those NAIS troops that hit us last night."

"A full RCT, here, on Northwind?"

Loren watched as one of the burning Galleons spewed a cloud of dark black smoke into the bright morning sky. "Probably not yet, but one thing's for sure, before long it's going to get pretty interesting around here."

= 24 =

Federated Commonwealth Consulate Building
Tara, Northwind
Draconis March, Federated Commonwealth
4 October 3057

Consul Drake Burns nervously read through the morning's diplomatic messages at his desk as he had done dozens of times before. With MacLeod's Highlanders off in pursuit of his Consul Guards he felt safe and secure in the neutrality of Tara. The families of the Northwind Highlander regiments had, for the most part, avoided trouble and confrontation. Sleep had been hard to come by for the Planetary Consul, though. He had always envisioned his posting to Northwind as a kind of pastoral vacation. Now it had become a nightmare of revolution and possible retaliation. Burns knew that he would not be able to sleep until MacLeod and his people had finally submitted to Prince Victor's rule, and that seemed like years away.

The briefings of the status of the war did nothing to ease his state of mind. The secession by the former Lyran Commonwealth was literally breaking the spine of most of the Federated Commonwealth garrison units posted there. Many units were splitting apart, while others chose to fight for one side or the other. These conflicts would eventually peter out, but in the process the Federated Commonwealth was fragmenting.

212   Blaine Lee Pardoe

Adding to the politics was the fact that Sun-Tzu Liao had transmitted an announcement that he was granting Northwind the same independent status as he had for the Wolf Dragoons' world of Outreach. It was a blatant attempt to incite trouble, that much Burns knew for sure. But one way or another Northwind was now the center of many forces pulling at it in different directions. The only good thing was that MacLeod wouldn't get word of Liao's pronouncement immediately.

So deep in these thoughts, Burns never heard Lepeta enter the office until the door closed behind him. Stephen Lepeta was Drew Catelli's aide and was filling in while Catelli was off fighting MacLeod. While Drake Burns disliked the Colonel, he found something downright eerie about Lepeta, something dark and brooding. The Consul feared him more than anyone else on staff, but Catelli had always managed to keep Burns from dismissing him.

Some of what Burns found so disturbing in Lepeta was his pale, emotionless expression. Some was his choice of clothing, which always included a long black riding coat. The fact that Lepeta worked directly for Colonel Catelli was the worst part, for the man obviously had neither respect nor regard for Burns but total loyalty to Catelli.

"Good morning, Consul," Lepeta said in his dull monotone.

"Mr. Lepeta, in the future please knock before entering my office," Burns snapped, irritated by the man's stealthy ways.

"It won't happen again," Lepeta replied coldly.

"I assume that you've looked over the dispatches this morning?"

"I reviewed them prior to your arrival this morning. The war is not going well for Prince Victor. Both Marik and Liao are hitting our worlds with overwhelming force. Some of our units are holding out well for now, but it's only a matter of time."

"Indeed. I am trying to have more faith than you and Colonel Catelli. And what is the word from the field? Has our esteemed Colonel managed to evade Colonel MacLeod yet?"

Lepeta seemed almost bored with his duty of reporting. "According to the message from the field that we decoded just a few minutes ago, the expected reinforcements will be arriving in-system today. Colonel Catelli is confident his task force will reach The Castle this afternoon, according to plan. Colonel MacLeod's force is still in pursuit and will not engage our people until after they reach The Castle, far too late to interfere with our plans."

"Excellent! The reinforcements, these Third Royals, where will they be deployed?"

"The force will land here at the spaceport as soon as the breakout from The Castle begins. Once they secure Tara they will deploy to destroy the Highlanders."

Burns' face immediately flushed beet red. "Here, in Tara? You must be mistaken, Lepeta. We've promised Colonel MacLeod and his Highlanders that Tara will remain neutral. Landing that RCT here is a direct violation of that agreement. Is Marshal Bradford aware that such an action will only invite a response from the Highlanders? Perhaps I'd better speak to him directly."

Lepeta nodded slightly, his head bowed slightly and his shoulders slouching. "Marshal Bradford has told Colonel Catelli that he wants his troops garrisoned within Tara. I think it's safe to say that by the time the Third Royals begin their landing on Northwind, the situation in Tara will demand that they land here. By then the Highlanders will already have broken the agreement to treat the city as neutral, and Marshal Bradford will be forced to order the Davion forces to hold Tara for its own protection."

"What are you talking about?" Burns demanded hotly. "Have you learned of some plot or trick on the part of the Highlanders? Are we in some sort of danger? Does Catelli know something I don't?" Drake Burns knew that Drew Catelli had once been a member of MIIO, the Federated Commonwealth's intelligence corps. The thought that he might be withholding information was not a new one, but that didn't make the Consul any less nervous.

Lepeta pulled the Sunburst pulse laser pistol from a hidden fold of his long riding jacket and leveled it at Consul Burns. Drake Burns stared back, his mouth dropping open in disbelief. In that instant Lepeta pulled the trigger slowly and smoothly, sending three bursts of laser light squarely into the forehead of the Planetary Consul. Burns' body was flung back against the leather chair. It slumped there lifelessly to one side without the man ever fully understanding the plot in which he'd become a mere pawn.

"Easier than I thought," Lepeta said, tossing the pistol to the floor. The symbol on its handle glimmered slightly, the insignia of the Northwind Highlanders. "The Colonel needs a pretext to take control of Northwind and Marshal Bradford needs an excuse to land his Royals here." Lepeta surveyed the sprawled body of the former Planetary Consul and nodded in satisfaction. Twice before, he'd failed—once in the attempt to hit MacLeod in the park and once when the Highlanders had discovered that their 'Mechs were sabotaged. But this time he'd succeeded. *I have given the Colonel exactly what he asked for—an excuse for the Davions to take Tara.*

25

Tilman River
Northwind
Draconis March, Federated Commonwealth
4 October 3057

"We've got a new crisis," Colonel Catelli began, addressing the ranking officers of his, Mulvaney's, and Bradford's commands. "Normally, I'd never have called together our key officers with an enemy hot on our butts, but this is important. I received word an hour ago that Planetary Consul Burns was assassinated, apparently by rebellious anti-Davion Highlanders."

"How accurate is the report?" Marshal Bradford asked.

"My aide de camp in Tara is heading up the investigation personally. According to the report he filed with me, a Highlander weapon was found on the scene and he has turned up several witnesses who confirmed that the assailant was wearing the field fatigues of MacLeod's Regiment."

"Damn," cursed Marshal Bradford. "I know some of the Burns family. I was never close to Drake, but he was a good man. So, Colonel Catelli, this makes you the ranking member of the diplomatic staff. It looks like you'll be wearing the hat of both field commander and Consul at large."

"Yes, sir." Catelli suppressed a smile of satisfaction. *This has been all too easy.*

"I don't believe it," Mulvaney said coldly.

216 Blaine Lee Pardoe

Bradford stared at her for a moment before speaking. "What do you mean? The Consul's own staff has implicated the Highlanders in the assassination. They have nothing to gain by making such an accusation."

"I heard the report, sir, but with all due respect that does not mean I have to sit and believe it. It's true we Highlanders can be ruthless in combat. But such a cowardly killing is not the style or in the nature of any Highlander I know."

"Perhaps your former CO has changed the way he operates since your formation of the loyal Davion Highlanders," Catelli offered. "Perhaps Colonel MacLeod ordered the assassination because he thought he would lose to us in the field. I wouldn't rule out this Major Jaffray either. He's a Death Commando and you know what they're capable of. While he's here on Northwind doing who knows what Liao treachery, his own government has launched a war against the Federated Commonwealth. You must admit it's all very logical."

Mulvaney didn't like her people being called loyal Davion Highlanders, like somebody owned them, but now wasn't the time for that discussion.

"Logical is the last thing this killing is," she said. "MacLeod is also the last person in the Inner Sphere to order an assassination. He's direct and he's honorable. He's not a murderer. No sir, I think that this is a trick to make it look like MacLeod's people are to blame for this crime."

"What I know is this," Bradford said, raising his voice to show that he was the one calling the shots, "we made an agreement to keep Tara neutral. Now the Highlanders, either under orders from MacLeod or by an element acting on their own, have violated that agreement. Tara is now without a rightful leader and possibly lacking the ability to govern according to the will of the Archon Prince."

"How will you deal with this new situation, sir?" Catelli prodded, almost as if on cue.

"The Third Royal RCT is due in-system in several hours time. I propose that they divert from a combat landing in the field to a garrison posting in Tara."

"Sir, that's in direct violation of our agreement regarding Tara," Mulvaney protested quickly. "You initially said they'd land near Tara but promised to honor its neutrality.

The presence of the Third Royals in the city will incite those Highlanders still within the city proper. Need I remind you that all this is being done on hearsay evidence, with nothing to back any of this story up? For all we know it wasn't a Highlander who killed Consul Burns but the work of some mad person. It could have been anyone." She shot a quick glance at Colonel Catelli. *You are the only one who stood to profit from the death of the Consul. I might never be able to prove it, but I'd bet my life that you're behind this murder and trying to make sure the Northwind Highlanders take the blame.*

Marshal Bradford seemed to be listening carefully. "What you say does have some merit, Colonel Mulvaney. But there's a war going on and we have to work with the best intelligence at hand. That data points to Highlander involvement in the death of the Planetary Consul and we are sworn to protect Davion interests on this planet. The most effective way to do that is to divert the Third Royals to Tara and have them use the city as their base of operations."

"Sir, such a move would place them at risk. If MacLeod learns of it he'll divert his forces away from us and back to Tara."

Catelli was shaking his head. "I think that Colonel Mulvaney may be incorrect on that assumption, Marshal. Our recon scouts place MacLeod's Highlanders close behind us. They apparently still believe we're going to ground at The Castle. Our intelligence monitoring shows that MacLeod has not yet been able to reestablish communications with The Fort. If our plan goes well we can still tie them down out here for days or longer while landing the Third Royals undetected. If he thinks we're trapped in that old bunker he won't pull his forces away no matter what's happening in Tara—that is, if he ever finds out. Hesitate now, and he'll manage to get a communications link back to Tara and find out about the landing of the Third Royals."

Marshal Bradford nodded in agreement as Catelli finished. "MacLeod is still deaf and blind to what's going on in Tara. The Third Royals will secure the city and protect the loyalist civilians from any other outbursts on the part of MacLeod's Highlanders. MacLeod will probably detect the Third during their final approach, but without his sophisticated communications and regimental tracking gear he won't know their vector or landing coordinates. Once in Tara we'll be able to prevent him from establishing communications with The Fort. Without that link-up he won't be able to spread word of his little rebellion to the other Highlander regiments. From Tara, the Third can move out and keep MacLeod cut off from the city, pinching him when we do finally emerge from hiding."

Mulvaney saw that her argument had failed. "What about Stirling's Fusiliers, sir? They're due back for regimental rotation. Last reports had them still heading for Northwind."

"According to our long-range sensors, a task force of unknown composition emerged three hours ago at a pirate point close to the zenith jump point. It doesn't take an NAIS scientist to figure out that it has to be the Fusiliers; at least three days ahead of our estimates. We hadn't counted on them using a secret jump point, but at least they don't know about the Third Royals. Given the units' relative positions, it's unlikely that Colonel Stirling will detect them. Thus far they've ignored all transmissions made to them and are moving at maximum burn-speed to Northwind and are anticipated to land in eighteen days time. Knowing Cat Stirling's reputation, she'll probably wait to appraise the situation on solid ground rather than jumping in blindly. Or better yet, she'll be waiting for word from MacLeod about where to land ... word we may be able to provide her.

"The only thing we have working for us right now is MacLeod's inability to communicate with her. The Third Royals will be here ahead of the Fusiliers and should be able to land undetected. Once down they can position themselves to prevent the two forces from linking up once Stirling does make planetfall. Mulvaney, you will be critical after they've landed. You must get the Fusiliers to either join us or remain neutral in the fight. Otherwise we'll have no choice but to destroy them."

"Sir, that won't be easy. There's no guarantee that Colonel Stirling will accept Prince Davion's will concerning Northwind. I have no desire to see blood shed, so I'll do what I can. But fighting them will be costly ... for you and Third Royals RCT. Even with Winchester's NAIS forces, the battle will be even and on the Highlanders' own turf."

"We can ill afford to hesitate," Bradford said harshly. "Another force has also jumped into system and managed to beat MacLeod's aerospace carriers to our diversionary force. The ships were ID'd as Capellan. Our decoy ships sustained some losses and managed to jump out of the system, but it means that MacLeod's fighters have turned around and are heading back to Northwind."

Marshal Bradford spoke in a low, almost menacing tone. "What are these Liao ships doing here? I don't know how Loren Jaffray managed to contact the Capellans, but if he did I'll make him pay dearly. Chances are these ships are linked to the message the Chancellor sent, perhaps to reinforce acknowledging the declaration of Northwind's independence. Their presence may cause us to change plans slightly, but it won't pose any real threat to our plan."

Mulvaney barely heard the Marshal's words. Her thoughts were of William MacLeod and his regiment and how fiercely they would fight to hold onto Northwind, the very womb of the Highlander regiments. Sun-Tzu Liao's declaration had no meaning to her. That was only the empty words of a politician far removed from the reality all around her on Northwind. Just words, and for Mulvaney, actions had more meaning.

She wondered if there was any hope even for the Royal/NAIS troops if Cat Stirling was able to reinforce MacLeod. *It could turn into a slaughter of the Davions, but they're too blind to see it coming. If Bradford can keep MacLeod and Stirling's forces separated and uncoordinated, the massacre might go the other way. Now the Capellans may have troops in the system as well. Will they sit this fight out or join in?* Her mind conjured images of long-time friends and allies suddenly dead and buried ... all because of her actions or inactions.

"Now then," Bradford was saying, "everyone had better get to their 'Mechs and continue on according to our plan. *The Despiser* has shuttled most of our ground vehicles out of the area to the planned coordinates. I fully anticipate MacLeod trying to stop us from reaching The Castle. Thus far he still has no reason to believe we're going anywhere else and that mustn't change. If he hits, break off engagement and fall back to The Castle. Mulvaney's maps will lead you to where we need to go. Remember, we're on a tight timetable." Marshal Bradford saluted quickly and his ranking officers began to leave the makeshift HQ.

"Please stay a minute, Colonel Catelli," Bradford said as the last of the officers departed.

"Sir?"

Bradford stepped close so that no one could overhear his words. "When I ordered you to stage an incident that would let us seize control of Tara, I didn't give you authorization to kill our own Planetary Consul, Colonel."

The color rose in Catelli's face. "Sir, I'm shocked at your insinuation. I didn't plan or authorize the death of the Consul. My plans called only for the fire-bombing of several empty government warehouses. I was as stunned as you to learn of Drake Burns' death. We two might not have been close friends, but I had come to respect the man a great deal." *I respected only his power, and now that power is mine.*

"Indeed," Marshal Bradford said, pulling out one of his ubiquitous cigars and carefully inspecting its condition. "For what it's worth, I won't record this conversation in my report. I'm a military man, Catelli. One day I hope to muster out and retire into some sweet little diplomatic post not too unlike this one on Northwind. However, I assure you, Colonel, that you will never work on any staff of mine. And if I learn that you had any involvement whatsoever in the death of Consul Burns, you will be apprehended and held for trial. Know this, I do not want to find anything that might implicate anyone other than the Northwind Highlanders in this crime. Do I make myself clear, Mister?"

"Yes, sir," Catelli said softly. *You won't be on Northwind for long, my dear Marshal. You toy soldiers are so poor at politics. You want an incident but only if you can keep your hands clean. You ask for plausible deniability. Fine. In return you'll do my dirty work and break the spirit and backbone of the Highlanders. When this is all over you'll be gone and Northwind will be mine. All I have to do is feed your ego until then.*

Loren and Huff leaned over the portable field display and stared at the map. The small transportable electronic map was all they'd been able to salvage from the ruins of the command post, destroyed what seemed like weeks before. It had been patched together and barely worked, but it was the best they had and neither of the men complained. Since the ambush at the river, MacLeod's force had pushed Mulvaney and Catelli's forces at a faster pace up the Tilman River. Now it had become a race, a dash for The Castle fortress. But their foe had a sizable lead, and the dim green glare of light from the electronic map only seemed to confirm that reality for the two officers.

"What's the word on reestablishing communications with The Fort, Major?" Loren asked.

"Another ten hours or so at best. The biggest problem we had was that a squad of those power-armored NAIS goons backtracked our trail and destroyed two of the relays. That kind of fighting just ties up our limited resources and steals time we don't have."

"What's next?"

"The Colonel asked that I go over these plans with you. If we're going to hit them it will have to be soon. Our recon forces upriver have them moving at flank speed," Huff said, running his hands back through the stubble of his crew cut hair. "We're also seeing indications that they might be using their DropShip to shuttle troops and vehicles."

"What do you and the Colonel propose?" Loren said, twisting his neck slightly. Wearing a neurohelmet for seemingly days on end had left his neck muscles tense and tight. They'd gone slowly trying to avoid the occasional mine and other booby traps in their pursuit of Mulvaney, but now the time had come to take the risks and try and stop her once and for all.

"We have almost a full battalion that we can throw at them if we push them to the red line. Colonel MacLeod has asked me to take the lead on this. He also asked that I use you as my number two." Huff reached out and pressed the controls on the battered field map. The image showed the lines of attack as well as the icons representing Mulvaney's and Castelli's forces. Loren studied them carefully. *Where could all this go wrong? What are we assuming that we shouldn't? If we know this much, then Marshal Bradford does too. How will he counter?* Loren would have liked to

222　Blaine Lee Pardoe

review the plans in greater detail, to try to plan contingencies against all the possible countermoves and tactics. But this was a battlefield, one that was highly mobile and one where they no longer had the luxury of time.

"You know they'll be expecting us."

"Yes," Huff replied curtly. "Colonel MacLeod and I fully expect them to either dig in or make an all-out run for The Castle. Either way we have to be there. I expect you to coordinate with the First Striker Company and take what's up front of the Regimental Command Company. You'll have the south bank of the river, I'll have the north. Hit them, punch through their line and get between them and The Castle. They're on the south bank of the river and I want to get on their flank and force them to a halt. Destroy their momentum and they'll be ours."

"Lieutenant Fuller told me a little bit about this bunker complex they're heading for," Loren said. "The entrance sounds like it's a holy terror to get through."

"You might say that," Huff said, almost letting himself smile. "The entrance is at the bottom of the falls and is only wide enough for two 'Mechs to pass through at a time. In Star League times they had a mechanism that diverted the waterfall to allow direct entry. Now it's broken and you have to enter underwater."

"And the firing platform? Sounds like some sort of breastworks for 'Mechs."

"Halfway up the falls is a ledge with heavy armor plating. From there, a handful of 'Mechs can hold off eight or nine times their number."

"So, Major Huff, do you want me to bypass the falls and move on the tunnel entrances on my side of the river?"

"Negative. The Colonel and I feel that blindly charging into those tunnels would be disastrous. They're too easy to mine or set up with fire traps. You can't get up the bluffs surrounding the falls, either. They're so steep that only the best jumping 'Mechs have even a chance of getting up them in one piece. And trying to go around the cliff faces will cost you three kilometers in either direction."

"What about cutting off their escape, Major?"

"Escape?" Huff asked, surprised at first, then his eyes sparked with realization. "Don't tell me you *still* think they're going to make a break for the mountain camp. I told you, Jaffray. We reviewed the possibility and flushed it. Their troops have been on the run for days and been pushed to the limit. They'll go the ground because they can't risk pushing themselves even farther."

Loren gave a small shrug to say he wasn't convinced. If he were in Mulvaney's shoes he'd never dig in at a bunker complex like The Castle. The key to the success for a small unit fighting against a bigger one was to stay on the move. Burrowing in at The Castle, regardless of how easy it was to defend, simply did not make sense. It would force a resolution of the conflict. No. Mulvaney was too much like him. She was a MechWarrior and she had been the Executive Officer of an elite fighting 'Mech regiment. She'd never make such a blatant tactical error. She would want to win on her own terms, and The Castle was not the place for that.

"I realize that you don't think there's any merit to my theory, but why not cover those tunnels anyway? I might be wrong, Major, but there's very little to lose making sure you're right. Deploy some of your forces on those exits."

Huff was obviously becoming irritated, his face flushed and his motions quick and jerky as he spoke. "Listen, Jaffray, I respect you as a fellow MechWarrior, but you're a visiting officer in this unit, not a bonafide Highlander. I *told* you that the Colonel reviewed your plan and ruled it out."

Loren didn't understand why Huff should be so upset. He didn't pose any threat to the man. "What's the problem, Major? I was simply pointing out an option."

Huff must have realized that he'd overreacted and managed to catch himself. He drew in a tight-lipped breath and let it out slowly as if trying to cool his temper. "It's not just this, Jaffray. You had Mulvaney in the palm of your hand and you let her go. Some of us in the command chain think you pulled your punch, and in this case, it was a punch that could have put an end to this fight."

Suddenly Loren understood. "Major, I assure you I didn't let her go. She escaped. I didn't blow her to bits because there was a damn good chance I would have been wasted first. We had to work together. If I'd known she was going to make such a fast exit I'd have done something different." Loren heard the words come from his own mouth but didn't believe them. Deep in his heart he knew that he wouldn't have done anything differently at the murky bottom of the Tilman River.

"I think I understand," Huff said, not sounding anymore convinced than Loren was. "I can't help but think that if you'd taken her out of action, all this would be over. Now, no matter how much we try to abide by the rules of engagement, good men and women are going to end up dead."

Huff was right, but that was war—fighting and death. They were warriors and killing other warriors was what they did. They could only do their duty.

"Let's get going," Loren said. "Let's hit them hard and get this thing over with."

26

SLDF Fortress N001, "The Castle"
Northwind
Draconis March, Federated Commonwealth
5 October 3057

By the next morning, Loren was in the middle of the advancing line of BattleMechs as they virtually ran up the sandy banks of the Tilman River. Despite the heat buildup that usually accompanied prolonged running, the *Gallowglas*'s heat levels were still low. All his operative heat sinks were still active and venting away the heat, but the cockpit temperatures would soar once he began using his weapons. MechWarrior's bane was what they called heat buildup, but it was an occupational hazard that could not be avoided, only managed.

The river was wider in this region, and the current much more rapid. The rock formations that had occasionally jutted up downstream were now more common, and more menacing somehow. Perhaps it was just the tension of the pursuit, but Loren sensed that the battle to come would be even fiercer than their first engagement.

Remembering Huff's jibe, he thought back to the encounter with Mulvaney at the bottom of the deep river. Was it fear that had kept him from firing at her when they'd been entangled? Loren had never cowered from death before, but what else could have driven him to cooperate with her rather than risk his own destruction? Was it the memory of hearing about his father's death on some forgotten world in some dark, mysterious, undeclared war?

As if all that weren't bad enough, Mulvaney's escape was at cross purposes to the success of his mission. Instead of the conflict ending quickly, it was dragging out into a prolonged fight.

These gloomy thoughts were interrupted when his short-range sensors suddenly began to paint targets up ahead. Loren immediately called up the map of the river and The Castle. According to the readout the river banks narrowed to a point at the falls that guarded the entrance to the bunker. The rise was nearly fifty meters high and impassable to most 'Mechs. With the dense forest on both sides, the battle zone would be a tight funnel ending at the waterfall entrance. At the moment their foes were spread out for three kilometers on both sides of the river leading to the falls. Some of them must have already made their way into The Castle, but the 'Mechs at the end of their column were still viable targets.

One of the forward recon lance commanders, a Lieutenant Dewkovich, was the first to officially call in the target list. "Medium and heavy 'Mechs, down-range and moving away from us." Hearing those words, Loren's heart began to race with excitement. He was nervous and excited at the same time, but none of that would be revealed to the troops he was tasked with moving. "Good call, Dewkovich. This is Jaffray. Everybody home in on those signals. Everyone piloting a jump-capable 'Mech execute Case Blue."

Just ahead of him he saw the flares as three of his 'Mechs fired their jump jets, turning slightly into the deep forest. Loren followed suit, firing the jury-rigged jets on his own *Gallowglas*. It lurched forward slightly and Loren's body sagged into the command couch as he leaned into the force of the thrust. The Sensation he always felt at such moments raced through his body.

Combat! Some men wrote of it, some witnessed it, others feared it, but Loren embraced it. His body and mind seem to merge with the *Gallowglas* around him. It was no longer a mere machine of destruction, but an extension of his own thoughts and actions—a part of him. The Sensation was like a drug, and Loren wanted more and more of it. But it was not the killing he craved. It was the graceful art of war that enticed him.

Loren had devised Case Blue to give his task force an advantage. All the jump-capable 'Mechs would leap into the deep forest just along the banks of the river. Instead of running forward, the 'Mechs would engage the enemy, then continue to jump up and past them as soon as they had. Their mission was to stay between The Castle and the renegade BattleMechs still trying to reach it. The non-jump 'Mechs would concentrate on knocking out the rear of the Davion/Mulvaney ground force.

Huff had gone for a more conventional tactic, a rushing offensive to plow his forces through the middle of the Davions in an attempt to seize the position upriver between them and The Castle. Loren had wanted to argue the choice of tactics with Major Huff, but in the end kept quiet. Huff was not as open as MacLeod and the last thing Loren wanted was to get into another squabble with him. The best test of his plan would be the results. And if all went well, the two plans combined would smash the rear flank of the Davion line.

As he sailed in his 'Mech nearly thirty meters in the air above the river Loren saw the layout of the land in a way that no cockpit tactical display could convey. Nearly three kilometers upriver, perfectly framed by the dense green forests, were the rising white mists of the waterfalls guarding The Castle. And just as Huff had described, the slopes on either side of the falls were too steep to scale unless a 'Mech were jumping—testimony to the skill of the engineer who'd designed the fortress so many centuries ago.

Moving toward the waterfall was nearly a company's worth of BattleMechs of assorted configurations and weights. Most were near the water's edge and seemed to be ignoring their pursuers, concentrating instead on reaching the safety of the hidden bunker. Both Loren and Huff's ground forces were racing up the open terrain of the south river bank to their rear, with MacLeod providing the support and reserve. Mulvaney and Catelli's 'Mech forces were centered on the south bank, with their remaining hovercraft skirting the river for protection. Jaffray concentrated on adjusting his 'Mech's flight path slightly, letting it take him just inside the dense tree line. As the *Gallowglas* began its descent he signaled his ground forces.

"Jaffray to task force, fire at will!"

As he plummeted into the wall of ancient trees Loren saw the first wave of long-range missiles streaking up past his right toward the Davions. The *Gallowglas* landed hard into the tree line, shattering several branches as it landed, and Loren had to fight the controls to maintain balance. The gyro of the massive war machine seemed to purr inside his ears as it fought to keep the 'Mech upright. A wave of vertigo passed over him as the neurohelmet feedback fought his balancing efforts. Loren was so intoxicated by The Sensation of combat that he barely noticed the cockpit's rising temperatures, a result of his short flight. He ignored it and triggered the jump jets again, once more sending his massive 'Mech upward into the bright Northwind sky.

As the river-bank battlefield came into view down below him Loren saw that first blood had been drawn. One of the Consul Guard *Griffin*s had apparently halted its flight and turned to face the onslaught of Loren's task force. It was firing its PPC with deadly precision at the 'Mechs charging straight at it. Missiles exploded in and around the water, but the 'Mech did not waver or try to retreat from the dangers. The Davion MechWarrior had probably positioned the *Griffin* in the shallow water to cool the 'Mech and was opening up with everything that he or she had. Steam rose from the heat sinks at the 'Mech's feet.

Loren glanced around and saw that his Case Blue team was airborne all around him. A series of missile volleys twisted upward through the air and past him, slamming into Fuller's *Shadow Hawk* and showering the treetops with armor fragments and shrapnel. Still in flight, Loren lowered his PPC and scanned for an easy target. There. A *Nightsky*, one of Mulvaney's Highlanders. The 'Mech was pivoting in mid-stride to fire at one of Loren's ground 'Mechs with a barrage from its large pulse laser. Loren triggered his PPC at the moment the HUD signaled a weapon's lock. But the brilliant blue bolt of energy missed the renegade Highlander 'Mech by less than a meter, sending an explosion of sand and rocks into the air.

The *Gallowglas* began its drop all too quickly for Loren,

and the cockpit was starting to feel like a sauna. Seeing no open terrain suitable for landing, he simply let the 'Mech come down on its own, which it did by crashing into a massive oak like a gladiator charging a foe. The centuries-old tree trunk was no match for the impact of the 'Mech's sheer mass. It split straight down the middle, giving Loren the necessary resistance he needed to keep the *Gallowglas* upright.

A quick check of his secondary monitor told him where the opposing forces stood. From the looks of it a handful had stopped and were attempting a holding action so that the rest could make a break for The Castle. Further downriver Huff's mad rush was forcing 'Mech engagements at point-blank range. From what Loren could make of the data on the monitor, Huff's force had not managed to penetrate the opposition as intended. Matters were getting worse as several hovercraft, Savannah Masters and Pegasuses, came sweeping in from the river and down on Huff's flank.

If they were lucky MacLeod would arrive soon enough to reinforce their thrust. Either way, Loren's force was cutting off the enemy's approach to The Castle. *We make a stand there and this all might be over in a matter of a few well placed shots.*

The next jump was rockier from the start. As soon as the *Gallowglas* rose above the tree tops the 'Mech took a peppering of laser fire from the rear, flank, and front. Many of the brilliant bursts of light missed, but several hit their mark, boiling off his 'Mech's thinner rear armor. As the sweat rolled down his arms the secondary monitor showed him the pockmarked damage of the random hits on an outline of his 'Mech displayed in green and brown on the monitor. Nothing deep and penetrating yet, but the battle was still young.

As Loren cleared the tree line he continued looking for a target and noticed the renegade Highlander *Nightsky* moving upriver parallel to his flight path. The *Nightsky* pilot must have spotted him at the same instant that Loren began his own target lock. Both BattleMechs seemed to slowly twist and aim their weapons at each other as the weapons lock warning siren began to blare in Loren's cockpit. In response he adjusted the flight of his 'Mech to keep it moving towards the riverbank again. Carefully this time, taking the time to aim, he locked his PPC and large lasers on the *Nightsky*.

The renegade 'Mech fired first. The red bursts of laser energy blasted through the sky like tracers, quickly tracking into Loren's flight path. He didn't try to dodge the shots or avoid them, but let the 'Mech's armor do its job. As the burst seared into the torso of the *Gallowglas,* Loren felt a sparkle of heat in his head from feedback to the neurohelmet. Then came a ringing sound that made him reel for a moment with dizziness, something he could not risk while in mid-flight. For a fleeting moment, vertigo swept through him again. Loren held back the bile rising in his throat with the wave of nausea from the feedback, and checked his weapons lock. Satisfied that the *Nightsky* was still a viable target, he triggered his PPC and twin Sunglow large lasers.

The *Gallowglas* tugged in its flight trajectory as the laser shots sought their target below him. A wave of heat blasted Loren's skin as the lasers unleashed their damage, stabbing like spears into the *Nightsky*'s right torso. The armor blasted away from the torso, severing myomer muscle bundles that sprung free from within, followed by a billow of white smoke as the lubricant inside burned. The PPC shot slammed into the elbow joint of the *Nightsky*'s right arm in a blast of arcing electrical and particle discharge. The impact of the weapons twisted the running path of the 'Mech, spinning it towards the water and sending it stumbling forward and down. It was far from destroyed, but Loren knew from experience that it would take several minutes for the pilot to get his 'Mech upright and in the fight again.

He touched down in a small glade and almost immediately leaped skyward again. Only two dozen meters away Jake Fuller's 'Mech landed and re-launched upward as well. Loren saw that the end of the next jump would place him at the base of the falls. No more river bank on either side. Just a sheer wall of rock and flowing water.

Loren's finely honed tactical senses, the product of years of training and experience, quickly assessed the strengths and weaknesses of the terrain and the firepower, movement and defense capabilities of both his force and the enemy. It wasn't even conscious thought, but instinctive, like a wolf stalking its prey. *Here we will make our stand.*

"Case Blue 'Mechs aim for the embankment. Dig in and fire on the 'Mechs we passed," he commanded. Loren scanned downriver and saw that his force was faring somewhat better than Huff's. Apparently his jumping tactics had thrown his side of the river into some disarray from which the Davions were only now beginning to emerge. From what his sensors told him Huff's problems against the Davions were about to come to an end as the advance 'Mechs of Colonel MacLeod's forces had begun to arrive, nearly doubling the firepower at Huff's disposal. That placed Loren's smaller force at The Castle, wedging the Davion/Mulvaney 'Mech's between them and the rest of MacLeod's Regiment.

The Case Blue 'Mechs landed along a hundred-meter stretch of the narrowing banks. Scanning the falls that fronted The Castle, Loren detected no activity or sign that the fortress was manned or active. Was it possible that none of the Davion/Mulvaney troops had been able to reach the complex? No. But there wasn't time to think about what had happened to the rest of the enemy force, there was only time to press their attack.

The enemy 'Mechs that had been in full retreat to The Castle suddenly began to rush forward, realizing that Loren and his small group were in position to stop them. They preferred to take on Loren's task force over digging in and facing the sheer firepower of Huff's and MacLeod's. Jaffray had just begun to transmit orders when the first long-range missiles began to shower in on him and the rest of Case Blue.

"Case Blue, fire at will. Advance towards them. Any stragglers that make a break for the center of the river are considered primary targets!" he ordered, at the same moment letting go with his PPC at an approaching renegade *Warmhammer.* Loren knew that if the Davion/Mulvaneys managed to make it into the river they'd be able to get into The Castle through its submerged entrance.

Fuller's *Shadow Hawk* advanced several meters and leveled its autocannon downriver. It discharged a steady stream of shells at several 'Mechs, eventually settling on an approaching *Rifleman* as its primary target. The shells exploded across the 'Mech, blowing one of its large lasers off in the process.

Then a renegade *Penetrator* fired its extended-range large lasers at one of Loren's people, hitting a *Griffin* in the left leg. The leg blew off to the back, leaving a stub of internal support and loose myomer bundling hanging where the limb had once been. The *Griffin* hobbled diagonally toward the water, its pilot eventually managing to regain his sense of balance. Impressed with the Highlander warrior's skills, Loren congratulated him or her by targeting the *Penetrator* with his own large lasers, sending his shots low into its legs. Even in the heat of battle Colonel MacLeod's rules of engagement had to be respected.

Loren fully expected the renegades and their Davion allies to charge into his ranks. It would reduce the effectiveness of his own force's firepower while at the same time get them further from MacLeod's and Huff's slowly advancing wall of 'Mechs and death. Loren was ready to have his own force pull back to deny them the close quarters combat they sought when suddenly he saw the approaching enemy 'Mechs halt their advance, digging in and firing at both Huff's and Loren's forces.

"Loren," signaled Fuller as he let go another wave of fire from his autocannon. "What in the hell are they up to?"

Jaffray didn't answer, but locked his medium pulse lasers onto the *Nightsky* that had returned to the battle. *It's as if they don't care about getting into The Castle. But why?* He loosed another volley of fire at the *Nightsky*, slamming its mauled arm with one of his lasers, missing altogether with the other. As the hatchet-arm of the *Nightsky* dropped off, sizzling into the cool waters of the river, the answer dawned on Loren. *They aren't rushing to take The Castle because they already have!* As he concentrated his sensors on the waterfall only 125 meters behind him, several magnetic disturbances appeared halfway up the falls.

Fusion reactors! Suddenly instead of the Case Blue force being the anvil and Huff acting as the hammer, the tables were turned. 'Mechs on The Castle's armored ledge were taking positions to attack his force from behind. *Not this time, Chastity. You've placed my mission in jeopardy since my arrival. Now is the time to bring the fight home. Not this time . . .*

"Case Blue, we have 'Mechs to the rear in The Castle. Charge the ground forces in front of us!" Loren pulled the throttle full back, and his massive machine lunged forward as the rest of his 'Mechs began to realize their predicament.

"Sir," Fuller broke in, "rushing into a stone wall isn't exactly what I'd call sane."

"There's no place for sanity here," Loren returned.

27

SLDF Fortress N001, "The Castle"
Northwind
Draconis March, Federated Commonwealth
5 October 3057

Loren's warning had come in the nick of time. From directly behind the roaring wall of water more than eighty long-range missiles streaked for the 'Mechs of Case Blue. The falls themselves had gaps, and from within those gaps and behind their armored breastworks, the attacking 'Mechs had fired out their deadly salvo. The missiles streaked at three of Loren's 'Mechs which, like him, had begun to run. That couldn't prevent them from taking damage, but their sudden movements had caused about half of the incoming missiles to explode. The explosions ripped up the sand and water all around Loren's task force as they raced forward.

"I show two *Archers*, a *Grand Titan*, and a *BattleMaster* up there," one of the other pilots transmitted. Loren bit his lower lip. Finding 'Mechs already deployed in The Castle had caught him off guard. Now he had to correct that error with a tactical solution. Just as before, his mind seemed to gear up to a level faster and more instinctive than thought.

"Keep moving, Case Blue. Rush the enemy in front of you. Engage them as close as possible. Once we mix it up with them it will be hard for their fire support to sort out the good guys from the bad guys!" Loren said. He took three steps and punched his left foot pedal to move the *Gallowglas* into the shallows of the water. Behind him a torrent of explosions rang out as two enemy *Archers* moved into their narrow firing positions behind the waterfall again. Then their deadly missile racks opened fire. Several missiles were lost to the falls, but most cleared the gaps in the falling water and reached out like the hand of death for Jaffray and his men.

One of his 'Mechs, a *Vulcan*, took the brunt of the missile salvo as well as a Gauss rifle slug in its lower right leg. Loren watched out of the side of his viewport as the Highlander *Vulcan* turned almost in a pantomime of agony and the pilot ejected. Her seat blasted clear across the river onto the other bank, where its chute deployed. As the pilot drifted downward Loren watched the shattered and charred remains of the *Vulcan* drop lifelessly into the water and disappear from sight.

Then the Davions began to converge on Loren's forces. The 'Mechs that had been at the rear hastily pulled back and began the long process of wading along the shore of the river while the harassing hovercraft swept about, turning to face Case Blue squarely. As the Davions turned away from Huff and toward Loren, he saw that his force would now face one that was significantly larger and growing by the minute.

"Sir? What are they doing?" a Captain Sullivan signaled from the First Strike Company. His *Crusader* was 50 meters ahead of Loren's 'Mech and blasting away with both its long and short-range missiles. "They're digging in here rather than plowing through us."

It was another trap, Loren knew. But where was it coming from? Loren scanned the surrounding forests and the waters of the river. "Check your sensors, everyone. Look for mines or hidden 'Mechs. Something strange is going on," he said while starting to target a Davion *Caesar*. The paint scheme showed it to be the same 'Mech from Mulvaney's ambush, though now burned and battered. But the battle-scarred 'Mech moved as if undamaged, even possibly repaired. Memories of that ambush were all too fresh, and Loren didn't want a replay of his failure. Huff's earlier words also hung in his ears. He could have ended the fight once and for all back there, but didn't. This time would be different.

As The Castle 'Mechs let loose another deadly salvo Loren was even more puzzled. The rising cloud of smoke from downriver told him that Huff and MacLeod were closing in tightly, but his eyes and sensors showed him that Mulvaney and the Davions were packing themselves almost on top of each other on his side of the river. He and the other Case Blue 'Mechs still pressed on, much slower than before, wary now of the situation that had changed before their eyes.

As Loren locked his weapons for another shot at the *Caesar,* his target came to a complete stop and fired its Gauss rifle at Sullivan's *Crusader.* Moving so fast it looked like a burst of light energy, the silvery slug slammed into the *Crusader*'s hip and the 'Mech staggered back, armor spraying into the river. Loren fired his PPC, sending a burst of charged particles deep into the right elbow of the *Caesar,* hoping to draw some of his fire. The *Caesar*'s forearm, with its own deadly PPC, fell limp at its side as the elbow joint sparked wildly from the damage.

Jake Fuller came on again. "They're all boxed in down the shore, just sitting and waiting for us, Major. What's your call?"

Of all the reasons Loren could imagine why a group of MechWarriors would behave as his opponents had, the likeliest seemed that they wanted to bait an enemy into an ambush. But in scanning the river bottom and forest he was unable to detect any forces in wait to spring such a trap. By the enemy's falling back Loren knew Case Blue wasn't rushing into a minefield, and had gained enough distance from The Castle attackers to reduce their effectiveness. *They're either trying to lure us into the open or trying to make it easy for someone to distinguish our forces. If they want us kept separate, I should respond by making that impossible. I don't know what they have planned, but our best defense is to try and foil their attempt.*

"Case Blue, this is Major Jaffray. All units, charge! Rush them. Engage in close quarters combat. Mix it up, and *mix it good!*"

"Sir?" came the voice of Lieutenant Fuller.

Loren rushed the *Gallowglas* forward as a wave of six

short-range missiles narrowly missed his left arm. "You heard me, Jake! Charge! They're trying to keep away from us and I'm not in the mood to play along." As his entire force reached flank speed Loren noticed that the Davion/Highlanders pulled back, still trying to maintain their distance. Then three ranks of them turned and opened up on the rest of Loren's nonjumping 'Mechs and those of Major Huff.

"Huff to Jaffray," Loren heard as the *Gallowglas* took two medium pulse laser hits to the chest. The heat alarms rang out loudly, but Loren shut them off, concentrating on his fellow officer's words. "Go, Huff," he responded, firing his pulse lasers at the *Caesar* as it waded backwards into the river bank.

"Long-range sensor contact. Break for the forests or river," Huff said, the edge of fear in his voice coming through even over the commline.

"Where . . ."

"Fighters!"

Just then Loren saw the ground near him explode as a rain of LRMs poured down from the blue Northwind sky and struck one of his *Stingers,* which instantly vanished in a flash of bright red and black explosions. The pilot couldn't possibly have survived.

Still running more on instinct than any sort of logic Loren opened his channel to the Case Blue team. "Davion aerospace fighters! Rush their BattleMechs now! All 'Mechs, charge!" *Our only hope is to get into the middle of their formation so we can't be strafed or bombed.*

The Case Blue 'Mechs slammed into their opponents like a wave of water rushing to meet a dike. Loren charged the *Gallowglas* squarely into a renegade Highlander *Wolverine* at the same instant his target leveled a punch at him. The giant metal fist buried itself deep into the *Gallowglas*'s shoulder, just missing the shoulder actuator. The impact of Loren's charge was so strong that his 'Mech's shoulder actually became lodged in the upper chest of his attacker. More important, the *Wolverine* pilot lost his balance and fell backward into another renegade Highlander *Valkyrie* on its way down.

Loren opened a tight-beam transmission to the *Wolverine*'s pilot. "Surrender or I'll leave your 'Mech crippled forever," he said. The heat from the close quarters combat was almost unbearable, and Loren's cooling vest only marginally protected him from searing warmth of the air. In the distance he saw Huff's and MacLeod's forces taking a beating in the aerofighter assault. Several thundering bomb blasts from down the river shook his 'Mech and filled the sky with billowing black and gray smoke.

"Aye, sir, I submit myself to yer justice," the *Wolverine* pilot answered, powering down her fusion reactor in a gesture of surrender. Jaffray didn't waste another moment, but turned towards his nearest friendly, Captain Sullivan in his battered *Crusader*. The older Captain was pulling back his 'Mech's right arm for a solid punch against the Davion *Caesar* that Loren had struck earlier, but the punch was never completed. Leaning his 'Mech forward so that the tip of its Gauss rifle was just under the lip of Sullivan's cockpit, the *Caesar* pilot fired.

The blast ripped off the head of the *Crusader* like a man beheaded by a broadsword. The point-blank range also destroyed the Gauss rifle, but Loren doubted whether that bothered the Davion pilot at all. MacLeod and Mulvaney's rules of engagement apparently had little meaning for the Consul Guards. To them all that mattered was the kill. But Loren knew that if they didn't understand honor, they would never be able to master the Northwind Highlanders.

How different they are, Loren thought. *One fights for a cause, the other fights for power. Barbarians! Best to kill the beast than let it commit the same crime again. Letting it live would be a crime!* He quickly locked onto the *Caesar* as it turned towards him, its right arm hanging uselessly. Jaffray triggered all his target interlock circuits at once. The PPC, twin large lasers, pair of medium pulse lasers, and even the small head-mounted laser opened up at once against the ungainly *Caesar*. At almost point blank range the PPC only arced a brilliant blue blast of energy that scoured the entire surface of the 'Mech. The lasers dug into the torso just under what was left of the Gauss rifle assembly, burning past the myomer and remains of armor and digging into the engine insulation. One shot ruptured the magnetic field that held back the reactor core.

In a brilliant ball of fire, the *Caesar* exploded into a million pieces over the remains of the fallen *Crusader*. Flying fragments of the 'Mech slammed into a Consul Guard *Hatchetman* and sent a renegade Highlander *Warhammer* sprawling. Loren was so intent on watching the *Caesar* die that he didn't see the volley of LRMs streaking at him. They slammed into both sides of his torso with such force that he lost control of the 'Mech. The *Gallowglas* dropped near the fallen *Warhammer*, throwing him hard about the cockpit despite his restraints.

In all the battles Loren had fought across the Inner Sphere, he had never felt death as close as it seemed to hover over his actions on Northwind. He didn't so much fear it as he feared facing it. But perhaps there would be peace in passing. Death would also put an end to his mission. No longer would he live under the shadow of dishonoring his grandfather's memory. Only the jarring of the *Gallowglas* under another weapons hit seemed to shock Loren back to reality.

He knew that firing all his weapons at once had overloaded the Mech's heat capacity. The *Gallowglas* toppled, then hit the ground. The sand softened the impact, but the fall still tossed him about in the command seat like a rag doll. Loren didn't move for several long seconds before attempting to activate his 'Mech. The switches and controls all seemed lifeless, and he feared the worst as none of the systems came on-line. Finally, after he gave the keypad a frustrated punch, the DI computer ran its start-up routine, casting a series of dim lights on the readouts. *It isn't much, but it's a start. For now, death will just have to wait.*

It took a full two minutes for his battle computer to come back on line, and they seemed like the longest two minutes of Loren's life. All around him was the dim roar of combat, but he wasn't part of it. *I reacted out of anger and look where it got me, crippled and missing the fight.* As his 'Mech ran a diagnostic Loren saw the extent of the damage. His frontal armor was peppered from the blast as if he'd been hit at point-blank range with a giant shotgun. The gyro had been knocked out of alignment and wouldn't even be operational enough for Lorne to get the 'Mech to a standing position. It could be repaired in the field, but he had the sinking sensation that he was out of the fight for now. Not a feeling he liked at all, one of loneliness and regret.

I've failed, he thought. *Grandfather always warned me about fighting from emotion, and I did just that. Now I'm out of the action. It's the same emotionality that I saw as a weakness in the Highlanders. The only difference is that for them, it will spell the end of the Northwind Highlanders—at my hands.* The only good news was that their side must have taken the field, otherwise the Davions would have been blasting Loren's remains to ashes. In disappointment tinged with shame, Loren set the fusion reactor to run at a low power level and locked out the security system of his fallen machine.

He surveyed the cockpit's interior with a sense of loss. If the 'Mech couldn't be repaired he'd have to resign himself to acting as a mere advisor to MacLeod's Highlanders. But the damage looked like something the field techs could handle, or so he hoped. If not, he'd lost his place in the war.

He looked up at the bright blue Northwind sky, dimmed only by the tinting of the viewport's polarized glass, and saw several streams of thick smoke drifting into view. Loren unbuckled his seat restraints and began to consider the prospect of a long crawl out of his fallen and crippled BattleMech. Pulling himself to the hatch, he hit the control stud to open it. The hatch cracked slightly, letting in a sharp rush of cool river air. Loren tried to push open the hatch, but it was tightly wedged.

Then a pair of hands appeared from the other side, pulling at the hatch. Loren couldn't see their owner but wasted no time in sitting back and pushing with his feet at the hatch. *I don't really care who's prying that thing open, as long as it isn't that worm Catelli.* As the hatch slowly opened, Loren had enough room to crawl out.

The bright sky and cool air were almost too much to bear. He saw that the fight was mostly over, with most of the remaining 'Mechs not firing but moving towards the treeline. *Just how long was I lying there? Minutes? Hours?* Loren looked over at the female MechWarrior who had helped pry open his cockpit. She was sweaty and bruised in several places, worn and weary from the fight. *I'm probably in the same shape, but it hasn't caught up with me yet.* He pulled off his neurohelmet.

"You're Major Jaffray, the Capellan, aren't you?" she asked, her voice sounding oddly familiar. Loren mentally searched for where he'd heard it before, but couldn't associate her face with the accent.

"Yes, I am. One of us is the other's prisoner, I assume," he said, looking over the battlefield and trying to see if he could make out which side had won.

"I'd be the lassie that's the prisoner. You bested me in combat," she said, pointing to the *Wolverine*. The 'Mech was badly mauled but probably repairable. Otherwise, this warrior had just joined the sad ranks of the Dispossessed.

"You're the pilot?"

"Aye. MechWarrior First Class Kathleen McKinley at yer service."

"Who won?"

"This battle? That would be Colonel MacLeod, fer now. But one battle a war does not make." She pointed at a series of eight small burning lights moving across the brilliant blue Northwind sky. To the untrained eye they looked like a cluster of slow-moving meteors streaking towards the planet. But to Loren Jaffray's experienced eye they were much more.

"DropShips. Damnation, it's DropShips. The Third Royals RCT," he muttered, shading his face and watching them as they passed overhead.

"You knew about the Third Royals?" She sounded very surprised.

Loren nodded, not taking his eyes off the ships.

"Then you must know that this fight is far from over, except maybe for the two of us," Kathleen McKinley said, walking towards Huff and MacLeod's position. Loren followed her, knowing that matters had suddenly just gotten much worse.

28

SLDF Fortress N001, "The Castle"
Northwind
Draconis March, Federated Commonwealth
6 October 3057

The regimental movers were still hauling and towing the remains of the downed BattleMechs back out of range of The Castle's defenders as Loren slowly walked over to the makeshift command post that Colonel MacLeod had established on the river bank. He'd made sure during the afternoon and evening of the day before that the field techs treated his *Gallowglas* carefully as they dragged it out of the riverbed. The crews had begun work, but still couldn't give him a status by the time he eventually drifted off to sleep.

Major Huff had taken the remains of both their task forces and seized control of the high ground bluffs and tunnel entrances to The Castle. The operation had continued on into the night, and with the first rays of the new day Loren was summoned to meet with the regimental command staff. There was only one reason for a such meeting: to plan the next phase of the operation. *I hope MacLeod and Huff have some sort of field assignment or a replacement 'Mech for me. Riding shotgun into this fight is not how I pictured spending this war.* Loren also knew that a combat assignment was his only hope of encountering Mulvaney again.

MacLeod's field HQ was little more than a rocky outcropping flanked by several 'Mechs, including the Colonel's *Huron Warrior*. As Loren walked towards the ad hoc headquarters he saw the short, weary form of Major Huff and several other offices gathered around the CO of the Highlanders like monks around a temple priest.

Seeing the look of frustration on MacLeod's face, Loren thought back suddenly to how proud and confident the Colonel had looked on that first day at the spaceport. How long ago it seemed. Things had seemed so much clearer then. Had Loren failed in his mission? Had he let the Chancellor down?

Loren saluted when he entered the tarp-covered, makeshift tent. "Major Jaffray reporting as ordered, Colonel." MacLeod snapped a quick return salute as Loren joined them around the portable electronic map.

When MacLeod began to speak, his voice was deep and somehow reassuring, despite what they'd just been through. "You've all done remarkably well under some tricky conditions. We've taken losses, but we hit them pretty hard in the process.

"And now I'm faced with a difficult decision. I'll let Captain Dumfries provide us with the intelligence we've gathered thus far." He gestured to the stocky red-haired and bearded Captain dressed in the field kilt some Highlander 'Mech pilots wore in lieu of the traditional shorts.

As Dumfries activated the map controls, the dim lights of the display showed the region surrounding The Castle. "Thanks to the efforts of Major Huff we've been able to secure the tunnel entrances to the west, but we've also found some of them recently sealed with explosives or protected by 'Mech and infantry. We can confirm that Mulvaney and Catelli hold The Castle, but we have no idea how many of them are there.

"Adding to the confusion is the evidence that some of their 'Mechs may have escaped The Castle prior to our arrival, heading upriver due northwest. We've been unable to determine how many left or how many remain."

Loren glanced over at Major Huff. The Highlander officer made only cursory eye contact with him, refusing to acknowledge that Loren had been correct about their foe's intentions.

"They aren't in there," Loren finally said. "Or at most it's only a handful. The rest are making a break for your mountain camp where they can refit while we sit bogged down here."

Huff was quick to leap back with the same old argument. "We don't know that, Jaffray. All we know is that some of them may be heading in that direction."

Captain Dumfries cut him off. "Actually, Major Huff, it is safe to assume that only a marginal force remains in The Castle."

"A guess, Richard?" Colonel MacLeod asked.

Dumfries shook his head firmly. "Simple logic, sir. First off, there's no sign at all of any Consul Guard ground armor. Considering the terrain on this side of the river they couldn't possibly have moved their tanks and vehicles into the tunnels."

"Then where did they go?" asked one of the other officers.

"I believe they've been using that DropShip to move the vehicles in the past few days. They could have used a low tree-top flight trajectory, and we'd never have picked them up with our limited sensor capability. It's a good bet they headed for the mountains, because from there they could use the established roads to get back to Tara.

"Second is the fact that we haven't encountered any NAIS power armor in our probes of The Castle, yet we know that a significant number escaped after the raid on our HQ. If I had such elements available I'd have used them to help my 'Mechs reach The Castle. But we haven't seen them at all, which is one reason we were able to hit their rear guard troops so hard."

"The situation isn't good," MacLeod said, stroking the full length of his graying beard. "Tell them what you were able to make of the DropShips we saw yesterday, Captain."

Dumfries stiffened slightly and nodded. "The DropShips were definitely not Stirling's Fusiliers. According to the wide-beam transmission we've received from Cat Stirling the Fusiliers are planning a drop at 1400 hours on October 20, so we know it's not them. She'd only have sent a message like that if she were unable to get a response from The Fort. Unfortunately without a communications link to Tara and The Fort's transmitter, we can't get word to her either. Our relay's in place, but The Fort doesn't respond. That tells us something is very wrong at their end."

It was bad enough that they'd lost their comm gear, Loren thought. Now it looked like the Davions might actually control The Fort.

"And just so we all understand, I tracked enough Drop-Ships to carry a full regimental combat team and necessary supplies. We cannot know their exact landing coordinates because of the loss of our equipment, but by taking the signal feeds from the 'Mech forces in the area I was able to target their landing zone within five kilometers."

"Tara," MacLeod said softly.

"That's not possible," Huff exclaimed. "We all agreed that Tara was to remain neutral in this fight. They wouldn't dare violate that, not now."

Loren shook his head. "You may be underestimating the lengths to which Victor Davion will go to keep Northwind and the Highlanders. I'd bet my life that they've landed either in or near Tara."

"I must concur with Major Jaffray," MacLeod said. "It explains why we can't contact The Fort to learn their status or inform Cat Stirling of the Davion presence on Northwind. I'll bet Bradford dropped right on top of The Fort. He kept us blind long enough to secure it as a base of operations. We left Tara with little to defend herself and now, for all we know, we may have a hostile enemy sitting right in the middle of Peace Park."

MacLeod's words seemed to stir every one of the officers present, including Loren. It was as if they'd been violated or raped. Comrades were dead on both sides, and now the enemy was breaking promises and agreements. There was not a face in the tent that didn't show anger or frustration.

"This isn't over yet," MacLeod said grimly. "So far we've played the dog chasing its own tail. We had them on the run, but now instead of being the superior force we're outnumbered. Fine. I've been there before and turned it into victory—more than once." The Colonel bent over and activated the map to display his plan for dealing with the situation confronting them. Icons on the electronic display grid came to life as did the key locations of Tara, The Castle, and the Highlander training camp in the nearby Rockspire Mountains. The bright light of day dimmed the glow of the field display, but not the glow on MacLeod's face as he surveyed the map.

"We have no way of knowing how large a force is in The Castle, which compels us to either lay siege to it or at least bottle it up so they can't get out. And we know that a force of unknown size is either on its way to the training camp or is already there. Not to mention the Third Royals near or in Tara. Mulvaney and Catelli will both think that I'll take this personally and simply sit here and slug it out at The Castle. Or worse, go on the defensive myself and flee to one of our other bases on the other side of the continent—knowing that the Third Royals will be hot on my tail the whole way. To be frank those were my first inclinations. Both choices would be easy. But it would only play into their hands.

"And as Major Jaffray is so fond of pointing out, we have to be a little innovative against the Davions. They aren't exactly fighting fair, in the Highlander sense of the word.

"Rather than run, we're going to take this battle home. Mulvaney and Catelli will think I'll try and hold out until the Fusiliers arrive, and that will be their mistake. A small recon force will start on a direct path to Tara to determine the status of our people there and the location and intent of the Third Royals. A small lance-size force can reach Tara a hell of a lost faster than the entire regiment and can do some pathfinding for us on the way. Meanwhile we'll attack and take The Castle. I estimate three days' worth of fighting to pry out whoever is hiding in there.

"As soon as we've suppressed The Castle we'll re-supply from the arms and parts there and set out for Tara based on the intelligence information being fed from our recon team. We need to reach Tara by the end of the month. By then Stirling's Fusiliers will be on final approach. Once they land the odds will be even numerically, though I doubt our Davion counterparts can measure up to our class and style." The Colonel's last comment brought a round of laughter from the officers.

Huff pointed at the map and illuminated a thin line that led back to Tara from the mountain encampment. "The plan is tricky. Assuming that Mulvaney or Catelli have a large force in the camp, they've got a nice wide highway leading directly from there to Tara. With their aerospace fighter advantage they'll be able to keep tabs on the bulk of our force, but the recon team may be able to get through undetected. Mulvaney could very easily be in Tara fast enough to cause us a lot of problems."

Captain Dumfries eyed the map with one raised red brow. "In drawing up this plan we were faced with another problem, and that is how to contact Colonel Stirling. With no way to send her a message we won't be able to communicate unless her DropShips are right on top of us. That means we need to know where she's going to drop."

"What are her standing orders for a Northwind landing with no communications?" Loren asked. He knew that most units had standing battle plans in place should a situation turn sour.

"Cat Stirling has orders to drop on Tara in the event of a communications blackout or if hostilities are presumed. But she could be dropping right into the middle of a trap and we'd have no way to inform her."

"Unless we were in Tara," Huff said.

"Or she figured out the trap," Dumfries added.

MacLeod straightened his stance and pulled his uniform taut. "I plan to have our regiment in position to take on the Third Royals by the time Stirling's Fusiliers begin their landing. Hopefully Cat will put two and two together and figure out what's going on. Maybe we'll be able to warn her, but if not we can at least light up the countryside enough to let her know that a battle is brewing."

Loren leaned over the map display and studied the rugged terrain between The Castle and Tara. The rough broken hills and dense forest were the very reason the Highlanders had followed Mulvaney's rebels along the flats of the river bed. Now Colonel MacLeod was proposing to lead his already weary troops across that rough country from one battle into another. Only an elite unit like the Highlanders or his own Death Commandos could undertake such a test of endurance.

"Sir, our battalion-level communications relays are laid on

the path we took to get here. How will you keep contact with the recon lance going to Tara?" he asked.

"Two other lances will fan out along the trail the recon lance uses. We'll build a manual relay of sorts. They'll piggy-back their signal in a line, 'Mech to 'Mech, and eventually back to the regiment. It will leave them isolated, but it's our best bet."

Major Huff pointed off towards the falls that concealed The Castle just within eyesight of MacLeod's makeshift field HQ. "Taking The Castle is going to be a little tricky, but I'm going to assume that Mulvaney left only a token force hidden there to tie us down. Using our Gurkhas infantry to hit the upper tunnels and our BattleMechs to pummel the entrance and the firing deck, we should be able to overwhelm them. No matter what, though, it's going to be an infantry battle in those upper tunnels, one meter at a time. Worst-case scenario is that it will take four days."

MacLeod pointed his swagger stick onto the map grid and physically traced a line from The Castle to Tara. "The key to this plan is a recon force that moves like lightning. I expect to take only three or four hours of sleep a night and to reach Tara before the Third Royals have a chance to establish a strong security net-perimeter. Otherwise we won't get the data we need. Plain and simple I need an old-fashioned cavalry operation."

Loren studied the invisible line that MacLeod had drawn. He knew that he was more than capable of the mission, but wondered if the other Highlander officers would be offended if he offered. He kept silent, staring at the map. *Hell, I've done this kind of thing before. Getting this mission could be crucial to fulfilling the Chancellor's. I need to know exactly where the Davions are and where Cat Stirling is.* As he lifted his eyes he saw that every officer was gazing at him, staring intently as if waiting for something.

"Why are you all looking at me?" he asked almost shyly.

MacLeod laughed slightly and even Huff gave a little smile. "So far you've gone out of your way to volunteer for every chance to throw yourself into battle. We all assumed you'd leap at this chance. Especially since you were right and I was wrong about them making a break for the mountain camp." Then MacLeod paused. "No pressure, Loren, but the mission is yours if you want it."

"Of course I want it, sir. I just didn't want to deprive these fine men and women of their rightful opportunity."

Captain Dumfries walked over and put his arm around Loren's shoulders like a paternal uncle. "Laddie, there isn't a MechWarrior or tech here who doesn't know you for what you are. In our eyes you're a Highlander. We all saw what you did during the battle, saw what happened to that ice-hearted murderer of J. D. Sullivan. Even the hard-liners like Huff are lightening their aim on you. From what McKinley told us you could have killed her and didn't. It's the spirit that makes us all one and the same, whether you realize it or not. The Colonel says you're perfect for the job."

"And my 'Mech?"

It was Huff who answered. "They tell me she's already up and running. You'll be a little short on ammunition and the crew is just finishing work on your armor replacement."

"Who's my lance?"

MacLeod nodded in approval at the way Loren was approaching the mission. "I'm going to keep the Command Security Lance attached to you. I gather that neither Frutchey nor Fuller has any objection to following you into combat again. Thanks to some damage, you're short one slot, though. Captain Carey here has agreed to fill it if you'll have her." Laurie Carey stepped forward and Loren nodded approval. Now was not the moment to debate skills and expertise. Time was critical.

"Welcome aboard, Captain Carey," he said. "Colonel, I'll need some gear, long-range electronic binocs, lightweight communications equipment and recording gear. Night operations suits for the team. The usual stuff."

A voice from the back of the crowd of officers spoke and Loren immediately recognized it as that of Lieutenant Gomez. "I personally assure you, Major, that your team will be equipped with the best we have to offer." Gomez was still pale, but obviously ready to re-enter the fight, pressure casts and all. Loren was more than slightly pleased to see that she'd survived the ambush downriver.

250   Blaine Lee Pardoe

Colonel MacLeod walked up and put both hands on Loren's shoulders. Looking into the Colonel's eyes, Loren thought he saw a glimmer of envy, as if MacLeod wished he were the one leading the mission. Loren saw something else too, memories of his grandfather. All the stories and legends of Northwind seemed to come to life in that one moment, and he understood his place with these people. *I'm not a Highlander just by birth. It's in me. It's part of me. Something in my blood that I cannot deny.*

"We'll be behind you by only a few days. Your communications support lance will follow your departure in six hours. Good luck, young man. May your forefathers tread with ye."

Chastity's *Marauder II* and her command lance slowly made their way along the rocky rapids of the breakwaters of the Tilman River. Behind her was the battle that she'd been denied the opportunity to wage. Behind her was her past, her friends and former allies. Behind her was Loren Jaffray, the man who'd turned her life and the lives of her followers upside down. The man who had single-handedly turned Northwind into a hotbed of political and military turmoil.

The man she could not forget. The man she was sure would destroy the Highlanders.

"Message on scramble from The Castle," Lieutenant O'Leary said over the comm channel.

"How did the operation go?"

"Apparently a task force from MacLeod's regiment used jump-capable 'Mechs to cut off our rear guard. They anticipated our troops on the firing deck and managed to inflict heavy damage. We have only two lances of 'Mechs and a platoon of Consul Guard troops in The Castle now. The rest of our forces in the rear guard were crushed."

Knowing the fortress well, Mulvaney was sure a small group was more than enough to hold off a large assault, but not forever. Attrition would take its toll. But the use of the jumping 'Mechs intrigued her. Too subtle for Huff, who always wanted a straight-up fight. MacLeod used similar tactics, but he rarely led the front line troops. No, there was only one man who'd have been willing to take that risk, Loren Jaffray. *Damn, can't he just leave my life alone?*

"Any new orders, Colonel Mulvaney?"

Chastity stared blankly out the viewport as her *Marauder II* moved over the broken stones and jagged rocks. "No, we move on according to plan. Marshal Bradford and Colonel Catelli are already at the camp. We meet up with them there and then link up with the Third Royals to finish off MacLeod." Her voice was lifeless and low.

"Do you think MacLeod will follow us?"

"No, O'Leary. Not right away. By now he's probably figured out that some of us are heading west, but he can't afford to ignore those troops in The Castle, however few or many they are. They could spring up and hit his rear flank. And for all he knows, most of our troops could be in The Castle. It will take him the better part of a week to learn the truth, and by then it will be too late." *The plan is sound. I know the Colonel and tailored it to fit his fighting style. Just like I know the styles of every MechWarrior in the regiment. The only wild card is Jaffray. If they start listening to him, it's all wasted. He'll see the trap and turn our victory into a stunning defeat.*

What shocked Mulvaney was that she wasn't afraid of losing the conflict any more. The insinuation of Highlander involvement in the death of Consul Burns had turned her against her new allies. Were Marshal Bradford and Colonel Catelli merely using her and her knowledge of the regiment? Had they twisted and perverted the truth to force the issue of landing Davion reinforcements in Tara? She knew that the truth would forever be lost, or worse, left to be rewritten by the victor. She no longer totally trusted the Davions.

The only thing that kept her from turning on them was the promise her people had made to the Federated Commonwealth. If military men or women started violating their word of honor with a liege lord, the Inner Sphere would be thrown into chaos. It was an act beneath her as a Northwind Highlander. Though she did not respect the men Prince Davion had sent to Northwind to protect his interests, Mulvaney felt that she personally represented those interests.

As long as she lived, the agreement with the Federated Commonwealth survived as well.

What frightened her was that for the first time she found herself hoping that MacLeod or Jaffray would hand her a defeat, or at least a reason to stop the madness.

29

South of Tara
Northwind
Draconis March, Federated Commonwealth
11 October 3057

Loren's *Gallowglas* cleared the ridge line, but it was hard to tell the difference. The dense forest and occasional jagged rock formation was more than enough to block out the surrounding terrain features. All he really had to go on were the readings from his BattleMech's computer system and a gut feeling for the lay of the land. After several long days' travel through the thick, almost twilit forest, Loren knew first-hand why MacLeod had not tried to march the entire regiment at once directly into Tara from the south. Moving a whole regiment through this kind of terrain was going to be a difficult task. With Loren and his recon forces mapping the way, the Colonel might be able to shave valuable hours off the trek back to the city.

With typical Davion efficiency the aerospace forces of the Third Royal RCT made passes over the area twice a day. The first time was always within an hour of midday, and the other was in the mid-afternoon. Checking the chronometer readout in his cockpit he saw that it was time to conceal the lance or risk their detection. Except for a daily transmission of their findings, the lance operated almost totally under a communications blackout. Loren only violated the stand for quick orders, usually warnings or directions.

"All right, people, stop and find some shade," he replied. Such a task was not difficult in the forest. If anything, it would have been hard to find a place where the bright yellow Northwind sun could get through. Loren gently backed his *Gallowglas* up against a massive oak and throttled back the 'Mech's reactor so that it produced only a trickle of power. Then he unbuckled his seat harness and pulled a thermal concealment tarp from a small compartment at the back of the cockpit.

Opening the cockpit hatch, Loren stepped out onto the shoulder of the *Gallowglas*. With a heavy toss he unfolded the heavy tarp over the cockpit and front chest of the BattleMech. Nearby he saw Lieutenant Frutchey performing the same ritual on his *Warhammer*, throwing additional smaller tarps over the crossed PPC arms of the weapons to further cloak their emissions.

The tarps were designed to suppress the heat and magnetic signatures of a 'Mech from a wide-area scan. Woven into them was filament that also helped shield the 'Mech's fusion reactor from magnetic sweeps. Such tarps had been common for centuries and were useful against aerospace forces running broad sweeping scans. Loren was counting on the tarps, combined with the heavy forest cover, to keep even a Davion satellite in orbit from getting a position fix on them.

Loren descended the ladder down the 'Mech's side and walked over to meet up with Frutchey, Carey, and Fuller and their 'Mechs in an area of thick grass. All three looked tired and worn. The little sleep they got was usually taken in the periods between the flyovers, and most of their movement and reconnoitering was accomplished during the night and early morning hours. Fuller's eyes were shadowed with dark circles, and Loren felt his own puffy from lack of sleep. Four days of sprinting across the rugged Northwind outback terrain was beginning to take a toll on them all.

The roar of the aerospace fighters overhead was reassuring, even though none of them could see any sign of the craft through the overgrowth. Loren checked his personal chronograph and shook his head. "There's one thing that a large military always fraks up. That is acting too consistently. Those Davion fighters are running their scanning patterns right out of a Federated Commonwealth regulations and procedures manual. Sloppy work for such a crack unit."

Jake Fuller took a long gulp of water from his canteen. "If I'm ever in command of a regiment I'm going to remember all this. Vary the flight times and patterns to keep the enemy off guard."

"*You,* in charge of a *regiment*? Talk about illusions of grandeur," Frutchey said, craning his neck in an effort to relieve the muscles there. His fresh new Lieutenant's bars showed up as black stripes in the dim shade.

"You should talk. At least the ink is dry on my commission, green-horn," Fuller retorted. "I've at least been in some real battles before this one."

"What was the latest communication dump from the regiment?" Loren asked Laurie Carey, deciding he'd heard enough parrying. Seated on a fallen log, Carey was methodically rubbing her right knee, stopping only long enough to hand Loren a printout of the daily transmission. Judging by the scar, she'd been injured badly before and the prolonged recon was making the old pain surface.

"Nasty scar you've got there," Loren said knowingly.

Carey looked up and nodded. "I got it during the so-called Second Skye Rebellion when we went in to help the Gray Death Legion clean up on Glengarry. Tough fight, too. It was a freak shot really, a nasty laser blast that fractured my cockpit glass and defragged on the broken shards. Burned my knee to the bone and then some." The two other Highlander officers winced slightly at her story, but not Loren. Instead he pulled off the harness straps of his cooling vest and pointed to the triangular pattern of hole-like scars on his right chest.

Carey grinned. "Where'd you get yours?"

"I can't tell you the name of the planet," Loren said. "Part of the fun of being a Death Commando—the location's a state secret. Hell, according to the Confederation the mission never happened in the first place. I was in a *Trebuchet* sprinting all-out when a full flight of LRMs slammed into my cockpit from out of nowhere. Three of the missiles blew the cockpit glass all over my lap. Shredded my cooling vest, but I guess I was lucky. The last warhead entered the cockpit but didn't blow. Instead its fuel cell fractured against the wall and I caught three pieces of shrapnel in the chest. Those little buggers were hot! My lung collapsed, but I was able to hang in the flight for another two minutes, long enough to send my would-be assassin to her grave."

"Damned lucky, if you ask me," Frutchey said in disbelief.

"Luck had nothing to do with it," Loren returned. "It wasn't my time to die, so I didn't."

"Your time to die?" Carey echoed.

"Ever since I was a kid I've believed I was put here for a purpose. Maybe that's why I've never given a thought to death in all my missions. That's changed since coming to Northwind. I don't know why."

Laurie Carey smiled knowingly. "It's because you feel part of the family—the Highlanders—and you're fighting for that. We're family and the Colonel has brought you in. In the past you've fought for nation and ruler. Now you fight for yourself. That's why it feels different."

Her words struck Loren deeply. *Was she right?* As a Death Commando he'd been a member of an elite unit. His missions were ones of the highest honor, protecting the interests of the Capellan Confederation. *I was part of the defense of House Liao, first and foremost. A part. But here it's different.* Was it true that he now felt more kinship with the Northwind Highlanders than the Great House he'd served for his entire life? *All those words my grandfather spoke, they prepared me for this moment. He couldn't have known that I'd end up here, but somehow it happened. Karma ... or fate? No. I'm a Death Commando, first and foremost. I wouldn't be here if not for the Chancellor.*

Loren felt that for the first time in his life he belonged to something rather than just being part of a great whole. The feeling was deep and stirring, almost overwhelming. To regain his composure, he began to read the printout Carey had handed him. The only anchor that kept his mind focused was his mission. *He must neutralize the Northwind Highlanders.* If Carey, Fuller, and Frutchey believed that he was one of them, so much the better.

Catching Loren's cue, Carey smiled but dropped the subject entirely. "Apparently the assault on The Castle is going well but slowly. According to the transmission, they've been able to take part of the interior, but some explosives work by the Davions have left them literally digging their way through. Those flights we see overhead everyday are making bombing runs on our troops in the river valley, but MacLeod has mounted a strong anti-air defense. According to this communication, the Colonel expects to complete capture of the bunker sometime this afternoon. The Gurkhas are fighting their way in against the infantry." Reading the details of the report, Loren noticed that casualties had been minimal in the assault, but that precious time was being lost.

Jake Fuller took out a small kerchief and wiped the sweat from his brow. "I'm beginning to think we were the lucky ones, drawing this mission over that one. The Castle is a tough nut to crack."

Loren was quick to cut in. "Don't delude yourself, Jake. This mission is no Marik tea party either. How's the communications signal with the regiment, Laurie?"

Carey held out her hand and waved it back and forth. "Shaky at best. The lance MacLeod sent after us is catching up, but the signal is hard to get locked. They're getting out data feeds though, and our pathfinding is going to eliminate a lot of hours from their trek once they start the link up."

"That's good news anyway. Now then, tonight we're going to move in a tight delta formation with Carey at point and me on the right flank. Just two more days of this hellish running and we'll be just outside Tara. I want everybody to be crisp and sharp. We can't be sure where the Third Royals are and I sure don't want to stumble into them blind."

"What are your plans once we reach the outskirts of the city, Major?" Fuller asked.

"We'll hide our 'Mechs in the marshland and make our way in on foot."

"Sir?" Frutchey asked in dismay.

"You have a problem with that, Lieutenant?"

"Well, sir, on foot we don't have much in the way of offensive gear. If we run into trouble, we're going to be pretty unprepared to deal with it."

"Frutchey, we're not here to run into trouble. We're here to gather information. I know that we're a lot safer in

'Mechs, but I have a suspicion the Third Royals are not about to let us tour The Fort in our BattleMechs. Sneaking into a city in a 'Mech is quite a stretch, even for me. A good MechWarrior always sizes up the limitations of himself and his foe. The 'Mechs remain behind.

"We'll enter the city on foot, shoot some film, get an idea of where they've positioned their 'Mechs and tanks and HQ. Then we leave. No firefights and no heroics. There'll be plenty of time for that when the Colonel and the rest of the regiment arrive. Without our information the regiment will be moving blind."

"We all go into the city, then?" Fuller asked.

"No. One of us will stay back with the 'Mechs. That person is our equivalent of a dead-man's switch. If we get captured he or she will escape with all the information we've gathered up to that point."

"Will it come to that, Major?" Frutchey asked.

Captain Carey answered for Loren. "It might, so we'd better be prepared for it. If the Royals are in Tara they're going to consider us hostile. No neutrality, no rules. The plain truth is that we might be captured or killed. If captured, chances are pretty good they won't handle us with kid gloves. They're likely to label us as terrorists just like they did with Major Jaffray. There's no telling what they might do, especially with a war on."

The two younger officers were listening with perfect attention. Carey had definitely made her point.

"All right, then, on that happy note everybody get some sleep," Loren said, breaking the tension. "We lay low until those flyboys return to their base. Once they're back home we move all night. Check your water collection units too. The last thing we want is to run out of provisions in the middle of the mission."

"You've barely touched your food, Major," Catelli said, pointing at Mulvaney's plate from across the table. Though Marshal Bradford's regimental cook had managed to scrape together a fairly good meal from the rations stored in the training camp as well as from supplies brought with the Third Royals, Mulvaney's mind wasn't on the meal, but on the coming battle. The few bites she did take had little taste for her.

"I guess I'm just not hungry," she said, tossing her napkin onto the plate.

Marshal Bradford studied her face carefully as he chewed his fish. "What's the latest field report on MacLeod's forces, Colonel Mulvaney?" he asked, fully knowing the status from his own reading earlier in the evening.

"From what we're able to determine from our daily flights, virtually all of MacLeod's Regiment is tied down at The Castle. We're unable to raise our task force inside, but thus far nothing indicates that they've been routed."

Catelli chuckled slightly as he took a deep drink of his wine. "And while the good Colonel MacLeod spends his days and nights trying to open an almost empty fortress, we've started repairs on our battle damage using the Highlanders' own supplies." His tone was so arrogant and cocky that Mulvaney quickly looked away for fear of what she might say or do.

"Indeed," Bradford said, raising his own wine glass in mock salutation. "My last communiqué with Colonel Morrow said that the Highlander families have begun some organized resistance. Minor incidents so far. Of course they deny any knowledge in the death of Consul Burns. Morrow has his troops positioned to keep peace in the city, though, and order is being maintained."

"Any word on Cat Stirling's regiment?" Mulvaney asked.

"Still inbound. They sent a landing confirmation signal to The Fort, and our NAIS forces holding the facility responded with the proper code. Chances are Colonel Stirling is waiting for some word from MacLeod, but when that doesn't come she'll land. When we took The Fort we got hold of the Highlanders' authorization codes and signals, though our NAIS troops paid a heavy price for it. Don't fret, Colonel Mulvaney, I assure you that the Third Royals are more than capable of handling the Fusiliers if they opt to slug it out.

"Our surveillance of the other Northwind Highlander regiments shows they've all abandoned their garrison postings and are apparently also on the way here. It will be a month before any of them pose any sort of a threat to our operation, and by then we'll have MacLeod under control."

"You seem so low lately, Colonel," Catelli said. "Most people participating in such a chapter in history would feel the invigoration of it. You seem almost disinterested."

"History, Colonel?"

"Of course it's history," Bradford put in. "War is erupting in the Inner Sphere. Great armies are on the march. And we're here—a part of the great unification of the Northwind Highlanders with the Federated Commonwealth. I'm shocked that you don't see the significance of this affair, Colonel. Your actions and our own will shape the face of this planet and the future of your people for centuries to come. This is an exciting time for all of us!"

Mulvaney shook her head slightly, the only defiant act she could muster. "No, sir, this is a matter of honor for the Northwind Highlanders. You are witnesses to it, but it's a matter that Colonel MacLeod and I have to settle. It's the only way for our people to survive as a whole. This fighting will purge one side or the other. Otherwise, the Highlanders would fall apart. This is not about our assimilation into the Federated Commonwealth. This is about us surviving as a people."

Bradford's voice had the slur of semi-intoxication. "You speak about this as if we were mere spectators. The political implications of what this Capellan Jaffray has proposed and what MacLeod is doing are staggering. The Federated Commonwealth cannot simply stand by while worlds demand independence. That would rock the very foundations of our government. Remember, no matter what anyone thinks, you are part of a greater whole, a mighty star empire that one day will become the core of a new Star League!"

He took up the decanter and poured himself another glass. "MacLeod and this Jaffray have forgotten the rules of law. But you must never forget who your liege lord is, Colonel Mulvaney. I would hate to think that your loyalty is in question as well." The threat was far from veiled and Mulvaney felt the heat rise in her cheeks.

Bradford stopped his barrage at the sight of the expression on her face. "Then again, I am a military man like yourself. Too often we're so busy executing the orders of state that we don't appreciate where we are and what we are doing. Like all good soldiers, you and I, Colonel, we follow orders."

When I was MacLeod's executive officer, I knew my place, Mulvaney thought. *Now I'm just a player in a great drama. They see this struggle for what it means to their little games of politics. I hate being just a player in a game. Before I was much more, I was part of a family. God, how I long for that feeling again.* She rose silently from the table and gave the Marshal a nod as she left. Catelli watched her walk from the tent, careful to wait until she was gone before speaking.

"She may prove to be a problem for us in the later phases of this operation."

Marshal Bradford swirled his wine in the glass slowly and methodically. "She will not be a threat for long. With Colonel Morrow holding their precious Fort and their communications code books in our hands, her usefulness is beginning to wane. We have enough information to lure Colonel Stirling and her regiment right where we want them. Straight down into the middle of Kohler Spaceport."

"And then?"

The Davion Marshal took a deep gulp of his drink, consuming the remaining wine in one shot. "Then there will be no more Stirling's Fusiliers. Gone! In an instant! Their loss, and the eventual crushing of MacLeod's Regiment will shatter the Highlanders. If Mulvaney is stupid enough to resist . . ." He tossed the empty wine glass into the side of a transportation case, shattering it into tiny crystal fragments. Bradford never finished his sentence. He didn't have to.

= 30 =

Peace Park
Tara, Northwind
Draconis March, Federated Commonwealth
11 October 3057

Tara had a dark, almost forbidding appearance as Loren Jaffray led his team along the side of a small building at the end of the street. Looking about he remembered how different the city had seemed to him before, fresh and untainted. Gone was the Tara of his grandfather's stories and whose sights had intrigued him only a few short weeks ago. What was left was a tomb, silent and morose, with danger and death waiting around any corner.

The clouds rolled past the slice of moon in the sky, occasionally dampening what light did reach the city. Lieutenant Frutchey had remained behind with the lance's 'Mechs in the swamplands just south of town while the three of them had slowly made their way through Tara's outskirts. Frutchey had protested vigorously, but Loren finally succeeded in impressing him with the importance of his part of the mission. Every few minutes Captain Carey typed in a message relaying the information they discovered and compressed it for a short microwave transmission. Such a short-burst transmission would be virtually impossible to trace and difficult even to detect. If the mission failed to report in,

Lieutenant Frutchey was to escape with the information they'd gathered up to that point.

"Awfully quiet," Jake Fuller whispered, pulling the dark knit cap over his blonde hair. "It's still not that late. There should be traffic on the streets, people enjoying the air. Where is everyone?"

"Holed up or gone altogether," Laurie Carey replied. "We've seen lights going on and off in the buildings. They must be running under a curfew. And a curfew requires enforcement, which must mean the Third Royals are already here."

Loren nodded agreement. There were other signs that his trained eyes had caught to substantiate Captain Carey's thought. One of the wider streets they'd passed a few blocks back had been barricaded and equipped with electronic sensors to detect any disturbances. If Loren hadn't been using surveillance binoculars he and the others might have set off the alarm. He'd also noted an empty Rotunda armored car positioned nearby to create the illusion of police troops in the area. Loren scanned the street with his electronic binoculars and made sure the path was clear before leading the team across the street toward Peace Park. Loren quickly tucked and rolled under a dense bush, followed by the rest of his team.

No sooner had they caught their breaths when a deep quaking sound filled the air. Looking down the boulevard Loren saw a light *Battle Hawk* 'Mech making its way down the street, possibly scanning Peace Park or the surrounding buildings. The 'Mech was impressive, the golden coiled rattlesnake emblem of the Third Royals Regimental Combat Team gleaming under the lights of the street lamps. Loren took out his small laser camera and captured the image of the 'Mech as it passed. *At least we know where one of their 'Mechs is. It's wandering down the street only a few meters away from us.* The *Battle Hawk*'s pace increased slightly as it passed them, moving into the darkness of the park. Fuller let out a long sigh of relief as the 'Mech disappeared from sight.

"Carey, transmit to Frutchey that we've finally found confirmation of the Third Royals' presence here. Stress that it's

'Mech forces. Let him know where we are," Loren whispered.

"Let's go to The Fort, Loren," Fuller said in a low tone. "If they've set up camp anywhere it will be there."

"Too risky, Jake. We'll approach, but the only way for us to know what they've got inside is to go over the wall. No dice." Loren checked his chronometer and the small map he carried, holding it up to catch the light. *He's like the others. They're taking this personally. This is their home and I have to remember that. They see occupation by an outside force as a desecration of everything sacred to them. Maybe that's one of the reasons Colonel MacLeod gave me leadership of this recon. He figured I'd be objective, not influenced by sentiment.* Loren would not fail MacLeod, especially since a successful recon would help lead to the fulfillment of his own mission for the Chancellor. Leading the Highlanders into even a marginal engagement with the Royals would weaken them enough that the Death Commandos somewhere over Northwind could easily mop up the survivors.

"We'll cut across the park and make our way to the spaceport. Time is short," he said, elbowing his way under the brush to the other side. Carey and Fuller followed slowly and cautiously.

Being in Peace Park brought back sharp memories of the attack on him and MacLeod. His wound had also begun to ache slightly, as if it had a memory of its own. Jaffray ignored the pain as they moved over the small hills and knolls of the tree-filled park. *I could have died here.* He narrowed his eyes as he looked at the treeline again. *I won't let it happen that way again. Next time I'll assume my foes are more devious than I am.*

They stopped to get their bearings near a cluster of small trees when the sound of someone running made Loren and the others freeze in place. The footfalls were fast but sounded odd, almost uneven as they smashed against the dried leaves and crashed through the underbrush. The running feet were heading almost directly toward them, the runner making no effort to conceal either his location or direction. Loren reached for his needler pistol and pulled it out. *Whoever it is seems intent on running right into us . . .*

HIGHLANDER GAMBIT 265

but I'm not going to go down without a fight. Blast! Everything was going so well.

The figure burst into the open across from the trees as Loren and his two team members leveled their weapons. Carey's pulse laser carbine was the most menacing of their team's firearms. Fuller carried an old battered and beaten laser pistol that he claimed had been in his family for over four centuries. From its age and condition Loren might almost have believed that fable. The figure staggered two steps, then fell face forward into the open.

Suddenly four other armed figures appeared behind the running man. They strode boldly into the open and stood over him as he attempted to roll over and get his breath. As he tried to rise one of the men swung the butt of his rifle, hitting him squarely. It was a blow to subdue, the force of it drawing a loud moan of pain from the man on the ground.

Davions! Their uniforms are Davion. I'd know those epaulettes and boots anywhere. Loren motioned for his compatriots to hold their fire as they watched. Their mission was to gather information. Opening up would expose their presence and deprive them of the chance to find out what was going on.

"Hey Danny, it looks like we caught up with your prisoner," the tallest of the figures said. As the speaker turned, Loren saw that he was waving a menacing needler rifle over the fallen form.

The smallest of them stepped up and gave the man on the ground a booted kick. "That we did, Mister Yoark. Hold it right there, old man." Using his foot he prodded the figure to roll over.

In the dim light of the quarter moon Loren saw the face of Sergeant Major Pluncket, master of the Highlanders' Pub. Wheezing in pain and exhaustion, he gazed up at his Davion tormentors with an expression of fury and contempt. Loren felt the pit of his stomach tighten as he watched the scene unfold. *They're going to kill him if he resists at all. He'll die if we do nothing.* The short Davion trooper leaned over him. "You wounded one of our officers pretty good with that carving knife. We can't let you run around doing that sort of thing. You're coming with us."

"What, for more of your fun and games?" Pluncket said.

266 Blaine Lee Pardoe

"This is our world, not yours. You invaded Northwind, and it's our duty to defend it. I'm not afraid to die protecting my home. But I'll be damned if I'm going back with you to spend the rest of my days in my regiment's own jail." One of the men pressed the muzzle of his needler rifle against Pluncket's forehead.

"We don't want any trouble, old man. Drop the weapon immediately."

Loren mentally struggled against the urge to pull his trigger. *Damn. I was right. That stubborn old man is a goner if we don't act. Is saving him worth the mission? Is the life of one man worth that of the entire regiment?* Not just a regiment, there were also his own Death Commando forces. Endangering the Highlanders might very well endanger his own mission.

"Mister Yoark, this man has some sort of a weapon and will not disarm," the middle figure said, lifting his rifle into a semi-firing stance. "Inform the gentleman that if he does not produce and hand over the weapon immediately we will be forced to take aggressive action."

If he does have a weapon he's a dead man here and now. No trial, no justice. He doesn't deserve to die like this. No one does except maybe Catelli. Deciding on whether to save the life of one man over saving those of many should be an easy decision. But this isn't. Letting him die wouldn't be the Highlander thing to do. Loren looked over at Carey and Fuller. Even with the black night paint on their faces, he was able to make out their expressions. Their worst fear was that Loren would order them to hold their fire, to stand and watch while one of their kind was executed.

I should let him die. He's only one man. Loren saw the logic of the situation. Hadn't he heard his own grandfather drill into him the value of thinking logically when everyone else was reacting emotionally? But now he was watching a defenseless man die and couldn't just sit back and let it happen. And wherever his grandfather was, Loren couldn't help thinking he'd never rest easy knowing that Loren had permitted one of their kindred to die such a pitiable death. *It's not how I'd want to go.* Loren locked eyes first with Jake and then with Laurie, nodding to them slowly. Carefully and silently he disengaged the safety on his weapon. His comrades each took careful aim with their weapons, pointing into the darkness at their own targeted Davion. *Wait for my signal* . . .

"You will no' take me back to that jail house. I will not surrender without a fight either." Pluncket groaned between breaths.

"I say again, disarm or we will use force." A weapons muzzle began to take aim at Pluncket. The man seemed nervous.

Hold your fire until I give the word . . .

Pluncket smiled and wearily rose to a sitting position, not seeing the recon team taking aim at the figures facing him. "Ye Davion dogs are a cowardly lot. How many of ye does it take to bring in a defenseless old warhorse such as meself?" He seemed to be holding his prosthetic leg with both hands, rubbing it as if it were sore.

The taller trooper, the officer referred to as Yoark, sneered. "I don't want to kill you, but we're not policemen. I'm not about to order my men to search you for a weapon. You wounded an officer. Disarm in three seconds or I will fire." He once again began to lift the muzzle of the needler rifle toward the Sergeant Major still sitting on the ground.

Loren was bringing up his own weapon. *Take aim carefully. We have to do this in one shot or this entire mission is lost, if it isn't already.*

Pluncket moved like a jaguar. From the ankle of his artificial leg he pulled a vibroblade and slashed out with it against the tall Davion officer. The microfiliment blade hummed at ultrasonic speeds and was enough to disrupt and cut even hard metal. The trooper's thigh offered no resistance as the blade gouged through the flesh. Yoark's needler rifle fired wide, missing its mark and sending a burst of plastic needles into the soft loam. The tall Davion trooper squealed in pain as the other two troopers stood dumbfounded, shocked by Pluncket's sudden and deadly attack.

The old Highlander took advantage of their shock. He rolled over and held the powered weapon in front of him, ready to throw or stab. The other two troopers began to raise their weapons, ready to finish off the downed man.

"Now," Loren said grimly as he fired his pistol at the

wounded officer. The nearly silent blast of razor-sharp needles slammed into the chest of the man called Yoark, sending him flying back into the darkness before he could raise his weapon in response to Pluncket's attack. Carey opened up with her laser carbine and the night lit up with a rapid series of laser pulses hitting the middle figure. The man crumpled to the ground. Fuller's laser beam hit the Davion trooper squarely in the face. The man uttered a brief cry as he died, letting go a light wail like a crying child. None of them stood a chance of surviving the attack.

Jaffray leaped across the distance to Pluncket. The older Highlander waved the vibroblade at his newfound allies, unsure of what had just happened around him. "Identify yerselves," he commanded under the light hum of the blade's action.

"Major Loren Jaffray," Loren said, reaching out his hand and smiling. "There's not a lot of time, Mister Pluncket." Nearby he heard the gurgling sounds of one of the men, probably Yoark, dying in the dark.

The Sergeant Major saw Loren's face and smiled broadly. "What in the bloody hell took you so long?" he demanded.

Loren lifted him to a standing position while Jake and Laurie made sure there were no other soldiers nearby. "You knew we were there?"

"No, laddie. I just knew that I was not to die this way. But we canna stay here long. Their HQ is only a short distance away." Loren motioned for his two compatriots to pull back. They all formed a silent wedge around Pluncket and started out of Peace Park.

"One thing is fer sure, I knew ye were a Highlander at heart, Mister Jaffray," Pluncket said, giving Loren a knowing nod.

31

Tara, Northwind
Draconis March, Federated Commonwealth
11 October 3057

The open basement was like a safe port on stormy seas to the team. Half-lifting the older man, Carey and Fuller helped the Sergeant Major down the stairs while Loren closed the door behind them. From this vantage point they had a clear view of the street and the park. Loren's heart was racing as he surveyed the street from one end to the other. *We were lucky. By all rights we should have ended up dead.*

"Are you hurt?" Fuller asked the older trooper in a low tone.

"No, not now. I think those lads will no' be in the mood to dance for some time. Nice piece of work, sirs, for a bunch of officers." Somehow he managed to maintain his crass sense of humor despite the near brush with death. "You must be part of the rescue force sent to get us out of here."

Loren knelt next to him. "I'm afraid not, Mister Pluncket. We lost our regimental communications weeks ago. But what do you mean 'rescue'? What's going on here?"

"You don't know, do ye?" he asked, seeing Fuller and Carey both shake their heads. "That blowhard of a Planetary Consul Drake Burns was assassinated and the bloody Davions are blaming us fer it. That puppet Lepeta claims he has evidence of Highlander involvement, but we ignored him. We thought it was nothing more than a trick to get the locals up in arms agin' us.

"Then those bloody rattlesnakes landed. They broke our neutrality. Dropped power armor troops right inside The Fort. Oh laddies, there wasn't a chance fer a fair fight. We dinna have any way of protecting ourselves. They secured The Fort and the spaceport in a matter of hours. Highlander officers and NCOs were placed under house arrest and the rest of the city is under strict curfew."

"Our families?" Captain Carey said in shock.

"Aye, lassie. I guess they used our files from The Fort to round 'em up. Placed them under house arrest too. Some of our lads protested, but what could they do against an entire RCT? We heard rumors that some were killed, but I think most are in jail."

"What *did* happen to the Consul?" Loren asked.

"Accordin' to Lepeta and the embassy staff, some of our people sneaked in and killed the bloody fool. By the news accounts he was shot with a Highlander laser pistol and there's some trumped-up evidence that highlanders were involved."

Loren drew himself up as he spoke. "And were they?"

Fury spread over the robust face of the Sergeant Major. "No, sir! I'm as close to the grapevine as anyone, and none of our people knows anything about it. We sent a party to meet with Lepeta to discuss the matter, but they were arrested on the embassy grounds. The truth didn't matter at all to those blasted hounds. They've painted us as killers and will make their story stick even if they have to kill us all to prove it!"

"Damn it!" Fuller spat. "Our people are being held hostage for crimes we didn't commit. There'll be hell to pay when the rest of the regiment hears about it."

Loren nodded. "You're probably right. Taking Highlander families hostage did nothing to help the Davions here. It will only solidify resistance against them. By the time the Fusiliers land it will be an outright massacre. I've never met Cat Stirling, but I'm willing to be she won't stand by and let this pass without a fight."

The Sergeant Major rubbed his good leg and shook his head. "Gods, man, you dinna know it all yet, do ye? Everyone knows the Fusiliers are a-landing in a week or so, laddie, but those snakes took the spaceport and are planning a surprise fer Stirling. They let me be, writing me off as an old cripple, making me tend bar fer them. But I learned what was happening."

"What are their plans, Mister Pluncket?" Loren pressed.

"For the past five days they've been unloading petaglycernie by the ton from their cargo haulers, packing the warehouses around the spaceport to the brim. I heard one of them say they've got another two ships' worth to unload and are having the stuff brought in from factories they captured in the city."

"What are they going to do with that much explosive? DropShip holds' worth of the stuff sounds like enough to take out the entire city, especially if they've got it in concentrated form. What have they got up their sleeve?"

Loren stared at Plunckcet as the realization came over him. His face felt flushed under the greasepaint and his mouth opened slightly. The older man nodded, seeing the comprehension coming into his eyes. "You understand, don't ye, laddie . . ."

"I don't," Jake said, looking from Loren to Plunckcet and back.

"Those warehouses are positioned all around the spaceport. They've stuffed them with massive amounts of explosives. All they have to do is lure Stirling's Fusiliers onto the spaceport and set off the explosives. The blast will be so big it will take out their DropShips, 'Mechs, and troops all in one swoop. Bang, in one shot no more Fusiliers."

"Sweet heaven," Captain Carey said.

"You can't be serious," Jake said in disbelief. "A blast that size would wipe out a huge piece of the city too."

Loren suddenly remembered one of his grandfather's sayings: "When politicians and military men meet, chaos and death reign." How right he was, Loren thought. "You're not thinking big enough, Jake. So what if they knock out a quarter of the city in the blast? It's a small price to pay to gain control of an entire planet. They wipe out Stirling's Fusiliers all at once and keep their own forces intact to mop up what's left of MacLeod's Regiment. Short and sweet. And all witnesses to the crime are blown to dust in the explosion.

Catelli and his cronies rewrite the truth to fit their own purposes and the Highlanders are crushed forever."

Loren understood the plan all too well. In some respects he admired it as one worthy of a Death Commando. What bothered him was the impact of his own mission. Wiping out Stirling's Fusiliers in a single swoop would leave the Davions with control of Northwind by the time his Death Commandos arrived. He couldn't let that happen.

Understanding finally dawned on Fuller's face. "Major Jaffray, what you're talking about is a holocaust. Thousands will be killed in such a trap."

Images of a rising mushroom cloud and fireball filling the Northwind night gave Loren a chill. Everything his grandfather had held dear in life wiped out in a heartbeat. *I've got to keep it from happening. Neutralizing the Highlanders is my mission, not mass destruction.* Then his mind focused. He remembered the words that Sun-Tzu had spoken about sacrificing even his personal honor. He would do what he could to prevent the loss of innocent lives, but if necessary, he would let them die. It was not an easy decision, and not one he could easily put from his mind.

"Sweet Northwind, it could work," Carey said, still stunned by the implications of what Loren had said. "They'd have to find a way to get the Fusiliers to drop onto the spaceport, though, and that won't be too easy. Cat Stirling is pretty cautious."

Loren frowned. "They took The Fort first thing. Your transmission codes are stored there and probably already in their hands and decoded. Unless they're total fools they'll signal Colonel Stirling that all is well and she'll land right in the middle of their trap. And with the regimental communications gear wiped out we can't warn her off." Loren knew that it was all speculation, but he was sure he was close to the mark. All the evidence fit the crime.

"We've got to do something," Jake said, anger rising in his voice. "Thousands will die."

Loren nodded. "First off, let's make sure that Mr. Frutchey has the whole story in case we get captured. Code a message to him, Laurie."

"On it." Her fingers flew over the small keypad of the portable transmitter. The message was hurried and short, but gave the Lieutenant enough that he would fully understand the implications.

Loren turned to Sergeant Major Pluncket. "Where did you say the Third Royals established their command post?"

The elder Highlander pointed out the darkened window across the street. "You were practically knocking at their door. They've set up in the middle of the Peace Park, they have. Any closer and you would've tripped their security screen and had a full company on yer butts. The bulk of their troops are spread out in the northwest end of the city. They've been digging in for the past few days, hiding their 'Mechs and tanks in buildings. The bloody dogs have ruined plenty of our people's homes to hide themselves."

"Mop up forces," Carey added, not even slowing her work on the tiny transmitter. "Anything that manages to survive their little ambush gets killed by the hidden 'Mechs."

Loren knew the tactic all too well, having used variations of it himself throughout his career. "We're going to have to confirm some of this, capture some images on disk as evidence. This building is five stories tall. Captain Carey, you and Jake get on up to the roof. Don't expose yourselves, but get some images of their HQ in Peace Park. Track the positions of any BattleMechs or tanks you happen to see." Jaffray checked his chronometer. "If we're not out of here in thirty minutes it'll be light."

The five-hour trek out of Tara and into the mired swamps south of the city was oddly silent. Pluncket needed to stop every hour and rest. Jaffray and the black-clad members of his recon lance halted but did not talk. What more was there to say? Their mood was dark by the time they reached Frutchey and the half-submerged 'Mechs in which they'd made the push to Tara. The Lieutenant's expression was equally dark, since he'd read Carey's transmission before sending it on to Colonel MacLeod. Loren sensed the lance's feeling of hopelessness.

The laser images captured by Fuller and Carey on the roof of the abandoned building confirmed much of what Plunket had told them. The ages-old Peace Park had been turned into a staging base of operations for the Third Royals. Tanks and BattleMechs ringed the mobile HQ and communications vehicles, which, ironically, were similar to those MacLeod had lost earlier in the campaign. The images of the spaceport were less conclusive but did confirm some of the story. At the very least they'd learned that the 'Mech-carrying DropShips had been removed to prevent their loss in the explosive ambush.

Lieutenant Frutchey was the only one with any good news. He'd received a transmission indicating that MacLeod's forces were already well on their way to the rendezvous outside Tara. He had no specific details except that the siege of The Castle had ended several days earlier. Meanwhile, MacLeod was apparently using a ruse to confuse the Davion surveillance and intelligence forces.

There was still hope. With troops heading this way Loren thought there as still a chance to do something, *anything,* to stop the Royals' ambush. He thought about Mulvaney, and wondered if she might be the one ace in the hole. *These are her people. She'd never sit back and let them get blown to kingdom come. No matter what kind of loyalty she feels to Victor Davion, she'd never turn her back on everything most dear to her.* Chastity Mulvaney was no cold-blooded killer. The deaths of innocents would hurt her, maybe even be enough to bring her back to MacLeod.

Loren stood on the small dry knot of land that rose up out of the swamp around them and looked the other members of his lance, including the newest member, Mr. Pluncket, in the eye. "I have to make a decision," he said. "With MacLeod's Regiment on the way and a good chance of a Davion trap in Tara, we have to move and move smartly."

Carey wiped the camouflage paint off her face while she spoke. Loren didn't have to see how much darker were the circles under her eyes to know they'd been pushed to their limit both physically and emotionally. "Major, we're with any plan you've got, as long as it makes sure those blasted Royals don't succeed in taking out Stirling's Fusiliers or the city. I'll do whatever it takes to stop them. If your orders aren't in line with that, then you can have me brought up on charges when I mutiny."

It also didn't take much to see that they were running on sheer emotions now. Jake and even Pluncket looked ready to take their guns and head straight back to Tara. But Loren knew that kind of thinking wouldn't solve anything—yet. They needed focus, something to guide them to a victory rather than a wasted punch against twelve to one odds. *I have to ask them to trust me and make them understand that this meets their needs for vengeance.* "I hear you clear enough, Captain. Trust me when I say I won't sit on my hands and let the Royals blast the Fusiliers off the face of the planet.

"The reality is that the Fusiliers are on their way, but the fact that they aren't due yet buys us some time. Captain Carey, if you want to run off and take on an entire FedCom RCT, go right ahead. You will be missed and your death will be in vain. Striking out in pure anger will just end you up as a casualty figure and won't contribute one bit to a victory. You'll be nothing more than a name on a caber. I won't stand in your way, but don't get in ours."

His words hit hard and Carey averted her eyes as she listened. "I mean for us to put an end to their little scheme. We have something now that we haven't had since the start of this entire operation, some intelligence as to what is going on. We now know where the enemy is and what their plans are. That's no small thing. With this knowledge we can put together a plan to crush the Third Royals. You don't need to sit around here in the mud depressed. Be glad. We finally have an advantage."

"I sure don't feel like celebrating . . . sir," Fuller replied coldly. "We're still outnumbered, what with Mulvaney and Catelli's forces in the mountains. It's only a matter of time before they spot our regiment and close in on us."

"I'm sorry, Jake, but looking purely at the odds is not a trait I would have associated with a Northwind Highlander. I was raised to believe that you were fighters. If you really think there's no chance, perhaps we should just surrender now and start praying merely to survive." Jaffray's voice was filled with mock contempt. Fuller looked angry, but did not retract his words. He only glared back at Loren, who ignored it. *I'm on the edge of losing them, but at least they're still listening—and I'd better take advantage of that while I can. They need a plan to follow. Something they can believe in. It's time to hit our enemy where he's weakest.*

"The key to all of this is Mulvaney," he announced boldly.

276 Blaine Lee Pardoe

"What?" Jake sputtered, his anger obviously risen a notch. "She betrayed the Colonel and the whole of the Highlanders. What do you mean she's the key?"

"She hasn't betrayed anybody, Jake," Loren returned. "She's given your people a way to preserve their honor. I haven't known her long, but I don't believe Mulvaney is one to stand by and let the Davions blow the Fusiliers to ribbons. Even if Colonel MacLeod himself had walked in and killed Burns, there's no way she'd submit to any plan to annihilate a full regiment of Highlanders without giving them a fighting chance. And she'd never stand by while there was the danger of innocent Highlander families becoming hostages or casualties. Chastity Mulvaney would never be part of a plan to level the city of Tara. And you know I'm right." *And if I'm not, what I'm about to propose might expose us all to death.*

"Major Jaffray is right," Sergeant Major Pluncket said from his seat on a small rock. "We've all known her for years. Chastity Mulvaney would never sit by and let all this happen. She's one of us, bonded by blood. A Highlander through and through. You've all fought by her side. Remember the Clans, laddie. Old Ironheart, you named her. Carey, you served under her on Glengarry against them bloody Skye rebels. If my memory serves, she saved your company's collective butts, eh, lassie?"

"What do you propose?" Carey said, looking as though Pluncket's words had been a cold slap of reality.

"I'm willing to bet that Mulvaney is being kept totally in the dark," Loren said slowly, feeling his way. "It's the only thing that makes any sense. If she finds out what's going on in Tara, she might just help turn the tables on Catelli and his crew. One of us will head toward the training camp with the mission of pretending to change sides and join Mulvaney's Highlanders. When you meet her, pass on all we've learned. Let her know what's happening, and more important, what we think is going to happen."

Jake's forehead was creased deeply in thought. "You realize you're asking us to take a pretty big risk. If you're wrong, she'll know we're wise to them and their scheme. Not to mention what will happen to us if we walk right into their hands."

"But I'm not wrong and you know it, Jake ... All of you know it in your hearts. If Mulvaney's Highlanders turn, there'll be no hope for Catelli or the Third Royals."

"Maybe we should check with Colonel MacLeod," Frutchey offered. "I mean this is a pretty big risk, not just who goes but for the entire regiment."

Jaffray shook his head. "There's not time. Hell, we could be discovered any minute and all of this would become moot. No. We must do it and do it now. I accept full responsibility for the decision." *I know I'm right. Everything tells me I am. I only hope we can get a message to Mulvaney.*

"I'll go," Lieutenant Fuller said. "I've known the Major the longest and she'll listen to me."

"No," Loren said, cutting him off. "I've got another idea." *I only wish I was going myself ...* "Someone she might believe even more." He turned to Sergeant Major Pluncket. "Sir, you and Major Mulvaney are fairly close, are you not?"

"Me, laddie? Aye," Pluncket said, patting his artificial limb. "But in all honesty it's been a lot of years since this warrior took to the field. Espionage and spyin' were never my strong suit."

"If any one of us goes, Mulvaney might suspect a trick or trap. If it's Mister Pluncket showing up on her doorstep, she'll know he'd never try to lure her out into some sort of ambush."

"Are ye sure, laddie? This old war mule has no' been in the field in some time."

"I'm sure, Sergeant Major. Jake, I saw one of those Rotunda armored cars at the edge of the city where we first went in. Do you remember it?"

"Yes."

"What are the chances of you and Mister Frutchey sneaking back and stealing that car?"

Frutchey and Fuller smiled at each other as if they were going to enjoy the task. "I'd say we can handle it."

"Good. Get going, then. Mister Pluncket, you go with them. Take the car and head up the highway to the training camp. I know we're playing a hunch, and I wouldn't ask you to if I wasn't so sure it would work. Mulvaney's the pivot point. Sway her and we can cut off the rest of the Davion plan at the knees."

"I'll try and no' let ye down, Major," Pluncket said.

"You won't. When you see Mulvaney, will you pass a message on to her?"

"Sir?"

"The last time I saw her she told me I'd be picking the place for the next time we meet. Tell her it's Tara. She'll understand." *One way or another Mulvaney will make sure she gets here, either to learn the truth for herself or to stop me. Either way I bring this fight to an end once and for all.*

The Sergeant Major nodded. "Understood, sir," he said crisply, and from the gleam in his eye, Loren thought that the old infantryman might at that.

= 32 =

South of Tara, Northwind
Draconis March, Federated Commonwealth
17 October 3057

Loren walked out of the water and wrapped the towel around his waist. Bathing was a rarity on a long campaign, but even by those standards he was feeling gamy. Regimental field quarters sometimes offered the luxury, but this time Loren had to content himself with a pond at the edge of the swamplands south of Tara. He doubted that the disinfectants and deodorizers in his field kit would do much good, but he sprayed them on anyway, knowing it would make him feel better.

The past few days had not been easy for him and the recon lance. Remaining in one spot too long risked eventual detection so he'd kept the lance on the move. Skirting the swamps, they'd made several sorties toward Tara, each time gaining more information and data. Frutchey and Fuller had managed to obtain some laser images of Kohler Spaceport and confirmed much of the story they'd heard from Mister Plunket. Cargo-hauler transports were being unloaded and the combat DropShips of the Third Royals had been moved away to prevent their destruction.

His lance members did not realize it, but Loren was carefully mapping out their path and their locations. In the time they spent dug in, he was often in his cockpit, running a series of calculations on his 'Mech's computer. There was a reason. Up in the sky, some two hours above Northwind, the Death Commandos were supposed to be in place, safe at their pirate jump point, awaiting word from him. Communicating with them was going to be difficult, but he thought he knew of a way.

Loren rubbed the ever-thickening stubble of his beard as he made his way to the *Gallowglas*. What concerned him most was the fact that the Royals had begun several recon missions of their own. Prompted no doubt by the deaths of the troopers in Peace Park, the security net around Tara was growing stronger and wider each day, forcing Loren to keep pulling back away from the city. *They aren't sure if our rescue of Plunckett was organized resistance or sheer coincidence. The Royals officers are probably getting edgy, worried that their little surprise might be exposed. Good. Let them sweat. Maybe it will lead them into making some sloppy mistakes.*

What had caught Loren most off guard was the blanket of communications silence that had suddenly been imposed between his lance and the main body of MacLeod's troops. Not wanting to risk detection, the Colonel had ordered a blackout of signals after their initial transmission. There'd be silence on that end until the two groups made contact again. Despite the lack of response to their reports, Loren kept on transmitting in hopes that someone from the regiment was receiving and analyzing their findings.

To the west were the Rockspire Mountains, and Loren stared at their dark, jagged shapes against the bright sky. *Somewhere up there is Mulvaney ... and hopefully Plunckett. She's up there by choice. He went on my orders, but seemed to think it was a good idea anyway.* Ever since the Sergeant Major had gone off, Loren had been wondering how the mission would turn out. He'd studied the maps, and knew the highway up into the mountains would bring the stolen Rotunda to the training camp in short order.

But how would Mulvaney respond to the information Plunckett was bringing? Had Catelli or Bradford twisted and distorted her thinking so much that she would no longer side with MacLeod and the rest of the Highlanders?

He'd also sent details of the mission to the regiment before the cut-off of communications. How would MacLeod respond when he received word? The Colonel was the embodiment of the Highlanders and their long and illustrious history. In that regard he reminded Loren of his grandfather, whose wisdom and approval he'd always valued.

He was climbing up the ladder footholds on the *Gallowglas* when he heard a light wail from the open cockpit. The emergency communications signal. How long had he been standing and thinking while his lancemates had been calling for him? Loren chided himself inwardly. He couldn't afford to get sloppy. Not now. Scrambling fast he reached the communications panel and activated the internal speaker.

"Jaffray here," he said, dropping the towel and pulling on his pilot's trunks.

The speaker spat back a hiss of static and garbled words as the 'Mechs communication system unscrambled the incoming transmission. "Carey here. We have targets closing in, bearing three-two-two at approximately five kilometers."

Loren toggled his fusion reactor to life as he snugged the neurohelmet over his head and down onto his shoulders. "I'm powering up now. Frutchey, do you confirm?"

"Yes, sir," the young Lieutenant's vice snapped. "Tracking the incoming targets now. I show four, no, make that five 'Mechs."

"You'd better pull along the right flank if you can, David," Carey returned. "I paint a total of eight 'Mechs on my long-range scan, light to medium configurations, moving fast in wide vee formation."

"No can do, Captain. Two of those I'm showing are moving into the moors and are cutting me off. My best bet is to pull north and link up between you and the Major."

Loren throttled his heat sinks on line and bypassed his own security coding to get the *Gallowglas* started as quickly as possible. The 'Mech seemed to vibrate to life as he pushed it forward into the swamp waters where only moments before he'd been bathing. *If it's the Third Royals, they've sent this task force a long way to get behind us. It was only a matter of time before they figured out we were here, I guess. If they push matters we'll be driven right into the city and into their hands.*

"Frutchey, they're trying to push you north. That'll trap us up against the city and the bulk of their forces. Hold your position. Carey and I will come to you and we'll punch our way out and to the south before they can solidify their position."

"Confirmed, sir," Captain Carey responded. "Hold on to your linen, Mister Frutchey. The cavalry is on the way." Loren stared at his long-range scanner and saw the line of 'Mechs approaching from the south as well as the positions of his own lance. Fuller and his *Shadow Hawk* were near Carey and moving in as well, but even so, they were outnumbered and outgunned nearly two to one. The terrain would help even up the odds but not nearly enough for a chance of true victory.

But perhaps there was no need for victory. "Frutchey, this is Jaffray. They're in short range. Run an IFF check on those targets, and fast."

There was a long pause as Loren came into visual sighting of Carey's *Guillotine* lumbering through the light swampland and trees. In the distance Fuller's *Shadow Hawk* pushed its way through a cluster of trees and into view as well. Loren's heart raced as they closed in on the mysterious 'Mechs that were closing on them. His sensors told him that the attackers were tightening their noose, but the moors were slowing them down.

"Sir! They're Highlanders. I show them as MacLeod's 'Mechs!" Frutchey's voice boomed.

"Are you sure, tinhead?" cut in Fuller's voice.

Suddenly the transmission signal was interrupted by a familiar voice that filled their cockpits and cut through the tension like a steely cold knife. "Major Loren Jaffray," came Colonel MacLeod's resonant voice.

"Jaffray reporting, sir," Loren replied as he and Carey came to a stop just short of Frutchey's *Warhammer*.

"This is MacLeod, laddie. I appreciate you holding down the front for us. Help has finally arrived." Loren let go a long sigh of relief, but that didn't release all his tension. MacLeod's arrival surprised him in more ways than one. Arriving several days early meant that MacLeod must have pushed hard to get here, perhaps even pulling 'Mechs away from the assault on The Castle. It was impressive and spoke volumes about the leadership of the Highlander CO.

Now he would have to explain why he had sent Mister Pluncket into the mountains to MacLeod. Major Huff, he was sure, would never approve. How could Loren be sure that even MacLeod would support that desperate decision?

33

South of Tara
Northwind
Draconis March, Federated Commonwealth
17 October 3057

All four members of Jaffray's recon lance stood in the shade of a massive willow as Colonel MacLeod went over their findings. The regimental intelligence officer, Captain Dumfries, and one of his aides were there too, poring over their notes and the laser images that the lance had managed to capture during their recon of Tara. Both men seemed to treat the information as if it were some sort of treasure, precious and delicate. MacLeod was silent for a long time, apparently thinking over his options. Several times he spoke to Captain Dumfries in a low whisper as they checked and rechecked the maps.

"You've all done remarkably well," he said finally to Loren. "The terrain information you obtained helped us moved the regiment out days ahead of schedule. More important you've uncovered a trap that would have taken the lives of thousands of Highlanders and our kin in the city. This is no small achievement and I thank you all for the work you have done. I know the communications blackout was hard on you, but you understand that we didn't want to risk tipping off the Royals that we were underway."

Loren relaxed slightly as he looked into the steely gray

eyes of the Highlander CO. "Sir, what happened back at The Castle?"

"It took us slightly longer than expected, but once we penetrated the upper tunnels it was only a matter of time. The Gurkhas infantry are topnotch and managed to do a pretty fair job, even though they were fighting their own kindred. I began to move some of our heavier BattleMechs out toward your position here while we secured the rest of the bunker. When all was said and done there turned out to be only ten 'Mechs and two platoons of infantry holding us at bay. As you predicted, Major, the bulk of their forces had been shuffled to the training camp in the mountains. They went there the long way, but now they're sitting on the highway only a few days outside of Tara."

Loren felt some satisfaction at this news. Major Huff had been adamant that Catelli and Mulvaney would not head for the mountains. It was reassuring to know that he, Loren, had been right on the money in predicting their actions.

"How did you manage to get the regiment moving this way without the Third Royals spotting you?" he asked. Loren knew that if the Royals had detected MacLeod's Highlanders closing on Tara they'd have mobilized and set out after them in force.

The Colonel beamed with pride. "Just a little sleight of hand. We took the crippled 'Mechs from both sides and moved them about on the river banks and on the topside of the falls. Our tech crews towed them from one end of the river to the other, repositioned them, and even painted them at night. Some were outfitted with salvaged weaponry parts so that every time the Davions did a flyover it looked like many different 'Mechs were moving in and around The Castle. In reality we were sneaking through the woods on your trail."

"So you're the vanguard of the rest of the regiment?"

MacLeod nodded. "In a manner of speaking. You've got to remember that our ground armor isn't really suited for the terrain between here and The Castle. I sent them to the upper Tilman, where right this minute they're providing the illusion that we're heading for the camp . . . just as Catelli and Mulvaney would have hoped. I had to commit some of our lighter 'Mechs to bolster the illusion, but I doubt they've pieced it together yet.

"The only bad news is that moving an entire regiment under cover is slower than moving one recon lance. We're spread a little thin, but Major Huff has assured me that when the Fusiliers land we'll be at full force here."

"Time's running out, sir," Captain Carey said. "Stirling's Fusiliers will be arriving on schedule and that puts them here in three days. You've seen our reports. If they get tricked into landing at the spaceport they'll be wiped out in one big blast."

MacLeod shook his head adamantly. "I assure you, Captain, that will not happen, not as long as I'm alive and able to fight. Captain Dumfries and I have put together a plan. It's risky, though, given the odds against us."

Loren stepped forward. "Tell us what you want us to do, sir."

"The plan is simple really. When we first got started on this little venture, Marshal Bradford knocked out my HQ and communications system. And now I plan to return the favor in spades. We'll hit Tara from three different directions at once. Two of those will be feints designed to lure out the BattleMechs they've been hiding. The third group will drive for Peace Park.

"Once there that force will do one of two things. Their first priority will be to take control of the communications van and transmit a warning to Colonel Stirling about the trap. If they can't take the van intact, the team will destroy it in hopes its destruction will tip off Stirling before she touches down. Frankly I'd rather use The Fort's or the spaceport's transmitter, but there's no way we can field enough forces to get either of them back in the time we've got."

Loren was impressed by the daring plan. "Sounds good, sir." The Davion Marshal would never expect the Highlanders to hit him like that.

"Cat Stirling is going to want some sort of verbal confirmation before landing, especially in a place as obvious as the spaceport," MacLeod continued. "I'm sure the Davion intelligence machine has come up with a way to impersonate me. The only hope we have is to get a direct warning to her—one that will make her question any other verbal orders the Davions might try to feed her."

"But if she ignores the warnings and lands—" Loren began.

"I've known Cat Stirling for years. She's always suspicious. I'm counting on her intuition as much as I'm counting on you."

"We'll do whatever you require of us, sir."

MacLeod smiled broadly. "Good. And your lance's knowledge of Peace Park and the current troop placement there makes you the best choice to lead the attack."

Loren had been hoping MacLeod would say that. *Leading an attack in a great battle is much more honorable than risking my life for a mere diversion.*

Captain Dumfries stepped forward to join the conversation, his combat kilt wrinkled and dirty from prolonged wear. "The Colonel and I feel that timing is the key to the success of this operation. Spring it too early and we risk facing the full force of the Third Royals RCT, who could wipe us out and still lure in the Fusiliers. Move too late and our brothers and sisters will be destroyed. For this to work we need to start the attack as soon as the Fusiliers begin their initial descent."

MacLeod cut in. "We have some portable ECM gear and some light mounted sets as well. We need to get the First Gurkhas to the spaceport to make sure that nothing gets set off accidentally. But that won't change anything. We may not be able to get them through, and even if we do, they may not be able to effectively cover the entire port. If you fail to divert the Fusiliers they'll still be easy prey for the FedCom troops."

Lieutenant Fuller let go a long whistle. "That's not going to give us much time. Once they're on approach, they'll be down in forty-five minutes time. We have to get the warning to them pretty damn quick or they'll end up as sitting ducks on the tarmac."

"Sir," Captain Carey cut in, "just how many troops will we have to work with?"

MacLeod checked his electronic notepad. "If all goes as planned and we manage to keep moving undetected, I estimate a total of twenty to twenty-four 'Mechs and three platoons of supporting infantry."

Frutchey chimed in. "Based on what we scanned in Peace Park, that should be enough to take on the park's defenders. This just might be a cake walk after all."

MacLeod shook his head. "Sorry to burst your bubble, Lieutenant, but that is the *total* number of 'Mechs we have at our disposal. Some of those will have to be committed to the diversionary attacks. That trims you down by two full lances and our Gurkhas infantry support."

Fuller raised his eyebrows and shrugged. "Maybe I spoke too soon."

Colonel MacLeod stroked his beard as he surveyed his warriors. "As I said before, you've done remarkably well. But now I have to ask more of you. This attack won't be easy, but we've got a few days respite before we're forced into combat. Let's break camp, pull back, and conceal our 'Mechs. We have a lot of detailed planning to do if this is going to be a success." The seemingly ageless Colonel saluted the officers and dismissed them. Loren was about to go, too, but the elder Highlander gestured for him to remain.

"You wanted to speak to me, sir?" he asked softly. *This has to be about Pluncket and Mulvaney. He probably decided to reprimand me in private rather than humiliate me in front of the others.*

"I think you know what this is about."

"Yes, sir, I think I do. And let me say that I accept full responsibility for my actions. What I did might not seem right at this time, but I firmly believe it was worth the risk. I believe that if Mulvaney knows the truth she'll cease fighting us and possibly even turn against the Davions."

MacLeod chuckled deeply and slapped Loren on the shoulder. "You think I'm upset by your actions, lad?"

Loren was confused. "You're not?"

"Not at all. I never know what to expect from you, but you've proven that you're a man of honor. Even hard-liners like Huff no longer consider you a threat but an asset, though I doubt he'd ever admit it. Your move was a master stroke. Mulvaney is still a Highlander, no matter what the Davions have tried to feed her. I refuse to believe she has or can turn her back on her own people."

"Thank you, sir."

"No laddie, thank you." MacLeod turned to look across the low bog to where his *Huron Warrior* stood waiting in the mud and muck. "You reminded me of something I learned as a brash young Lieutenant training with Colonel Marion's Highlanders."

"What was that, sir?"

MacLeod stared off into the distance as if he were searching for his memories among the heavy woods and moors. "Marion was a devil and a half. He would drill us as new cadets day and night. All during our training he would tell us, '. . . the key to victory is to take the high ground. Hold the high ground and you can never lose a battle.' For two years I thought he was talking about terrain—hills and ridges and the like. It made sense at the time. I was still wet behind the ears and full of fire and spirit."

MacLeod turned back to Loren, his eyes suddenly showing both his age and his weariness. "We got involved in a little skirmish on Ningpo before we left the Capellan Confederation during the Fourth Succession War. Nasty series of battles in the flatlands there. What strikes me as so ironic now is that the unit we faced was the Third Davion Guards RCT."

"The same unit on its way here now."

"Twice should be enough for any commander in a lifetime. Anyway, we were engaged with the Guards when the Colonel linked up with me in a small clearing. On the hill above us were three Davion BattleMechs that had been mauled over by another company and left for near dead. They were practically radioactive scrap when we spotted them trying to escape to their own lines. I remember locking on my *Archer*'s LRMs and arming them when the Colonel signaled me to shut off my T&T."

"Why?"

MacLeod chuckled once to himself. "He told me to 'take the high ground.' I told him that I was trying to do just that. That was when he told me what he really meant.

"You see, Loren, he wasn't talking about the terrain. He was talking about the moral high ground. Hold a higher set of moral standards than a common MechWarrior. Those warriors that I was locking onto did not pose a threat and they had no way to defend themselves. Colonel Marion told me the important thing was to hold myself high as a Highlander, to be an example to others. To do that was to be a leader.

"Since then that is where I've tried to fight my battles, on the moral high ground, siding with the good. I've taken stands for right against might even though they weren't always popular at first. I've taught Mulvaney just as Colonel Marion taught me. She'll come around."

Loren was silent for a while before speaking. "I appreciate the chances you've given me, Colonel. Things I only dreamed about as a boy; a chance to fight in our family's regiment. Not just against a common foe, but to lead Highlanders into battle. This has meant more to me than I can ever express, Colonel. I only wish my grandfather were till alive to see a Jaffray again in the ranks of the Highlanders."

"He'd be proud, Loren. It's odd, though. You always mention your grandfather but never your father."

Loren lowered his head and stared at the ground for several seconds before speaking. "My father and grandfather never seemed to agree. I guess that's common between fathers and sons. He thought that Grandfather put too much store in the Northwind Highlanders and not enough in House Liao and the Confederation. So when the time came my father enlisted in the Capellan Armed Forces and became a Death Commando. He was gone a lot while I was growing up. I never really go to know him. Except that they say he died with honor.

"When the Commandos offered me a position in their ranks I accepted, especially since it was to the same unit as my father. Now I feel torn between my duty to the Confederation and to the Highlanders. I hope I can honor both my father and grandfather . . . if that's possible."

"You've done well, Loren. Don't worry about honoring the memories of your family. The time has come for you to make your own place in history. The only balance you have to strike is one with yourself. If you can't wake up in the morning and look at yourself in the mirror, then you've failed. Trying to live up to the expectations of other people is a sure way to fail.

"You have a drive in combat and a way of creating a battle plan as you go. You seem to be able to sense your enemy and understand what's going on in their minds, and that is no small gift. You also have a knack for seeing the moral high ground yourself. Otherwise you'd never have had the sense to send Pluncket to find Mulvaney. You've proven me right all along.

"There is only one thing that I don't understand . . ."

"What is that, Colonel?"

"Why didn't you go find Chastity yourself?"

Why didn't I go? Loren stared into the eyes of the Highlander Colonel, not sure how to respond. "A part of me wanted to, sir. Mulvaney and I have developed a kind of love-hate relationship. We had each other in our sights at the bottom of the river, but something kept us from killing each other.

"I guess I knew that my duty was here. And if she was going to listen and believe anyone it would be the Sergeant Major. If I'd gone she might have felt a nagging doubt. With Mr. Pluncket she won't hesitate to accept the information he's bringing her."

"You seem worried and I'm not sure I understand why. You've done all you could."

"It's not just what might happen with Mulvaney, sir. I have a concern that maybe only you could understand. There was a moment there when I almost lost control of the lance. When they realized what was happening in Tara and saw their city under enemy occupation, for a minute I thought they might break ranks."

"But you retained your command."

"What worried me about it is that our people might fight this one more from emotion than thought when we launch our attack. Against these odds it's going to take a superior plan to beat the enemy. We're not going to charge into Tara to wipe out every last Davion, but some of our troops will think we should. If they do, and refuse to follow orders, this will turn into a disaster."

"What you're saying is that they've got to push aside their feelings and do their duty. Well, Major, I can tell you they will. Not just because I order it, but for the sake of the Highlanders."

"Then we have nothing to worry about, sir."

MacLeod pointed to their BattleMechs looming in the

swamp. "It's time for us to prepare to take that high ground I told you about and hold it against a dark foe. The odds aren't in our favor, but we've got to try."

Loren nodded slowly in response. William MacLeod was a man living in the past, future, and present all at once. The Chancellor was right to send Loren to Northwind. The fact that the Jaffray line intertwined with MacLeod's past made Loren the perfect instrument to destroy the Highlanders. He felt the same familiar pang over what he had to do, but as in any mission he undertook, Loren knew he must succeed—or die in the attempt.

Colonel Drew Catelli ran across the ground at a trot to where Mulvaney stood near the sleek outline of the Rotunda armored car. Dressed in the standard shorts and cooling vest of a 'Mech pilot, she stood talking with the mysterious man who had just arrived.

Catelli's heart was racing. He'd taken extreme measures to keep Chastity Mulvaney in the dark about what was unfolding in Tara. With the departure of Marshal Bradford, she'd been ordered to report directly to him. Now a stranger had arrived in the twilight hours and Catelli was afraid that his tight control over her might be destroyed in a matter of seconds.

Damn fools! I told my men to make sure that no one approaching our position be allowed through to the Highlanders. That blasted sentry who let this happen is going to end up as point in our attack, that I guarantee. If Mulvaney's learned what the Royals are doing in Tara the entire operation could be at risk. She would strike out instantly and cripple my force. Not to mention what she and her Highlanders might do to me. This can't happen. Too much is at stake.

He strode up alongside Mulvaney, half-expecting to see that her visitor was Loren Jaffray. Instead he was relieved to see a stranger in front of him.

"Colonel Mulvaney," Catelli said as he eyed the man from top to bottom. *This is not a MechWarrior, that much I'm sure of.* The Sergeant Major was portly and the field infantry fatigues he was wearing were drenched with sweat from his journey. From the bags and dark circles under his eyes, it was obvious he'd been driving the Rotunda for some time, if not days. "Who do we have here?"

"Colonel Catelli, this is Sergeant Major Pluncket," Mulvaney said evenly. "He approached us on the highway signaling surrender."

"Indeed. What brings you to us, Sergeant Major?"

The old man threw Mulvaney a glance before answering. "Sir, I was with Colonel MacLeod's Regiment but decided that my loyalties were best served with the likes of you and yer Davion troops, sir. I'd learned you were headed for the training camp and thought this would be a good time to join up with ye. I was a little surprised to come across ye so soon, only two days' march from the camp."

"This isn't your vehicle, is it?" Catelli was suspicious. Something just wasn't right about the story this old codger was spouting.

"No, sir," Pluncket returned proudly. "I'm an infantryman like my father and grandfather before him."

"I've known the Sergeant Major for years," Mulvaney chimed in. "I can vouch for his integrity."

Catelli ignored her comment and concentrated on Pluncket. "You arrived driving a Highlander armored car. That is fairly odd for someone of your background and training."

"Stolen, sir. A good infantryman knows how to use an advantage whenever he can. I am a *very* good infantryman, sir."

"I see," Catelli said smoothly. "Well, I'm glad to have you, Sergeant Major. Allies are always appreciated, but enough of this chatting. We're on a bit of a schedule."

Again the man shot Mulvaney a glance. "Looks to me like yer headin' for Tara."

Catelli nodded. "We're going to assist in the garrison duties there. Have you been to Tara recently, Mister Pluncket?"

"No, sir. I came through the woods on the southern bypass to get here. Tara is neutral, is it not?"

"*Was* neutral. Things have changed. Indeed we're operating under tight security restrictions. As such you'll have to report to one of my Consul Guard units for posting and debriefing. Meanwhile, Colonel Mulvaney, if you would take the lead we can get a few dozen more kilometers behind us tonight." *Simple. Divide and conquer. Keep them apart. My men will interrogate this Sergeant Major while I keep my little Highlander busy.*

"With all due respect, Colonel," Mulvaney said, "I'd like Mister Pluncket posted to my command company. As I said before, I've known him for some time."

Jeopardize my dreams on a whim and a promise? Never! "Now, now, Colonel. This is a military operation, not a social event. There will be plenty of time for you two to get reacquainted once we reach Tara. In the meantime, our standing security orders remain in place. After all, if our newest volunteer has recently been with Colonel MacLeod's forces, I want to make sure we get as much information out of him as quickly as possible."

I've caught this one in time, Catelli told himself. *If Mulvaney knew about the Third Royals trap she'd have my blood by now. And if this Pluncket knows something he'll never get a chance to pass it on to her. She's still in the dark about what's going to happen when we reach the city, but by then it will be too late. Soon, Northwind and its precious Highlanders will be mine to do with as I wish.*

34

South of Tara
Northwind
Draconis March, Federated Commonwealth
18 October 3057

Loren volunteered for the first evening watch, though his motives had little to do with protecting the regiment's security. As he moved through the swamps he thought back to his meeting with MacLeod the day before. The memory of their conversation tugged at his emotions, twisting his thoughts as he traveled to the carefully calculated coordinates he'd been working on for the past week. But no matter how he tried to clear his mind, he couldn't shake the memory.

MacLeod had become his grandfather in his eyes. He was every childhood memory and dream of the Northwind Highlanders. And somehow his memories of his grandsire seemed to be overlaid with images of MacLeod. But it wasn't only that on his mind. Having seen the Highlanders at both their best and their worst, he considered them to be remarkable warriors. They were not merely mercenaries. Even the Death Commandos would find them a stern and deadly challenge. Hadn't he nearly been bested at the Castle? It had only been his own Death Commando training that kept him from being killed in the ambush. Loren felt he'd been fortunate to survive.

And even when fighting each other, the Highlanders still managed to maintain their honor. Thinking about his conversation with MacLeod about the moral high ground, Loren wondered if the Highlander CO suspected him of duplicity. Loren would do his duty, yet couldn't help feeling a kinship not just with the Colonel but with the Highlanders as a whole. They were family—something that had been missing in his life since the death of his grandfather.

That was what made his next actions so difficult.

Loren checked his secondary monitor and saw that he'd reached the proper coordinates. Somewhere out there two battalions of Death Commandos were waiting at a pirate jump point in close proximity to Northwind. He knew the coordinates, having committed them to memory during his trip to Northwind weeks before. Coordinating their position and his own, as well as the spin of the planet relative to the jump point had been challenging but it was something he'd done before. Without large-scale communications, contacting a JumpShip from a BattleMech was almost impossible. But Loren's training in covert operations gave him more than a few tricks up his sleeve. To solve the problem he would resort to a technique used centuries earlier.

He checked the area to make sure he wasn't being scanned or viewed. Once confident of his security he loaded a special communications program into his battle computer. It had taken him days to write the code, but he was sure it would work. Tied into the DI computer's chronometer, the program started its countdown. Loren watched as the program slowly ticked away the seconds.

At the thirty-second mark the left arm of the *Gallowglas* began to rise, almost straight up. The twin Magna Quasar pulse lasers charged another five seconds later. *Somewhere out there my comrades wait.* The medium pulse lasers were fully powered four seconds later and the 'Mech's gyro stepped up its humming as it further stabilized the *Gallowglas.*

Loren knew there was only a ten-second window of operation. As the chronometer ran down Loren watched in satisfaction as the pulse lasers fired intermittently. The bursts of crimson light streaked upward into the mid-evening sky, off into the darkness of night. They did not fire full bursts but instead let go with a series of timed and calculated pulses, all in accordance with his program. The left arm of the *Gallowglas* rose slightly with each burst, tracking an unseen point in the Northwind night. Somewhere, out in the vastness of the stars, his unit waited.

Loren watched with dark satisfaction as the program came to an end. The pulse lasers powered down and Jaffray once again took control of the 'Mech's arm. He was proud of his actions. He had behaved like the perfect Death Commando. But it was also hard knowing that he was betraying his honor and bond with the Highlanders. It chewed at his mind like a hungry rat, gnawing at his thoughts as he slowly moved the *Gallowglas* back on its security sweep pattern.

The Capellan JumpShip *Eban Emael* hung waiting at a pirate jump point in the Northwind system. The starship's one-kilometer jump sail was fully deployed in charge mode, pulling in photons and converting them to the energy required for the ship to make its instantaneous hops between star systems. The Death Commando corporal assigned to the battery room had what seemed to be a dismal duty: watching for any abnormal microjoule spikes. To most personnel, even seasoned spacers, such spikes were meaningless. To the Death Commandos they meant something more, something significant.

The corporal verified the readings. The spikes were small but obviously not solar flare activity. It was called pinging, a way to communicate where such communications were usually impossible. Satisfied with his diligence, the young officer printed a hard copy of the readings and signaled the commanding officer's quarters. It was late but there was a standing order if such an anomaly arose.

"Colonel Hertzog, this is Corporal Kwang."

There was a short pause before he heard the husky voice of the Death Commando CO, apparently forcing himself awake. "Report, Corporal."

"Signal pulses on the solar sail, sir. It's definite pinging, sir. They're faint but I believe they are our protocol."

The voice of the Colonel seemed to come to life. "Excellent, Corporal. Send them to the file under my directory

298 Blaine Lee Pardoe

structure. Contact the command staff and tell them to join me ASAP. I'm on my way to the bridge."

Colonel "Tank" Hertzog reached the bridge five minutes later. At that hour only a skeleton crew was on duty, but Hertzog had disrupted their usually silent routine by ordering his command staff to the bridge. The gathered officers looked sleepy but ready for action. They'd been sitting at the jump point for some time waiting for word from Northwind. Now, finally, there might be some action. The instant they saw the Colonel they snapped to attention.

Hertzog returned their salute and leaned over the bridge's computerized command table. "I appreciate the late-night roll-out. Our sail monitor in the battery room picked up a reading. I believe we may have finally heard from our contact on Northwind." The big man pressed several control buttons, and then the spike signals scrolled out on the table monitor. Each of the officers watched the small series of spikes and the intervals between them. A message, small and encrypted, almost invisible, yet present.

"That's Jaffray, all right."

One of the officers, Major Stafford Xhu, looked over the signal as Hertzog ran the pattern through the secured library of the current coded messages the Death Commandos used. "Things must be getting hairy down there for him to resort to this method of getting word to us."

Major Quaid watched as the computer arrived at a match to the signal pattern, stroking his shaven ebony-skinned head as he spoke. "Give the damage our fighters did to that Davion DropShip convoy, it's safe to assume that the Federated Commonwealth has committed troops to their Northwind initiative. This may be Jaffray's only way of getting us a message without attracting attention."

Hertzog ceased the discussion. "The message is a standby to drop signal."

Quaid smiled broadly at the confirmation. "So, it's finally the end of the Northwind Highlanders. The day of reckoning."

Colonel Hertzog said nothing, merely giving his subordinate a nod. He looked over at the JumpShip's duty officer who was at the far end of the bridge, keeping his distance from the Death Commando field commanders. "Captain

Loring, we will be disengaging from the *Eban Emael* within thirty minutes." The duty officer nodded and immediately began to give orders to his two ensigns as Hertzog turned his attention back to his ground officers.

"I want each of you to return to your DropShips and prepare for immediate departure. We'll break free and hold near the JumpShip for a fast drop as soon as we get word. We're only a two-hour burn from Northwind and I want full tactical database assimilation within the hour. Go over the intelligence and our satellite data. This is very real. Our Chancellor's mission directives are clear—destroy the Highlanders and any remaining Davion resistance."

"Are we going in, sir?" Xhu asked.

Colonel Hertzog nodded firmly. "It looks like it. There are only two men in the universe who can stop us now. One is on Northwind and the other sits on the Celestial Throne of the Capellan Confederation."

35

Duggan's Marsh
Northwind
Draconis March, Federated Commonwealth
20 October 3057

The two companies of MacLeod's BattleMechs and their supporting troops and techs huddled in a horseshoe formation under an umbrella of thick willow trees as their commanding officer's own *Huron Warrior* strode to a position in front of them. The technical crews carefully undraped the tarps and other electronic concealment gear covering the equipment.

Seeing how skillfully MacLeod piloted the *Warrior,* Jaffray wondered if the Colonel had done the 'Mech's reprogramming himself. How else could he have achieved such a harmonious blend of man and machine?

When he began to speak, the Colonel's voice was like that of a kindly father talking to his children. The authority was there, but also revealed were the care and concern of a true leader. These were not just his troops, they were his kin, each and every one of them. "The last flyby of the Royals fighters was ten minutes ago. That gives us less than an hour to reach Peace Park.

"You've all reviewed the battle plans and maps at length, but let me stress the importance of adhering to the plan. Our two diversionary forces will drive in to where our families are being held under house arrest. Once in the city they will not attack, but only make enough noise to get the Davions' attention. Lots of false communications chatter in the recon lances, that kind of thing. We need to make them think that most of our troops are heading there. Remember, for the main force to reach the center of the city we've got to pull the bulk of their forces away from the perimeter.

"I'll be leading the primary attack force, which will wait just outside the city until the attack is underway and we're sure the Davions have sent troops after the diversionary forces. When we do emerge we'll drive into the heart of Peace Park from the south. The First Gurkhas under Captain Cohlm will move into the spaceport if at all possible. No matter what, we cannot miss our primary objective. Our goal is simple. Either capture or destroy their communications van.

"Each of you in the primary task force has a laser disk with a coded message for Colonel Stirling and the Fusiliers. It carries a data message about the trap and my verbal warning as well, just in case. If we take their communications van intact, use the disk to warn the Fusiliers of the ambush. We can't know exactly when Cat Stirling's going to land, but our best estimates and calculations based on their last orbit show them dropping in approximately ninety minutes."

"How will we know if they receive our transmission?" Lieutenant Frutchey asked.

"Unfortunately there's no way for sure. My guess is that if we're successful you'll hear the wail of bagpipes over the commline—which will be Stirling trying to jam the lines to keep the Davions from being able to coordinate their forces."

MacLeod emphasized the gravity of the mission. "If Cat Stirling lands in that spaceport, the Fusiliers, along with most of the city of Tara, will be wiped out. Our families and a lot of innocent civilians will also die in the blast. Without honor, without hope of survival. We cannot permit such a slaughter of our kinsmen." Loren felt a lump rise in his throat as the Colonel spoke.

"Many of you have a lot of confusing thoughts and emotions running through you right now. Yes, this is our homeworld and these invaders are occupying our capitol.

But this isn't the time to fight from your emotions. If *any* of you leap into battle and disregard your orders because you think those damnable Davions owe us a pound of flesh, this entire mission could fail. We're not going into Tara to wipe out the occupiers or to recapture even one block of the city. We're going in to save the lives of every man and woman of Stirling's Fusiliers. These are your family and friends. Remember the mission, focus on your duty."

Loren smiled in satisfaction at those last words, glad MacLeod had decided to make a point of every man doing his duty. As he watched the relatively small force, his mind raced through a dozen possible outcomes. Combat in an urban environment was not something any MechWarrior looked forward to. It was something to dread. He had trained and fought in such an environ, but now he would do so alongside the Highlanders.

The same people who, in a very short time, would be destroyed by his actions.

MacLeod was still talking. "From this point forward we're likely to be visible to the enemy. Hit them hard and fast and remember to keep moving. Don't get bogged down in a fight because we're outnumbered nearly six to one and don't have a chance of winning. Hit your objectives, then get the hell out. Understood?" The commline rang with the affirming voices of MacLeod's Highlanders.

Loren checked his heat levels and bit his lower lip slightly in concern. Ever since the battle at The Castle, the 'Mech's fusion engine had intermittently been running hot. Now it was acting up again. He watched as his heat sinks bled off the excess, hoping the problem wouldn't surface in combat. The techs had assured him it wasn't serious, but of course none of them would be riding the 'Mech into the fray. Out of necessity he ignored the potential problem.

As always, he was feeling The Sensation, and it was stronger than any other time in his life. The chills and bursts of heat wracked him like an intense fever. His heart raced until he could hear it pounding like drums in his ears. Loren felt sharper, more ready than he ever had before battle.

I've fought a lot of battles in my time, but this is the most important one. It's not just being outnumbered, I've seen that before too. No, this is something more. He remembered

MacLeod's discussion of the moral high ground and wondered if that was what was feeding The Sensation rushing through his veins and mind. *It's almost like he knows what my mission is and wants me to save the Highlanders instead of calling down the Commandos. There's more here than just my mission, I'm a part of this battle. I'm not fighting for myself or for the Chancellor. I'm fighting for family. MacLeod knew it and even Carey saw it in me on the trip here. These are my people despite all the politics and the passage of time. Now I must sacrifice my honor to destroy my own kin.*

The diversionary lances broke out of the marshes first. They would hit Tara from the north and west while the primary attack force under MacLeod would hit from the south shortly thereafter. All parties would try to stay away from the spaceport, knowing it was a deadly trap that not even a powerful BattleMech could hope to escape. Loren watched as the others lumbered off, and then he turned his attention back to MacLeod's *Huron Warrior*. The remaining BattleMechs were waiting for the order to march. Once given there would be no turning back.

"Highlanders . . ." came the booming voice of the Colonel. "Roll!" The *Huron Warrior* strode through the trees and moors just outside of Tara like a knight charging into battle. Loren and his lancemates followed quickly, turning the lone charge into a raging stampede. The trip seemed to take no time at all. Halfway to the city Loren realized that he couldn't remember any details of the trek thus far. It was as if it had never happened. He, like the others, had been so focused on the march that he hadn't noticed anything other than piloting his 'Mech.

Less than half an hour later the city of Tara came into view, framed against the majestic Rockspire Mountains to the west. The Colonel led the reinforced company into a huge drainage ditch that was empty now. The trench was nearly a kilometer long with space enough for three 'Mechs across. It wouldn't offer any cover from the air, but it would block any direct line of sight observations by the enemy.

Loren knew that it was only a matter of time before the diversionary forces hit the city. Once they did the Davions would counter the attacks . . . and then MacLeod and the main force would strike. It was an old tactic, but one that rarely failed when the element of surprise was added in. So far, it looked like MacLeod's plan was working.

The Third Royals headquarters van was stuffy and humid despite its climate control systems. "Sir, I have reports of several lances closing in to the west and north of the city," the communications technician announced. "It looks like they're converging on the area where the Highlander families are housed. According to our scouts the force is slightly less than company size."

Marshal Harrison Bradford smiled broadly, took out a fresh cigar and leaned over one of the tactical displays. "This is better than I'd hoped for. Apparently MacLeod decided not to head for the mountains or stay at The Castle after all. Trying to get here in time to link up with the Fusiliers at the last minute, eh? Well, Colonel MacLeod, you may not know it now, but I already have a full regimental combat team here. And for the past three days I've also been moving Catelli and Mulvaney's forces in, just in case Cat Stirling decides on her alternate landing zone. I must thank the Colonel, if he survives, for saving me the time and trouble of having to hunt him down."

"Orders, sir?" the communications officer asked.

"Recall our aerofighters. Inform all commands of the positions and locations of the attacking forces. Pull four companies out of our other sectors and divert them toward the Highlanders. Dump Colonels Catelli and Mulvaney what you have on track so far. Let Catelli know that at least some of MacLeod's Regiment has surfaced, but that we won't need him here yet."

Colonel Morrow, the Third Royals 'Mech commander, stepped forward. "Sir, perhaps this is a diversion."

The Davion Marshal shook his head as he studied the tactical display showing Tara and his troop placements. "I don't think so. Our recon flights are still showing a lot of activity in and around The Castle and a ground armor recon effort up the Tilman toward the mountain camp. If MacLeod did somehow get a force here, it's probably nothing more than a token offering."

"But there is still a possibility that this is a ruse. For that matter the activity we've photographed and scanned at The Castle might be false, designed to confuse us."

Bradford mulled over the idea as he studied his cigar. "I didn't become a Marshal by being stupid, Colonel Morrow. If you're right, the most likely place for them to attack would be where? The spaceport."

"Yes, sir. The spaceport, sir. If they learned of our ambush they'll try to keep the Fusiliers from landing or making use of the communications facilities there. The Fort is too heavily defended so they'd have to press for the spaceport. Because of the ambush we have almost nothing in that part of the city."

"Divert troops to that sector, at least two companies' worth," Bradford said. "That should be sufficient to keep them from interfering with the Fusiliers' date with destiny. Is Stirling's regiment still on approach?"

Morrow nodded. "We checked them a few minutes ago. MacLeod has no way to warn them off. Stirling will land at the Kohler Spaceport in fifty minutes—as scheduled. Mister Lepeta dropped off the dubbed tape of your verbal confirmation at The Fort and the message has been transmitted to her. So far there's no indication that she doubts the coded signals we've been sending them or the fake message from MacLeod."

"Was the message recorded exactly as Mulvaney and I specified?"

"Exactly, sir. With Mulvaney's knowledge of Highlander procedures and protocols and your text, it was perfect. Here . . ." He reached out and inserted a laser disk into a playing slot, turning up the volume.

The voice over the speakers was that of William MacLeod, computer-generated and compiled from a variety of recordings and carefully meshed to sound like the Highlander CO speaking direct and in person. "Colonel MacLeod to Colonel Stirling. Authorization Code Scorpio, Libra One. The Davions have thrown an RCT against us, Cat. We're holed up in Tara and need your reinforcements bad. Your orders are to land at the Kohler Spaceport and proceed directly to The Fort to assist in its defense. We believe that the Davions are tapping our communications and this will be the only message we send before blackout. We need your help."

Bradford smiled craftily. "Excellent. If I didn't know better I'd swear it was MacLeod myself. Now then, hold your reinforcements at the spaceport until fifteen minutes to their landing, then pull them back out. If MacLeod does try to take the spaceport he'll be wiped out right along with Stirling."

"Yes, sir." Morrow was grinning too, like the proverbial Cheshire.

"Well, Colonel Morrow, now I think we can just about wrap up this minor disturbance. After today there'll be an end to all this foolishness about Northwind independence. Maybe then we can get to the real action on the Marik-Liao front." The Marshal took out his cutter and snipped off the end of his fresh cigar. "I'm going over to the west zone and watch the mop-up myself." He was out of the van in two quick steps, then disappeared into the green of Peace Park.

36

Outskirts of Tara
Northwind
Draconis March, Federated Commonwealth
20 October 3057

The tension in the drainage ditch was so thick that Loren could hardly tell the difference when his reactor heat level peaked again. And if not for his external microphones he'd never have heard the distant rumbling of explosions as the diversionary lances charged into the city, engaging the Third Royals. Suddenly MacLeod gave the command they'd been waiting for. "Lads and lassies, follow me!" In four long strides the *Huron Warrior* crested the lip of the drainage ditch, with the rest of the Highlander 'Mechs close on his heels.

Coming to the suburbs of the city they encountered the first sign of the Third Royals as a platoon of infantry opened up with short-range missiles as they passed. Most of the attack force did not even slow pace. The only 'Mech that broke ranks was a Highlander *Firestarter* that fired its jump jets and lifted into the air long enough to target the building where the Davion troops were positioned. With a blast from every one of its weapons the *Firestarter* wiped the small building off the face of the planet, leaving in its place only billowing black smoke and roaring flames.

It wasn't until they were three blocks from Peace Park

that MacLeod's task force ran into its first true resistance when a combined arms lance of Royals appeared from an alleyway to slam into their flank. A Davion *Victor* and a *Centurion* led the assault, backed up with fire support from an antique Von Luckner heavy tank and a Harasser light missile platform. They drove straight into the center of the Highlander force, firing at the Highlander 'Mechs both in front and in back of them. The attack nearly shattered the momentum of MacLeod's race to the park, but only briefly.

Fuller's *Shadow Hawk* squared off against the *Victor* as it passed, tearing into it with both lasers and Streak SRMs. The missiles dug into the neck-ring of the *Victor* just under the cockpit, cracking the canopy with a spider web of hits. The *Victor* pilot responded with a haymaker-style punch that turned the long-range missile slots into a mangled mess on Fuller's torso. The Highlander 'Mech reeled from the impact but continued on towards Peace Park.

Carey's *Guillotine* caught a wave of missiles from the Von Luckner and responded by unleashing her medium and large lasers in a wall of brilliant light that ate the right treads of the tank, sending it twisting into the corner of a building. Loren slowed his pace slightly, firing his PPC at the *Victor* at the same time that MacLeod targeted the 'Mech with his Gauss rifle. The combined hits to the 'Mech's upper torso were too much for the *Victor*'s pilot to compensate for. The massive assault 'Mech tumbled backward into a building, becoming buried under the debris of the structure as it fell.

The Harasser driver knew that he was outclassed and tried to make a break for cover, getting peppered by missiles and lasers from the other Highlanders that passed. The crippled Von Luckner refused to give up the fight, twisting its turret and firing a barrage of cannon fire into Frutchey's *Warhammer*. The exploding rounds ripped away replacement armor from the previous fights and the young Lieutenant almost lost control of the *'Hammer* mid-step. Two of the shots left streaks of bright pink coolant oozing like blood from a stab wound.

Before Loren could lock his weapons onto the tank he saw Laurie Carey rush up to the Von Luckner at point-blank range and knock it in with a series of rapid kicks. The massive tank never stood a chance, and its missile ammunition went off as soon as she stepped away. Pieces of the Von Luckner crashed into the surrounding buildings, but the Highlanders had already moved on.

The sight of Peace Park was somehow reassuring to Loren as he and the rest of the assault company raced toward its lush green trees and grass-covered knolls. A place named for peace and created to reflect calm was about to be turned into a battlefield. It was both ironic and disturbing that in all the years of Davion occupation of Northwind, Tara had been spared the horrors of the Succession Wars. The city was a jewel of the Inner Sphere, a monument to the fallen Star League. *Now the very people who cherish this world are going to turn this monument city into a battle zone.*

Loren suddenly realized that the lives of many of Tara's citizens must also be forfeited if his mission were to succeed. There would be nothing left of the famous unit. Perhaps not even much of Tara.

For a heartbeat Loren thought that MacLeod's force might be able to simply charge the park with little resistance. But then his short-range sensors blared a warning howl as the surrounding trees fell in on him, knocked aside like twigs by a row of advancing BattleMechs. The Royals fired wildly, not waiting for weapon locks. While some shots hit the Highlanders, others struck the road and buildings, shattering glass and ripping ferrocrete asunder.

"Drive straight through them, lads and lassies!" MacLeod's voice boomed. He charged forward like a dervish, firing as he went. A shot from his Gauss rifle ripped a gash across the chest of a *Hatchetman,* tearing a gaping hole in its armor and searing off a thick bundle of myomer muscle. Loren fired his jump jets almost on instinct, piloting his 'Mech directly at the Royals' advancing line. A Davion *Stealth* riddled his legs with short-range missiles mid-jump, each hit shaking the *Gallowglas* like a piñata under attack by a mad child. As the heat rose in his cockpit Jaffray fought the controls to keep the 'Mech from plunging to the ground.

His T&T locked onto a *Thunderbolt* at the front of the Royals line, outlining it with bright red on his heads up display. Loren thumbed the trigger of his PPC and his large laser interlock on the weapons joystick, then watch as both weapons hit their mark in the 'Mech's right torso. The armor evaporated under the boiling effect of the two weapons simultaneously striking the ferrofibrous plating like Thor's mighty hammer. The *Thunderbolt* staggered back as its missile ammunition exploded. The rear CASE blast hatches blew clear, jettisoning some of the force of the explosion but making the *Thunderbolt* lose its footing. It had fallen in a black cloud of smoke and debris by the time Loren touched down behind the Davion 'Mechs.

He spun around in time to witness Carey's *Guillotine* take a savage attack by a Royals *Rifleman*. The ultra autocannon rounds slashed her leg and arm armor while her center torso suffered a blistering attack from the large lasers. Her 'Mech seemed to sag and Loren knew she must be fighting for control. As the *Guillotine* regained its footing Carey lifted her medium lasers and fired at the *Rifleman*'s cockpit. Though not enough to knock out the 'Mech, it pushed the machine back several steps as Carey pressed on. Then Fuller's *Shadow Hawk* finally moved in to block the fire from the *Rifleman*. His own ultra autocannon fed on the *Rifleman*'s armor like a shark on raw flesh. Each hit seemed to peel away the 'Mech's armor plates until the *Rifleman* pilot broke off and pulled back, just saving his 'Mech from certain destruction.

Loren was just going to finish the job that Carey had started when a pair of Pegasus hover tanks cruised in behind the Highlanders, both taking a bead on MacLeod's *Huron Warrior* as it staggered toward him through the Davion line. Loren locked his PPC onto the first tank and fired, missing by less than two meters. The discharge arcs from the PPC blast hit the tank and threw off the aim of the gunner, who missed MacLeod. However, the other tank was much more fortunate, slamming the rear of the Colonel's 'Mech with a dozen short-range missiles at almost point-blank range. The air filled with a thin haze of smoke as the battle raged on.

Lieutenant Frutchey had managed to push through the broken line of Davion 'Mechs and saw the plight of his commanding officer. He and Loren opened up with their lasers on the pair of Pegasus tanks even as they were locking onto MacLeod's *Huron Warrior*. The young lieutenant's PPCs both struck the lead tank that Loren had missed, literally cutting the vehicle in half. Its engine and ammunition went off in a ball of fire at the same instant Loren's lasers found the second *Pegasus*, hitting the turret and front of the hover tank. The driver threw the vehicle into a tight turn, sparing MacLeod from another attack.

Loren felt his jaw clench as he turned and broke the *Gallowglas* through a small cluster of trees, the limbs and trunks snapping with virtually no resistance. His short-range sensors told him that the Davion communications and mobile HQ were only a scant hundred meters away. What they also told him was that BattleMechs were closing in from almost every direction. Time was running short.

A wave of short-range missiles struck Loren's right arm and sides before he could even respond. As he turned, a platoon of jump infantry lit their packs and leaped away into the tree and brush cover of the park. Loren cursed to himself. *Damn these RCTs! 'Mech combat is bad enough, let alone the combined arms of 'Mechs, vehicles, infantry, and fighters.*

Frutchey came up alongside as an enemy *Stalker* moved to cut off their advance. *Stalker*s had a reputation for firepower and armor and most MechWarriors preferred to avoid the massive assault machines, but it didn't look like the young officer had much chance of dodging this one. As if to confirm that fact, the 'Mech let loose a storm of long-range missiles directly at Frutchey's *Warhammer.*

"Hey, you guys, he's not alone," came Captain Carey's voice over the commlink. On his other side Loren saw three Highlander BattleMechs fighting it out with an equal number of Royals. As one of the Davions fell, the *Atlas* and the *Orion* broke free from the fight and moved in to join the *Stalker* as the last line of defense. Beyond the wall of BattleMechs was the assault group's target, but one thing was sure, at this range there was not going to be any way to avoid the defending 'Mechs.

Loren locked his PPC onto the *Stalker* and fired, shearing off several intervening tree limbs before hitting the 'Mech's massive legs. Despite the weapon's power, the shots apparently did nothing. The *Atlas* and the *Stalker* returned with fire on Frutchey's *Warhammer.* Most of their shots went wide, but the Lieutenant's own aim was thrown off so severely that he didn't even try to fire back.

Loren struggled to adjust his heat sinks manually as the battle computer showed three of them drop off line. Carey fired at the *Stalker* with her extended-range laser, her shot true but not seeming to even chip the paint on the massive 'Mech. His short-range sensors told him that the rest of MacLeod's assault group was getting mired down in a prolonged fight with the Third Royals around them. None seemed to have any chance of breaking through and flanking the wall of BattleMechs they faced. And Loren's heat levels were peaking again, a sign that his engine shielding was beginning to fail. This, combined with the erratic heat sink controls, was bad news.

"We can't just sit here and slug it out with these big boys," Loren said to his lance, just as an *Atlas* scored against him with its Gauss rifle. The spherical slug slammed hard into the 'Mech's leg, severing the myomer muscles as it passed, and shot out the back. The *Gallowglas* lurched forward in a wave of heat as its leg heat sinks disintegrated under the impact. The leg itself was still operational but only barely.

"I'm open to suggestions, Major," Captain Carey said as she waded her *Guillotine* into a clump of trees, where the foliage might provide some degree of cover.

Loren drew in a long breath. *If I don't reach that communications van I won't be able to contact the Death Commandos. I've come too far for things to end like this. Saving the Fusiliers for the Commandos is important. Cat Stirling and the others don't deserve to die in an ambush without a chance of survival. They deserve an honorable end in real combat. It simply can't end this way. Sacrifices must be made ... Sun-Tzu all but told me that. It's time I live up to his expectations.*

"Colonel MacLeod, this is Jaffray. We need your fire support and every available 'Mech up here now. Objective is in sight, but we have some problems." *Big problems.*

"This is MacLeod. It looks like I *am* every available 'Mech, Major. We've got to get past those bloody heavies or this mission is a scratch." It was an understatement that did not escape Loren. In this case "scratch" meant the death of hundreds, if not thousands. It would also interfere with his own plans for the destruction of the Highlanders, possibly leading to weeks of fighting instead of hours.

These thoughts somehow galvanized Loren. If there was any way to save the lives of the innocent people of Tara and still fulfill his mission, he would try. He hoped he'd not have to make a choice between the two. But even if he did, there was still another option. It wasn't one he wanted to dwell on, because its outcome would mean his own end, if not physically, then morally. It was a choice that until now he had been able to avoid.

"Too much at stake for that, sir," Loren said as he triggered another blast of laser and PPC fire into the *Stalker*, with little or no effect. The Davion 'Mech had almost parked in place and was sitting back with its cohorts, ready to pummel the Highlander assault force into slag rather than let them pass. As if to enforce its point it let go a wave of long-range missiles at Fuller's tattered *Shadow Hawk*, hitting him and the trees next to him. Flames lapped up at the legs of Fuller's 'Mech as he brought his autocannon around to return the attack.

"I have a plan. Unless you hear from me, finish off the comm van. Otherwise I'll see you when this thing is all over with."

"What are you doing?" MacLeod demanded.

Loren ignored him as another wave of LRMs sprayed down on his position. One hit his left arm while all the rest merely succeeded in blowing up the turf near his heavily battered *Gallowglas*. "Sir, with all respect, get up here now. They're going to need your help to get out of here in one piece." Instead of staying back and using his long-range weapons, Loren walked the *Gallowglas* into a clearing and broke into a full charge straight at the Davion *Atlas*.

"Holy crudstunk ..." That was Fuller.

"Oh my God," Carey said in disbelief, moving up to cover for Loren as he charged forward. "Colonel ... he's going to get himself killed ..."

MacLeod turned toward the *Stalker* and fired a Gauss round into the 'Mech. "No he's not, lassie. Not if we don't let him down."

37

Outskirts of Tara
Northwind
Draconis March, Federated Commonwealth
20 October 3057

Drew Catelli pulled at the ends of his handlebar mustache and smiled as he saw the report running across his secondary monitor as it was being transmitted from the outskirts of Tara. MacLeod had finally surfaced, or at least some of his force. Instead of attacking the mountain camp he'd tried to break into Tara herself. With a crack Davion Regimental Combat Team hidden there, the acting Davion Consul knew there was little chance of survival for MacLeod's Highlanders. And, if all went as planned, Stirling's Fusiliers would also be nothing but a memory in a matter of hours.

And even if it didn't go as planned, there was still little chance that MacLeod's Highlanders could survive. Some of Winchester's NAIS force was with Catelli, as were Mulvaney's Highlanders. For three days they'd been on the march down the highway from the training camp, maneuvering into position just outside the city. If the battle went poorly, they were less than thirty minutes from Tara and could easily turn the tide of battle. Catelli chuckled softly in his cockpit, proud of what he had accomplished.

Thanks to Lepeta I've managed to discredit the Highlanders by implicating them in the death of that imbecile Burns.

I've splintered MacLeod's forces and will see the end of Stirling's. The other regiments will capitulate rather than see their families and home world burned to a cinder ... and I'm fully prepared to do that. Bradford can think he's in charge as long as it suits my needs. It's only a matter of time and he'll either be gone, dead, or reporting to me. Soon Northwind and her precious troops will be mine to govern and rule. Everything is unfolding as I planned, with nothing left to chance. A transmission from one of his officers interrupted his reverie.

"What is it?" he demanded as soon as the channel was opened.

"Sir, per your instructions we've let the last of Mulvaney's Highlanders clear the front marker. I thought you should know."

"What are you talking about?" *Instructions? Front marker? Where in the hell was Mulvaney taking her—No!*

"She had orders from you, sir, deployment to Tara."

"No!" Catelli screamed at the top of his voice in the cockpit of the *Atlas*. "You idiots, why didn't you confirm that order?"

The officer was obviously shaken by Catelli's rage. "You asked not to be disturbed, sir ..."

Catelli took in a long breath and did his best to curb his temper. "Send a message to all our troops. Order them to break camp immediately. Contact Major Winchester and let her know we're going in pursuit of Mulvaney. Tell them that we assume Mulvaney and her troops are hostile. They are to fire at will."

"Sir?"

"You heard me, you incompetent buffoon! I want a full pursuit immediately. I don't care if the pilots have to push their BattleMechs by hand to get them moving!" He pounded his fist against the communications control panel, shutting it off and drawing blood where one of the studs cut his wrist. As he pulled the neurohelmet onto his head, Catelli realized that he was as hot as if his BattleMech were in battle. For the first time since he'd formulated his plan he feared that it might now come apart. He wouldn't let that happen. Too much was at stake.

* * *

Loren Jaffray watched as the light blue crosshairs of his heads up display flared red over the torso of the *Stalker* as he charged the *Gallowglas* forward. Triggering his medium lasers and PPC he watched with satisfaction as his fire whittled away the massive 'Mech's armor. As the heat in the cockpit became more and more stifling, he pivoted the large lasers to fire but was unable to get a lock in time. In response to his charge the *Orion* and *Stalker* both fired their vast array of missiles, sending a wall of flaming projectiles hurtling at him as he ran forward. As the flames of the streaking missiles filled his primary screen Loren clung tightly to the joysticks, bracing for the impact. His speed shook the lock of some of the warheads, but more than half found their mark across the front of the *Gallowglas*.

A glance at the 'Mech's outline on the secondary monitor showed dozens of red marks where armor had been breached and internal damage done. And his head readouts were so high that the failure of another heat sink would shut the 'Mech down completely. Two lasers raked his 'Mech's chest and cockpit, the latter hit making the cockpit sealing joints pop with a snapping sound. The heat inside the cramped cockpit was like sitting next to a raging bonfire. It was a dry, bitter heat and was rising to the point where the 'Mech was going to be uncontrollable.

His sensor sweeps told Loren that MacLeod and Dewkovich had taken his place, with Fuller, Frutchey, and Carey attempting to give him some cover fire. Still, there seemed to be little hope of getting past the line of Davion 'Mechs without getting destroyed. *My loss is acceptable. It's now or never.* He licked his parched lips at the thought, then did what none of the Third Royals expected; he activated his jump jets and aimed straight at their position.

MacLeod understands what I'm doing, so at least I have that going for me, Loren thought as the 'Mech's controls seemed to fight him as if they had a mind of their own. *Losing a 'Mech is a small price compared to losing two regiments and an entire planet. All I have to do is get clear of these biggies and I might actually be able to pull this off. Otherwise it won't matter.*

Unlike his jump at the fight for The Castle this flight was far from smooth for either Loren or his 'Mech. The battle-weary *Gallowglas* seemed to protest every meter of the trajectory, shaking and vibrating madly as it rose into the air. Its jump jets no longer fired a smooth stream of propulsion, but seemed to spit and sputter as the 'Mech lifted off. Loren swung his large lasers on the *Atlas* and fired at the apex of his flight. His target lock failed, most likely a result of overheating in the cockpit, but Loren didn't need it—firing more on instinct than anything else. He told himself several times that he wasn't there to knock out the Davion 'Mechs but to simply get past them ... no matter what the cost.

One shot missed while the other cut into the left arm of the *Atlas* just below its large laser, blistering and burning the armor plate. He looked up at the emergency exit controls at the top of the cockpit's main screen and wondered if he'd be able to eject from the *Gallowglas* in time. *Punching out in the middle of a bad jump is hell. I hope it doesn't come to that but it's best to be prepared.*

He barely heard the wail of his own target-locking system telling him that the *Stalker* and *Atlas* were engaging against him, but it had already lost the ability to show where the shots were going to hit. Looking out, Loren saw the missiles and bursts of light from the pulse lasers seeming to reach out for his smaller BattleMech. His entire body stiffened under the impacts and he closed his eyes, half expecting the cockpit to explode around him.

The *Gallowglas* vibrated madly under the impacts as if it were coming apart. Loren pushed the 'Mech's flight forward as he felt his right leg jump jets cut off totally, blasted apart by a stray laser pulse. The 'Mech tipped to one side as it dropped, landing only twenty meters behind the *Stalker*. As the *Gallowglas* landed the mauled leg collapsed under the weight of the machine, tipping it to the side, the cockpit glass shattering as the 'Mech plowed into the soft soil of Peace Park. As before Loren was tossed against his seat restraints as he tried vainly to move the *Gallowglas* to a better firing stance—eventually giving up. The cockpit controls flashed in sparks and the smell of ozone filled the cockpit. His legs stung from hot metal flakes searing into his bare flesh, but the pain kept him from losing consciousness at the impact of the fall. Darkness followed instantly and a feeling of vertigo and a massive impact. In the smoke and dim light

318 Blaine Lee Pardoe

Loren saw a small piece of cockpit glass sticking out of his arm. He didn't even flinch as he pulled it out.

Still alive! All around him was smoke and darkness lit only by bursts of white sparks as the cockpit controls were slowly destroyed. Had he been fighting to save the 'Mech Loren might have taken certain steps, but the 'Mech was not his main concern. Unstrapping his restraints, his body dropped to where the soil and sod had been forced into the crushed cockpit. Then he pulled his personal satchel from under the cockpit seat and detached the cooling vest and neurohelmet, setting them carefully on the floor of the fallen 'Mech. Rather than attempt to open the hatch he crawled through the shattered and spider-webbed chunks of cockpit glass and out onto the grass of the park.

Looming beyond him he saw the *Stalker*'s boxy form withering under a PPC attack from one of the Highlanders. *Probably Frutchey. At least he's still in the fight.* He checked that the needler sidearm was still on his belt and also that he had the laser disk. Only one task remained. From the satchel he took two other diskettes. If he made it to the communications van alive, he would need them.

Once outside Loren saw for the first time the damage the *Gallowglas* had taken during the battle. Huge rips in the center torso exposed sensors and severed myomer strands smeared with coolant and other chemicals hung from the guts of the 'Mech. Some spots glowed from the heat and still-burning fires inside, and smoke trailed from the cracks and holes that were all over the armor. The 'Mech's left arm was totally crushed and the badly damaged leg had been torn off. It lay forlornly on the ground. Loren felt a loss, the kind every MechWarrior feels when a BattleMech is destroyed from under him. But time was short and he must press on. Too many lives were depending on him. Not just the Fusiliers, but MacLeod and even the Death Commandos were depending on his success.

A thundering roar of explosions from the nearby battle seemed to shake new life into his weary body as he ran across the open ground toward the communications van. He'd gone almost seventy-five meters before hitting a squad of Davion infantry. Dressed in city camouflage jackets marked with the golden coiled rattlesnake symbol of the

Third Royals, they stood with weapons trained on him as he ran into the open. The leader, a sergeant, barked out his command loud and clear.

"Halt."

Loren slowed his pace, still fighting to draw in the cool air after the searing heat of the cockpit. There were two ways to handle this. One was to try to take on the entire squad, all five of them with weapons already drawn. The other way was a little more deceptive ...

"They're right behind me!" he yelled in mock terror, pointing to where he had just emerged from the undergrowth.

"Hold your position. Don't move."

Loren pulled his needler pistol from its holster and aimed it in the general direction of the *Stalker,* then fired off two shots. "Don't just stand there!" he called, leaping to a tree as if to take shelter from the battle he'd just left. "Move up and take positions before they swarm us."

The sergeant and the squad were dumbfounded. Here was a man who did not seem to fear them as an enemy and who seemed to be firing at their foe. They made a poor decision, assuming that if Loren wasn't afraid of them he must be on their side. They ran forward, then dropped to the ground, aiming toward where Loren had fired.

"They took out my 'Mech and are heading this way!" he shouted, firing another shot into the brush and undergrowth.

"Who?" the Sergeant asked.

"Highlander infantry! My God, there they are!" Loren shrieked, rising and firing again. "Form a defensive perimeter here, Sergeant," he ordered. "I'll go and warn HQ to pull back until it's safe." The Royals sergeant just stood there, looking confused and unsure how to proceed.

Loren decided to up the ante. In a full command tone he barked out an order to the squad. "Damn it, Sergeant. I order you to deploy your men. Do it now or I'll take your command myself!" That apparently was enough. The Davion squad rapidly deployed into the trees and foliage against an enemy that didn't exist.

Loren turned slowly and saw his objective looming in front of him. Having sent its sentries against a nonexistent threat, he now had only the occupants of the communications van to contend with. As he jogged up to the door he heard the distinctive crackle of PPC fire and the thundering boom of autocannon and missile explosions behind him as MacLeod and his forces continued to press the assault. Without hesitation Loren opened the door to the van and stepped in.

The crew inside were so intent on their duties that none seemed to notice him at first. The guard standing watch inside the van also seemed unconcerned at his entrance. *With the battle right at their doorstep they're probably thinking more about getting away from here than worrying about anyone trying to break in.* Loren swung the needler pistol in front of him, holding it at eye level of the guard.

"Drop your weapon and move to the back of the van," he said in a low tone. The guard flinched and nervously dropped his weapon. As the man stepped back, several of the other officers and technicians saw what was happening and froze.

"All right, everyone," Loren announced loudly, activating the lock on the door behind him. "I am Major Loren Jaffray of the Death Commandos and you are my prisoners. Everyone drop any and all weapons, remove your headsets, and move to the back of the van! I want to see hands overhead or I'll start firing." A wave of the needler was more than enough to convince the technicians and communications officers that he was deadly serious.

Loren moved around one of the terminals, not taking his eyes off his prisoners as they shuffled into the tight confines at the back of the van. He pulled out the laser disk that MacLeod had given him and fed it into the transmission slot. The system read the tracking and searching program on the disk, then began to search the skies for its intended target. The drive whirred with activity as it sought out the correct frequency and began broadcasting its message to Stirling's Fusiliers. The message was on continuous loop, running over and over again. Loren listened as the drive ran, but he also kept a sharp eye on his hostages.

"You can't get away with this, you Liao pig. We know who you are," one of the officers said, relaxing his stance slightly and lowering his hands to mid-chest. He was ready to challenge Loren regardless of the odds.

Loren was unimpressed by the posturing. He leveled the needler and fired a blast of the plasticine needles into the back wall of the van just above the officer's head. That was enough. The man's hands instantly shot back over his head and his face showed stark terror.

"It appears we disagree. I'd say I've already gotten away with this," Loren retorted in a matter-of-fact tone. Loren reached over and removed the diskette, then slid it back into his belt pouch. The Fusiliers were warned. That part of the mission was complete. There was one other. Two battalions of Death Commandos also awaited his signal at their pirate point. His last message had been a standby code, holding them ready to drop on Northwind. They were two hours away.

The timing was right. The Fusiliers would divert and reinforce MacLeod against the Third Royals RCT, and the two sides would grind themselves into pieces. Then, in the middle of their exhausted fighting, the Death Commandos would drop and annihilate whatever was left. The Highlanders would be destroyed and Northwind would truly belong to the Capellan Confederation.

Only Loren could order them to drop or abort. He had prepared two transmissions to the Commandos, one for each alternative. The time had come for him to fulfill his destiny. He pulled out the transmission disk and loaded it, sending the final orders to the Death Commando troops.

Chancellor Liao had told him that his personal honor was expendable on this mission. As he watched the transmit light flash, Loren knew he'd fulfilled that sacrifice. Any honor he might once have claimed, he now felt was cast to the wind. No matter what choice he made, no matter which transmission he sent, Loren knew that a part of him was dying. At that moment he wore two coats of arms. He was a Death Commando and he was also a Northwind Highlander. Loren would have to live with the choice he'd made for the rest of his life, no matter how brutally difficult had been the decision.

I did as you asked, Chancellor. My honor is now gone.

The transmission complete, he turned back to the Davion hostages crowded across from him. "Ladies and gentlemen, I thank you for your hospitality. We should do this again soon. I suggest you exit the rear door as soon as I leave." To emphasize his point he drew a grenade and pulled the firing tape free. Ten seconds after he let go of the blast-stud the communications van would be little more than a memory. From their expressions of horror every one of the Davion troopers knew it too.

Loren leaped through the doorway of the van, leaving the grenade sitting in the middle of it. Sprinting had put fifty meters between him and the van by the time the device went off. The blast seemed small and muffled at first, confined to the vehicle's interior. Loren turned and watched as white smoke and orange flames lapped from the open door and from the front of the vehicle. He watched for a moment, fearing he might have only crippled the van and not destroyed it. But then came a secondary explosion that engulfed the rest of the vehicle in a perfect sphere of orange fire and debris.

The blast was so strong it knocked Loren off his feet and onto the soft grass of a small knoll. For more than a full minute he watched as the fireball shot into the sky, burning nearby tree branches as it rose. There was nothing left but the frame of the van, and it was melting under the heat of the fire over it. A small smile drifted over his lips. *Payback for what your NAIS power armor did to the Highlander mobile HQ. I only wish Catelli had been inside when it blew.*

Loren rose slightly and turned to run. He wasn't sure which way to head; he hadn't projected that far in his planning. All he knew was that he couldn't remain there. Getting to his feet he saw the stark outline of a *Marauder II* in front of him, looming less than fifteen meters from where he'd fallen. He recognized the battle-scarred paint scheme all too well, and realized that he'd won the battle but perhaps lost the war.

Mulvaney. He had faced her 'Mech before, and now it towered over him like a harbinger of death. Loren could only hope that Plunket had gotten to her.

The 'Mech's external speakers crackled to life and filled the air around him with her voice. "It appears I have the upper hand, Major Jaffray. Consider yourself my prisoner. Drop your weapons and gear and climb up here immediately." As if to underscore her advantage over him, she leveled her twin PPCs in his direction. It was an empty gesture. Loren had no intention of trying to flee.

Prisoner? He felt his heart sink. *Pluncket must not have made it. She doesn't know what's just been averted, and worse yet she probably won't believe it if I tell her.* Loren dropped his gun and bag and raised his hands.

Falling into the hands of an enemy dedicated to killing him was not the ending he had planned.

38

Outskirts of Tara
Northwind
Draconis March, Federated Commonwealth
20 October 3057

"Marshal Bradford, we have a problem," Catelli said in his best diplomatic voice.

"No, my dear Colonel," the Davion Marshal shot back. "You have a problem. I have a situation."

"Please let me explain," Catelli pleaded as his troops fanned out in the outskirts of the city.

"There is nothing to explain. You were to keep Colonel Mulvaney and her Highlanders in the dark about our plans for Stirling's Fusiliers and you failed that. Now she could be anywhere in the city. Blast it all, man. MacLeod was driving straight at my HQ all along. I don't have time to be mopping up your messes!"

"We don't know for sure what Mulvaney'll do, sir. We aren't even sure at this point that she knows about the ambush." For the first time since the two had met, Marshal Bradford sensed fear rather than arrogance from Drew Catelli. Unfortunately, he didn't have the luxury to enjoy it.

"Take your Consul Guards and proceed to the east side of Peace Park. We have to make sure that MacLeod's troops don't try and get onto the tarmac of the spaceport to warn off—" The transmission suddenly died, replaced with the low hiss of static.

Catelli scanned the command frequencies. *The regimental comm network is off-line. What in the name of the Prince is going on? The Marshal said that his HQ was under fire. Is it possible MacLeod actually destroyed it? No! The last intelligence placed his troops either heading for the training camp or dug in at The Castle. This in inconceivable!* The Davion Colonel turned his *Atlas* toward Peace Park, signaling his Guards to follow. *I'll find Lepeta. If nothing else he can tell me what's going on.*

As Loren climbed the handholds up the massive leg and torso of Mulvaney's *Marauder II* he could still hear the rumble and roar of combat nearby. But around him he saw only a handful of BattleMechs, all familiar as those of Mulvaney's Highlanders. Reaching the cockpit hatch, he took a moment to glance behind him. The Royals' communications van was still ablaze, but, surprisingly, there were no support troops trying to put out the flames. He was even able to make out the fallen form of his own *Gallowglas* on a small rise nearby. What he did not see was any sign of the Davion assault 'Mechs or of MacLeod's forces, something that confused and more than slightly worried him.

The almost smothering crampedness of Mulvaney's cockpit was made even more uncomfortable by the heat the BattleMech generated. Mulvaney in her cooling vest had some respite except for the extremes of heat generated in combat, but Loren had nothing to help him. The air was stifling and the sweat from his brow stung at his eyes with each new bounce of the *Marauder*'s gait. As he climbed in, he found himself staring down the barrel of Mulvaney's laser pistol. Much of her face was hidden by the neurohelmet, but what was visible looked consumed by rage and fury. Had she called him all the way up to her cockpit just to kill him?

"I assume I won't need this," she said, gesturing with the pistol.

Jaffray shook his head. "I surrendered to you. I've lost my BattleMech and completed my mission. If I'm going to capitulate to anyone in this fight I'd rather have it be you. At least you might try to get me a fair trial. Catelli and his goons would have me executed as a threat to the security of the state."

"You warned Colonel Stirling, didn't you? I assume that's why you hit the comm van."

Loren nodded. "Yes. I sent a warning. I have no way of knowing if she got it, though." *She knows about the ambush, she must. Or does she think we're warning the Fusiliers about the Third Royals holding Tara?*

"You seem pretty relaxed for someone who's just become a prisoner of war. How do you know I won't kill you?" Mulvaney said, still not lowering the gun. There was a frigid tone to her voice.

"Too much is at stake. You've been trained to kill, but you're not a cold-blooded murderer. If I were in a 'Mech facing you one on one, you probably wouldn't hesitate. But we both have too much honor in our bones to see the other die without so much as a fighting chance. You could've killed me when we were at the bottom of the Tilman River, but you didn't then and I don't think you will now." Loren turned around and closed the cockpit hatch behind him, listening as the air seal cycled and locked it shut.

Chastity stared at him with intense concentration. "Do you know why I'm here?"

"I can guess." *Don't show all your cards yet,* he told himself. *Let her tell you.*

"I was a little shocked when the Sergeant Major showed up. We were only able to spend a few minutes together before Catelli took him away, but it was enough to get the gist of what's been happening."

"You know, then?"

"I don't 'know' anything for sure anymore, Loren. But all the evidence seems to substantiate what you said. You took a hell of a risk in sending Mister Plunket to me. How did you know that I'd even give him the time of day?"

Loren settled to a low squat in the narrow space of the cockpit. "I didn't know for sure. Seeing you two at The Pub gave me the strong impression that he was someone you trusted. I'd have come myself, but I figured you'd have too many doubts about me trying to play some kind of trick. Plunket is an old infantryman. Men like that don't turn traitor easily or lead fellow troops to their death just for the hell of it."

"Good call, then. My troops have secured this area and whatever is left of the Third Royals HQ. I contacted MacLeod and he's holding our exit point from Peace Park. MacLeod's Regiment is one and whole again. If I know Marshal Bradford at all, he'll be throwing the entire regimental combat team at us before this is done. I only hope that your message got through."

With those words Mulvaney throttled the fusion reactor to full power and started moving out. Loren almost fell over as the *Marauder II* began to lumber forward. He held onto the back of her command couch and stayed low, letting out a sigh of relief that no one but him could hear. There was still a chance to pull off the mission and survive.

"Do you mind if I tie in to your auxiliary headset?" Loren asked, his hands already reaching for the set. "I might not be piloting my way through this fight, but I sure as hell can lend a hand on the communications front."

"Go ahead," Mulvaney said absently, all her attention on maneuvering her *Marauder* through a thick tree line. On their flanks the other formerly-renegade Highlander 'Mechs fell into line. No order was given; they simply followed Mulvaney as though telepathically linked.

"MacLeod, this is Jaffray," he said even before the headset was fully adjusted on his head.

"Laddie! Tell me you did it, Loren my boy."

"Done deal. I sent the message three times. No response, though. Any word from the Fusiliers?"

"Nothing yet. But they're due down in a matter of minutes. Cat might be waiting to pull off a surprise of her own. Good work, laddie, but too bad about your 'Mech. She was a good piece of machinery and will be missed. I assume that Major Mulvaney is on-line as well."

"Present, Colonel."

"Major, I need you to move a wee bit faster. I have some tanks and some of those nasty NAIS troopers here."

The *Marauder* lurched forward as Mulvaney skillfully sent it running up the small knoll. "Our ETA is now, Colonel!" she said as the 'Mech reached the top of the hill. Loren looked out the cockpit display and saw the battle that was raging. A massive Demolisher tank was crawling across a mowed field, blazing away with its huge autocannons as it tried to reach a small cluster of light trees. Around it were nearly a dozen NAIS infiltrator suits, popping up into the air in, around, and on top of Frutchey's *Warhammer.* Carey's *Guillotine* was so blackened from shell and missile hits that not even a spot of untouched paint was visible. Loren bit his lip and fought back the urge to seize the controls from Mulvaney's hands. *This fight is far from over.*

MacLeod's *Huron Warrior* fired its lasers across the surface of the Demolisher's turret as it tried to make it to the shelter of the trees. Shells from the massive tank tore up the turf in and around the Colonel's 'Mech, but failed to hit their mark. Mulvaney fired her own medium laser at the tank, ripping a string of gashes across the front of the vehicle. Instead of turning on the tank to finish it off with her massive PPCs, she stopped and aimed at three of the power armored troops using one of the many park statues for cover as they battered what was left of Frutchey's 'Mech.

"O'Leary and Darley, take out that tank. Everybody else go for that power armor now!" she commanded to the 'Mechs still pledged to follow her. Before anyone could react she fired both her PPCs at the statue across the green field. The lightning-like bursts of charged particles lit the air and disintegrated the statue in less than a millisecond. Two of the armor-suited troops were killed instantly while the other half-crawled, half-ran trying to escape from the charred crater where they'd been hiding.

Mulvaney pivoted slightly and locked every one of her weapons on the power armored troops that were attempting to maul Frutchey's *Warhammer.* The 'Mech was pockmarked from their claws attempting to rip off the armor around his actuators and weapons. Locking onto three of the troopers as they prepared to jump away, she fired her Magna Mk II medium pulse lasers. The air around Frutchey's *Warhammer* seemed charged with bursts of laser light. In less than an instant only a handful of the power armored troops remained. Those that survived the onslaught broke and jumped away, preferring survival over facing the sheer firepower of Mulvaney's *Marauder.*

Jaffray turned toward the Demolisher and watched as

O'Leary's *JagerMech* tore into it with wave after wave of autocannon fire. The shells ate away at the massive tank like a spray of acid. As armor flew in every direction, the driver turned tail and tried to flee. But the tank's rear armor was thinner and no match for the firepower that O'Leary had let fly. The huge stores of ammunition went off and destroyed not just the tank, but the entire grove of trees it had entered. All that remained was a rolling cloud of gray smoke that obscured the fighting beyond.

"Thanks, Major," Frutchey signaled, sounding as if the wind had been knocked out of him. Trying to fight off infiltrators in a 'Mech with PPCs where its arms should be was no easy task. Judging by the damage his *Warhammer* had taken, the young officer had barely escaped destruction.

"I've been there myself, Frutchey," Mulvaney returned, rubbing the scar on her arm. Then she leaned over to where Loren was huddled near her controls. "That NAIS power armor was posted with us only a few hours ago."

Loren realized instantly what she was trying to say. "That must mean that Catelli is . . ."

Mulvaney nodded and opened her commline again. "We've got some problems, Colonel. Colonel Catelli is in the area as well."

MacLeod responded quickly. "And according to my short-range scans we have about a battalion's worth of troops closing in from the south, north, and west. We're going to have to start moving and quick." Loren checked Mulvaney's secondary monitor and saw the images. *This isn't good. They're leaving us only one way to go, to the east, to the spaceport.*

"Colonel, we can't move too far, not yet anyway. They're trying to drive us into the same trap they set for the Fusiliers," Loren returned.

A voice cut in on a different channel. "This is the end for you, MacLeod. You, that damned Jaffray . . . Mulvaney . . . all of you." It was that viper Catelli. Loren watched as the Colonel of the Consul Guards broke from cover, his *Atlas* staring down at them with that evil grin on its skull-like cockpit.

MacLeod was being goaded into a fight against very bad odds, but his voice dripped contempt. "You bloody demon," he shouted. "Highlanders have at them!" His *Huron Warrior* let go a volley from its Gauss rifle, hitting Catelli's *Atlas* squarely in the torso. Had the 'Mech been a man the shot would have struck him in the heart. MacLeod was just lining up another shot when a Royals aerofighter strafed the green in front of him, forcing the Colonel to pull back the shot.

Then, from the north and south came a wave of light and medium BattleMechs all bearing the golden markings of the Third Royals. Mulvaney turned into the wave, blazing away with every weapon. A Davion *Hatchetman* took the brunt of her laser fire in its legs, one of which ripped away and went sprawling across the grass as the other 'Mechs moved past.

"Damn it," Loren muttered under his breath. They were in way over their heads. "Concentrate on the Consul Guards," he said tersely. "They don't have the experience that these Royals do. If we can punch through anyplace it will be there." Mulvaney did not speak, but turned her 'Mech toward Catelli's troops. Loren watched as her heads up display began the locking process on the lead *Atlas*.

Three tiny Savannah Master hovercraft cut across the field and swung toward Frutchey and MacLeod. Despite the damage Frutchey had taken he was as ready as ever to fight, firing his missiles and medium lasers. The lightning-fast hovercraft artfully dodged each blast, swinging behind MacLeod's *Huron Warrior* and riddling its legs and torso from behind.

Loren had often seen fast-moving hovercraft use such tactics. They were too small to do much damage, but fast enough to keep from getting hit. Commanders liked to use them to force enemy 'Mech pilots to waste time and firepower trying to knock them out. He raised the thin microphone to his mouth. "Don't waste time on those little bastards, Frutchey. Concentrate on the real targets!" Then he was distracted by a hit from a Gauss slug that dug so deeply into the *Marauder* that the whole 'Mech was set to quaking.

"Catelli!" Mulvaney hissed, fighting the joysticks and other controls, which were bucking under the impact of the round.

Captain Carey and Lieutenant Darley were concentrating their firepower on a Consul Guard *Enforcer*, bathing the 'Mech in a spray of laser and missile fire. For the first time since rejoining the battle Loren saw the seemingly charred figure of Jake Fuller's *Shadow Hawk* emerge from a cluster of thick pines, its autocannon blazing into the side of the *Enforcer*. When the blasts stopped, the *Enforcer* toppled over, its reactor riddled with holes. Mulvaney concentrated her laser fire on Catelli in the distance, ignoring two pulse laser hits across her *Marauder*'s lower torso.

Loren wanted nothing more than to see Catelli's *Atlas* sent up in flames, but the approach of one of the Royals' new *Salamander* 'Mechs caught his eye. It was charging unimpeded across the field directly at Colonel MacLeod, who was facing the Consul Guards in the distance. Jaffray nudged Mulvaney and she responded by blasting the *Salamander* with everything she had.

Every shot hit the soft rear armor of the 'Mech, turning it into something resembling Swiss cheese. The machine's charge suddenly skidded to a halt as its ammunition stores erupted, blowing the CASE hatches clear. Mulvaney's final PPC shot ate away at the *Salamander*'s gyro housing as the 'Mech suddenly spun on its heels like a mad dancer doing a deadly tango. Its legs twisted and contorted under a stress they'd never been designed to handle, finally shattering at the hip actuators. Loren's eyes were transfixed during the death dance of the 'Mech, marveling at its elegant destruction. "Damn fine shooting," he grunted.

"Thanks," Mulvaney said coolly.

Loren studied the short-range sensors and bit his lip. "I only hope it's enough," he said as the short-range sensors painted a gloomy picture. "There's more coming in at us." As two squads of NAIS power armor swarmed a Highlander *Whitworth*, the 'Mech managed to kill two of the troopers but was unable to shake the others. Jaffray watched in horror as the NAIS troops ripped open the cockpit canopy and fired their lightweight chainguns inside. He never saw the results because the next moment a black cloud of smoke from another fallen 'Mech obscured his view.

Then a bright light suddenly appeared over the small field where the battle raged. A DropShip, an *Overlord*, its fusion engines flaring brilliantly, hovered over the scene of battle. Mulvaney did not look up but kept firing at one of the Royals who was attempting to pull out of the fray. Loren strained to see the markings but could catch only the ship's name—*The Bull Run.*

If it's Davion reinforcements we'll be done for in a matter of seconds. From the open doors, jump-capable 'Mechs rained down onto the battlefield all around them.

"Who in the hell . . ." Frutchey's voice began.

Suddenly the communications channels blared with a sound that seemed to shake and penetrate every cockpit on the field. "Bagpipes! Stirling's Fusiliers have arrived!" A voice barely managed to speak over the peaks and valleys of *"Scotland Forever,"* the Highlanders' unit march. The strains of the music and the heart-tugging wail of the bagpipes seemed to reach out and stir the hearts of every Highlander warrior struggling to survive on the ground below.

39

Tara
Northwind
Draconis March, Federated Commonwealth
20 October 3057

"Sorry we're late, William. We appreciated your rather timely message," Colonel Cat Stirling announced to MacLeod and all of his surviving 'Mechs. Even as she spoke most of the Consul Guard 'Mechs were starting to pull back, realizing the threat they were suddenly facing. As Catelli's Guards broke ranks and fled, the Third Royals began to fire wildly at the dropping 'Mechs, unwilling to yield the battlefield to the newcomers.

"Welcome to the party, lassie," MacLeod replied.

Loren watched in fascination as Stirling's Fusiliers swept up alongside their comrade units, weapons raging like a hurricane of death and destruction. The moans and cries of the bagpipes seemed to sweep the very air of Peace Park. Loren checked the comm controls and found that every channel carried the tune. On one he could hear Davion officers and MechWarriors trying frantically to shout their orders and commands over the sound. The words were garbled, but he could sense the fear and panic in their voices as their messages were jammed by the wailing of the Highlander bagpipes.

Loren watched the secondary monitor, reaching forward to

enhance its scanning as the Fusilier DropShip departed, its pilot wisely avoiding the spaceport. *Catelli,* he thought. *Where is he?*

Mulvaney seemed to know what Loren was doing even without the need for words. She adjusted her secondary monitor controls, filtering out the images on the tactical display. All that remained were the 'Mechs and vehicles of the Davions. Keying in on the 'Mech type, the icon of the *Atlas* the two of them sought showed up flashing on the overlay of the map of Tara's streets. "He's heading for the spaceport, probably thinking we won't dare follow him there," Loren said. *Sly little fox. Only a madman would follow him into that trap.*

Mulvaney looked hard at Loren, staring deeply into his dark eyes. They still had no need for words. They both wanted the same thing . . . the same man.

"Colonel, we're in pursuit of Catelli and his remaining Guards," Loren barked over the bagpipe music.

"I'm with you, laddie," the elder officer replied. "That rat-bastard can't find a place to hide from me. Frutchey and Carey, fall in on my signal. The rest of you report to O'Leary and remain here. Work your way to our Highlander families and get them out of the city in case this whole thing falls apart on us. We're going to save the Assembly the cost of a war crimes trial."

The Kohler Spaceport was the most silent place in Tara. The Consul Guards had been reduced to no more than a lance of BattleMechs and a handful of semi-functional tanks that had somehow managed to escape the chaos of Peace Park. In the confusion of the Fusiliers' hot combat drop, Catelli had managed to retreat with at least some of his unit intact. But it wasn't much. His dream of breaking the backbone of the Northwind Highlanders was now in the hands of Marshal Bradford's Third Royals.

They don't stand a chance. The odds are even, but the Davions will never beat the Highlanders. True, MacLeod's forces are weary, but Stirling's Fusiliers are fresh and they're fighting for control of their own capitol. No. Victory is gone. All that's left is escape and somehow making this look like Burns' fault. Better yet, if Bradford dies I can paint him as a renegade. Perhaps there's still something to be gained in a Highlander victory after all.

Catelli's only hope was to find Lepeta and a way off Northwind. With the spaceport heavily mined and filled with explosives he doubted any of the Highlanders would risk pursuing him there. By the time they secured this part of the city, he planned to be on a DropShip already leaving the world far behind.

Catelli had led what was left of his unit into a warehouse at the edge of the spaceport, a large building more than big enough to hide the BattleMechs and surviving vehicles from view.

Use of normal communications channels was virtually impossible, thanks to the Fusiliers' primitive but effective means of jamming the signals with an overriding wail of bagpipe music. He frowned in irritation. *I never liked that bellowing sound and now I hate it even more,* he thought. The commercial channels were still open and it was through these that he'd managed to contact Stephen Lepeta. Entering the warehouse in his battle-weary *Atlas* Catelli saw his aide de camp standing beside the door, wearing his black riding coat and carrying a laser carbine. *All along he's been my tool, a means to an end. I still need some of the information he possesses. But when all this is over, Lepeta will be only a nasty reminder of my failure here. It is unfortunate, but he will have to die once his usefulness is finished. I can't afford to have him live to tell anyone about my involvement in this debacle. It will be hard enough to deflect the political attacks the Marshal is likely to make, should he survive.*

Catelli opened his hatch and Lepeta wasted no time climbing up the side of the *Atlas*. Though holes from damage done by MacLeod and Mulvaney's forces hampered his ascent, in a matter of minutes he was safe and secure in the cockpit of the *Atlas*.

"Have you arranged for an escape?" Catelli asked.

"Not exactly, sir. I just got here. As you know we never planned for matters to turn out this way. Only one DropShip is still out there, Jaffray's *Leopard* Class. I assume that will be sufficient. I would have searched further, but I saw several 'Mechs moving in and around the spaceport perimeter and some of MacLeod's infantry begin to deploy nearby. I

336   Blaine Lee Pardoe

assume they're trying to defuse our explosives at the other end of the port."

Catelli was exultant. "Jaffray's ship—perfect! And what about crew? Those ships don't fly themselves."

"Of course," Lepeta said as he settled into the back of the cockpit. "But I studied navigation and piloting of DropShips as part of my intelligence training. It will take some work, but we should be able to get away."

You're lucky I need you, Lepeta. This has simply prolonged the inevitable. "Let's get going. The longer we stay here the more risk we face." Catelli began moving the *Atlas* forward, motioning for the other 'Mechs and vehicles to follow him. Suddenly the mournful sound of the bagpipes was broken by a voice that was the last one he wanted to hear. "Colonel Drew Catelli. In the name of the Northwind Highlanders I order you to surrender."

MacLeod's words were firm and direct. He and the other three Highlander BattleMechs were lined up in perfect formation in front of the warehouse nearly seventy meters away. To their left were more warehouses blocking Catelli's escape. To the right was the wide open space of tarmac leading to the DropShips. Catelli's force outnumbered MacLeod's, but he stopped at the sound of the Colonel's voice just inside of the warehouse where they had been hiding.

"You fool," Catelli retorted. "I still outgun you. Surrender now and I might let you live."

MacLeod was unshaken, raising his right arm Gauss rifle and aiming it squarely at the cockpit of the *Atlas*. The massive, skull-like head of the Davion 'Mech seemed to be grinning back at them as Loren leaned over Mulvaney's shoulder. She too raised her arms and pre-heated the lasers housed there. At this range, PPCs would be worthless and she knew it. Besides, for Drew Catelli this was how she preferred it, up close and personal.

"Looks can be deceiving. Surrender, Catelli. I promise to give you as fair a trial as you offered Mister Jaffray," MacLeod said coldly. Loren studied the warehouses and knew they were loaded with explosives intended to wipe out Stirling's Fusiliers. While MacLeod and Catelli bantered, he scanned the huge stockpile of explosives stacked to the ceiling behind the Davion force. *At least fifteen tons of explosives in there and the surrounding buildings. Probably shaped charges too. Enough to wipe out anything on that tarmac. Considering the number of warehouses around here, the Fusiliers wouldn't have stood a chance of surviving. I hope that my other transmission got out.*

"This battle isn't over. The Third Royals can easily take the Fusiliers. And it wouldn't be the first time they mauled one of your regiments. Your own unit is too battered to survive, especially with your impending death, old man."

"If you believe victory is at hand, why flee?"

Silence followed for several moments. "I tire of this, MacLeod. You're too stubborn for your own good. Prepare to die." Catelli signaled his 'Mechs and their weapons came on line.

Colonel MacLeod repeated his demand. "Surrender your forces or be destroyed—the choice is yours."

"You won't fire on me," Catelli taunted. "This warehouse is filled with explosives. You fire at me and I send the signal that detonates these explosives. I'll die, but so will half of Tara, Highlander families and all. If I can't have Northwind, no one, not even the Highlanders, will."

Another 'Mech moved forward in the Highlander line, a massive *Grand Titan* bearing the bright red lettering of "The Cat" on its shoulder. Then came the voice of Cat Stirling over a broad channel all the Highlanders could hear. "Colonel, your troops have disarmed a number of the buildings and deployed some jamming gear. I took the liberty of dropping a lance of ECM-equipped 'Mechs near the spaceport. They can't transmit anything more than seventy-five meters. It will do some damage, but not very much."

Frutchey cut in, "Are you sure—sir. I mean if you're wrong . . ."

Stirling laughed on the line. "My word is my bond. Do you think I'd be here if this area wasn't jammed, laddie?"

Mulvaney needed nothing else. She raised her lasers slightly, aiming just beyond the *Atlas* in front of her. Loren watched, stunned with disbelief. Later he would wonder if he'd been unable or simply unwilling to move. "This is for your betrayal, you bastard." Before anyone could speak she fired.

The laser blast streaked past the *Atlas* and into the explosives stacked in the warehouse. There was a momentary flash of fire, then a devastating explosion. The fifteen tons of explosives erupted instantly, engulfing the Consul Guards in a ball of yellow and orange fire. The 'Mechs evaporated as their ammunition and reactors disintegrated a full millisecond after the explosives erupted. There was no hope for ejection, no hope for survival.

The concussion and wall of debris struck the Highlander 'Mechs another millisecond later, knocking them back and down like a row of toy soldiers. Mulvaney's cockpit glass cracked in several places as she fought unsuccessfully to keep the *Marauder II* upright. Loren, not having the advantage of a seat harness, flew to the back of the cockpit, then forward as Mulvaney lost control to the shock wave.

Loren saw tears streaming down her cheeks inside the neurohelmet. "Are you all right?" he asked, crawling up beside her and looking out at the massive black mushroom cloud that rose into the air over the spaceport. The *Marauder*'s damage display came on line, lit up red in the places where the explosion had slammed into the 'Mech. Loren quickly surveyed the roadway where the Guards had been. All he could see were a few piles of slagged and charred hulks, most likely the remains of the Guard 'Mechs. Nearby he saw the blackened form of MacLeod's *Huron Warrior* stir and shift. Cat Stirling's own *Grand Titan* had somehow remained on its feet, its massive array of weapons scanning the smoldering debris as if the Guards might rise up like the phoenix of legend.

"This test of honor is over," Mulvaney said. "Did I win or lose?"

Jaffray wrapped his arm around her and pulled her closer in the tight space of the cockpit. "This one's a victory for you."

40

Celestial Throne Room Antechamber
Sian
Sian Commonalty, Capellan Confederation
1 November 3057

"Chancellor," Colonel Hertzog said, his head bowed. "I am here as you requested."

"Tell me," Sun-Tzu said, "what happened to the operation on Northwind? I want your opinion on what unfolded there." The Chancellor took a long sip of his wine as Hertzog took a seat across from him.

The Death Commando Colonel raised his head and met the gaze of the Chancellor. "Sir, we were betrayed! Major Jaffray sent us the abort order just as Stirling's Fusiliers were landing. The timing was perfect. We could have landed and destroyed both the Davion and Highlander forces. Instead we followed orders and returned to base."

"Major Jaffray decided to spare the Highlanders, despite having a perfect opportunity to crush them. Is that what you are telling me, Colonel?"

"Regrettably, Chancellor."

Sun-Tzu did not seem surprised by the information, nor did his temper flare as Colonel Hertzog had expected. He seemed wrapped in thought, considering the alternatives and outcomes. By now his mother Romano would already have issued a death order. The son, however, was different, very different.

"And what do you think that I, as Chancellor, should do about it?"

The question was not something that Hertzog had been prepared for. "Several of my officers have requested permission to travel to Northwind to assassinate Loren Jaffray."

Sun-Tzu Liao tilted his head to one side as he contemplated the Death Commander CO. "In your mind he should be killed, then?"

"Jaffray broke his oath to both you and the Confederation. Such actions cannot go unanswered. We have always treated such failures in the ranks of the Commandos in that manner. His death will not be swift. It will send a message to our own ranks as well as those of our enemies. Betray the Confederation, fail the Chancellor, and you will be crushed." His tone with filled with bravado and enthusiasm. Sun-Tzu had no doubt that Hertzog himself would be honored to undertake the assassination of Major Jaffray.

"Do you play chess, Colonel Hertzog?" the Chancellor asked, almost as if his mind were wandering.

"Sire?"

"Chess. You have played it?"

"As part of our training, I have learned more than a hundred games of strategy and tactics. I know chess. Indeed, I am good at it. But what does this have to do with Jaffray, Celestial Wisdom?"

Sun-Tzu smiled thinly, his eyes narrowing like a cat about to spring at a mouse. "Loren Jaffray did everything I expected him to do."

"But we were to destroy the Northwind Highlanders, Chancellor. Their regiments are still functional despite the damage they've taken. They can rebuild in a matter of a few months."

"You miss the point. Jaffray's mission was to neutralize the Highlanders and deny the planet to Victor Davion and the Federated Commonwealth. In that, he has been more successful than any of us could have hoped. Even as we speak the Highlander Assembly of Warriors is voting for full independence. Do not forget, Colonel, that in the process

Loren Jaffray managed to utterly destroy a crack Davion Regimental Combat Team and an NAIS cadre to boot."

"He betrayed us all, sire. Because Jaffray aborted our landing, the Highlanders still exist. From where I sit he is as vile a traitor as Stefan Amaris or Phelan Kell."

Sun-Tzu chuckled slightly at Hertzog's growing frustration. "Loren Jaffray did exactly what he had to do, Colonel. For him there was no other option, though I'm sure he thought otherwise up until the end. The Northwind Highlanders were his family. He could no more betray them than you or I could voluntarily amputate a limb. They are a part of him. I gave him the choice to abort the mission because I knew he would. If he'd gone in any other way, he'd never have been able to win the Highlanders' confidence. This way, he arrived at my solution of his own accord."

"I don't understand."

"Chess, Colonel, it is chess. Loren Jaffray was expendable. For he played the part of a gambit, a pawn of sorts. I could not have ordered his actions, for he wouldn't have been believable. But by giving him the free will to make his own decisions, he has acted as I knew he would. I doubt that even now he knows the truth."

"But the Highlanders . . ."

"They survive, yes. That did not matter to me when I ordered this mission. Their survival was not the matter. I have still won a great victory. One man has managed to take an entire world from Victor Davion. Katrina Steiner has claimed the planet. As do I. But those were just words, the words of House Lords. What Jaffray has done is to deny the planet of Northwind to both of Hanse Davion's whelps, delivering it to me by default. And the Highlanders won't fight for House Davion any time in the future, especially after the Third Royals' attack on them.

"You are a military man. You must have wondered why I am so concerned over a world like Northwind—impossible to support or defend and so near the Kurita border to boot. Now, thanks to Jaffray, the Highlanders see me as an ally of sorts—someone who supports their right to independence."

"Then why did you send us to Northwind if you never intended us to destroy the Highlanders, sire?"

"Do not misunderstand me, Colonel. If the chance had

presented itself, I would have crushed the Highlanders. They did once betray House Liao. As it turns out, however, such action was not called for." The Chancellor did not have to add the word *yet*. Though unspoken, it hung in the air loud and clear.

"Then what about Loren Jaffray, Chancellor? What do we do about him?"

"Nothing. Take no action against him. He was an expendable round of ammunition, Colonel Hertzog. If he had failed, the cost to me would have been one man. If he succeeded, as he did, I would deprive the Federated Commonwealth of four of its best regiments as well as an entire world." Sun-Tzu paused as though contemplating the whole affair, and he looked most pleased.

"My people will not understand this, sire."

"Your people are to follow my orders. Tell them that Major Loren Jaffray is on a special mission, an extended mission. He is considered to be on active duty. Only you and I will know the truth."

"As you desire, Celestial Wisdom."

"And Colonel," Sun-Tzu said.

"Yes, sire?"

"See my secretary and set up a time for us to have a game of chess."

Colonel Hertzog nodded, then bowed and backed slowly out of the room. As the door closed Sun-Tzu couldn't help but beam at the thought of his success. He opened the desk drawer and pulled out a packet of holovid pictures. One of them was of a man whose features closely resembled his own. The same eyes and high cheekbones. The face of his grandfather, Maximilian Liao. Sun-Tzu held the holopic in front of him and stared deeply into his own eyes staring back.

"For nearly three hundred years we attempted to re-take Northwind from House Davion, grandfather. And then you were cruelly betrayed when Hanse Davion seduced the Highlanders from your service. And when they left, dozens of planets fell. We lost the war, and half our worlds.

"I have righted that wrong. The worlds of the Sarna March—*our* worlds—no longer belong to the treacherous Davions. And I have also taken from him a potent symbol, the planet of Northwind and its Highlanders. What armies of BattleMechs and military minds could not do, I did with one man." In a single swift action he had also stolen the world from Katrina Steiner. The cost had been the honor of one man. For the Chancellor of the Capellan Confederation that was a cheap price to pay. Sun-Tzu Liao set the holopic down and took another sip of the delicate Foochow wine. The taste was sweet, like the taste of victory.

"Ah, Grandfather, rest easy wherever you may be. This is only the beginning ..."

41

The Fort, Tara
Northwind
Draconis March, Federated Commonwealth
6 November 3057

Loren watched with a bored expression as the technicians rolled another BattleMech into The Fort. The days following Catelli's death had been hectic, filled with turmoil. For the first time in the two weeks since the fighting, he had managed to get a full night's sleep and a fresh change of clothing. It had revitalized him physically, but now he felt empty, as if he had nothing to do. All that was left was the waiting. He had gone to watch the initial landings of the Second Kearny Highlanders and marveled at the pomp and circumstance of their parade through Tara. With the fighting over, Loren was painfully idle.

His only regret of the entire campaign was having to sit out the battle for Tara rather than being able to pilot a BattleMech in the fight. The destruction of Catelli and the Consul Guards had not stopped the battle. Marshal Bradford had almost encircled Stirling's Fusiliers in the city as devastating pitched battles raged building by building at the peak of the fighting. The return of MacLeod's aerofighters fighting alongside those of the Fusiliers broke the back of the Royals' offensive and gave Stirling some desperately needed breathing room.

The Davion forces attempted to flee to the south of the city and had almost succeeded in escaping when Major Huff arrived with several companies' worth of MacLeod's forces. Huff was heavily outnumbered but managed to turn his knowledge of the moors to his advantage against the Royals. As Huff held the Davions mired in the swamps, Colonel Stirling and her infamous Red Kilsyth Guards hit them from the rear. Huff's own 'Mech was so badly damaged that it took the techs and medics a full hour to cut him free from the cockpit when the battle was done. Given the losses in his command, most considered him lucky just to have survived.

Stirling's own executive officer had not been as lucky. From reports Loren had read, Major MacFranklin had been swarmed by NAIS power armor and died when his own ammo exploded and blew off the head of his 'Mech. Loren had been on the battlefield and had helped recover the survivors. What he saw inside the severed head of MacFranklin's 'Mech was something he would never forget: the charred form of the Major trapped in a perpetual scream, still attached to the carbonized seat of his cockpit.

Marshal Bradford and what was left of his command broke through to the west, pursued by MacLeod leading a handful of surviving 'Mechs, tanks, and ground troops. The Regimental Old Guard infantry and the First Gurkhas sprang an ambush on Bradford, pinning him in an abandoned industrial complex until his 'Mechs were all but crippled. From what Loren had heard from Jake Fuller, the Marshal had been held in the bowels of The Fort since his surrender. For most Highlanders his claims that Drew Catelli was the real manipulator of the events surrounding the invasion fell on deaf ears. There had been talk of a war crimes trial, but most agreed that the best interests of the Highlanders would be served by simply sending Bradford and his officers back to New Avalon in shame.

Loren's friends, on the other hand, had fared well. Frutchey's stature as a young officer had grown considerably. Loren had seen him in the commissary recounting his exploits while other young Highlanders listened in awe to the once green lieutenant. Carey had lost her 'Mech in the fighting, but was first on the list for a replacement and had received a field commission for her efforts. Jake Fuller had received a promotion to the rank of Captain, but had lost his *Shadow Hawk* in the furious fighting in Peace Park. Loren was proud to know them all, and he secretly hoped that one day they might have the chance to fight together again.

Cat Stirling had brought with her a quorum of the Assembly of Warriors. And in the week that followed, long closed-door debates were held in the Hall of Warriors. The local news covered the highlights as public opinion behind the drive for Northwind independence built and grew stronger. Loren considered that good news, but it did nothing to lighten his own feelings of dread and gloom.

Other public opinion polls were split on the matter of Mulvaney's and even MacLeod's roles in the fighting. Some of the more outspoken critics claimed that one or both should be held for trial, though the charges were not specified. The Northwind Highlanders had won, after all. Perhaps that was the most important thing to the general public. It was no surprise that the Davion loyalists who had protested outside the gates of The Fort a month ago all but disappeared with the Highlander victory.

Loren turned and walked along the edge of the parade grounds toward The Pub. He had been on Northwind only a short time, but to Loren it seemed like a lifetime had passed. In that time he had taken part in a full-blown civil war within the Highlanders. He had seen Northwind break its decades-long ties with the Federated Commonwealth. Northwind, no matter what the vote, was never going to be the same.

And neither was Loren Jaffray.

He watched a lance of light 'Mechs assume a review stance at the far end of the field as he thought back to the choice he had made. Chancellor Sun-Tzu Liao had given him the authority to either bring down or avert the destruction of the Highlanders. On Krin the Chancellor had told him to sacrifice even his own honor if necessary. *Good thing, too. I did sacrifice it. I chose to save the Highlanders. I doubt this is how he thought it would turn out.*

Up until the battle in Peace Park, Loren had not known what he would do, for sure. He'd carried two copies of the command orders, one for each solution. Having fought beside these people, lived with them, seen some of them die,

Loren could not betray them. To do so would have shattered his soul and all but destroyed the memory of his grandfather. Loren was also sure it would have turned him into a heartless killer like Catelli.

I honored the intention of my orders. The Highlanders were neutralized and Northwind is no longer part of the Federated Commonwealth—not like it was anyway. But the choice I made leaves me all alone. I can't return to the Capellan Confederation. My former comrades would kill me on sight. I broke my oath of service and blood to the Chancellor. Now I am dispossessed. No 'Mech, no unit, nothing.

To some men, the loss of everything in their life would have crippled them emotionally. But not Loren. He had known loss before. His mother had died when he was a child, his father had disappeared, and eventually his grandfather had left him too. What he had in the way of personal possessions would constitute a minor loss at best. Though he had virtually nothing left, he felt at ease with himself. *No matter what happens from this point forward, I know that what I did was right.* Knowing the difference between right and wrong and knowing that he had chosen the moral high ground, made his life, and his choices, easier to deal with.

Loren stepped into the darkness of The Pub and slowly made his way to a booth in the back. "Lad, ye shouldna be so down," Plunket said, sliding a stein of amber Northwind ale in front of him. Loren had been pleased that the Sergeant Major had managed to escape from the Consul Guards and make his way to Tara on foot by the time the fighting had ended. The story of his exploits had already been circulating among the Highlander command staff and he was fast becoming something of a legend . . . a role he did not resist.

Loren wanted to tell Plunket about what he had done. It hurt him to have to keep it bottled up, not to be able to talk about it to anyone. But if it ever got out, even The Pub would not be safe for him. No, it was a secret he could never share.

Loren took a long, thirsty drink of his ale. "I'm not returning to the Death Commandos," he said, setting the stein down on the table. "I just don't think my place is there anymore." It was as much a lie as the truth.

A group of five figures entered The Pub and before

Plrcket could reply, walked up to Loren's booth. Sergeant Major Plrcket stood rigid and stepped back and away, wordlessly. Loren looked up and the sight of Colonel William MacLeod brought a smile to his face. He jumped to his feet and extended his hand to find it warmly grasped. "May we join you, Loren?" MacLeod said.

One of the faces he knew already, that of Chastity Mulvaney. She met Loren's eyes only briefly as he glanced one by one at the various members of the group. MacLeod made the introductions lightly. "This is Colonel Stirling, Major Senn, Colonel Cochraine, and I think you already know my executive officer." Loren was honored. These men and women were the leaders of the Northwind Highlanders' four regiments. More than that, they were the leaders of the people of Northwind.

To the Colonel's right was Andrea "Cat" Stirling, long dark hair framing her lean face. Even in the dim light of the room Loren could make out her green eyes. Apparently what he had heard several days before was correct; Colonel Senn had not yet arrived on Northwind but had sent his son, Major David Lee Senn, to take his place. The young man looked almost out of place among the seasoned Colonels of the Highlander command staff. The other ranking officer was Colonel James Cochraine. His weathered and worn face seemed to command respect and demand attention.

Loren gestured to the table, suppressing his emotions of awe and respect. The leaders of the regiments took seats one by one. Loren sat between Stirling and MacLeod, two sharp contrasts. "I am honored to meet you," he said.

"There's no need for formality here, Major Jaffray." Cat Stirling rested her elbows on the table and nudged him slightly. "Bill here has briefed us all on your exploits since arriving on Northwind."

"In painful detail, I might add," Colonel Cochraine said, his sarcasm seeming odd for a man wearing such a serious expression.

"From what we've heard," said Major Senn, "you've proven yourself an outstanding MechWarrior. Having reviewed some of the battle ROMs, I'd say Colonel MacLeod's praise is not exaggerated."

"Thank you," Loren said.

"It's time to cut to the chase, laddie," MacLeod said. "There's a reason we came looking for you."

"Other than to get out of another boring Assembly session and debate," Colonel Stirling put in.

"Both Colonel Stirling and I lost a number of veteran MechWarriors in the recent fighting. We're going to have to rebuild our forces. Better yet, reorganize the battalions and command structure.

"I know you came here at the request of your Chancellor and that you're still on active duty with the Death Commandos. But you are blood-bound to the Highlanders. And in all honesty, Loren, we need people like you; fresh blood, with training and experience outside of our own ranks. I, we, wanted to ask you to consider resigning your commission with the Capellan Armed Forces and joining us." MacLeod's words rang with emotion.

"As a Highlander?"

"Indeed," Chastity Mulvaney said. "You have more than proven you are a Highlander."

Loren was stunned. He could imagine how hard it was for her to speak those words. He knew once and for all that he had earned her respect.

He shook his head in wonderment. "I was trying to get up the courage to ask if there was a place for me, and now you come asking me to join. Having fought alongside you, I've learned there's something I needed here." *A sense of belonging. The Highlanders are my family. I didn't think I had one anymore. All I had were memories. I executed orders, but never really for my own reasons. The Highlanders are the embodiment of reason for me. Besides, the only thing that awaits me at home is execution at the hands of one of my former Commando brothers or sisters.*

"Excellent," MacLeod said. "The position we were thinking of is a difficult one, however. Of course you'd retain your rank, but I must warn you that you'd be reporting to someone notorious as a hot-headed firebrand. She's been known to disregard orders, and is said to be unpredictable. None of our officers are exactly clamoring for this open slot."

Loren shot a glance at Mulvaney. It had to be her. But she was smiling and shaking her head as she pointed to his side.

350 Blaine Lee Pardoe

Loren turned and saw Cat Stirling eyeing him like a challenge. "As my executive officer, you'll find me more than willing to keep your life interesting," she said, carefully placing a badge of the Kilsyth Guard in front of him. "Besides, I want to see how you are away from Bill's influence."

Loren laughed slightly and caught MacLeod's eye. *I'm being offered something of great value. Not in terms of money, but in terms of life. This would be the first time that I've fought for Loren Jaffray and not another man or a nation. There is nothing else in life I'd rather do.* "I accept your gracious offer."

Loren Jaffray knew that no matter what, he was at home. And after thirty years of exile Clan Jaffray once again took its place among the ranks of the Northwind Highlanders.

Epilogue

Davion Palace
Avalon City, New Avalon
Crucis March, Federated Suns
1 January 3058

Jerrard Cranston poured himself a snifter of brandy and sat down opposite Prince Victor Steiner-Davion, his friend and his lord. "Matters are more interesting than either of us would have expected," he said, leaning across the table to pour for the weary Prince. "There are several dispatches that we need to review."

Victor Davion's expression was dark despite the holiday atmosphere that had overtaken the city and the palace. The full weight of the throne was beginning to take its toll on the young Prince. He sat back in his chair, opening his unbuttoned dress uniform coat further and kicking his spurs loose. "I take it that these aren't matters that can wait till tomorrow."

"Maybe so," Cox said sheepishly, looking first at Victor, then studying the brandy in his glass as if it might offer some answers. "But they involve Sun-Tzu and the events on Northwind. I think we should at least consider them."

Victor winced slightly at the sound of Sun-Tzu Liao's name and gulped down a big swig of his favorite liqueur. "Jerry, please tell me that it's not another dispatch filled with bad news," he said in a tired and strained voice. Jerrard

352 Blaine Lee Pardoe

Cranston fully understood. The events of the past few months had not gone well for the Federated Commonwealth. Victor's sister Katrina had split the once mighty realm in two, calling her half the Lyran Alliance and refusing to help Victor when both Liao and Marik invaded the Sarna March. That invasion had taken back almost all the planets Victor's father had conquered in the Fourth Succession War almost thirty years before. What had formerly been the Sarna March, a political division of the Federated Commonwealth, was now being called "the Chaos March." While Liao had taken back a number of his worlds Marik reclaimed every planet he had lost in the Fourth War, other Sarna worlds had gone independent. Now Victor sat at the same desk where those conquests had been planned decades ago, and watched as his father's dream seemed to evaporate into thin air.

Cranston raised his glass in salute, then took a long draught of brandy. "It's not so much news as arrivals. I just received word that Marshal Bradford and his aide have arrived insystem from Northwind. According to the message we received from Colonel MacLeod the Highlanders have decided not to press charges against him but are returning him as a gesture of good will towards us. He came on a slow commercial jump transport and is now en route to Avalon by DropShip. He's due to arrive in about a week, and has asked for an audience with you when he does."

Victor shook his head, not in anger but in frustration. "Northwind . . . what could that idiot possibly have to say to me about it? He and that blasted MIIO agent of yours . . . what's his name?"

"Catelli, sir," Cranston said softly, recognizing the barely controlled anger in the voice of the Prince.

"Yes, Catelli. The two of them concocted this little operation to crush the Highlanders without any approval whatsoever. I didn't send him there to defeat them. I sent him there to restore order. Only a fool would attempt to seize control of the Highlander families and to wipe out their regiments. Damnation, we needed those troops to help hold the Terran Corridor together. Now Northwind proclaims itself independent, and with all four regiments in the system, there's no way I'd even consider reclaiming the world for a long time."

"From reports I've received from our other operative on Northwind, Lepeta, this Catelli apparently went rogue on us. We may never know for sure since both of them are missing without a trace and the Highlanders aren't exactly telling us what happened to them."

Victor was unimpressed. "Those fools cost me Northwind. What my father took, I lost because of petty little men wanting to play overlord. Tell the Marshal to report to his quarters and consider himself under house arrest until I say otherwise. With all that's happening the last thing I needed was some power-hungry field commander cooking up a scheme to further his career and power. Let him simmer for a few months and think about what he did. He's lucky I don't bring him up on charges of insubordination."

"I'll make sure the orders go out. I must admit that I'm shocked, though."

"Why, Jerry?"

"The Victor Davion I knew a few years ago would have stripped him of his command, publicly humiliated him."

Victor Davion looked at the electronic map built into the desk top. The former outline of the Federated Commonwealth was split down the middle. The worlds that were calling themselves independent showed up as amber. Northwind was one of those.

"If you're going to say that I've mellowed I'll have to find a new intelligence advisor as well."

"That's not it. You have matured, though."

The Prince looked around the office that had once been his father's, and lifted his hands. "This place does that to you, as have the events of the past three years. Bradford Harrison is a good field commander, he just got greedy. At some time in the future I may need his skills. And that will let him repay his debt to me and House Davion."

"Understood."

"Good. Is there anything else?"

"There still is the Sun-Tzu issue. A package arrived in system today for you. It came with full diplomatic markings from the Capellan Confederation. We scanned it thoroughly

354 Blaine Lee Pardoe

and it appears harmless. It is addressed to you personally from Sun-Tzu Liao."

The mention of the Capellan Chancellor made Victor's expression even grimmer. Galen placed the package on the table, and the Prince activated the opening hatch. The lid retracted back to reveal a stack of fine china plates. Victor pulled them out and looked at each one carefully. On the top plate was a note and two epaulettes.

"On the day your mother and father married, your father had dinner china like this made for the reception." Cranston was looking at the plates one by one. Each one had the name of a planet in the Inner Sphere. "I'll give it to Sun-Tzu," he said. "He's pretty brazen to send a gift like this."

"Why's that?"

Galen pointed to the fine lettering on each plate. "Every one of these dishes is painted with the name of a planet Sun-Tzu has either taken in this war or that we've lost to Thomas Marik." He showed Victor several of the plates, the ones showing the names of Liao and Wazan. The top plate was painted with the name of Northwind.

Victor took the plate from his intelligence advisor, then examined the epaulettes that were sitting on them. One was Marshal Bradford's—emblazoned with the golden rattlesnake of the Third Royals RCT. The other was a smaller piece of shoulder regalia with the markings of the Second NAIS training cadre. Testimony to Sun-Tzu's contribution to the loss of Northwind.

Victor's face turned red at the sight, then he read the note aloud.

" 'Now that Northwind is a free world, be assured that the Capellan Confederation not only recognizes her independence, but will assist in defense of the world should you ever challenge her right to self rule.

" 'These dishes represent the Sarna March and your former holdings there. Enclosed are those china plates for worlds that are already mine. In the years to come I promise to give with the rest of the set, the rest of the Inner Sphere worlds that I will take for myself. The illusion of a Star League under the thumb of a Steiner-Davion is shattered. The future is mine. Sun-Tzu Liao.' "

Victor took the epaulette and squeezed it with his fist, ignoring the pins that cut into his hand. A tiny drop of blood fell onto the desktop map.

"We must be vigilant, Jerry," he said, watching the smear of red spread across worlds that were still his. "He just might succeed..."

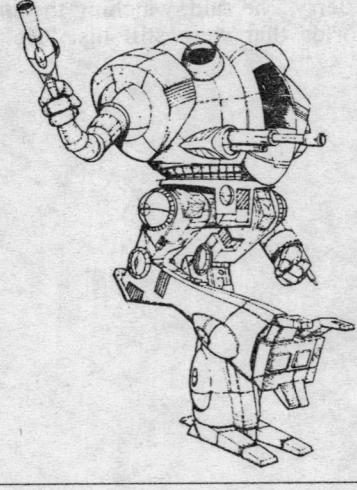

Caesar

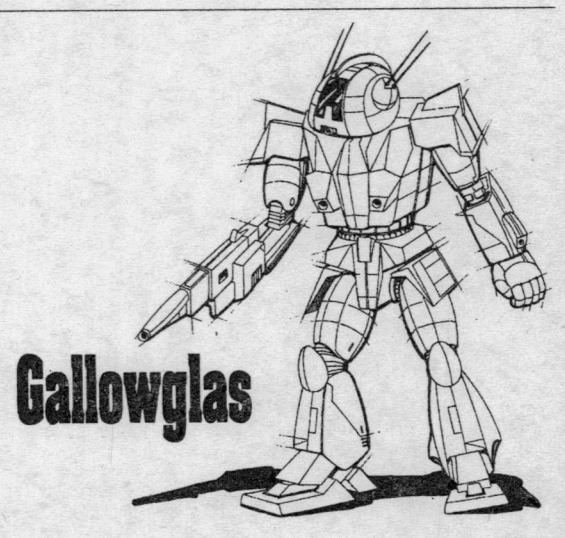

Gallowglas

Grand Titan

Griffin

Guillotine

Marauder II

Shadow Hawk

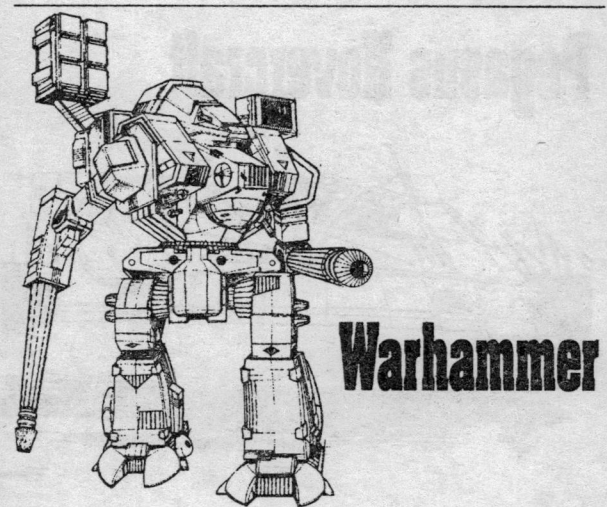

Warhammer

Huron Warrior

Pegasus Hovercraft

Von Luckner Tank

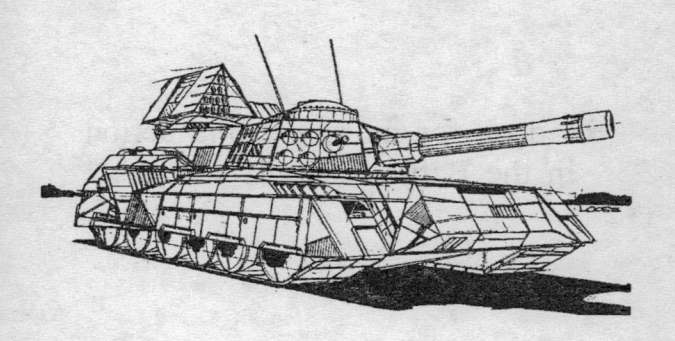

Savannah Master

Read on for more exciting action in the Battletech universe....

Battletech 1: WAY OF THE CLANS, Legend of Jade Phoenix
By Robert Thurston

In the 31st century, the BattleMech is the ultimate war machine. Thirty meters tall, and vaguely, menacingly man-shaped, it is an unstoppable engine of destruction.

In the 31st century, the Clans are the ultimate warriors. The result of generations of controlled breeding, Clan Warriors pilot their BattleMechs like no others.

In the 31st century, Aidan aspires to be a Warrior of Clan Jade Falcon. To win the right to join his Clan in battle, he must succeed in trials that will forge him into one of the best warriors in the galaxy, or break him completely.

In the 31st century, Aidan discovers that the toughest battle is not in the field, but in his head—where failure will cost him the ultimate price: his humanity.

Battletech 2: BLOODNAME, Legend of the Jade Phoenix 2
By Robert Thurston

TRUEBIRTH—Born in the laboratory, these genetically engineered soldiers train to be the ultimate warriors. They are the elite pilots of the Clan's fearsome BattleMech war machines.

FREEBIRTH—Born of the natural union of parents, these too are soldiers, but pale imitations of their truebirth superiors. Despised for their imperfections, they fight where and when their Clan commands.

Aidan has failed his Trial of Position, the ranking test all truebirth warriors of the Clan Jade Falcon must pass. He is cast out. Disgraced. His rightful Bloodname denied him.

But with a Bloodname, all past failures are forgiven. With a Bloodname comes respect. With a Bloodname comes honor.

Aidan will do anything to gain that name. Even masquerade as the thing he has been taught to despise.

A freebirth.

Battletech 3: FALCON GUARD, Legend of the Jade Phoenix 3
by Robert Thurston

A CLASH OF EMPIRES
In 2786, the elite Star League Army fled the Inner Sphere, abandoning the senseless bloodshed ordered by the Successor Lords. Now, almost three hundred years later, the Clans, heirs of the Star League Army, turn their eyes back upon their former home. Nothing will stop them from raising the Star League banner over Earth once again.

A CLASH OF ARMIES
For two years, the Clans' BattleMech war machines have overwhelmed the armies of the corrupt Successor Lords. Now, at the gates of Earth the Clans must fight one final battle, a battle that will decide the fate of humanity for all time.

A CLASH OF CULTURES
For Star Colonel Aidan Pryde of Clan Jade Falcon the battle is more than a question of military conquest. It is an affirmation of the superiority of the Clan way, a way of life he has sworn to uphold despite his fear that the noble crusade has fallen prey to the lust and ambition of its commanders.

Battletech 4: WOLFPACK
by Robert N. Charrette

THE THIRD AND FOURTH SUCCESSION WARS
THE MARIK CIVIL WAR
THE WAR OF '39
THE CLAN INVASION

WOLF'S DRAGOON WON THEM ALL

Now, in 3005, the Dragoons have arrived in the Inner Sphere. No one knows where they came from—no one dares ask. They are five regiments of battle-toughened, hardened MechWarriors and their services are on offer to the highest bidder.

Whoever that might be....

Battletech 5: NATURAL SELECTION
by Michael A. Stackpole

THE CLAN WAR HAS ENDED IN AN UNEASY PEACE....

Sporadic Clan incursion into Inner Sphere territory supply mercenaries like the Kell Hounds with more work than they can handle.... border raids sharply divide the Federated Commonwealth's political factions, bringing further instability to the realm standing between Clans' goals and anarchy.

And while secret ambitions drive plans to rip the Commonwealth apart, Khan Phelan Ward and Prince Victor Davion—cousins, rulers, and enemies—must decide if maintaining the peace justifies the actions they will take to preserve it....

Battletech 6: DECISION AT THUNDER RIFT, The Saga of The Gray Death Legion
by William H. Keith, Jr.

WINNER TAKE EVERYTHING

Thirty years before the Clan invasion, the crumbling empires of the Inner Sphere were locked in the horror of the Third Succession War. The great Houses, whose territories spanned the stars, used BattleMechs to smash each other into rubble.

Grayson Death Carlyle had been training to be a MechWarrior since he was ten years old, but his graduation came sooner than expected. With his friends and family dead and his father's regiment destroyed, young Grayson finds himself stranded on a world turned hostile. And now he must learn the hardest lesson of all: It takes more than a BattleMech to make a MechWarrior.

To claim the title of MechWarrior all he had to do is capture one of those giant killing machines by himself.

If it doesn't kill him first.

Battletech 7: MERCENARY'S STAR, The Saga of The Gray Death Legion
by William H. Keith, Jr.

AN OPEN BATTLE OF MAN AGAINST MACHINE

The Gray Death Legion. Mercenary warriors born out of treachery and deceit. Now the time has come for their first assignment serving as the training cadre for farmer rebels on the once peaceful agricultural world of Verthandi. And although MechWarrior Grayson Carlyle has the knack for battle strategy and tactics, getting the scattered bands of freedom fighters to unite against their oppressors is not always easy. But the Legion must succeed in their efforts or die—for the only way off the planet is via the capital city, now controlled by the minions of Carlyle's nemesis, who wait for them with murderous schemes....

Battletech 8: THE PRICE OF GLORY, The Saga of The Gray Death Legion
by William H. Keith, Jr.

THEY RETURNED AS ENEMIES
WHEN THEY SHOULD HAVE BEEN
HEROES

After a year-long campaign in the service of House Marik, Colonel Grayson Carlyle and the warriors of the Gray Death Legion are ready for a rest. But there is no welcome for them at home base. The soldiers return to find the town in ruins, their families scattered, and their reputations destroyed. Rumors fueled by lies and false evidence have branded them as outlaws, accused of heinous crimes they did not commit. With a Star League treasure at stake, Carlyle's need for vengeance against unknown enemies thrusts him into a suspenseful race against time. But even if he wins, the 'Mech warrior must ally himself with old enemies in a savage battle where both sides will learn.

Battletech 9: IDEAL WAR
by Christopher Kubasik

FIGHTING DIRTY

Captain Paul Masters, knight of the House Marik, is well versed in the art of BattleMech combat. A veteran of countless battles, he personifies the virtues of the Inner Sphere MechWarrior. But when he is sent to evaluate a counterinsurgency operation on a backwater planet, he doesn't find the ideal war he expects. Instead of valiant patriots fighting villainous rebels, he discovers a guerilla war—both sides have abandoned decency for expediency, ideals for body counts, and honor for victory. It's a dirty, dirty war....

Battletech 10: MAIN EVENT
by James D. Long

BATTLES FOR A BATTLEMECH

Dispossessed in the battle of Tukayyid, former Com Guard soldier Jeremiah Rose wants nothing more than to strike back at the Clans who destroyed his 'Mech and his career. Dreams of swift vengeance turn to nightmares when every effort he makes to rejoin the fight to protect the citizens of the Inner Sphere is rejected.

Forced to win a new BattleMech by fighting on the game world of Solaris VII, Rose recruits other soldiers from the arenas to create a new mercenary unit and take his grudge back to the invaders.

Unfortunately, Rose is long on battle experience and desperately short on business skills. Turning a band of mismatched MechWarriors into an elite fighting unit becomes harder than he imagined when Rose is forced to fight his fellow MechWarriors in order to fight the Clans.

Battletech 11: BLOOD OF HEROES
by Andrew Keith

HEROES FOR A DAY

Melissa Steiner's assassination ignited fires of civil war, and now secessionist factions clamor for rebellion against the Federated Commonwealth. The rebels plan on gaining control of the Skye March, and thus controlling the crucial Terran Corridor. Throughout the March, civil and military leaders plot to take up arms against Prince Victor Steiner-Davion.

The final piece of the plan requires the secessionist forces to gain access to the planet Glengarry and the mercenary group that calls it home: the Gray Death Legion.

When Prince Davion summons Grayson Death Carlyle and his wife, Lori, to the Federated Commonwealth capital, the rebel forces seize their chance to establish a garrison on Glengarry.

The rebels didn't expect the legion's newest members to take matters into their own hands. . . .

Battletech 12: ASSUMPTION OF RISK
by Michael A. Stackpole

THE FUTURE OF THE REALM

Solaris VII, the Game World, is the Inner Sphere in microcosm, and Kai Allard-Liao is its Champion. Veteran of the war against the Clans, he daily engages in free-form battles against challengers who wish his crown for their own.

There is no place he would rather be.

Then the political realities of the Federated Commonwealth intrude on Solaris. Ryan Steiner, a man sworn to dethrone Victor Steiner-Davion, comes to Solaris to orchestrate his rebellion. Tormano Liao, Kai's uncle, redoubles efforts to destroy the Capellan Confederation, and Victor Steiner-Davion plots to revenge his mother's assassination.

In one short month, Kai's past, present, and future collapse, forcing him to do things he had come to Solaris to avoid. If he succeeds, no one will ever know; but if he fails, he'll have the blood of billions on his hands.

Battletech 13: FAR COUNTRY
by Peter Rice

THE DRACONIS COMBINE

claimed the loyalty of regular soldiers and mercenaries alike. But while the soldiers fought for honor, the mercenaries, the MechWarriors, fought for profit, selling their loyalty to the highest bidder. When a freak hyperspace accident stranded both Takudo's crack DEST troopers and Vost's mercenary MechWarriors on a planet for which they had no name, survival seemed the first priority. But that was before they captured one of the birdlike natives of the planet and learned of the other humans who had crashlanded on this world five centuries before. Then suddenly the stakes changed. For Takuda was sworn to offer salvation to the war-torn enclaves of human civilization, while Vost was only too ready to destroy them all—if the price was right!

Battletech 14: D.R.T.
by James D. Long

DEAD RIGHT THERE

Jeremiah Rose and the Black Thorns, flush with success against the Jade Falcons on Borghese, head to Harlech to draw a new assignment. Their only requirement: Their new job must let them face off against the Clans.

They find more than they bargained for. Their assignment: Garrison duty on Wolcott—a Kurita planet deep in the heart of the Clan Smoke Jaguar occupation zone. Wolcott is besieged, but protected from further Clan aggression by the Clan code of honor.

Wolcott makes a useful staging area for Kurita raids on Smoke-Jaguar-occupied territory.

The pay is good. The advance unbelievable.

But they have to live to spend it.

Battletech 15: CLOSE QUARTERS
by Victor Milán

SHE WAS THE PERFECT SCOUT

Resourceful, ruthless, beautiful, apparently without fear, Scout Lieutenant Cassie Suthorn of Camacho's Caballeros is as consummately lethal as the giant BattleMechs she lives to hunt. Only one other person in the freewheeling mercenary regiment has a hint of the demons which drive her. When the Caballeros sign on to guard Coordinator Theodore Kurita's corporate mogul cousin in the heart of the Draconis Combine, they think they've got the perfect gig: low-risk, and high pay. Cassie alone suspects that danger waits among the looming bronze towers of Hachiman—and when the yakuza and the dread ISF form a devil's alliance to bring down Chandrasekhar Kurita, only Cassie's unique skills can save her regiment.

All she has to do is confront her darkest nightmares.

Battletech 16: BRED FOR WAR
by Michael A. Stackpole

A PERILOUS LEGACY

Along with the throne of the Federated Commonwealth, Prince Victor Steiner-Davion inherited a number of problems. Foremost among them is the Clans' threat to the peace of the Inner Sphere—and a treacherous sister who wants to supplant him. The expected demise of Joshua Marik, heir to the Free Worlds League, whose very presence maintained peace, also endangers harmony. Victor's idea is to use a double for Joshua, a deception that will prevent war.

But secret duplicity is hard to maintain, and war erupts anyway, splitting the Inner Sphere and leaving the Federated Commonwealth defenseless. And when Victor thinks things can get no worse, word comes that the Clans, once again have brought war to the Inner Sphere.

Battletech 17: I AM JADE FALCON
by Robert Thurston

SHAME OR GLORY?

For years, Star Commander Joanna has had to live with the shame of the Jade Falcon defeat at Twycross, and the nightmares of the heroic Aidan Pryde flaunting his bloodname in her face.

Now, with the arrival of the new Star Colonel Ravill Pryde, who will lead them against the Wolf Clan, Joanna must once again fight for her chance to recapture the glory of her victory at Tukkayid. But will her advanced age bring her to defeat again, or will being a Jade Falcon be enough for her to take on the legendary Black Widow in a repeat battle at the Great Gash on Twycross?

AUTHOR'S BIO

Manassas
Commonwealth of Virginia
United States of America, Terra

Virtual Geographic Society Biography:
Blaine Lee Pardoe

Blaine Pardoe was born in Virginia, Terra, pre-Star League 1962, but spent the majority of his life in Michigan. At an early age he developed a love of science fiction, primarily the works of Jack Chalker. He graduated from Central Michigan University with a degree in Business Administration.

Soon after graduating he contacted a small publishing firm called FASA with a proposal to write a book based on their *Star Trek* game. They accepted this proposal, but first wanted to know if he was interested in writing about a strange *new* universe involving giant war machines called BattleMechs.... That was ten years and thirty books ago.

Blaine has written and contributed to a wide range of FASA products, but his first love has always been the BattleTech universe. *Highlander Gambit* is his first novel set there.

During the day Blaine is a Supervising Associate for Ernst & Young's National Tax Group in Washington DC. His wife, Cyndi, and their two children, Victoria Rose and Alexander William, lovingly tolerate his nightly trips into the 31st century. They all live just outside the Bull Run battlefields—the perfect place for an armchair general and historian to plot and plan the wars of the future.

YOU'VE READ ABOUT IT...
NOW PLAY FOR KEEPS!

BATTLETECH®

At **VirtualWorld**
EXPLORATION · ADVENTURE

Locations in: San Diego, Dallas, Las Vegas,
Walnut Creek, Chicago and Houston

FASA (0451)

DISCOVER THE ADVENTURES OF BATTLETECH

- [ ] **BATTLETECH #9: IDEAL WAR by Christopher Kubasik.** Captain Paul Master, a knight of the House of Marik, is well versed in the art of BattleMech combat. But when he is sent to evaluate a counterinsurgency operation on a back water planet, he doesn't find the ideal war he expects. He discovers a guerilla war—and it's a dirty, dirty war. (452127—$4.99)

- [ ] **BATTLETECH #10: MAIN EVENT by Jim Long.** Former Com Guard soldier Jeremiah Rose wants nothing more than to strike back at the Clans who destroyed his 'Mech and his career. But dreams of vengeance turn into nightmares when every effort he makes to rejoin the fight to protect the citizens of the Inner Sphere is rejected. (452453—$4.99)

- [ ] **BATTLETECH #11: BLOOD OF HEROES by Andrew Keith.** In a battle between the rebels trying to gain control of the crucial Terran Corridor and the Federal Commonwealth comprised of the legions, the rebels never expected the legion's newest members to take matters into their own hands.... (452593—$4.99)

- [ ] **BATTLETECH #12: ASSUMPTION OF RISK by Michael A. Stackpole.** When rebellion threatens the Federated Commonwealth, Kai Allard-Liao, Champion of Solaris VII, the Game World, is forced to do things he had come to Solaris to avoid. If he succeeds, no one will ever know, but if he fails, he'll have the blood of billions on his hands. (452836—$4.99)

- [ ] **BATTLETECH #13: FAR COUNTRY by Peter L. Rice.** The Draconis Combine claimed the loyalty of regular soldiers and mercenaries. But while soldiers fought for honor, the mercenaries, the MechWarriors, fought for profit, selling their loyalty to the highest bidder. Stranded on a distant world by a freak hyperspace accident, would their greatest enemies be themselves? (452917—$4.99)

Prices slightly higher in Canada.

Buy them at your local bookstore or use this convenient coupon for ordering.

PENGUIN USA
P.O. Box 999 — Dept. #17109
Bergenfield, New Jersey 07621

Please send me the books I have checked above.
I am enclosing $_____ (please add $2.00 to cover postage and handling). Send check or money order (no cash or C.O.D.'s) or charge by Mastercard or VISA (with a $15.00 minimum). Prices and numbers are subject to change without notice.

Card #_____ Exp. Date _____
Signature_____
Name_____
Address_____
City _____ State _____ Zip Code _____

For faster service when ordering by credit card call **1-800-253-6476**

Allow a minimum of 4-6 weeks for delivery. This offer is subject to change without notice.

YOU'VE READ THE FICTION, NOW PLAY THE GAME!

Third Edition 1604

BATTLETECH
A GAME OF ARMORED COMBAT

IN THE 30TH CENTURY LIFE IS CHEAP, BUT BATTLEMECHS AREN'T.

A Dark Age has befallen mankind. Where the United Star League once reigned, five successor states now battle for control. War has ravaged once-flourishing worlds and left them in ruins. Technology has ceased to advance, the machines and equipment of the past cannot be produced by present-day worlds. War is waged over water, ancient machinery, and spare parts factories. Control of these elements leads not only to victory but to the domination of known space.

FASA CORPORATION

BATTLETECH® is Registered Trademark of FASA Corporation. Copyright © 1992 FASA Corporation. All Rights Reserved.

YOUR OPINION CAN MAKE A DIFFERENCE!

LET US KNOW WHAT *YOU* THINK.

Send this completed survey to us and enter a weekly drawing to win a special prize!

1.) Do you play any of the following role-playing games?
   Shadowrun _____ Earthdawn _____ BattleTech _____

2.) Did you play any of the games before you read the novels?
   Yes _____   No _____

3.) How many novels have you read in each of the following series?
   Shadowrun _____ Earthdawn _____ BattleTech _____

4.) What other game novel lines do you read?
   TSR _____ White Wolf _____ Other (Specify) _____

5.) Who is your favorite FASA author?
   _____

6.) Which book did you take this survey from?
   _____

7.) Where did you buy this book?
   Bookstore _____ Game Store _____ Comic Store _____
   FASA Mail Order _____ Other (Specify) _____

8.) Your opinion of the book (please print)
   _____
   _____
   _____

Name _____ Age _____ Gender _____
Address _____
City _____ State _____ Country _____ Zip _____

Send this page or a photocopy of it to:
FASA Corporation
Editorial/Novels
1100 W. Cermak Suite B-305
Chicago, IL 60608